Luke Talbot was born in Suffolk, England, in 1979 and moved to the south of France when he was eleven. He spent his early years exploring the mountains and ruins of the Languedoc and became obsessed with the ancient Romans and their architecture.

Returning to the United Kingdom to study archaeology at Southampton University, he graduated with honours and moved on to technology, achieving a Master's in Information Systems from Portsmouth University in 2002.

Since 2003 he has worked in telecommunications and he currently lives in Southampton, England, with his Spanish wife, two children and their goldfish, Pancho IV.

KEYSTONE

LUKE TALBOT

KEYSTONE

First published in the UK in 2013. This edition published in the UK in 2014 by Perseo Books Limited.

Cover art by Tiago da Silva, www.tiagodasilva.com

A CIP catalogue record for this book is available from the British Library

ISBN 978-0-9576019-1-8 (B Format)

Printed and bound in Great Britain by Clays Ltd, St Ives plc.

Typeset in Adobe Garamond and Adobe Trajan Pro Regular

MIX
Paper from
responsible sources
FSC
www.fsc.org
FSC® C018072

To my wife, Sonia
for taking my dreams and making them real.

PROLOGUE
EGYPT - 1337BC

It was an unsatisfying knock, hesitant, the hard wood swallowing the dull thud almost instantly and making him wonder if it could possibly have been heard from within. He tried again harder, more assuredly. *Too much*, he flinched as the noise echoed down the corridor behind them.

"Enter!" a wheezy voice snapped from beyond the small, heavy door.

He looked sideways at his partner, by an inch the taller of the two and holding a leather satchel against his chest, before lifting the latch and pushing inwards. The door groaned on its hinges like an old man turning in his sleep.

They ducked into the room, a mess of papyri and clay-dust. The walls were covered in shelves stacked high with documents, and a vast workbench made of stone and wood filled almost all the remaining space. The dry, musty smell of scribe's ink hung in the air.

Perched on a stool at the far end of the workbench, holding a simple reed quill, was the source of the voice: a small, leathery man, his wispy remnants of hair held back by a colourful band of cloth across his forehead. He quickly hid his work under a flat, polished piece of wood, and gave them both an irritated look. "Oh, it's you again," he said dismissively.

They looked at each other and then back at the scribe. The one with the satchel opened it and pulled out a large clay tablet. "We bring news from Shuwardata of Keilah," he said, walking forwards and placing the tablet next to the old man.

The scribe looked at the clumsy document and sighed. The simple indentations in the clay were like the random impacts of rain in sand compared to the graceful hieroglyphs to which he had devoted his life. Even his shorthand was more elaborate. Tapping the nib on the side of his ink-palette, he placed his quill in a slot on the workbench and glanced over the end of his nose at the cuneiform tablet.

"More requests for money, soldiers, and a dozen other things," he said, clucking his tongue. He pulled the tablet off the desk and walked slowly towards a shelf at the far end of the room. "And I know what the king would like me to do with your news," he said as he tried to find the perfect place to file it. "Whine, moan, never happy when we're around and when we're not just complaints that they need help. Thank the Aten this doesn't need to go on much longer," he muttered under his breath.

The man with the satchel leaned over the workbench to look at the papyrus the scribe had been working on, its top half still protruding from under the piece of wood. The scribe spun round. "And spies, indeed!" he threw the tablet on top of a large pile of similar rectangles of hardened clay and dashed back to cover his work, waving the two messengers away with his hands.

Ignoring his gesticulations, the man who had knocked on the door stepped forwards.

"We have travelled for many days to bring this news to your king," he said. "We will not simply turn on our heels and go back. We demand an audience with Akhenaten."

The scribe looked at them both and sneered.

"No, you don't. Nobody demands that. I am not just Suten Anu, the royal scribe," he breathed in deeply, seeming to grow taller by several inches. "I am the royal architect. I am working on the commission of my king and queen. That commission has significance beyond these four walls, beyond the royal city of Akhetaten, beyond this great kingdom of Egypt and yes indeed, beyond even that of your beloved Shuwardata of Keilah.

"And yet even I do not demand to see them. You arrived without fanfare, but nonetheless they know that you are here. If your presence was desired or even required, they would already have sent for you by now."

They shifted uneasily on their feet at this statement from the diminutive scribe, royal architect, who then softened and gave them an insincere smile.

"Mahu!" he shouted unexpectedly at the top of his voice. The messengers looked towards the door.

"But of course," he continued sympathetically, the wheeze returning to his voice, "I am sure you will be welcome to stay and enjoy the evening's festivities!"

At that moment Mahu, chief of police, burst in with two foot soldiers and after a short scuffle the door closed behind them, leaving the scribe alone with his work.

He uncovered his papyrus and looked at it uneasily, his shoulders sinking as the adrenalin in him died. There it was: his treason, his betrayal in black and red ink as clear as obsidian and blood on sand. But it had to be that way. He couldn't let this secret, this terrifying truth, be buried in the desert for all eternity.

Carefully, he rolled the papyrus up and slotted it into a wooden tube, which he then capped with canvas bound with twine. When his tasks in Akhetaten were complete, he would travel south, away from this crumbling kingdom. He didn't yet know what to do with his treacherous document, but instinct had taken him this far and would lead the way again, he was sure.

The next morning, just before the sun rose above the hills to the East and enveloped the regal capital of Akhetaten with its warm embrace, the scribe greeted Queen Nefertiti on a cliff-top a mile to the north of the city. The king, Akhenaten, was already too weak to make such trips and she had now, albeit unofficially, assumed almost full control.

In her absence from the palace, the king usually busied himself playing as best he could with his son, the disobedient and contrary Tutankhaten. The child was not Nefertiti's, and even though he was barely four years old she could sense where his defiant nature would ultimately lead. Akhenaten would not last much longer, and on her own she didn't know for how long she could retain control of the already fragmenting kingdoms of Egypt.

The scribe directed her to a hole in the ground hidden inside a large tent. Steps hewn into the bedrock descended into darkness.

"How safe will it be?" She was all too aware of the grave robbing that took place in the kingdom; sometimes mere months after a tomb had been sealed.

"The most secure there has ever been," he said proudly. "The workers are brought here blindfolded. On the surface they work only at night, and underground none have visibility of the overall plan. When we finish only I shall know where and how to enter, and what is inside."

She looked him up and down. This small man and old friend had already devoted most of his working life to this task and she held him in the highest regard. That he was the only one apart from the king and queen to know the full details of what lay beneath their feet was a great comfort to her.

He shuffled over to his portable work-bench and picked up a small wooden tablet and a lump of charcoal with his right hand, an oil lamp with his left. Together they went down the steps, the empty tent above them beginning to fill with the golden hue of dawn.

"Suten Anu," Nefertiti's soft voice barely echoed in the narrow tunnel, "what you have built here is important, but what it conceals even more so." She stopped before the end of the steps and turned to him. For a moment he looked her in the eyes but quickly looked down. "No," she continued, lifting his chin with her hand. "I want you to see me when I tell you this."

He let his eyes draw uncomfortably-level with hers.

"What lies within must not be found," she pleaded with him. "Not by our people, or by the kingdoms we barely keep at bay. It must be held secret and safe for thousands of years, and what you have built must protect it."

It was difficult to hold her gaze and he found himself once more looking to the floor. He tried hard not to think of the scroll hidden away inside his workbench.

"Suten Anu," she pulled his chin up again. "The secret of what lies beneath us must die with you. Can you guarantee me that?"

He clutched his tablet and charcoal tighter still and fixed her penetrating gaze as best he could.

"Yes," he lied.

PART ONE

SOUTHAMPTON, ENGLAND - JUNE 2036

CHAPTER 1

The sun broke through the slow-moving clouds and bounced off the glass side of the Faculty of Humanities building before plunging into the depths of the dark, cool water of an ornamental pond. The sound of birdsong broke the silence of the square, and a couple passing by stopped to hold each other in a loving embrace. Overhead, the vapour-trail of a passenger plane connected the two banks of grey cloud, through which the deep blue summer sky could be seen.

Moments later the sunlight retreated from the water, past the glass side of the building and up into the sky as the clouds connected once more. The loving couple broke their hold on each other and moved on. The optimistic chaffinch sang in bursts for several minutes before silence returned.

Gail Turner rushed past without noticing any of this because she was, as usual, late. The glass doors of the building slid open as she approached, recognising the tiny chip embedded in her forearm. The chip ID system could, technically, record her every movement around the campus, although it was effectively rarely used for anything other than opening doors and logging on to computers.

The security guard looked up in surprise as she burst into the long connecting corridor which led to the main foyer. Recognising the short, dark-haired woman, he shook his head and returned his gaze to the small tablet computer propped up on the desk in front of him. Gail crossed the foyer and took the steps to the second floor two by two, ignoring the lift. She knew that she would be the last person there, so she didn't have time to wait while the machine made its way down to the ground floor to pick her up.

Being late for a lecture during the first year of your degree was par for the course, in your second year excusable, and in your third and final year probably a bad idea. But being late at the end of your master's degree, for a study group that only had three other members and was supposed to help lay the foundation for the PhD she intended to begin that year, was bad even by Gail's standards.

She pushed the door inwards softly and slid inside.

"Sorry," she said quietly as she closed the door behind her.

The two other students looked up in amusement and she got a reprimand from Mr David Hunt, in the form of a quick shake of the head and an almost inaudible tut, which was about as severe as reprimands went where David was concerned. It was in his office that the study group was being held, and Ellie Pyke had to make space by shifting a huge pile of manuscripts and ring-binders from the chair beside her. Gail sat down, rescued her tablet from the mess of her handbag, flipped open its cover and sat back in her chair before looking at them all expectantly.

David gave her a wry smile.

"Anyway, as I was saying before Mrs Turner decided to pop in: Burynshik has really forced us to recontextualise pretty much every other site in Europe and central Asia, from the late Palaeolithic to the early Mesolithic."

Gail leaned forwards and tucked her tablet against her chest. She may have been late, and she may not have done all the reading she should have, but there really was nothing like a David Hunt monologue to really capture the imagination.

What always amazed Gail was that despite her interest in the subject, no matter how fascinating the prospect of uncovering artefacts that had been lost to the world for hundreds or thousands of years, she would always end up late to most things. As one of the more mature students, being thirty-two while most others were in their early to mid-twenties, her excuse to David, should the subject ever come up, was that she had a family to look after and a house to clean.

This wasn't true of course; not that she didn't have a family, taking George out of the equation would have broken his heart, but rather that as children weren't even on the radar and George mostly worked from home, there was honestly little for her to do other than study.

"I can't believe that no one knows where that structure came from" a voice said beside her.

"Sorry?" Gail looked up over her coffee cup on the table. The study group over, they had gone to the Faculty's small café for one of their usual mid-morning chats. "Oh, sorry Ellie, I was thinking about my research proposal." Ellie's face was a mixture of sympathy and amusement. Gail slumped down on the table and stared at her coffee, which was cooling down nicely. "It's useless. One minute I think I've got it, and then before you know it I lose interest and give up," she sighed. "I don't know, I just look at the way David talks about his research and I get it, you know?"

Ellie nodded. "He does make it sound interesting, for sure."

"It's not sounding interesting, it *is* interesting. That's what I want, something big, something different," she looked out of the window at the clouds moving across the sky; it looked like rain. "I give up, it's useless. I'm useless."

"That's true, you are," Ellie agreed. "You have a degree in politics, which you aced by the way, you used to work for a Member of Parliament, then you did a second degree in archaeology, now you're just finishing your master's degree, and you're about to submit a research proposal to do a PhD," she counted everything out on her fingers. "You see? Absolutely useless, I mean, what have you been doing with yourself?"

One of the reasons Gail loved Ellie was for her sarcasm. And she was right; her career path had been a little odd, starting in politics and ending up here in the Faculty of Humanities café over a decade later worrying about her PhD thesis. It was always the first question that came up when people found out what she did: how did you end up moving from politics to archaeology? And every time her answer was the same.

Gail had always wanted to make a difference. She had wanted to change things for the better and really achieve something. For as long as she could remember she had been ambitious, and deep down inside had felt that she was destined for something big. A first-class honours degree in Politics and International Relations had been her first step along that path, after which she had opted not to continue as a postgraduate but instead take a position working as an assistant for her local MP. Which was where it had all started to fall apart.

There had been nothing wrong with her employer, far from it: Janet had been just as full of integrity as Gail aspired to be. But gradually, over the several years she worked with her, she had become frustrated and disillusioned with the inner workings of politics. It was a job in which she felt she could make little real difference, despite Janet's assurances to the contrary.

It was at that time that she met George, and everything changed. Seeing how unhappy she was in her job, he encouraged her to go back to university to pursue something she loved, not become bitter working in something she was quickly losing faith in.

So politics went out of the window, and in came a degree in archaeology. Because alongside her burning desire to make a difference in the world came a passion for ancient civilisations: of the scarce vivid memories she still had of her father, her fondest were of going to ancient Roman ruins with him. He'd pick her up in his arms and explain everything to her in amazing detail, so much so that her early childhood dreams had been filled with chariot races, gladiators, vast temples and the Roman Forum.

Ellie had heard all this before. She knew how much Gail loved archaeology, she just needed a spark to get going again.

"Look, we're both just frazzled from working so bloody hard on our master's, so having to think about what we're going to work on for the next four years is a bit like asking someone if they fancy swimming the Channel right after finishing the London marathon," she joked. "The only difference between me and you is that I'm just going to take what I did in my master's and build my research on that. But you're not me, you need a new challenge. I'm sure something will come up, it always does."

Gail scoffed and took the first sip of her coffee.

"That has to be cold by now," Ellie commented.

"You know I always drink my coffee cold!" Gail replied with a grin. "And no, before you say it, it isn't easier to ask for iced coffee. It's not the same."

Ellie looked back at her and laughed. Four years earlier they had happened to be sitting next to each other in their first lecture, 'The Archaeology of the Roman World'. Whether it had been that they shared the same sense of humour, or simply the fact that they were both the same age, they had instantly clicked. They had spent the next three years pretty much joined at the hip, even going so far as to choose parallel dissertation topics. Gail had then gone on to do a master's in Social Archaeology, while Ellie had taken Ceramic and Lithic Analysis, something Gail had always loathed since her first taster unit as an undergraduate.

Now, here they were about to do PhDs. And along with her

husband George, Ellie was the closest Gail had to family.

"You'll find your Burynshik sooner or later, I know you will. Just make sure it is sooner rather than later: you've pretty much got a September deadline for your proposal, which is less than ten weeks away!" Ellie exclaimed. "Why don't you ask David if you can look into those Caspian Sea structures with him?"

"I don't know," she mused. "I do find it really interesting, but then is that really a good idea?"

David Hunt obviously enjoyed his subject matter enormously, and his enthusiasm always rubbed off on his study group, but he was by no means what you would call a traditional academic, having written more than one bestseller on the subject of ancient conspiracies and so-called forgotten history. His theory was that the history of the human race had been vastly underestimated by scholars, and that there were advanced civilisations tens of thousands of years before the rise of even the earliest known written records. This usually led to unfortunate parallels with Atlantis theories, which never went down well with his peers, regardless of how enthralled his students were.

He was in the middle of investigating some new finds in Kazakhstan; pretty much all of his spare time was spent on site, and he was preparing to return for the summer break.

The rapidly receding waters of the Caspian Sea had uncovered some perplexing archaeology near the small town of Burynshik, on the north-eastern coast of the country. What the remains had once been was certainly nothing unusual: wooden posts sunk deep into the mud, forming the foundation of what had almost certainly been small buildings above the water, possibly a fishing village. The technology and architecture were similar to that found in early northern-European Iron Age settlements, before the arrival of the Romans. But experts had started to scratch their heads when the results of dating analysis had returned from Moscow State University.

At first, they had tried to use radiocarbon dating, and their first samples were found to contain less than five percent of Carbon-14. This meant that the wood had to be over twenty-thousand years old. Not believing this to be the case, further samples were sent to Moscow, all returning similar results. The wood was also sent to Cambridge in England, to be dated using dendrochronology, or tree-ring dating. The combined results were conclusive: the Burynshik remains did not fit into any known long tree-ring sequences, meaning they could not be chronologically linked with any other wood found to date.

As he had told them this, he had put his tablet on his desk and leaned forward, fixing them all intently with his gaze. He then almost whispered, as if letting them in on a closely-guarded secret, that the structures were confirmed to be between 23,560 and 23,760 years old. The general intake of breath from his small audience made him smile, and they had finished the study group with an animated debate on the subject of dating accuracy and sample contamination.

In the café, Gail was now scrolling through her notes on the site while Ellie went to get another cup of tea. She was just about to open a browser and start surfing the net when David Hunt's face popped up on the side of the screen.

She tapped it.

"Hi Gail," he said as his face filled the screen. "Studying hard, I see?" he smiled.

"Just having a chat with Ellie about your dig, actually," she told him.

He grinned. "Excellent! Look, I've got some great news. Do you want to come and see me in my office?"

As Gail walked with Ellie along the main corridor of the Department of Archaeology, she thought about Mr Hunt and his passion for upsetting the natural order of things. In her mind, such a tack was a bit risky for her thesis; knowing her luck she would be shot down in flames for it, and she couldn't risk her PhD like that. She and George had invested heavily in her academic career and had spent the last four years relying principally on his income. To throw everything away now wouldn't go down well.

"What I really need is a good mystery that doesn't involve upsetting half the department!" she said aloud, causing strange and amused looks from a group of future first-year students being shown around the campus.

For all their similarities, two more physically distinct people could not be found on the entire campus: while Gail was athletic and dressed in fashionable jeans and blouse, with smartly-combed chestnut hair tied back in a short ponytail, Ellie was plump and round, wore baggy combats and a loose t-shirt, and her hair was a mess of long dreadlocks.

"What I need is something different, something –"

"What you need is another coffee, maybe Irish it up a little this time though!" interrupted Ellie.

"Isn't 11am a little early for that?" she grinned.

She knocked on David's door and they both entered before waiting for a response.

"Ah, my favourite future doctorates!" he said rubbing his hands together. "Ellie, you're welcome to stay."

She nodded, though she hadn't really offered to leave.

"Gail, I have just been speaking to an old friend of mine. I happened to mention your lack of inspiration for your thesis, and it just so happens that he is leading some expeditions this winter that you might find interesting. He's short a couple of spaces, and I persuaded him he could do with a PhD student on the books," he tapped his tablet a couple of times. "I've sent you some details. I told him that you are one of the brightest students here, and as such he would be a fool not to offer you a place immediately. I'm sorry I lied, but needs must," he winked.

Gail flipped open her tablet and the brief summary from David flashed up.

"Egypt?" she gasped.

Ellie looked at the small, colourful, slightly amateurish summary brochure on her screen. She looked at her friend's face, then back again at the screen. "Egypt, for a month? You can't do a thesis on Egypt!"

David shook his head. "The Department doesn't specialise in Egyptology, for sure. But I think your Social Archaeology master's sets you up perfectly, Gail."

"It looks interesting, different," Gail was nodding enthusiastically. "Besides, we've touched on Egypt before, in 'Classical Mediterranean' and I'm sure there was a first year course that covered it."

David grinned. "One of mine in fact: 'The Emergence of Civilisation'."

"And the cost?" Ellie continued. "It's for volunteers, Gail. They even underlined that bit, so they're not going to pay for a free holiday to Egypt for you; you'll probably even have to fork out for the accommodation and food yourself!"

They looked up at David, who sat on the corner of his desk and put his tablet down. "You've both been on digs before, and this is no different: they will have some reasonable accommodation and catering on site. From what I've heard it's in the middle of the desert, so everyone will be in the same situation. As for flights, I can't imagine they're too expensive."

Gail grinned. "I'm sure I can persuade George that it's a good idea." She knew she was probably going to have to soften him up a bit beforehand, though.

"Speaking of which, what about George?" Ellie replied. "You can't just leave him on his own for a month," she sounded almost sorry for him, "and over Christmas!"

Gail knew this would hardly be a bar: she had no living relatives, her parents having died in a car crash while on holiday in France when she was nine. Her foster parents had younger children to care for now, so they rarely imposed on them for anything more than a coffee and an exchange of presents. For his part, George's family were spread across three continents and his parents had moved to Canada the year before. Christmas was going to be a quiet affair.

Gail thought about this for a moment and checked her calendar. She looked up at David and smiled. "I'll think of something, don't worry."

"Great!" David clapped. "Look, you still have to apply for a place, but I'll put in as good a word as I can. In the meantime do some brushing up, I've sent you a reading list so you should have some documents waiting for you." The University library had digital copies of all its textbooks, and free access to most other digital libraries in the academic network. As her master's supervisor, David was able to select any texts from these resources and assign them to her automatically, at which point they would become available in her tablet's digital library. "If you want to do this, you need to send me your thoughts on your proposal by the end of next week, that way I can help you to make sure it's perfect in time for your PhD application deadline."

Gail thanked him and turned to go, leaving Ellie standing next to David. "Well, are you coming?" she asked her. "We've got another study-group in five minutes."

Ellie looked at David and then laughed. "My God, that Egypt thing really has affected her, hasn't it?"

"What do you mean?"

"Gail Turner: on time!"

CHAPTER 2

George was in the living room when Gail got home, stretched out on the settee. His bare feet were resting on a small chair in front of him and his t-shirt was riding up, exposing what had recently become a slightly podgy belly. His short, dark hair was a mess and his face was covered in what he called 'designer stubble,' but what Gail called the result of working from home for a whole week. She often joked that as George worked from home, it was as if she was doing the studying and he was living the life of a student.

His career as a marine biologist often meant that he had to go on extended field-trips, though he had so far failed to be sent any further than the freezing waters of the Baltic. In between trips, he spent most of his time building simulation models for micro-organism behaviour.

He was facing the video wall, their latest toy. It had been installed the previous week, and was literally a normal everyday wall, which at the flick of a switch could display from any one of a number of multimedia sources, or even all of them simultaneously. George's favourite setup was watching the football on eighty per-cent of the wall, with the remaining fifth split between browsing the internet and social feeds. Having just splashed out on such a big gadget, she knew she had leverage for some flights to Egypt if she needed it.

As she sat down beside him she gave him a peck on the cheek, at the same time leaning over and grabbing the remote. Before he could complain she had changed the channel.

"Good day then?" he laughed.

"Not bad, not bad." She continued to look at the video wall intently. "You?" she asked nonchalantly.

He looked at the wall and smiled: the History channel. When Gail wasn't watching programs on archaeology she was watching history, and she preferred to view it full screen. She claimed that you simply couldn't concentrate on more than one source at the same time; anyone

17

who said they could was obviously trying to impress someone. George had thought this to be slightly out of character, considering how she tended to jump from topic to topic at the drop of a hat.

"OK, I suppose," he sat up and shifted his body to face her on the settee. "I couldn't do much today because most of our data from Latvia was corrupted, again. Apart from that, just the usual."

"Corrupted?"

He sighed. "The data from another one of the sensors we put on the seabed came through all garbled, missing half the packet information. It might just be the data transfer, but they're organising a dive team to go and replace it. Then they'll send us the memory chips to see if we can salvage anything."

"That's the fourth one, isn't it?"

"Yup," he said with a sigh. "It'll push that trip back by a few weeks now, probably at least a month."

"Pushed back a month, eh? When was that supposed to happen?" she asked, still looking at the wall.

It was a loaded question and he knew it. She had sent him a strange email that afternoon, asking him how much holiday he had left for the year. He only had a couple of weeks. "Late December, early next year. Doesn't matter now."

Gail turned to face him with a huge smile on her face. Although she was eager to go to Egypt, going to such an amazing place with George by her side would make it extra special.

"Oh, no. What are you planning?" he asked.

"What do you think of going to Egypt this Christmas?" She could barely contain her excitement.

George took a moment to react. When he did, Gail was reminded why she had married him two years earlier: his smile turned into a grin, and he leant forward to kiss her. "Tell me all about it, honey."

She had immediately been interested in the idea of going to Egypt for a dig. But as the hours had gone by and she looked ever deeper into the background of the excavations, that interest had turned into raving enthusiasm. She had completed her application form for the dig online and had spent the rest of the afternoon surfing the Internet for more information.

It turned out that the story of Tell el-Amarna was very simple, which was what made it so captivating. For over seven hundred years, the financial and political capital of ancient Egypt had been at Thebes in the south of the country. Royal palaces, temple complexes at Karnak and Luxor, commercial centres, agriculture, everything was within convenient reach. By the reign of Amenhotep III in 1382BC it was the centre of an expanding, powerful and ambitious kingdom. The international influence of the Egyptians was unquestionable, and their armies were fast becoming unbeatable on foreign soil. The kingdom was enjoying a period of unprecedented wealth and power.

Then, at the start of his reign, the young pharaoh Amenhotep IV started work on a new capital, far away from Thebes to the north, on the edge of the Eastern Desert and the banks of the Nile. Shortly afterwards, Amenhotep IV changed his name to Akhenaten. The Aten suffix was derived from the name of a newly promoted god of the sun, suddenly the primary deity of the Egyptian people. Within four years, the seat of government had been moved to the new capital, named Akhetaten.

Akhenaten himself moved to this new capital with his wives and children and at the height of his reign, the city of Akhetaten boasted a population of over twenty thousand people.

Nine years later, Akhenaten died and power quickly shifted back towards Thebes. After barely twenty-five years of occupation, Akhetaten was abandoned. There was evidence that the tombs of the later Aten kings, such as Smenkhkare and Tutankhamen, who even changed his name from Tutankhaten to distance himself from his father's legacy, were purposefully tampered with so that their occupants never found eternal peace. The succeeding pharaohs ensured that no record of the city or its heretic kings remained intact. Engravings were chiselled and scratched from stone and plaster, written records were buried or destroyed, and the city was razed to the ground and abandoned.

So thorough was their work that it was not until 1887, over three thousand years later, that Egyptologists became aware of the ancient city, when a woman from the modern village of Tell el-Amarna came across a hoard of clay tablets.

For Gail, the most enigmatic of all this was Akhenaten's famous queen, Nefertiti; with an imposing appearance in artwork, most notably her bust in the Berlin Museum, it was difficult to imagine that she had not played an important role in Akhenaten's kingdom. And yet to date, her burial place and remains had never been identified and in all likelihood were yet to be discovered.

As Gail finished telling George all of this, he had little doubt that she had indeed found the mystery she had so been longing for. That the capital city of a great kingdom moved from one place to another was important enough, without the Egyptians having changed from polytheism to quasi-monotheism at the same time. But it was what happened afterwards that really made the story intriguing: the Egyptians had made every effort to erase Akhetaten and everyone involved in it from their history.

Gail was so excited that they stayed up until the early hours of the morning talking about the mystery of the site, searching her textbooks on her tablet and surfing the Internet. Over half a million websites made some mention of it and after several hours George would have sworn that they had looked at most of them.

"Are you sure this is the sort of thing you're looking for?" he asked her as he looked at a page on the video wall. He gestured with the remote to scroll down and read more.

"What do you mean? It's perfect!" she answered.

"This website here looks a bit far out, to be honest, talking about aliens and the pyramids and all that."

Gail looked up from one of her own hardcopy textbooks from her undergraduate years: it turned out that there was a whole chapter on Tell el-Amarna that she had never noticed before. "There's always going to be at least one, isn't there? I mean there are still people who think that we didn't land on the Moon!"

"Did we?" her husband joked. In the last ten years, man and woman had landed on the Moon no fewer than three times. The most recent of these, a joint Sino-Russian mission, had visited the historic Apollo 11 landing site and transmitted live video footage to Earth. The conspiracy theories continued, unabated.

"Whatever," she laughed and continued to look through her book.

George touched her arm. "Gail, isn't this the sort of thing you wanted to steer clear of, you know, conspiracy theories and cover-ups? Isn't this what David Hunt goes on about?"

"No, not at all!" She put her book down and took the remote from George, motioning back several pages to a website they had looked at earlier. "This is history," she gestured with the remote and highlighted a paragraph in yellow. She turned towards George and smiled. "You see,

David likes to pick up on where people have made mistakes, trying to find bad dating and conveniently ignored evidence. He's made a career out of it, and he's certainly not the only one."

"And for every piece of evidence in favour of one of his theories, I bet there's a whole ton of evidence *he* ignores," George commented.

Gail smiled. "A bit harsh; he's a scientist just like you and I, a damn good one at that. He does love going against the flow, and that's not always the easiest path, but this is the brilliant thing: Amarna isn't some twentieth century cover-up," her eyes lit up. "it's a cover-up made nearly three and a half thousand years ago, by the Egyptians themselves, and that's what archaeology is all about. We're just like police at a crime scene, except that we take a really long time to turn up. And no one has yet been able to fully solve the mystery of Tell el-Amarna."

"Until you showed up, obviously," he poked her in the ribs and grabbed the remote back from her.

She ignored him and carried on. "And anyway, it doesn't matter, I'm going for it. I sent off my application already." Gail looked at George and put her hand on his arm caringly. "I don't imagine many people want to spend the whole of Christmas holidays away from home, do they?"

"Or pay for the privilege," he snorted. "Well, I guess it's lucky my Baltic sensors are all messed up so I can go with you then, isn't it?" He looked at her with mock suspicion. "Which talking of conspiracy theories certainly is a remarkable coincidence, don't you think?"

Gail laughed and pulled him towards her. "I planned everything," she told him, before kissing him passionately.

CHAPTER 3

The corridors of the Peabody Museum were eerily quiet as Seth Mallus worked his way to the research labs on the first floor. A small group of Mayan figurines watched him go up the ornate late-nineteenth century staircase, past a large pop-up stand advertising an exposition of indigenous identities in the twenty-first century.

He had been to Harvard University's Anthropology Department many times over the past few years, though this was his first visit to the Peabody Museum after normal opening hours.

Dr Patterson was waiting for him.

"Great to see you, Dr Patterson," Mallus said going in hand first.

Patterson shook his hand and smiled nervously; he had his agenda and he was going to stick to it. He didn't want this calculating businessman catching him off-guard.

"Mr Mallus, good to see you too. I expect you will want to see the fruits of our labour first?"

Mallus looked at him and raised an eyebrow. "First?"

Patterson bit his lip. He was better at his day job and barely a heartbeat after shaking hands was already at risk of slipping up. He chose not to say anything else and led Mallus into a small room off the main corridor. Its walls were sterile-white with a long work bench along one side. On it was a strange machine that looked like a cross between an old-fashioned mangle and a newspaper press, enclosed in an acrylic glass box

"Here it is," he said unceremoniously.

Mallus walked up to the machine and looked inside; the beautifully intricate red and black symbols can't have been any more vivid the day they were inked. Patterson had done a superb job. "It's beautiful," he whispered. "Is it safe to touch?"

"No, it will never be safe to touch. The oils of your skin would cause lasting damage. It will also need to be kept inside a pressurised, acclimatised container to ensure that it doesn't deteriorate. It will need to be kept out of direct sunlight."

Mallus turned towards him and smiled. "I know what you are about to say, Dr Patterson. Henry," he emphasised the more personal touch. "We've been working together now for almost five years and I've been waiting for this exact conversation, so trust me when I say you do not need to skirt around the subject."

"It should remain here," Patterson said frankly. "At your request, and thanks to your generous donations thus far, I have been able to keep this project relatively quiet. But I'm already coming under some pressure from my peers, those that I have had to involve, to secure this artefact for the Museum."

Mallus shook his head. "I'm afraid that's out of the question. I will be taking the document with me this evening, and a final donation to the Anthropology Department will be made in the morning. I'm quite prepared to make a personal donation to you, too."

It was Patterson's chance to shake his head.

"I won't be bribed, Mallus." It had taken considerable effort to setup the laboratory environment required to open the ancient papyrus, and he wasn't about to give it up without a fight. Even more so considering the level of secrecy he had been forced to keep during the long years it had taken for the document to finally be laid bare. "This papyrus is perhaps one of the most finely preserved outside of Egypt, and it does not belong in your private collection."

Mallus walked up and down the room before standing to face the nervous-looking scientist. "I'm going to be completely honest with you, Henry. You know this isn't about the papyrus; it's about where it leads. I want to start planning excavations in Egypt; dozens of people digging up the desert to find it. That's the prize, and that's what I'm interested in. Now, I've got a feeling that when they do find it, there'll be a lot more work, and what we'll be looking at then will be far more interesting than some ancient treasure map."

"So this is all about money?"

Mallus looked down at the floor, for the first time in Patterson's eyes looking lost for words. "No," he said quietly. "No, I have a feeling there's something more important here. Something that could change everything."

Patterson looked at him with interest. "Like?"

He looked up, the confident businessman Mallus gone, replaced with an anxious Seth. "I just have a feeling," he said. "We can work on this together, Henry. I'm not bribing you. Just let me take my papyrus back and I promise I'll bring you something so big you'll forget the damn thing ever existed in the first place."

CHAPTER 4

Gail woke with a start.

What a strange dream, she thought. She had been standing on the top of a cliff overlooking a vast plain. Running through the middle of it was the river Nile. Suddenly, the ground had shaken beneath her and a huge glass tower erupted into the sunlight. Up, up it had risen until it must have touched the very edge of the atmosphere. Its base filled the plain, bridging the gap between the Nile and the cliff on which she had been standing.

The smooth walls of the tower had reflected the surrounding cliff-top and the rising sun behind her in perfect detail. It had however been unsettling that the only thing they didn't reflect was her.

Awake now, she fancied she could still feel the humid air of the desert on her skin, and touching the sheets realised they were damp with sweat. She rubbed her eyes and checked her tablet sitting on the bedside table: three minutes to six. Barely dawn.

George lay sleeping beside her, his pyjama top was twisted round so that half the buttons were on his back. In her still-sleepy state she couldn't quite work out how that was possible, so she decided to think it through while she went downstairs to the kitchen to get a glass of water.

On her way back she stopped in front of the video wall. It was certainly good fun to play with, and the novelty had not yet worn off. She picked up the remote from the coffee table and shook it. The wall came to life and she quickly pressed the mute button; the system came with an incredibly powerful speaker setup that Gail could not see a use for in her normal-size home. Unlike George whose exact words were "It's like being at Wembley!" to which Gail had shouted "What did you say?"

She tilted the remote on its side, and an Internet browser appeared next to the news presenter. Her thumbprint on the remote automatically logged her in to her social feed, which came to life with pictures and videos from her friends and family. She focussed her attention on direct messages and emails.

The first was from Ellie. She had sent it barely half an hour earlier, and from the way it was written she must have been drunk. Gail almost laughed out loud as she realised about halfway down that Ellie obviously thought she was writing to her mother. Closing the message she scrolled down, ignoring several general emails from the University until she reached the previous day's auto-reply message from Professor Mamdouh al-Misri of the Egyptian Museum of Cairo, regarding her application form. She sighed and scrolled back up to the top.

Rotating the remote lazily she refreshed the feed. It was only six in the morning, but you never knew who might be up sending funny things. Her heart missed a beat as she saw the new email appear: 'RE: Tell el-Amarna dig.' She quickly opened the message and read it, her eyes resting on the last line: 'Look forward to seeing you soon! Mamdouh.'

Within seconds she was shaking George. "Honey! I got the place!" she screamed, her voice so high-pitched it was almost unintelligible. "We're going to Amarna!"

George broke into a huge sleepy grin and tried to reach out to hug her. His twisted pyjama top stopped him from lifting his arms, and he spent several frantic seconds freeing himself from it. "Well done," he said eventually. "I knew you would. Now all you have to do is write your research proposal."

But she had already left the bedroom, and was taking the steps back down to the living room two by two. "I know," she shouted back up the stairs. "I know!"

PART TWO

AMARNA, EGYPT - DECEMBER 2036

Chapter 5

The hot tarmac of the road gleamed in the late-afternoon sun as their car moved slowly south. The encroaching desert threw tentative fingers of light yellow sand across both carriageways from their right. In the distance, mostly hidden behind the low mounds of sand, the tops of a group of palm trees could just be seen, swaying gently in the light breeze.

Gail looked above the desert at the deep blue sky. It seemed almost alien to her, having arrived the previous evening from the cold and wet winter climate of England. On top of that, she could not remember the last sunny day in Southampton. One, perhaps two weeks of sunshine over the summer months, but the relentless clouds mostly won the battle for the skies of northern Europe. Here, it seemed the other way round; a small, cotton-like cloud, devoid of rain, glided slowly across the horizon to their left, but it was totally alone against the azure background.

For thousands of years, the Sahara desert had fought an ongoing battle with the fertile banks of the river Nile. In the time of the most ancient pharaohs, the Great Pyramid on the Giza plateau had overlooked a landscape of fields and palm groves, which had helped to feed a young and expanding kingdom. Every year, the Nile would spill over into the surrounding fields, bringing with it the necessary nutrients that made the area so welcoming to farmers and their animals. And every year, the sands of the desert would fight back. The incessant tug of war between the desert and the river meant that for a great deal of its length, only a narrow band of cultivated land separated the Nile from the sands.

Better irrigation and modern technology during the twentieth century had meant that the land could be used all year round with less reliance on seasonal flooding. However, the beginning of the twenty-first century had already seen a rapid change in climate, and for the past twenty years the desert had been steadily gaining ground.

On their left, the sand quickly turned to grass, which within ten yards had developed to a rich variety of trees and other plants, their green leaves a welcome break from the yellows and blues of the desert and sky to their right. George slowed down to give way to an oncoming van. The road was barely wide enough for both of them to fit, but the driver seemed unconcerned as he smiled at them and nodded his thanks. Since they had left the motorway fifteen minutes earlier, this was the first human they had seen. Gail was increasingly excited as she looked between the car's satnav screen and the road, scanning the horizon for something familiar that she would recognise from the hours spent online looking at satellite images. They were less than three kilometres away from their destination, and she knew it wouldn't be long before something familiar cropped up.

"There!" she exclaimed, moments later. "Over there, those houses!"

George had just taken the car around a blind corner, revealing a group of flat-roofed houses a hundred yards in front of them. It was almost dreamlike, the scene so typical of a postcard of Egypt that Gail laughed; a couple of children ran across the street chasing a football, a lone chicken stood proudly on a low stone wall. George let a large black sedan pass them, its rear windows obscured, the stone-faced driver barely nodding at them in return.

"Are you sure?" George said glancing at the satnav, which still claimed another two kilometres to go.

"Absolutely! Just past here on our left is a turning, which you take to cross the canal. Ignore the satnav, it's wrong." Gail bounced in her seat as they drove past the two children, who now appeared to be arguing about whether or not the street lamp was the goalpost or not. "Just after that house," she was almost shouting now, and George couldn't stop himself from grinning. "Now! Turn here!"

George indicated left and turned onto a small side street, sandwiched between two rows of houses; telephone and electricity wires criss-crossed the street, like the intertwined branches of trees meeting above an English country lane. "Are you sure? This looks like a bit of an alley-way."

"Yes, I'm certain. Just keep going along this street, it widens out!" As the road did indeed widen she slapped George's leg and held it firmly with her right hand. "See?"

The rows of houses on both sides ended abruptly, and the street gave onto the concrete banks of a canal. A few hundred yards to their right, a flat bridge crossed the calm black water ten feet below. Along its edge ran a series of short concrete blocks designed to stop cars falling whilst also letting water and debris pass unhindered over the bridge in times of flood. The precaution seemed very optimistic, as currently the water couldn't be more than a few feet deep at most. There were a few cars and people on the roads, but Gail had expected to see many more. Indeed, this was far from the bustling small town full of activity that the satellite images had shown her.

"It's not very busy," she said with a disappointed tone.

George changed gear and brought the car to a halt at a traffic light. The left indicator flashed patiently as the engine ticked over, the fan from the air conditioning whining in the heat. "They're probably all watching Indemnity," he said. They had watched the dubbed American sitcom in amusement for half an hour in their hotel room the previous night. From the frequent commercial breaks, they guessed it must have been a very popular show in Egypt, too.

The light changed to green, missing amber completely. George had grown used to this by now, it seemed that the middle light was there purely as a spacer. He moved the car forward and turned onto the bridge across the canal.

"Where to now?" he asked.

"Carry on straight, we should be entering Beni Amran soon," she looked up and pointed at a small sign in Arabic with an English translation written below. "There! Well, it says 'Ben Imran', but that's close enough."

Passing through the small, mostly deserted village, they could see memories of a more prosperous time; the sand was piled high in the doorways of houses and most shops lay empty, the paint from the signs peeling and faint. There were some cars and people, clearly the area was still inhabited, but dying. Gail's 'Idiot's Guide to Egypt', a tongue-in-cheek present from Ellie before they had left, did not cover the modern area of Amarna or its surrounding towns and villages, choosing instead to focus on the ancient Egyptians, but Professor al-Misri had already warned Gail that the location was not known for its amenities.

They would be spending their first night in the only hotel in Beni Amran, which had fifteen empty rooms and was run by an old man and his wife. They also provided all of the meals, as it was the only restaurant in the village. The tourist industry at Amarna had dissipated over the past thirty years, as visitors tended to go to the more famous and immediately impressive sites of Thebes and Memphis. The frequent cruises running along the Nile no longer came as far north as Tell el-Amarna, stopping instead over a hundred and eighty miles away at Dendera. In a world of package holidays to the north and south, Tell el-Amarna was in the no-man's-land between.

"Amarna!" Gail exclaimed. Their car passed under a modern gateway in the form of an ancient Egyptian pylon. On it, barely visible in the cracked and faded paintwork, were the words 'Welcome to Tell el-Amarna'. George grinned.

Beyond this gate, they were barely twenty yards from the Nile. But the road did not end on its bank, instead vanishing beneath the water down a gentle slope. A barrier had been lowered to stop people from driving any further, whilst a small sign advertising ferry times in both Arabic and English politely advised them to buy tickets in the hotel before boarding.

The hotel wasn't hard to find, as it was right next to the slipway, its three stories rising high above the small flat-roofed homes, the elaborate writing on its fading sign hinting at a more successful past. George parked their car on the side of the road while Gail searched through the papers in her backpack for their reservations; she didn't think that there would be much of a problem if she didn't have the printout, but felt better for bringing it anyway.

The dusty heat of the early evening was in stark contrast to the cool controlled climate of the car, but nonetheless Gail was happy to be on her feet as she faced the river. She filled her lungs, throwing her chest out to catch as much of the atmosphere as possible.

Instead of the humid heat she had been expecting, she found herself breathing in fresh clean air, and for the first time since their arrival in Egypt she felt a cool breeze against her cheeks and bare arms. In front of her the width of the Nile stretched out over a hundred yards until it reached the opposite bank, beyond which she could see the cliffs that had once enclosed the city of Akhetaten.

"Come on George," she turned and opened the boot of the car. "Let's get our things inside and get ready. There's a ferry across in half an hour, we can go and see the site before it gets dark, can't we?"

"Is there anywhere we can eat on the other side?" George asked cautiously. "It's been hours since our last stop, and I'm famished!"

In a service area earlier that afternoon they had enjoyed their first

Egyptian fast food, couscous with spicy sausages, but they had not stopped since, and the smell of cooking emanating from the hotel beside them was obviously giving him ideas.

She already had her bags in her hands and was heading towards the main door of the hotel as she shouted over her shoulder. "We'll be quick, I promise!"

Once Gail had presented her letter of acceptance to the excavations at Amarna, sent to her by the Professor from the Egyptian Museum in Cairo the previous week, the owner of the hotel had happily sold Gail and George tickets for the ferry. Normally, he had explained, the local tourism police would have had to escort them both on the other side of the Nile, but the letter was proof enough not to warrant alerting them. If they intercepted them boarding the ferry, they may insist on accompanying them anyway, but it was worth avoiding such a thing if possible, if only to save the cost of the baksheesh. A baksheesh was a tip, but was often synonymous with bribe.

He advised them that the evening meal was normally served just before eight o'clock, giving them enough time to drive to the archaeological dig on the other side of the river and introduce themselves quickly, before catching the seven o'clock ferry back.

The police nowhere to be seen, they shared the ferry with an old man at the wheel of an ageing Land Rover Defender. The 4x4 and its driver both came from the previous century, but nevertheless towered over the small, modern rental car and its occupants. It was far better suited to the rugged terrain ahead, and while George had enjoyed the luxury of the air conditioning that afternoon, he couldn't help feeling that they would be better off in the Land Rover from this point forwards.

Leaving the ferry, they drove onto the eastern bank of the Nile for the first time. They passed a small, seemingly deserted village on their way and George laughed nervously. "I'm not surprised they abandoned this place, it's desolate!"

"The photos I saw on the Internet showed that until recent years this whole area was green and fertile, maybe not on this side of the river, but certainly where we've just been."

George gestured to the remains of an even older village, mostly buried in the sand and stone. "It looks like this place has been like this for quite some time."

"I think this side of the river was probably always less cultivated. It's very rocky," she pointed at the cliffs ahead of them to illustrate her point. Their car moved slowly along the road; by now, the tarmac was mostly hidden beneath the shifting sand. They had followed the directions given to them by the Professor, who must clearly have owned a more appropriate vehicle like the old man on the ferry. "We're not that far, only a few hundred yards or so." She could sense that George was nervous about the car getting stuck. It was already starting to drift unpredictably at each turn.

There were a couple of ongoing archaeological excavations at Amarna, but only the Professor's was uninterrupted over the holiday period. He had been very happy to enlist Gail's help for the four weeks, which made her think that he had been having difficulty getting people to sign up.

She couldn't have been more wrong. Up ahead they could see half a dozen white square tents, neatly lined up next to a row of six cars, mostly 4x4s. To the left of the tents, a group of a dozen or so people were sitting or standing around the edge of a trench, covered by a gazebo that during the day would keep out the harsh sunlight. They were talking animatedly while pointing inside the excavation. A tall, thin man with a neatly trimmed grey beard stood over them smiling, his wide-brimmed straw hat casting a shadow over his face.

The car stopped and Gail jumped out, followed by George on the other side. To his amusement, he noticed the spring in her step as they approached the gazebo.

"Which one's the Professor?" George whispered.

Before Gail could answer, the tall thin man turned, removed his hat, and ran his fingers through his short grey hair. Seeing them he grinned, displaying his impeccable white teeth that stood out in contrast to his dark skin. He placed his straw hat back on his head gingerly and started towards them.

"*Assalaam aleikum!* The beautiful one has come!" His English was perfect, tinged with an American accent that betrayed his time at Harvard over thirty years earlier. "The beautiful one has come!" he repeated.

George looked at Gail quizzically and she laughed. "Nefertiti," she said looking back at him. He raised an eyebrow and looked back at the Professor who laughed at his reaction.

"Welcome to Amarna," he exclaimed throwing his left arm out

behind him to show the site while thrusting his right hand out to shake their hands. "I am Professor Mamdouh al-Misri, but please, call me Mamdouh!" he grinned at Gail. "You have arrived at just the right time: come and see what we have found!"

They shook his hand and he turned to lead them to the trench, where the group of people were now laughing and patting each other on the back. A young man in his early twenties climbed out of the hole in the ground, grinning widely.

"Nefertiti?" George asked under his breath.

Gail squeezed his hand tightly. "Yes," she said. "That's what her name means."

"I must have missed something. What's what her name means?"

Gail detected a hint of jealousy in her husband's voice and looked up at him. "George, don't be upset, it's just a joke." She smiled and looked back at the Professor, who was now getting down into the trench. Some of the group had turned towards them and were getting ready to introduce themselves. "That's what Nefertiti's name means," she looked at him again and grinned, feeling happy that the Professor had paid her the compliment. "Nefertiti means The Beautiful One Has Come."

CHAPTER 6

Since the late nineteenth century, the ancient city of Akhetaten at Tell el-Amarna had captured the imagination of historians and archaeologists across the world. But by the twenty-first century the site had still failed to gain the popularity and renown that other discoveries, such as the tomb of Tutankhamen, had enjoyed. The remains of Akhetaten were by no means spectacular in comparison to those of Thebes and the Valley of the Kings; characterised by short walls and foundations, most buildings were mere outlines in the sand. In effect it was difficult to see, in the dusty plain sandwiched between the Nile to the west and the cliffs to the east, that Akhetaten had at least briefly been one of the most impressive cities of the Egyptian world.

Imagination alone could take the rare visitors on fantastic journeys to the time of Akhenaten and his most famous wife, Nefertiti, walking through bustling streets past grandiose temples and towering public buildings. For that, and because site access to tourists had traditionally been made difficult by the Egyptian authorities, the finds at Amarna went mostly unnoticed to the world at large. Now, one hundred and fifty years after its discovery, Akhetaten was at risk of being consumed once more by the shifting sands.

Despite this the mystery lived on. Every now and then, the sands would reveal a surprise to the delight of the persistent archaeologists. A collection of clay tablets documenting sales of livestock and grain had in recent years sparked interest far away in Cairo, mainly because it had been found in a previously unexcavated part of the city, close to where Professor Mamdouh al-Misri was now basing his expedition.

Gail and George had arrived in the middle of one of those rare moments of discovery. Three days of digging had uncovered countless pottery sherds and dozens of crumbling clay bricks, and all the evidence had been pointing to the fact that they were excavating a pile of rubble and rubbish. As unromantic as it sounded, that was exactly the sort of place the best archaeological finds were made, and just as George had been driving their car off the ferry, one of the young Egyptian students had lifted what he had thought to be just another clay brick.

"It's incredible," enthused the Professor as Gail peered down into the trench, the bottom of which was by now quite obscure in the fading light. "We have been here for little over half a week, and already we have found more than we could possibly have hoped for."

She squinted to see, and the Professor passed her a torch. Its powerful beam threw the shadows back, and she could now make out in more detail the rectangular tablets, each approximately the same dimensions as a hardback novel. She counted ten of them in the bottom of the trench, plus the one that the Professor was holding out to her. Taking the tablet, she cast the torch over its surface. "It's not hieroglyphs," she muttered. "More like cuneiform?" she said tentatively. Behind her, George raised an eyebrow and looked at the Professor with interest.

"Absolutely, Gail, I see you have done your homework! The writing is cuneiform, and the language it is written in is in fact Akkadian. You can see from the first lines that the letter is probably addressing Akhenaten, as it starts with the phrase 'To the king, my lord, my god and my sun'. It is the formal address of a letter destined for the pharaoh himself. Akkadian was the most widespread language of the time, like English is today. As such it was the accepted diplomatic language in the city of Akhetaten. It will be interesting to decipher further to see if we can date it precisely to Akhenaten's rule or not."

He took the tablet back from Gail and entering the nearest tent placed it in one of many plastic find trays on a trestle table. Covering it in bubble-wrap, he turned his head to them and smiled. "Like me, most of the team speak English, so you should have no need to worry during your stay. However, I expect you to learn some basic phrases by the end of the week."

"Of course," Gail nodded seriously.

"Let us start with greetings: next time I say *assalaam aleikum*, you should reply *waleikum salaam*."

"Waleykoom salum?"

The Professor smiled. "Not bad. People aren't saying hello, they are saying 'peace be with you.' That is why you should always reply 'and also with you.'"

He finished protecting the tablet and turned to George. "And I understand you will be leaving us tomorrow to do a bit of sightseeing?"

It seemed almost too touristy to be visiting Thebes after having been introduced to the excavation at Amarna, almost as if to say 'I've seen this, but I'd much rather take a look at some towering temples and impressive tombs!' Conscious of this, George simply nodded and agreed. Mamdouh did not seem to mind though, and as they walked back outside he proceeded to give George a rundown of all the best things to see in the other ancient capital. As they approached the back of the tents, they saw the other dig members gathering around a freshly-lit campfire, drinking from bottles and clearly in high spirits. Gail and George had arrived just at the onset of dusk; with the departure of the sun, a lot of the heat had already left the barren landscape and Gail looked at the fire longingly.

"Mamdouh," Gail said cautiously. It was obvious she felt uncomfortable using his first name, but he had already insisted twice. "What will I be doing on site?"

The Professor laughed and patted her on the back. "Gail, don't worry about that, I have a very interesting job for you for the next couple of days, which I am sure you will find very useful." He gestured for them to sit down next to the fire and they were given bottles of Coca Cola by a young student, who had enthusiastically introduced himself to them as Ben on the edge of the trench earlier.

"Thanks," Gail said to him.

"*Shukran,*" the Professor corrected.

"Shoe-cram," George said with a grin.

Ben laughed and clinked the side of his bottle against theirs. "*Shukran.*"

For the next hour, conversation centred predictably on their finds. Ben seemed to be the centre of attention, and the running joke was that had the Professor not been watching over him, the priceless artefact would have found itself at the bottom of a pile of worthless clay bricks on the other side of the trench. For his own part, Ben seemed more interested in getting to know Gail and George. In his early twenties, he was fairly short and of medium build, his long hair held back by a baseball cap he wore backwards. His English was good, though heavily accented, and before long George was in the middle of a fascinating debate about football, religion and whether or not Indemnity translated well into Arabic.

Looking at her watch, Gail realised with shock that they were about to miss their ferry; they were the only two people not staying at the dig that night, as everyone else was camping onsite. So they excused themselves and left the group of archaeologists celebrating around their campfire.

"I feel bad, leaving so soon." Gail mused as their car laboured along the track back to the river.

"We can always go back," her husband replied quickly, putting his hand on her knee. "There is a later ferry, we're only getting this one so we can eat back at the hotel."

Gail thought for a moment then shook her head. "No, it's better if we eat at the hotel, I wouldn't want to impose on them tonight, and I'll be camping there tomorrow anyway." She looked out of the passenger window and across the sands, the black silhouettes of swaying palm trees catching her eye. Dusk had now given way to early night and the moon had yet to rise. The car was bathed in the silvery-blue light of a million stars.

A smile grew on her face as she looked over to George in the driving seat; his hand was still on her knee and she covered it with hers and held it tightly. "Besides, I think that as this is our last night together until Christmas Eve, we should get an early night, don't you?"

George looked back at her and grinned. "Hotel it is!" he exclaimed and accelerated towards the ferry.

CHAPTER 7

The next day, George set off towards southern Egypt, dropping Gail and her luggage off at the dig and briefly saying goodbye to Ben, the Professor and the other students at the site.

Gail was used to seeing her husband leave on work trips, and sometimes even enjoyed the time alone. But the foreign setting made this feel different, like more of a separation, a parting of ways, than a 'see you later.' As she watched George drive away in their little rental car, his arm waving out of the window, she knew she would miss him enormously, despite being busy. But there was also a feeling of jealousy, that George would see the incredible temples of Karnak and Luxor without her.

Professor Mamdouh al-Misri coughed gently to get her attention, and she hurriedly wiped her eyes before turning round with a smile.

"It looks like we've come across the remains of an ancient filing cabinet," he explained to Gail as they walked towards the trench where the tablets had been found the previous evening. "The letter we found yesterday is from Shuwardata of Keilah, a Canaanite town under Egyptian influence."

Gail looked down into the trench, a rectangular hole twelve feet long by six feet wide. At its deepest it was about four feet down, where Ben had found the tablets. Carefully balanced over the tablets was a measuring grid: a square wooden frame with pieces of string stretched across like a tennis racket. It was exactly one metre square, each piece of string ten centimetres apart.

One of the younger students stood over the apparatus, and through its one hundred small windows meticulously translated the finds onto a large piece of graph paper, periodically flicking her long hair out of her eyes.

"Canaanite. Ancient Palestine, right?" she tested herself.

"Absolutely, as much a source of tension three and a half thousand years ago as it remains today. In the letter, Shuwardata is complaining of another ruler, Abdu-heba, who has reportedly occupied some of his land by force." Mamdouh peered down into the excavation, holding his hat to his head. "This mass of clay is the remains of the exterior walls of the building. The rest of the office should be over there," he gestured beyond the edge of the trench, where three other archaeologists were already clearing away the top-sand ready to extend the excavation.

"Most of the buildings at Amarna were built in a hurry. They used a combination of smaller limestone blocks that were faster to transport and build with than the larger blocks used in older sites to the south, and these poor quality clay bricks. The outside walls were then plastered and painted so that their outward appearance would have been no different." He pointed to a particular brick, thickly coated along one edge with plaster. "Have you ever been to the old Soviet Union or one of its satellite states?"

The USSR had disappeared over ten years before Gail had even been born, in another century. She had never heard anyone refer to it before as if it had actually existed. It was as if someone had just asked her if she had ever visited the old Roman Empire. She shook her head in reply and looked at Mamdouh curiously.

"At the end of the Second World War, the Russians occupied many countries on its western front," he explained, "a buffer-zone between it and capitalism, more specifically the Americans. Many of these countries had been at the very centre of European politics and economics for hundreds of years, countries like Hungary, Bulgaria, Poland and Romania. This was replaced with Communism, a harsh, unforgiving regime controlled by Stalin in Moscow." He was now walking towards where the new trench was being started, Gail followed. "You can't take everything away from people and give them nothing in return. You have to win hearts and minds, you have to make them believe that everything is alright, while at the same time re-asserting your power and authority. They tried to achieve this partly by constructing huge ostentatious buildings, government offices, and monuments. They built them quickly and poorly, weak concrete blocks covered in cheap plaster."

As he said this, he pointed behind him, towards the pile of clay bricks next to the first trench. "I went to Sofia, the capital city of Bulgaria, many years ago at the end of the last century. As I arrived at the main train station, I was awestruck by the sheer scale of the platforms, as wide as motorways and stretching far away into the distance. Leaving the station's huge main building, you could see whole sections of plaster that had simply peeled away, leaving the rough concrete visible beneath, and breaking the illusion of a monumental stone block structure. "

Gail looked around at the barren terrain they were in: the sun was already high in the morning sky and the temperature was rising rapidly. She tried to imagine a city of elaborate buildings dominating the skyline, but found it quite difficult. It was hard even to imagine the fertile plains on the other side of the Nile that had been there barely twenty years earlier.

"Do you think that Akhenaten was like Stalin?"

Mamdouh laughed and gave her a friendly pat on the back. "There are parallels, certainly. Akhenaten didn't run a democracy, that's for sure, but all evidence points to his rule being above all peaceful and happy." He looked across the sands at a group of palm trees, motionless in the still air. "It's almost as if this were a twenty-year vacation away from normality, ignoring duties such as pleas for help from other kings, including Shuwardata."

"So he was a pacifist?" she asked.

"Or an idealist, or a religious fanatic, or a lunatic, take your pick."

Gail thought about this for a moment. "That would be a good thesis title: 'Akhenaten: Idealist or Lunatic?'" she laughed. "By the way," as if joking around had jolted her memory, "David sends his regards."

"Ah, yes. He had good things to say about you, Gail," he said looking at her with interest. "He said you were struggling for inspiration, that you wanted something exciting: a good mystery to sink your teeth into," he laughed. "And he did mention that you didn't fancy classifying pottery sherds."

She blushed.

"There are many questions you can ask yourself about this place, many mysteries that have no answers yet, and only some of them have established theories. Why did Akhenaten change religion? Why did Akhenaten change the site of Egypt's capital city? Why did Akhenaten remove himself from the outside world?" he looked at Gail and smiled. "But I think the question you are most interested in is not regarding Akhenaten, is it?"

"No," she replied.

"Social archaeology is about people, not events. So if it isn't about him, it must be about –" he left the sentence hanging in the hot air for her to finish.

"Nefertiti," she looked Mamdouh in the eyes. "They say that behind every successful man there is a woman." Pushing him out of bed and nagging him, George would have added. "I've been reading about Akhenaten ever since I heard about this dig, and I don't know why but I feel that all of the changes he made were linked to her. We don't know where she is from and we don't even know where she is now. To me, she is the mystery."

Mamdouh laughed heartily and put his hand on Gail's shoulder. He led her away from the trenches and towards the tents. "Come with me and I will show you what I think you should do this week."

Gail's heart sank as they approached the large square tents: she was going to be cataloguing finds. "In here?" she asked. She could hear Ellie giggling childishly in the back of her mind.

"Yes, in here." He smiled as he led her under the white canvas, towards a trestle table covered with paperwork and laptop computers.

She approached the table and looked down at the mess of forms and maps and computer hardware. An A3 pad of fresh graph paper sat on top. The Professor put it to one side and uncovered a map of the area, the Nile running up the left hand side. Gail's hopes rose slightly as she saw this: cataloguing finds should involve diagrams of the trenches, not larger scale maps like this.

"I feel the same as you do about Nefertiti," he started. He was looking at her intently, as if what he was about to say was of utmost importance. "I feel that she was at the heart of Akhetaten." He paused and looked down at the map before continuing. "And I believe she still is."

"You think she is buried here?"

"I do."

Gail looked down at the map. It was covered with spidery writing, Arabic shorthand, with crosses and circles highlighting what she assumed were archaeological finds.

"Gail, whatever the subject of your thesis, I am thrilled that it will be centred on this great, ancient city and its people. But before you can write even one sentence, you have to feel Akhetaten. You have to know this place, its air, its soil and its mountains, before you can come close to understanding the people who lived and died here, and that includes Nefertiti." Pointing to several large circles on the map, he continued.

"There are many famous excavations around here, a palace here, some small dwellings there, the tombs in the cliffs. There are even some columns that stand out from the sand, which you will have noticed on your way here."

Gail nodded. The previous evening it had been too dark to see them in the dying light. But in the morning, she and George had easily picked out the low lying remains.

"This is your first visit to Amarna, and I do not want to throw you in a trench or hide you in a tent for the whole of your four weeks." Gail's sigh of relief was noticeable, and he laughed. "Your enthusiasm for this excavation has been apparent from your constant emails and has yet to be matched by any one of my students."

Gail blushed. She had not been aware of having sent constant emails, but on reflection she had probably become a little too chatty over the past few weeks as her excitement for the upcoming dig grew.

"I was once like you, though not quite as attractive," he smiled, "a young Sherlock Holmes of the ancient world wanting to find mysteries and solve them."

He studied the map for several seconds, during which time she wanted to say something but couldn't find the right words. It seemed to her that Mamdouh was opening up on quite a personal level, possibly a result of the rapport built between them by the constant emailing, possibly as a result of something more sinister.

"And did you?" she finally managed to say, feeling slightly uncomfortable.

"I wanted mysteries too and I got one," he said. "Amarna found me nearly thirty years ago, and I have been obsessed ever since." He was looking deep into the map, beyond the writing and the marks, toward something else.

Gail waited almost a minute before breaking the awkward silence that followed. "So how can I help?" she said quietly.

Her voice pulled him back to the present and he jerked his head up and away from the map with a smile. "I would like you to spend the next couple of days getting to know Amarna, the sands, the cliffs, the ruins. There are two reasons for me giving you this task. Firstly, I know that Nefertiti is here somewhere, but I have looked for so long I am blinded by experience. I need fresh, excited, idealistic eyes, and I trust David when he tells me that you're the person for that.

"I would recommend that you head to these plateaus to the north.

From there you will get a great panoramic view of the valley, and it's a good place to start before heading to the tombs to the east." He folded the map up and passed it to her, along with the keys to a Land Rover. "There is a 4x4 outside, which I prepared this morning with everything you will need. And after two days, there will still be plenty left to do here, such as cataloguing finds," he said with a wink and a grin.

Gail took the keys and the map. "Shoocran," she said.

"You're getting better!" he grinned. "*Shukran*," he corrected, shortening the u and rolling the r.

She couldn't quite believe her luck: four months ago she was floundering, without even a research proposal or any idea of where to find one. Now, she was in Egypt with the keys to a 4x4 and an open road to discovery.

"What's the second reason?" she asked.

He laughed. "Ben will be coming with you for safety. Not yours, but archaeology's. I need to get him offsite for a while: he's a complete liability with these fragile tablets in the trench!"

Half an hour later Ben started the engine of the Land Rover and pushed it into first gear, moving slowly forwards in the sand, he turned towards the main track and found second with a screech of the clutch. Gail poked her head out of the passenger window and grimaced at the Professor, who laughed silently and waved goodbye.

As they accelerated into the distance, he stopped waving and removed his hat. He pulled a mobile phone from his trouser pocket and hit the call button twice.

A telephone on the other side of the world began to ring.

CHAPTER 8

"My God, it's hot!" Gail exclaimed as she scanned the rocks ahead for a foothold. Seeing a suitably flat one, she shot her foot forwards and hopped on to it, holding her arms out to maintain balance. "And it's only eleven!"

"The sun, it is heating the rocks. The rocks are," Ben paused thoughtfully for a second before continuing. "Cooking us?" He glanced at Gail and she looked up at him and smiled.

"The rocks are absorbing the heat," she corrected, although she wasn't entirely sure herself whether absorbed was the correct term for it either. Kneeling down, she touched the surface beneath her feet and pulled her hand away quickly. "Ouch!" she said, standing up again.

Ben mentally repeated the word absorbing to himself several times, before shrugging and jumping across a deep hole onto another rock. "There is nothing up here," he shouted back as he reached a ledge in the cliff face. "This is just a cliff."

Gail reached his side and looked around them. The cliff rose at least another twelve feet above them, while the ledge they were standing on jutted two feet out at its base. They had just crossed at least ten yards of tightly-packed rocks of varying sizes. She knew nothing about geology, but guessed that they had, until sometime in the past, been part of the cliff. "You're right," she conceded eventually.

"Unless you like rocks?" Ben had intended this to be a joke, but it had clearly not translated well.

She didn't particularly like rocks. But something had drawn her to this specific cliff, and now she was determined to get to the top of it and look back out over the ancient city of Akhetaten.

"How do we get up there?" she asked, pointing to the top.

"By helicopter?" Ben suggested. This time he was rewarded with a short laugh from Gail, which boosted his confidence. "Or we can use the lift?"

"Don't be silly, we'll take the escalator." She looked at him and laughed. "Stairs that move, Ben, stairs that move."

"Ah! Escalator!" he said, accentuating the first syllable to suggest that he knew the word but she had pronounced it incorrectly. They both laughed as they made their way along the ledge.

Farid 'Ben' Limam was not the worst archaeologist in Egypt, but he wasn't far off. It was his last year at university, and the Amarna dig was earning him valuable credits towards his bachelor's degree, so he wasn't so upset that Mamdouh had seen fit to get him out of the way just as the exciting finds had started to emerge.

Truth be told, he was actually enjoying himself, climbing over rocks looking for something that wasn't there.

And in any case, he thought as he looked up at Gail, who had shot ahead and was nearing the top already, the view was pretty good. He looked down again and cursed himself. He had immediately clicked with George the previous evening, and felt bad for staring at Gail's rear. He looked up again just in time to see her legs disappearing over the top. Ben stopped climbing and looked down. It wasn't as steep as he had imagined, but it was higher. He had already climbed a good twenty feet up from the Land Rover and had another ten feet to go before he joined her.

Hearing Gail's voice from beyond the cliff-top, he shouted up at her. There was no response. Again, he heard her voice and hurried to reach the top. He was just about to clamber over and reveal himself when he heard her again, but this time much clearer.

"No, not yet, just climbing around some cliffs with Ben," she said. There was a short pause before she laughed and added: "No, of course not! He's helping me. The Professor sent me away for two days to search the desert for Nefertiti! Can you believe that?"

George, Ben thought. As he realised this was a personal call, he crouched down just below the cliff top and decided to wait; he didn't want to disturb Gail while she was talking to her husband.

"When do you arrive? So you'll have lunch there then?"

At this point it occurred to Ben that he was in actual fact eavesdropping, which was far worse than interrupting a private conversation. Debating what to do, he pulled out his own phone and opened the directory. He contemplated calling his father, to avoid the awkward situation of him standing there waiting while Gail struggled to say her goodbyes. But then he shook his head, realising that should his conversation take longer than Gail's, she would be in the same situation. Suddenly he thought of the solution.

"Hi!" he exclaimed as he popped his head over the edge of the cliff and waved, a huge grin spread across his face.

Gail was sitting on a small rock, about six feet away, with her back to him. Turning round, she waved and smiled, then gestured at her phone and made an apologetic shrug.

Smooth, Ben thought to himself as he pulled himself up and walked along the cliff's edge. Very smooth.

"See," he complained sitting down on a large, flat stone about thirty yards from the edge of the cliff. "Nothing but sand and rocks. And over there, a palm tree!" he pointed at the lonesome palm swaying gently in the breeze that had made its way up from the valley below. "Welcome to Egypt!"

"But no camels?" Gail laughed.

He shrugged and pointed to the valley and where the Professor's expedition was based. "Probably doing a better job than me over there in the trench," he half-joked.

Gail looked over at him and grinned. "Why do you call yourself Ben?" she asked.

"My real name is Farid, the same as my father. For as long as I can remember, people have called me Ben, I was even called that by my teachers at school!" He looked down at the sand and laughed. "I have no idea where it came from," he said.

Gail contemplated this for a second before responding. "When I was a child, I could never understand why my parents had named me after the wind. A gale is like a hurricane," she explained to him. "Names are funny old things, don't you think?"

"Yes?" he answered cautiously.

"Like Nefertiti," she continued. "'The Beautiful One Has Come'. What a strange thing to call someone. Where could she have come from, and where could she be now?"

"I imagine she is dead, Gail," he joked. "And she is certainly not around here."

Gail stood up and walked towards the lone palm tree, away from the cliff's edge and the stone on which Ben sat, looking out towards the desert. "She has to be somewhere!" she said. Despite the fact that they had seen nothing all day with the exception of a couple of landslides and a few lizards, she was filled with happiness at simply being in Egypt, in the desert, with ancient ruins barely half an hour's drive away.

Reaching the base of the palm, she turned and looked at Ben. He was still sitting on the stone about twenty yards away, but had shifted round to see what she was doing. She looked at him and started to wave, then stopped.

"What is it?" he shouted. He got up and jogged over to her. "Gail, what's wrong?"

She pointed to the stone they had been sitting on, and began walking towards it. "Look!"

Ben turned back to the rock and froze. Even he knew what it meant. The flat stone they had been sitting on was about eight feet long by at least six feet wide. It stood about eight inches high, almost buried in the sand, and was perfectly flat. There were many flat stones dotted around the landscape, a natural by-product of the stratified rock formation caused by millions of years of sedimentation, and this one had seemed no different as they had approached it from the cliff and sat down to rest. But it was obvious, seeing it from the other side, that it had once been shaped by man.

Whereas on the other side it was rough and ragged, this side was perfectly smooth and flat, the vertical face at right angles with the top. From where Gail and Ben were now standing, it looked like a giant stone building block that had simply fallen from the sky and landed in the middle of a barren cliff-top. Naturally occurring geological marvels were not unheard of: Gail had seen pictures of the Giant's Causeway and plenty of underwater sites around the world where natural rock formations had been wrongly attributed to man. And if it had only been for the right angles and the smoothness of the surfaces, Gail could have doubted her judgement. But it was not just this that made her heart swell with excitement.

Engraved on the stone, just poking out from beneath the sand, were the unmistakable lines, loops and curves of hieroglyphs.

They started clearing the loose sand at its base until an area approximately two feet high by eight long had been exposed.

On her knees, Gail ran her hand over the engravings, following the outline of what they could now see was a cartouche with her fingers. She looked up at Ben.

A cartouche is an oblong shape containing some hieroglyphic symbols. Both ends of the cartouche are always rounded, and if a straight line runs along the bottom edge, then the characters within the oblong typically represent the name of a royal figure. The term *cartouche* comes from the French word for cartridge, as French soldiers in Egypt during Napoleonic times noted their likeness to their ammunition casing.

This cartouche was definitely for someone important.

"Ben?" Gail asked.

Ben was rummaging in his backpack and brought out a well-thumbed textbook.

"Hieroglyphs, my favourite," he smiled. Running his finger along the symbols, he read out loud. "The four symbols at the top are *Ra*, *e*, *t* and *n*. The god Aten. The symbol at the bottom of the cartouche, of a woman, means a queen."

"Ben," she started. "Is that Nefertiti?"

He looked between the cartouche and his textbook. "What looks like a church steeple is actually the heart with a windpipe attached. One on its own, *nfr*, means beautiful. He skimmed through the pages quickly.

"I was never good at this," he complained, rubbing his forehead.

"You're doing brilliantly," Gail encouraged him. "Better than I could!"

He smiled and pointed to the next three hearts and windpipes.

"These three together, are *nfrw*, similar to the first, but meaning beauty. Ah, OK!" He pointed to a page in his book. "Beautiful is the beauty of Aten. It's like a part of the name, but not the name, if you see, like saying long live the queen."

Gail was disappointed. "So, it's not *the beautiful one has come*? It's not Nefertiti?"

"Be patient! OK, the next bit is another heart and windpipe followed by *neb*, the basket. This is *nfr-t*, a beautiful woman, or simply a beauty. The last bit, I have no idea. Wait, let me try something."

She looked at the cartouche and the surrounding symbols. "Beautiful is the beauty of Aten, A beauty *something something*. It's pretty close! What do you think, Ben?"

Ben was flicking through the pages of his textbook and jotting down some notes, muttering to himself in Arabic. Finally, he showed them to Gail.

"OK, I did it backwards. You want this last bit to be has come. The

verb to come is tall reed with two legs that you see here in the cartouche, but followed by two man legs walking. It is pronounced *ii*. The two vertical bars in the cartouche are a short form of two walking legs. The problem is the symbols are in the wrong order. They should be, reed, then walking legs, then the last one, which you can see here next to the sitting queen, which is pestle, from mortar and pestle for mixing herbs," he made a mixing motion with his hands. "The pestle makes a soft *t* sound, and it makes the feminine of the past of the verb *come*."

Gail read through the scribbled notes then took his pen. She jotted down the phonemes one by one: *Nfr-t*, a beauty, *ii-t*, has come.

"*Nfr-t-ii-t*," she whispered in wonder.

"Finally," Ben said with a grin. "Now you pronounce it like a true Egyptian!"

They both sat back on the sand, looking at their find with a mixture of disbelief and excitement.

And Gail thought to herself: *a beauty has come*.

CHAPTER 9

George edged the rental car down the track and cursed the sand as he looked enviously at the 4x4s parked a hundred yards ahead of where he was going to have to stop. Getting out, he donned an old fashioned explorer's hat that had been thrust upon him by an eager salesman in Luxor. He checked his backpack for his camera and took a swig from a plastic bottle of water before setting off.

As he rounded the bend in the road ahead, he was surprised to see the number of cars lined up at the foot of the small cliff. On top of the white 4x4s he had seen a few days earlier at the archaeological dig there were three luxury off-roaders, more used to driving in cities but clearly enjoying their trip in the country. On the side of one was a logo for the Al Jazeera news network.

It had been four days since he had left Amarna. Christmas Eve back in England, he thought to himself in wonder as the heat from the midday sun beat down on his shoulders. Back home, people would be doing their last minute shopping and panicking about whether there were enough sprouts for everyone; here, a procession of people had gathered in the desert around something his wife had found. "What on earth could it be?" he wondered, images of a surreal modern day Nativity playing out in his mind.

"*Assalaam aleikum,* George!" a shout came from above him. "Nice hat!"

Looking up he saw Ben's huge grin and waved. "*Waleikum salaam*! How do I get up?" he shouted.

"Keep going, you'll see a path in front of you!"

"George!" Gail shouted as she joined Ben.

He laughed and made his way to the path. "Hello honey. Been having fun, I hear?"

The stone stood six feet tall from the bottom of the excavation. A

53

crowd of people stood looking at the other side of it. George thought he recognised three of the students from the dig, but there were five men with them he had not seen before. A photographer circled the stone taking pictures. A tall man in his early thirties, he was wearing khaki shorts and a blue sleeveless jacket covered in pockets, a camera bag slung over his shoulder. He assumed that this had to be the reporter from Al Jazeera.

At one end of the excavation was a massive pile of sand and rock rising nearly five feet high.

Gail took George's arm and gave him a kiss on the cheek. "I missed you," she whispered in his ear.

"You found *this*?" he replied in disbelief. "On your own?"

"I was with her!" Ben complained with a grin.

Gail laughed. "It was just sitting here," she explained. "And now it's been excavated, it looks like there's a lot more to it."

George stood at the edge of the trench and looked at the stone. The two sides he could see from where he was were rough stone, in contrast to the flat, smooth top. From this angle, it looked totally unremarkable.

"We thought that there may have been hieroglyphs under the sand on this side," Gail said, "but we were wrong. It simply goes down to the base like that. It also looks like it was buried deliberately, judging from the deposits we excavated."

George walked round to the back of the trench and was met by the Professor, who shook his hand and asked him how his trip south had been.

"Not as exciting as this," he gestured towards the stone. "What is it?"

"It's covering something, but we don't know what yet."

"And what does *that* say?" he pointed to the hieroglyphs. Compared to those that he had seen elsewhere in Egypt that week, the engravings looked sloppy, almost *rushed*. The top half were noticeably more worn from where they had been exposed to the elements.

"Basically," Gail said from behind them, "it says Nefertiti."

He glanced over his shoulder at her and raised an eyebrow. She grinned from ear to ear. "So how do you know there's something underneath it?" he asked, looking at the Professor.

Mamdouh climbed into the trench and stood at the end of the rectangular block. "Because of these." He pointed with his index finger at a series of rough, straight lines scratched into the bedrock and ending at the edge of the stone. Where the Professor was standing, the trench had been lengthened by at least fifteen feet. The lines stopped just before the end of the trench.

"It was pushed into place, and it now sits a couple of centimetres deep on what we assume must be a small sill that runs around the edge of a hole beneath it," Mamdouh said. "If it was not covering anything, why would it have been pushed nearly five metres along these grooves and placed so carefully at this precise point." He put his hands on his hips and looked up at George. "That was a clue, Mr Turner." He nodded towards three people standing next to what looked like a water cylinder connected to a personal computer. "That and the fact that their X-ray shows that there is a large open space beneath my feet."

"You got here just in time," Gail said. "The Professor received the authorisation a while ago to go ahead with the excavation and remove the block."

George grinned. "I would like to see that."

"See it?" Mamdouh raised an eyebrow. "If you don't mind, you can help us by pulling on one of the ropes!"

One end of the stone was to be lifted from its seat using a large industrial jack. It looked like a scaled down forklift truck about two feet high, and was being operated by three engineers from Cairo. Two small indents had been drilled into the bedrock against the end of the engraved stone, to allow the jack's small metal feet to be wedged underneath it. Compressed air was forced into the machine's pistons, and the stone rose slowly. As its base crept above the bedrock, a long metal rod, flat on one side, barely an inch thick but made of high density carbon steel, was slipped under from one side and pushed through until it protruded out on both sides like an axel. Its flat edge was facing down, stopping it from rolling out from under the heavy stone.

One of the engineers crouched down and shone a torch underneath the stone to verify that the lip on which the stone sat ran uninterrupted around the perimeter of the hole.

"If the ledge is only partial, or damaged, then when we pull on the stone it may fall into the hole, which would make things rather complicated." Mamdouh had told them.

After several seconds the engineer stood up nodding and said one word in Arabic to his captive audience. "He saw steps in the hole," Ben translated for Gail and George.

Air began to escape from the jack's piston as the engineer gently lowered the stone to sit comfortably on the carbon steel rod. The engineer who had positioned the rod gave a thumbs up signal to his colleagues, and they proceeded to remove their machinery.

A hundred foot synthetic rope was then wrapped twice round the stone. The two loose ends, one coming from either side, were passed through a steel ring three inches in diameter positioned at the raised end. The two ropes were then given to two groups of three people wearing gloves and standing a foot above the bedrock, outside the trench. From above, the two groups, rope and stone looked like a giant letter Y; they would be pulling it back to where it had first stood, thousands of years earlier.

Ben and George positioned themselves at the back of one of the groups.

"Pull gently," Mamdouh ordered as he watched from inside the trench.

The two ropes became taught and the loops around the stone creaked as the six people nervously applied their weight. It gently shifted towards them, uncovering six inches of the stairway beneath.

The engineer who had shone the torch under the stone proceeded to spray its path with a water-based lubricant, to facilitate its passage. The Professor walked to and fro around the stone as it slid slowly away, until after barely five minutes of pulling it was clear.

He held his hand up to stop the eager Al Jazeera photographer from approaching the hole and shouted out in Arabic. The photographer backed off, pushed up the rim of his baseball cap and shook his head in confusion before taking several dozen photos from a short distance, outside the trench.

"We must catalogue the finds first, for archaeology, before letting Al Jazeera in." Ben explained in English.

"Is it just me, or does Mamdouh look a little nervous?" Gail quizzed him. "More nervous than excited?"

Ben thought about this for a while before responding. "I cannot say what the difference between nervous and excited is, Gail. If it were me, I would be running down the steps already," he paused. "But then that is probably why he is a Professor of Egyptology and I am almost failing my degree."

"Whatever he is," George interrupted them. "I think he's calling you."

The Professor got out of the trench and met Gail half way.

"I am certain, Gail, that you have seen or heard stories of archaeologists entering tombs and crypts over a hundred years ago, haven't you?" he started.

"Like Howard Carter in the Valley of the Kings, you mean?" she asked.

"Yes, absolutely. Well, we have come a long way in science, in methods and in practice since then, but no matter how much technology we have and how many studies we undertake, the basics of what we are about to do remain the same now as they were when Carter first took his pick to the mortar that sealed Tutankhamen inside his tomb." He paused for her reaction, one of mild surprise, before continuing. "I think that with what has happened over the past few days, you have more than enough material to start your thesis."

She laughed and looked to her left, at the steps leading down into the depths of the rock. "I think so," she said.

His eyes followed hers and he looked up at her, smiling. "Your enthusiasm, not to mention lots of luck, has helped to find something very special in Amarna, Gail. Some of the most incredible finds in archaeology have been found by luck, and mostly not by archaeologists. But you have the benefit of not only being lucky, but also an archaeologist, and as a reward you will be the first student to enter this tomb."

"Thank you, Mamdouh, but Ben found the site with me and translated the hieroglyphs." Gail liked Ben a lot, and thought it unfair to remove any credit from him for the discovery.

"This is true, but would Ben have reached this cliff top were it not for you?" he smiled and looked over at Ben, who was having an animated discussion with George. "And he is not an archaeologist at heart, he will find passion in something else. You on the other hand, are an archaeologist, and always will be no matter what you do. What lies beneath our feet at this very moment may be the biggest find you ever make."

She looked over to her Egyptian friend and smiled. "I will ask Ben, and offer to go down the steps with him," she decided. "If that's alright with you, Mamdouh?" she added quickly.

Mamdouh grinned. "Whatever you think is best, Gail, the choice is yours." He took a step past her and raised his voice to get everyone's attention.

The students, engineers, photographer and George had all been biding their time following the uncovering of the steps several minutes earlier. The thrill of the unknown, coupled with the Professor's desire to control the descent into the tomb, had fuelled their impatience, and it had been hard for everyone to content themselves with a simple glance or two into the hole.

He lifted his head and addressed the crowd in Arabic as the Al Jazeera photographer took a flurry of shots. "I will descend the steps first, along with an engineer who will ensure that the structure is safe. I will then come back up and we will discuss what to do next. OK?"

They all nodded, and watched as he descended with a powerful hand torch, followed by an engineer with a large black case that presumably held instruments with which they would assess the structure.

Gail looked at George and Ben, who were standing on the edge of the trench, and grinned from ear to ear.

Almost ten minutes passed before anything was heard from the hole. Suddenly, the engineer suddenly hopped up the steps, out of the trench and over to his two colleagues with their X-ray system.

After a brief exchange of words, the men gathered their equipment together and carried it over to the steps. Within two minutes they had all disappeared underground, much to the frustration of the Al Jazeera photographer, who returned from relieving himself just in time to see the engineer's head vanish down the hole.

"Is this normal?" George said out loud to no one in particular.

"The last tomb to be excavated in Egypt was over thirty years ago. And the last before that was over a hundred years ago." Gail answered. "With that track record, *normal* probably means breaking in, stealing all the gold and taking the finds out of the country. So no, this isn't normal."

George looked at his wife and shook his head. "That's not quite what I meant, honey."

"I do not know if it is normal," Ben said. "But it is annoying. I want to know what is down there!"

Gail looked at him and summoned the courage to ask him the question she had been reciting in her head. "Ben, Mamdouh has suggested that when he gets back, I go down the steps first on my own, followed by you and the other students," she said. There was a brief pause. "Do you want to come with me first instead?"

Ben looked at her with a smile. "Gail, this is your find, I merely sat on it to keep it warm."

"But you were with me, we found it together," she was almost pleading with him. She felt bad for wanting to leave Ben and be alone, it was not a sign of a competitive streak, she convinced herself, if she tried to make him come with her. But deep down inside she knew that she would not have asked him, but told him to come with her first, had she not wanted to go down alone.

"I wanted to turn back before we got to the top of the cliff, Gail, you did not," he explained. "If it wasn't for my requirement to pass this year, I would probably be in Cairo still. You came from England to be here, and climbed over many rocks against my judgement. This is *your* find."

"Thank you, Ben," Gail said, the emotion rising in her throat.

There was an awkward silence during which they all looked towards the steps.

"How was Karnak?" Ben suddenly asked George, changing the subject.

He smiled and pointed at his hat. "*That* good," he replied. "Is anyone else hungry?" Saying this, he opened his backpack and removed a couple of packets of biscuits and a large bottle of water.

They shared the snacks around, though almost everyone was too excited to eat, and did their best to enjoy tourist anecdotes for the next fifteen minutes, making sure to keep an eye on the trench for signs of the Professor and the three engineers.

It was while Ben was interesting everyone with a story of an overzealous border guard in Algeria, translating into English at the same time, that the Professor finally emerged from the hole.

Within seconds everyone had crowding round him.

Mamdouh looked up at them all seriously for several long moments before breaking into a huge grin, his white teeth shining in the afternoon sun. He said a short sentence in Arabic and received a great cheer in reply, while the photographer's camera flashed crazily in the background.

"Mamdouh?" Gail asked over the sound of a hundred questions being asked at the same time in Arabic.

He turned towards her and laughed out loud. "Gail," he sounded relaxed and enthused, in complete contrast to his behaviour before descending the steps half an hour earlier. "I said you had enough to start your thesis with what we have seen since you arrived, didn't I?"

"Yes, you did."

"I am sorry, Gail, I was wrong." He put his hand on her shoulder and looked her in the eyes. "Gail, with what you have found here in Amarna, you have enough for your entire career!"

Gail's heart missed a beat. "Is Nefertiti down there?"

"We don't know yet, we can't tell."

"So what is it?" she urged.

CHAPTER 10

Gail took her first step cautiously. She now understood what Mamdouh had meant, talking about Carter and entering a tomb for the first time; no amount of science and studying could have prepared her for the sheer excitement of knowing that apart from four men within the past hour, she was the first person in over three thousand years to descend these steps, and certainly the first woman.

The engraved stone they had removed from the surface had been sitting on a flat sill, six inches wide and two inches deep that ran uninterrupted along all four edges of the hole. The passageway in between was five feet wide, enough for two people to walk down side by side without touching each other. She took a mental note to thank Ben once more for letting her go down alone.

After thirty-odd steps, she found herself on a small landing, five feet square, where the steps took a ninety-degree left turn, away from the cliff outside, and continued to descend.

The walls of the staircase were completely smooth. As far as she could see, there was not one hieroglyph, engraving or painting all the way down. From what she knew of Egyptian tombs and monuments, this was not entirely uncommon; there may well be more to see further down.

The bottom of the steps opened onto a large room, about three times as wide as the staircase and just as long. She shone her powerful torch around, the passage of the Professor betrayed by the recently disturbed dust that danced lazily in its beam. In the four corners of the room and twice at regular intervals on each side, straight undecorated columns connected the floor and ceiling. On closer inspection, Gail noticed that they had not been built, but rather carved out of the bedrock, and were connected to the wall behind. The entrance she had emerged from was in the middle of one of the walls, in between two columns.

There were no other openings.

As with the staircase that led to it, the walls of the room were unmarked and the twelve columns stood out as the only decorative features.

The engineers' X-ray machine was on the floor opposite her, one flat end of the cylinder touching the wall between two columns, the other pointing towards the centre of the room. Sitting on the floor next to it was a laptop computer, open and unlocked. She walked over to it and looked at the screen.

At first, she was not sure what she was looking at, the monochrome display showing a series of dark and light shapes within a circular frame, but soon her mind adjusted to the input, in much the same way it usually did after several seconds staring at a three dimensional image. She twisted her head slightly, then looked at the wall the cylinder was propped against.

"No way," she said to herself.

She knelt down in front of the laptop and studied the grey and black shapes more closely for several minutes, briefly looking back at the wall several times in disbelief before resuming her in-depth appreciation of what lay beyond the rock.

It was a sight that, as a student, she was all too familiar with.

The echo of footsteps and excited voices from the corridor behind her brought Gail back to reality; she turned round just in time to see three students, a young boy and two girls, enter the room. Behind them, she could make out the distinctive tones of Ben trying to explain something to her husband.

"Look!" she said, standing up and pointing to the laptop display. "Look at this! Isn't it amazing?"

The three students gathered round and stood in silence as they struggled to interpret the picture. After a brief moment, one of them recognised an object with a shriek, and within seconds they were all pointing eagerly at various shapes and talking quickly in a mixture of English, for Gail was still with them, and Arabic, because they were too excited to be able to find all the words they needed to explain what they were looking at.

In this time, Ben and George had entered the room and now stood behind the small group of archaeologists.

"All those steps lead to *this*, a room with no doors?" George complained.

She grabbed him by the arm and pulled him towards the laptop. "*This* room isn't it." As she gestured towards the wall, he saw the look of excitement in her eyes and looked more closely at the display before him. "It's just an ante-chamber," she said.

George leant closer, the puzzled look on his face telling Gail that he was unable to interpret the monochrome feed. "What am I looking at?"

The Backscatter X-ray system being used by the engineers was an experimental piece of hardware, developed mainly for seeing through rubble after earthquakes. The traditional X-ray, as used on patients in hospitals, was able to 'see through' objects by detecting varying levels of resistance to the radiation passing through them, therefore giving a very obvious representation of the human skeleton for instance, where the density of the bone is significantly higher than that of soft tissue. In order to be able to measure resistance through an object, traditional X-rays require the use of a radioactive emitter and a photographic receiver, in between which the object to be examined is placed.

In contrast, the *Backscatter* X-ray, as the name suggests, exploits a different phenomenon in the field of radiation detection – that of the amount of subjected radiation *returned* from an object. At the end of the twentieth century, this new form of X-ray garnered some interest from the search and rescue community, but it was not until the twenty-first century that it was fully taken advantage of; indeed, an urge to improve airport security in the United States following a string of terrorist attacks forced the government to invest heavily in advanced security technologies. The Backscatter X-ray had many advantages over other detection methods, primarily in its speed. Whereas it would take nearly thirty seconds for a person to manually search a passenger, the new system was able to accurately scan and detect offensive items in less than a second.

The other benefit of the Backscatter X-ray over traditional X-ray was that as it measured radiation returning from a target object, the emitter and receiver could be contained within one box, giving it the same flexibility as radar and sonar. Rather than placing the object between the X-ray and a photographic plate, it was simply a matter of pointing the X-ray at the object you wanted to see through.

Unfortunately, public opposition to the X-ray eventually proved too strong and the technology was never successfully implemented. It was not that the amount of radiation passengers were subjected to was unacceptable; in fact the Backscatter technique produced far less radiation than traditional X-rays and was deemed to be harmless. Even the price of the technology was not prohibitive, as the end cost of a production passenger scanning unit was cheaper than running a traditional security checkpoint. In the end, the system was abandoned as it presented an infringement on passenger privacy. Because of the low levels of radiation employed by the system, it did not see through soft tissue to show bones; instead, it saw through clothes to show soft tissue. During its first years in live trials, it became obvious that the quality of the images produced by the system was so high that it was no different to asking people to pass through security completely naked, and with airport management unable to commit to the reliable safekeeping of all of the resulting indecent images, the Backscatter X-ray lost its high government funding, and it was relegated once more to the search and rescue community, where funding was low and public interest minimal.

The cylindrical system they were looking at now had therefore been specifically designed for search and rescue, and was more portable and significantly more powerful than its airport ancestors. The level of radiation it was outputting, whilst still significantly lower than that of a traditional X-ray, allowed it to see through solid objects and detect whatever lay beyond, within a distance of up to one hundred and fifty feet. The software installed on the laptop computer was developed not only to render the resulting images in monochrome, but also display relative distances and scale; the further objects were from the cylinder, the lighter their colour on the display. To help in measuring these variations, a scale was shown at the bottom of the screen, from black to very light grey, zero feet to one hundred and fifty. The view was very cluttered, as the user interface had not been particularly well designed, but as Gail and the group of students had shown, only a brief period of mental adjustment was needed to interpret the images.

"Hang on," George said slowly, before Gail could help him. "I think I know what that is."

"Yes?" she smiled.

Running horizontally across the X-ray were two very dark lines, approximately ten inches apart. Behind these were a series of six lighter lines, and behind those, ten more, lighter still. The pattern repeated itself a dozen times until the colour of the last set of lines showed them to be at least one hundred and twenty feet from the room they were standing in. An appreciation of the diminishing perspective as objects approached the limit of the X-ray's reach made it clear that each line was equally spaced vertically, and that the sets of lines were the same distance from one another. Also, although they were not visible for the first two sets of lines, from the third set onwards regular vertical lines seemed to intersect the horizontal ones.

"The machines scope spreads out in a cone, doesn't it? So we can only see a couple of feet square for the closest objects, but when it reaches the furthest ones we're seeing a lot more?" George asked.

Gail looked at the display again and did some mental arithmetic. "As far as I can tell, at its furthest its showing us an area over thirty feet wide; it's like a very expensive fisheye lens on a very old Egyptian front door," she said.

George looked more closely and started to focus on the detail. On top of almost every single horizontal line were dozens of thick, short lines and circles. The lines tended to be placed next to one another, both horizontally and vertically, whereas the circles, of varying diameters, were generally on top of one another forming triangles, like sets of bowling pins seen from above. As he understood the images more, it became evident that the Backscatter X-ray cylinder had not simply been placed against the wall randomly; the position had to have been chosen very carefully so as to show as much of the more distant objects as possible. If a series of the short, thick lines had been present on top of one of the horizontal lines in the foreground, they would have blacked everything else out.

"I see it!" Ben shouted, making the others all jump. "Books! And the things you put books on!"

"Shelves. Dozens and dozens of shelves," George said under his breath.

"And hundreds and hundreds of books," Gail added. "It's not a tomb, it's a *library*."

George found Gail's hand and held it tightly. "And there's something else, too," he said.

It was strange that when faced with such an overwhelming number of priceless written records, anything could have been more impressive. But as George pointed with his index finger at the screen, everything Gail had seen so far that day seemed to dissolve in her mind, to be replaced with an excitement she had not felt for many years. Suddenly, she was seven again, looking at the presents below the Christmas Tree, and only seeing the one huge, beautifully wrapped box towards the back.

In the bottom half of the screen in very faint grey, at least one hundred and thirty feet away from them and beyond the farthest set of shelves, was a rectangular object. It was very small on the screen, but despite the resolution Gail could just about work out that *there was something else on top of it*.

One of the students looked at the controls of the laptop, and cautiously moved the cursor on the display until it was over the object. Bringing up a menu in Arabic, he selected an option and the X-ray image disappeared. After a heart-stopping moment, the image reappeared, but this time, the rectangular object filled the screen.

"Oh, wow," Gail managed to say. She'd practically stopped breathing.

Of all the hundreds of books inside the library, there was now only one that mattered. It was placed on a plinth, at an angle, like a Bible at the altar of a Church.

George leant over to his wife and kissed her on the cheek. "Merry Christmas, honey," he said quietly. "Merry Christmas."

Standing on the edge of the cliff outside, Professor Mamdouh al-Misri snapped his phone shut and placed it back in his trouser pocket.

He scanned the rocky terrain below him, from the Nile on his right to his original archaeological dig ahead of him to the south. Shaking his head slowly, he turned round and made his way back to the trench, where the Al Jazeera photographer was impatiently waiting to be escorted down the steps.

On the other side of the trench, the three engineers stood together, watching him carefully. At their feet stood the large black case that had been taken with him down the steps.

The Professor pulled his eyes away from them and jumped down into the trench, landing next to the photographer with a thud.

"OK, come and see what all the fuss is about," he said in Arabic, ushering the photographer into the hole. He shot a nervous look over his shoulder at the engineers, whose steely gaze followed him as he descended once more.

PART THREE

SEPTEMBER 2045

CHAPTER 11

Captain Yves Montreaux had always dreamed of going to Mars. Born in California to a French-Canadian father and American mother, his first vivid memory was of an image beamed back from NASA's *Spirit* mission, in 2004. He had been barely six years old at the time and his mother, a US Navy pilot, had shown him the picture on the Internet early one morning before school. Even now, forty-one years later, he still dreamt of being there, with the *Spirit* rover, as it edged its way carefully out of its landing craft and onto Martian soil for the first time.

He pulled himself over to the small circle of Plexiglas, his window onto the eternal sunshine of interplanetary space.

A month earlier, the view had been dominated by aluminium cranes, connectors and cylindrical pods in orbit around Earth; the precision-built chaos that was the International Space Station. After half a century of operation, most of the original modules were now lost in a maze of metal and foil, somewhere towards the centre of the station. It had taken all of those fifty years to get to its current state, and was still exceeding the expectations of its original designers, now mostly dead.

Looking out of the window now, Montreaux had a front row seat to the stars. There was no horizon, no up, no down; a confusing state of affairs at first, but it was not something that he had simply been thrown into from one day to the next. For the past eight weeks, as the spaceship had gradually accelerated beyond the pull of the Moon and into interplanetary space, he had watched as his home planet had grown smaller, until now he was able to hold his thumb up and completely block it out. Within another week it would be but a bright star, and it would be time to look the other way, towards Mars.

There was a knock on the plastic door-frame of his quarters.

"Come in," he said without turning.

Despite the lack of actual doors to separate them, the ingrained protocol was hard to shake.

"Sir," the female voice said. "We are in the Lounge."

Montreaux smiled to himself as he held on to the handle on the wall and slowly pivoted round to see her. Her jet black hair was pulled into a tight ponytail, revealing her pretty, pale face. "Su Ning," he said. "We have known each other for over a year, trained together for months, and lived in the same metal tube for over two months, haven't we?" His voice was kind, soft.

She smiled. "And I still call you *Sir*," she confirmed.

Montreaux's Chinese was hopeless. A few basic commands and greetings were all he had managed to master since meeting Lieutenant Shi Su Ning the previous summer. For this reason it amazed and humbled him that she could not only speak perfect English, but do so with barely a hint of an accent. That she had also never lived outside of Beijing in her entire life only made the feat more incredible to him.

"I'll join you shortly, I have to quickly finish this log entry first," he explained.

She left, and the Captain returned to the window and gathered his thoughts. "Captain Daniil Marchenko, Russian cosmonaut, Second in Command of the *Clarke*, is twenty-nine years old today." He paused and repeated the number to himself under his breath; it seemed impossibly young. "We are having a small celebration in the Lounge this evening." He focused on the small brilliant disc that was Earth, its continents no longer distinguishable, and smiled. "Next log entry in one sol. *Stop recording.*" The last two words were said more loudly in a monotonous voice. He was rewarded with an audible confirmation from his computer.

The *Clarke's* crew had been working to the Martian day, twenty-four hours and thirty-nine minutes, for over a year, and were by now completely adjusted to it. As soon as they had been accepted for the mission training, they had all been given new wrist-watches, and their computers had been updated with new software to add the extra minutes into each day. The easy part of the transition had been to start referring to a *day* as a *sol*; the hardest part was to turn up to work nearly three quarters of an hour later every 'morning'. Within two weeks they were working at night instead of during the day, and it was two months before Montreaux learnt to stop looking towards the Sun for guidance.

While on Earth this had been a chore, in space it was much easier due to the lack of natural daytime and night time. Space made it more natural to fall asleep during what their watches told them was the Martian night. The *Clarke* was designed to simulate the cycle of the Martian sol by providing ambient light at pre-programmed times, in perfect co-ordination with the planet itself based on the time zone of their projected landing site.

Looking at his watch now, Montreaux knew that there were barely two hours of *sol-light* left.

CHAPTER 12

As Montreaux entered the Lounge, he saw Captain Daniil Marchenko sitting next to Su Ning on the sofa. He had a huge grin on his face as he donned his birthday hat. His head was completely shaven, and the hat slipped down to rest on his brow, partially blocking his sight.

"Wait, Danny!" Su Ning laughed as she lifted the paper hat off and crimped the back to make it smaller. "That's better!" she placed it back on his head, ensuring it fitted perfectly.

"Thank you Su Ning, I will bring you my suit to fix in the morning." He laughed as he avoided Su Ning's playful dig at his ribs before reaching for his drink. Placing the straw in his mouth he pressed down on the bag's contents until it was empty.

"Happy Birthday, Captain Marchenko," Montreaux said as he glided across the room, extending his hand to the Russian. They had, of course, already greeted each other that sol, but it seemed appropriate to repeat the congratulations given the festive appearance of the crew.

"Thank you, Captain," Marchenko replied gracefully.

Montreaux was glad that the *Clarke*'s official language was English, as his Russian was worse than his Chinese. While Marchenko's accent was not as good as Su Ning's, his English was similarly impressive.

"*S Dnyom Rozdyeniya*, Danny!" came a voice above Montreaux's head.

It was bad enough that the crew did not follow the regulatory naming convention of rank and surname, thought Montreaux, but if there was one person who would reliably break any possible protocol, including that of official language, it was Dr Jane Richardson, the mission's civilian scientist. She was the only crew member without a military background, a fact that was usually reflected in both her attire *and* attitude. The Captain glanced up at her and tutted.

The Lounge was the main social hub of the *Clarke*. A huge spherical room, it was fifty feet wide, with slightly flattened poles like a beach ball that was being pressed against the ground. Two cylindrical tubes connected the Lounge to the other parts of the ship, and four small windows, identical to the one in the Captain's quarters, were placed at regular intervals around the equator. Between two of the windows and directly in front of Montreaux, who had approached from the sleeping area, was the Lounge's red sofa, sixteen feet long with four backrests. It was designed for everyone to sit facing the low coffee table in front. Lieutenant Su Ning and Captain Marchencko had used the sofa's straps to stop themselves from floating away from the drinks and meals that stuck magnetically to the table's surface.

Behind Montreaux's head, on the wall above the entrance, was a large recessed television screen, protected by thick Plexiglas against out of control floating astronauts. Every night they would be able to sit in front of the screen and watch a variety of programmes and movies, held in the *Clarke*'s library. It was also where the crew would get regular video broadcasts from Earth. Private communications would invariably be played on the smaller screens, inside their own quarters.

The sofa and coffee table formed the logical 'floor', while the small recessed cupboards and drawers on the opposing side of the sphere were the 'ceiling'. However the lack of gravity meant that the *Clarke*'s crew were by no means restricted to such definitions.

It would be another month and a half before they would need to get used to an actual feeling of down and up, but even on Mars it would be at a third of Earth's oppressive gravity.

For this reason, he was unsurprised to see Dr Richardson sitting quite comfortably on the ceiling above him, sipping through the straw of her drink.

"Hi, Yves!" she waved.

"Good evening Dr Richardson," he said quite politely. "I would remind you that the official language of this vessel is English." He knew he was perhaps being a little harsh, given the circumstances, but his upbringing had been one of utmost respect for seniority and rank, none of which was forthcoming from the doctor. He reached the sofa with a push and strapped himself in. Pulling a drink from the table, he forced himself not to look up at the scientist. "Will you be joining us today?"

"Actually, yes, I will," she replied.

She suddenly appeared on the seat beside him thanks to a perfectly judged push against the room's wall. She clipped herself in and raised her drink for a toast. Some people took a long time to get used to zero gravity, and simply moving from one place to another was a chore. But not Dr Richardson; Jane was a natural, and it annoyed him no end.

"To Danny!" she said with a grin.

The light-hearted party had lasted three hours, during which special congratulatory messages from Earth had been played on the Lounge's television screen. It had finished when it became evident that both Captain Marchenko and Dr Richardson had clearly consumed too much alcohol, a dangerous situation in space. The Russians had a far more relaxed attitude to alcohol than their western counterparts, and had lobbied hard to allow some drinks on the mission for special occasions. But Montreaux been had brought up under the NASA doctrine, where alcohol was a complete no-no.

As a consequence, he had called an end to the night slightly earlier than planned, with Marchenko retiring merrily to his quarters to watch the more personal greetings that his family had transmitted during the day.

Back in his own room, Montreaux placed the headphones carefully over his ears and pressed them down firmly with his hands, before touching the screen lightly. As the music began to play, he lay back and let his mind wander.

On the wall opposite was a framed picture: a three dimensional rendering of the *Clarke*, set against the backdrop of Mars. The Sun shone from the left of the picture, casting the *Clarke*'s shadow over the Red Planet.

He closed his eyes and put his hands behind his head as Barber's *Adagio for Strings* reached its first climax in his headphones. Sudden silence, then a lone double-bass mournfully recited the American composer's melody.

Montreaux's imagination took him through his quarters' small window and he sailed out into space. He felt himself rotating slowly in the vacuum, before coming to rest in a reclined position, his eyes wide open.

Before him lay the *Clarke*.

CHAPTER 13

The *Clarke* slid through space effortlessly and silently at just over eight kilometres per second. The bright blue beam of charged ions escaping the spaceship's exhaust, powered by a nuclear particle accelerator, made it the fastest manned craft ever built. Despite this, the gradual acceleration over eight weeks made the sensation of incredible speed practically imperceptible to its crew, who continued to float inside.

The ion drive and particle accelerator were housed within a large grey oblong structure to the rear of the *Clarke*, narrowing at the end to a slit through which the ions were forced. The structure was connected by a one hundred feet section of titanium scaffold to the main living quarters. Running the entire length of the scaffold, through its centre, was a series of thin metallic tubes containing xenon gas, the fuel for their entire journey. On their arrival in Mars orbit, the spent canisters would be jettisoned carefully in space, away from the planet, to save on mass for the return journey; mass still had the same effect on objects as it did on Earth, even in the weightlessness of space.

Closest to the ion drive was a group of four cylindrical pods bunched together in a circle, each one fifteen feet high and ten feet in diameter. There was one pod for each crew member, containing a bunk, computer, cupboard and drawers for personal items, and a small desk and chair with strap to retain its occupant. The remaining space was used for storage; enough food for one person for eight months.

These personal quarters all led to a single cylindrical pod, ten feet high and twenty feet in diameter. Known to the crew as the 'Hygiene Bay', it housed the toilet and cleaning facilities. From the inside, it was a long way from a normal domestic bathroom; the walls and floors were made of thin stainless steel plates and fibreglass moulds. Any water used whilst cleaning would go through a purification process and return to the water canisters housed around the outside of the pod. Similarly, all bodily fluids were also recycled and returned to their reserve supply.

From the Hygiene Bay a small opening led to the southern pole of the Lounge.

The Lounge was designed to be a multi-purpose living area in which the crew would spend most of their time. Recessed cupboards opened out to reveal exercise mats and treadmills, and along one wall a complex scientific laboratory could be assembled. The Lounge's sheer scale allowed it to perform several functions at once, meaning that the crew of four could all use the space at the same time while not being restricted to the same activities. The flexibility had been deemed indispensable by the mission psychologists, who had also made efforts not to separate the crew. For this reason, aside from emergency airlocks between each pod, there were no closable doors throughout the ship.

Attached to the northern pole of the Lounge was the ten-foot long Command Module, containing four bucket seats in which the crew would be strapped during any navigation or propulsion changes. Surrounding the seats, an array of computer screens and old-fashioned flick switches covered every possible surface. Several portable fire-extinguishers were fastened to the walls.

Whereas the other modules, with the exception of the Hygiene Bay, were designed to be welcoming and friendly, using pastel colours and soft lighting, the Command Module was exactly the opposite; from its grey rivet-covered walls to the un-enticing control panels, entering the pod felt like getting into a World War II submarine. It was designed for functionality only, and doubled as the *Clarke*'s optimistic emergency escape pod. *Optimistic* because everyone knew that save for incredible good fortune, to enter the Command Module and leave the *Clarke* mid-mission was a one way ticket, as if they did so at any appreciable distance from Earth, it simply couldn't sustain life for long enough to allow a rescue party to reach it.

A single, closed hatch left the Command Module.

The final element of the *Clarke* interplanetary spaceship had been the subject of years of debate and research between the participating nations: the Mars Lander Pod. The MLP would be the first *manned* landing craft ever to touchdown on another planet. Larger objects had been placed on the surface of the Moon, but its lack of any substantially abrasive atmosphere naturally meant that aerodynamics did not need to be factored in; any sufficiently powered and controlled town house could be placed on the surface of the Moon with relative ease. Only the relatively small return modules needed to re-enter the Earth's atmosphere.

The MLP had eventually been developed as a compromise between volume, mass and form. At thirty feet in diameter and ten feet tall, shaped like two shallow soup bowls, one upside down on top of the other, it bore more than a passing resemblance to a nineteen-fifties flying saucer. Despite this, its method of entry into the Martian skies would be very conventional, sliding in like a Frisbee at such an angle as to ensure friction did not destroy it, but not so shallow as to cause it to bounce off the atmosphere and back into space.

Montreaux opened his eyes. His personal music player had stopped shuffling through his favourites list, and the ship's lighting had auto-dimmed, which told him it was Nightmode. Glancing at his watch, he noted with interest that he had been sleeping for nearly four hours. Lifting the headphones from his ears, he listened intently for voices.

Silence, save for the gentle hum of the *Clarke*'s air circulation system.

Although the ship was in Nightmode, thin strips of light ran along the edges of his door, and along all of the passageways outside it, throwing an eerie blue glow across his room. Looking round in the dim light, he unclipped himself and moved carefully through the door and into the Hygiene Bay.

The sound coming from Captain Marchenko's quarters was proof that it was possible to snore in zero gravity, and Montreaux smiled as he headed for the Lounge.

He reached for a small sliding switch on the inside of the connecting tunnel and the lights inside the Lounge turned on, faintly at first, then more brightly, until it was bathed in a soft, day-like warmth that reminded him of a summer afternoon in California. Were it not for the fact that he was now floating three feet above the sofa, he could almost imagine he was there, on the porch of the beach house, the sun touching his face gently.

"Couldn't sleep, Sir?"

Due to the lack of gravity he didn't so much jump as contract in surprise. He also couldn't stop a small gasp of shock from leaving his mouth.

"Sorry, I didn't mean to scare you," Su Ning apologised.

He looked up and saw her, lying flat on the ceiling, on her stomach, looking out of one of the Lounge's four windows. Her body and legs, held against the curved hull of the *Clarke*, made it look like an impossibly uncomfortable position.

"That's OK, Lieutenant. No, I had no problem sleeping, If anything I overslept! I'm just doing my rounds to make sure things are ticking along nicely, albeit a little later than usual. You?"

She continued to look into space. "I come up here every night, for an hour or two; when the ship goes into Nightmode, there is no reflection in the Plexiglas, and I can see all of the stars." Her voice drifted off, almost to a whisper.

"I had no idea you did this."

Su Ning arched her head up to look down at him. "You may be the Captain, Sir, but with respect you don't know everything."

She had spoken in her usual, kind voice. But something about the choice of her words, possibly her intonation, raised his suspicions. He was, after all, the commanding officer of the first manned mission to Mars. The mission's most valuable asset was its crew, and their well-being was always his highest priority. The revelation that Su Ning stared out into the depths of space every night wasn't concerning on its own, save for the fact that the controllers on Earth should have alerted him in his weekly psych report. However, the way in which she'd addressed him did seem a little out of sorts.

He pushed against the sofa and made his way to her, anchoring himself on the rung beside the window and lying down opposite her. He looked into space with her for several moments. She was right: with the light on, the window was more like a mirror. In it, he saw her worried look.

"Lieutenant, is everything OK?" He pushed away from the window to face her.

She looked away quickly.

The Captain allowed a long, uneasy silence to play out before opening his mouth and drawing breath. Before the words could come Su Ning continued, speaking quietly as if she did not want anyone to overhear.

"I am not sure if it is an issue, Sir," she whispered. "I would not worry you with anything unless I was certain." She took a final look out of the window, before pushing off towards the door. "I am very tired, Sir, please excuse me."

Montreaux lay confused for several seconds before turning quickly.

"Wait, Su Ning!"

He was alone.

Her parting words echoed in his head for minutes, although he decided to let her be. He could easily have reached her pod and confronted her; after all there was no door to close between them. But his experience told him that people, and none more so than astronauts, cosmonauts and taikonauts cooped up for months on end, sometimes needed their own space.

He launched himself from the wall to finish his inspection of the *Clarke*.

CHAPTER 14

Jane sighed and looked towards the small window on the opposite side of the Lounge. Danny Marchenko sat beside her, his bottom lip curled upwards in an amused smile.

"The United States is no longer a superpower, Jane," he said calmly, enjoying every minute of their debate.

She unclipped herself and launched towards the Lounge's ceiling. Halfway there she expertly twisted her lower body round so that she was facing him, while at the same time holding her arms outstretched to catch the edges of two metal rungs attached to the wall. Wedging her arms behind the rungs, she crossed her legs and looked him in the eyes.

"Danny, whilst I am all for the *International* nature of this mission," she said sarcastically, "NASA remains the main stakeholder in *Clarke.*" From where she was now perched, she could see both entrances to the Lounge. She squirmed as she saw Captain Montreaux enter from the direction of the living quarters.

He glanced up at her and laughed at the look on her face. "Captain Marchenko, are you winding Dr Richardson up again?" he said as he made his way to a small drawer recessed into the opposing wall.

"I know I shouldn't, but she bites so easily," Danny laughed.

She scowled at them both before returning her eyes to the darkness of space with a flick of her chin.

"Like it or not, Dr Richardson, this *isn't* an American expedition." He opened the drawer in front of him and removed a writing pad and pen. "This is the twenty-first century, and no matter how much lobbying goes on in Washington, this mission will not be putting the Star Spangled Banner into the soil of another planet."

Captain Danny Marchenko found himself in the unusual position of being in complete agreement with his American counterpart. "Absolutely," he made himself say. He had been leading Jane on for a quarter of an hour on the subject, as was their almost-weekly ritual, but while he did it purely for the look on the doctor's face, he recognised that sometimes things did get out of control. Twice already there had been heated arguments on board the *Clarke*, arguments that Earth had been quick to reprimand.

Today was one of those days, and Jane was taking the subject particularly badly.

"I don't see why we can't put all of our flags on Mars, that way everyone is happy!" she complained without looking away from the stars outside.

Montreaux closed the drawer and pushed himself towards the living quarter's entrance. "And can we put a Canadian flag, also?"

"Why not?"

"How about Japanese? I believe that Su Ning's Grandfather is from Kyoto," Captain Marchenko added.

"Naturally," she pursed her lips.

"Oh, wait a minute," Montreaux said theatrically. "My Grandfather was French, so how about a *Tricolore*? And a European Union Flag, so as not to upset everyone?"

Jane did not reply.

"Dr Richardson, this is part of our mission brief, and it does not matter how strongly you feel about the matter, the *Clarke* mission will be planting *no* flags in the Martian soil." He waited for a response, but none came. "Furthermore, whilst I happily encourage topical debate, I do believe that we have already covered this subject several times."

He had reached the door and was about to pull himself through the tunnel to leave the Lounge when Jane shouted out in his general direction. "You're an *idealist*, Yves," she made no attempt to mask her sentiment. "The world you dream of can't exist, and never will!"

Captain Montreaux stopped himself on the metal hand bar which ran the full circumference of the doorway. He pulled himself round slowly to face her, leaving his notepad and pen floating in the tunnel behind him. What amazed him wasn't that the topic of flags seemed impossible to put to bed; instead it was that of *all* the crew, with their military backgrounds and patriotism, it was the only *civilian* among them who seemed to take it all so personally.

"You are absolutely correct, Dr Richardson: my ideal world cannot exist. Not on Earth," he said carefully, looking straight into her eyes. "But on Mars, maybe. So why spoil this opportunity by setting off on the wrong foot?"

Danny nodded in sombre agreement as Montreaux pulled himself through the door, grabbing his notepad and pen as he went. The parting words weighed down on the Lounge for some time, before Jane finally spoke.

"It's only a flag," she muttered bitterly under her breath.

Marchenko unclipped his retaining straps and let himself float towards the centre of the room, giving the sofa a brief nudge with his toes as he went. This caused him to spin slowly as he crossed the Lounge, and as his body turned to face Jane, who was still lodged into the ceiling but was now looking down at him, his face burst into a huge grin, showing his large, perfectly white teeth.

"Exactly, Jane," he said gleefully as he span, like a child on a fairground ride. "It is *only* a flag."

Back in his pod, Montreaux set the notepad down on his desk and let the pen float as he secured himself in his chair. Grabbing the pen, he pressed down on the end to expose the writing tip and placed it against the paper.

After a brief pause, he lifted the tip again and looked over his shoulder at the door behind him. There was no way of closing it, but the faint noise of the crew's voices still emanating from the Lounge assured him he would not be disturbed.

Touching the paper with his pen once more, he started writing.

The *Clarke* was a true technological marvel, and was breaking practically every record in the space exploration book.

It was the biggest and most expensive space craft ever conceived, designed to take its crew of four on a seven-month round trip to Mars, punctuated in the middle by a nine-month sojourn orbiting the Red Planet while its occupants had their shore leave. In total the mission would last nearly a year and a half.

The simple logistics of such a task had been a headache for the mission planners, who had spent the last fifteen years meticulously calculating volumes of water, oxygen, food and even hygienic wipes. Every ounce of mass was accounted for, agreed and triply signed-off. In their favour, the laws of physics had given the *Clarke*'s designers grace when it came to putting the ship together. As far as science was concerned, it wouldn't have mattered if the Hygiene Bay had been jutting out at right angles to the Command Module and the crew's quarter's connected end to end in a train eighty feet long: the vacuum of space simply didn't care for aerodynamics.

Constructed using a modular design, the *Clarke* followed the same basic principles as the ISS. When it came to putting it together, it was simply a question of choosing a layout that looked good, and the decision to go for a familiar structure had been widely approved, not least of all because it suited the public relations officers and marketing departments; a spaceship that actually *looked* like a spaceship, and not an upside down foil-covered colander with tripod landing gear, the likes of which littered the moon, had been most welcome and had led to a marked increase in public attention.

The modular approach had another, more serious benefit. The ship's computer was programmed to monitor every cubic inch of the *Clarke* for environmental anomalies, ranging from loss of pressure to temperature irregularities. At the slightest sign of danger, it was able to completely shut down the affected areas and minimise the impact on the rest of the ship until the problem could be addressed. In worse-case scenarios, the faulty module could be jettisoned into space, leaving the rest of the *Clarke* completely unaffected.

Everyone knew that if they were in a faulty module at the time, they only had thirty seconds from the alert being raised to reach a safe part of the ship. Getting stuck on the wrong side of a sealed doorway could have fatal consequences.

To help the crew interpret these situations accurately, the ship's lighting had been developed to change colour and pattern: in a danger area, the lights would go red, and the marker strips along doors and passageways would indicate the nearest safe route by flashing.

They had practised all possible evacuation scenarios, from the Lounge imploding to the Hygiene Bay losing pressure. During training exercises simulating everything from fires to meteorite strikes, they had not always 'survived'.

Additional safety came in the form of the lead-lining in the Command Module. Exposure to radiation from space weather, caused by solar flares and coronal mass ejection on the surface of the Sun, could at best lead to a high probability of developing cancer. At worst, it would result in death. It was a risk that the inhabitants of the Earth's International Space Station had been coping with for many decades, rushing to specially shielded areas whenever the warning of a major solar event came.

It was a sobering thought that such precautions were relatively recent additions to space exploration. In August 1972, between the manned Apollo 16 and Apollo 17 missions to the Moon, a solar flare blasted past Earth. Had it occurred four months earlier, or four months later, it would certainly have proven fatal to the unprotected crews.

The modular design had brought flexibility, safety and had also reduced building time and cost. This had combined to create the hundred and eighty foot long *Clarke*.

But the most technologically advanced feature of the *Clarke* was not something that could be seen.

The early twenty-first century had been marked by a massive improvement in miniaturisation. Everything from small combustion engines to computer processors was benefiting from advances in the field of nanotechnology: while with the *Clarke* human spaceships had grown in scale, everything else was getting smaller. Much smaller.

The *Clarke* was leaving a world obsessed by size. Whereas the Industrial Revolution of the nineteenth century had been typified by a desire to make things bigger, the brave new world of the 2040s required things that not only fitted in your pocket, but also performed better. *Gadgets* were by now a necessity: everyone needed the latest telephone, because not only did it weigh less, it could also take your calls for you, set up meetings and call people back, and all while it sat silently in your coat.

As a consequence, in contrast to the ship's vast dimensions, the *Clarke*'s on board computers were neatly stowed away in small recesses in the ship. But the computers' external sensors were everywhere. Every single module of the ship was constantly being monitored, assessed and recorded by hundreds of mobile *nanostations*. Barely big enough to see with the naked eye, nanostations incorporated a camera, microphone, light sensor, smoke detector, environmental pressure sensor and thermometer. They were each powered by a minute motor with six tiny 'jets' on all sides, forcing air through to allow the station to move in any direction in three dimensional space.

They were normally fully automated, but could be guided by the main computer at any time, which in turn would take its directives from Mission Control on Earth.

Each module contained a small, saucer-sized surface, on which the nanostations would occasionally sit to recharge their batteries. They did not need to dock precisely on the surfaces, as the energy would transfer by magnetic induction directly into their power cells.

The nanostations sent all of their information back to the ship's computers. These were located in not one, but in *all* of the *Clarke*'s eight habitable modules. Each pod was fitted with a wafer thin rack, hidden inside a wall, which at all times was receiving input from every nanostation on board, and at any time could assume main control of the *Clarke*. By default, this control was normally taken by the computer housed in the Command Module, but it would periodically shift for a few hours every day, so that over a period of seven days every computer on board had taken control for a short time at least. It was an effective way for the computers to auto-test themselves, and something the crew took completely for granted.

They expected that in the event of an emergency, they would not be jumping into a mindless module, leaving the ship's brains to jettison themselves into the space.

CHAPTER 15

Sitting at his desk, Montreaux finished writing and let go of the pen, letting it float gently just above the desk. He waited for half a minute before tearing the piece of paper from the pad and folding it twice, placing it carefully in his breast pocket and opening a drawer in his desk. He grabbed the pen and put it with the pad in the drawer before closing it carefully.

He knew that the nanostations would have been watching him.

Everything they did, and indeed wrote, on board the ship was being sent back to Earth. At the current distance of approximately thirty eight million kilometres, it took roughly two minutes and six seconds for the data to reach Earth, network switching at both ends notwithstanding. Between each phrase in a standard conversation would therefore be a delay of over four minutes.

Anything over that could be put down to human deliberation.

It had now been barely four minutes since he had finished writing his message. He expected there to be a few more minutes waiting for a reply, at least. Suddenly and without warning, the screen on his desk lit up. It was a video feed from Mission Control, with no sound. In the middle of the picture, two hands were holding up a neatly written message.

He read the message twice before the screen went blank of its own accord.

Neither video nor audio feeds were accessible by any crew member, including the Captain, without authorisation from Mission Control. Whereas Earth could see and hear everything, and the information was always stored in the *Clarke*'s memory, it had been decided that the crew should not be able to systematically see potentially sensitive information.

For the mission planners this had provided a useful method of private communication.

Emailed messages could be read by indiscreet eyes, and conversations could be overheard, so it had been decided that in the event of an emergency, the commanding officer of the *Clarke* could use the very low-tech Private Message Protocol, or PMP, to speak to Mission Control. It was not something they had expected would be used, but when Captain Montreaux had taken the notepad and pen from the drawer in the Lounge, two nearby nanostations had been alerted, and had followed the officer back to his quarters, where they had watched him write down his enquiry.

The brief reply, held in front of a camera on Earth by steady, anonymous hands for several seconds, had not done much to satisfy him.

Psych request for crewmember Lieutenant Su Ning denied.
No incidents reported.

- Mission Control

Montreaux leaned back in his chair and looked at the blank screen where the message had appeared moments earlier. He made an effort to control his facial expression, knowing that they would still be watching, or at the very least recording.

He did the arithmetic in his head. They had written their message in less than thirty seconds and placed it in front of a working camera. In thirty seconds, they had been able to look into his enquiry, write a message and broadcast it directly back to his quarters. *That* was quick.

But nonetheless possible, he thought. Maybe they had been proactively monitoring the feeds since Su Ning's comment during the night, and were expecting him to use the PMP. It was certainly possible.

He unclipped himself from his chair and let himself float away from it towards the door. He thought about the handwriting on the message; neat and deliberate. The steady hands holding the message up to the camera had been calm and practised. *Thirty seconds was fast.*

He took the written note from his breast pocket and unfolded it before screwing it up into a tight ball with both hands and pushing it into the waste recycling tube recessed into the wall of his quarters. He felt the suction pulling the hairs on the back of his hand as the tube sensed the paper and sucked it through a series of twists and turns quickly leading to the waste processing plant situated in the walls of the Hygiene Bay.

Why didn't Mission Control want to look into it? He was the commanding officer, their eyes and ears on the ground, in charge of crew wellbeing and safety above all other concerns. He had raised a legitimate concern over the status of the Lieutenant. A psych report would give him a breakdown of her habits on board, analysis of stress and intonation, and even the meaning, of everything she had said, chemical balances, or *imbalances*, in her blood and even the composition of her waste material. It would, effectively, give him a good idea of how she was, in 0s and 1s. The computer's answer to the question 'how are you doing?'

The more he thought about it, the more worried he became. It wasn't a question of *why* they had rejected his request, but *how?* After all, a techie sitting at a desk in Mission Control had, for all intents and purposes, just denied one of his crew a reasonable medical request. *Under whose authority?*

And then it hit him: *Mission Control.*

No one signs off as Mission Control! Montreaux tried to keep his face as impassive as possible as the realisation sank in.

Under normal running, the only position in Mission Control to communicate with *Clarke* was CAPCOM, or Capsule Communicator. It was a legacy of the early space pioneers and a protocol that was affectionately defended. For the *Clarke* mission, all correspondence, audio, video and written, had so far signed off with two simple words: *CAPCOM OUT.*

Playing it over and over in his mind, it did not take him long to reach the only logical conclusion: something was wrong. And a little voice in the back of his mind told him that Lieutenant Su Ning knew what it was.

The only question now was that with the nanostations monitoring his every word and movement, how was he going to get close enough to her?

CHAPTER 16

Christophe Larue paced up and down in front of his desk before coming to a halt in front of the large, tinted window of his office. It had been a very busy day during a particularly stressful period for the European Space Agency's Head of Policy and Future Programmes.

He was a short man with wispy, almost transparent white hair falling down either side of his plump, flushed face. His expensive tailored suit did not hide the fact that too much good food and good wine combined with too little exercise over the past few years had started to affect his health, and the pressure he had been put under had not helped at all.

Shooting a hand into his pocket he pulled out a small box of pills, which he opened clumsily. After swallowing the medicine, he felt the rhythm of his heart return to normal, and he focused on the buildings outside the window to help him calm down.

It was an exceptional September day in Paris: the sun had been shining brightly since dawn and its warmth was notable through the triple glazing. Directly opposite his office was a small block of flats, each one displaying a proud, perfectly nurtured window box. Behind the flats he could see the top of the UNESCO buildings, a mass of twentieth century architectural wonders and a popular destination for Parisian workers during their lunch breaks. It had been a boost for France, he thought to himself, for the headquarters of two international bodies to be situated within a few hundred metres of each other in the capital city, but while UNESCO had been going from strength to strength in recent years, the ESA had been riding a torrent of public criticism that had already seen the closure of three major projects and the downsizing of six more.

Funding was being withdrawn, sponsors were getting cold feet, and it was all he could do to keep his head above water from day to day, maintaining the hope that something or someone would throw him and the Agency a lifeline and pull them onto dry land.

Furthermore, he knew it was pretty much his responsibility.

He was shaken from his reverie by a knock on the thick oak door of his office.

"*Entrez*," Larue barked.

The tall, attractive man, wearing a white tie-less shirt open at the collar, entered the office and closed the door behind him. He saw Larue looking out of the window and tensed up: it was a bad moment.

"*Monsieur Larue?*" he said, tactfully. His French accent was flawless.

Larue turned on his heels and looked the man up and down. He was young, as he once was, and handsome, like he had never been. Had he been a petty man he would have resented Martín Antunez for this, but the aide had helped him through some difficult times of late, so he was able to see past their physical differences. "Martin," he said, pronouncing the Spaniard's name the French way. "Some very bad news, I'm afraid."

"*Monsieur?*" He wondered how his boss' situation could possibly get any worse.

Larue's eyes flicked nervously away from his aide's inquisitive gaze and he focused on a framed picture of the Ariane 5 heavy-lift launcher taking off at night from the European Spaceport in Kourou, French Guyana, nearly half a century earlier. Still the ESA's most successful venture, he thought.

"Our scientific cooperation with NASA has been suspended, Martin," he admitted. "We will still receive some direct feeds from the Mars mission, but will no longer hold the same status as Russia, China or even Japan." His voice was resigned, as if the news had been inevitable.

"Why?" Antunez asked in disbelief.

"We have not invested in the Mars mission. As I understand, it has been decided that we are not to have immediate access to all of the data returned from the *Clarke*. Our ability to control nanostations remotely, for instance, has been revoked effective from six o'clock tomorrow morning, *heure Française*. From then on, we will receive a passive live feed, which they control," Larue said.

Martín Antunez knew this would be one of the last nails in Larue's coffin, both figuratively and possibly literally. It had all started with his first decision as Head of Policy and Future Programmes, nearly ten years earlier.

"I know what you are thinking, that we should have continued working on the *Clarke* with the other agencies all those years ago," Larue said. "But it just wasn't feasible. All of our scientific research at the time was in the area of robotic probes and landing craft. We were already tied in to dozens of missions we could barely fund. The mission's demands, both financially and in terms of human resource, were simply too high!"

"I understand, Monsieur." Aside from hundreds of satellites around Earth, the mainstay of the ESA's business, their only remaining significant scientific venture was the *Beagle 4* rover, roaming alone in the cold winds of Mars for the past three years.

Larue looked at him. "As far as the *Clarke* is concerned, we barely have one up on the press. We'll probably have to watch the landing on CNN." He sneered as he said the acronym.

"What can I do, Monsieur?" Antunez offered.

"Give me something to be optimistic about!"

Antunez looked at his boss with pity. There was nothing.

Larue returned to the window and held his hands behind his back. The urge to start biting his nails again had grown, but a respectable man restrained himself, he had decided. "Find something," he said over his shoulder. "Watch everything." He looked over at the UNESCO building. Education, Science, Culture. It was all there. *But above all,* he thought, *opportunity.* "NASA is a business, they only tell us what they want us to know, and then keep the juicy bits to themselves." His mouth had started to water; he was hungry already.

"Espionage, *Monsieur?*" Antunez sounded shocked.

Larue shot round and pointed a finger at him. "No! Not espionage, but liberty!" A thought was brewing in his mind and he revelled in his new-found enthusiasm. "Mars is *not* American, we all have the right to it, and this *Clarke* mission is from Earth, not the United States. NASA have no right to withhold information —"

"We have no evidence that they have, or will," Antunez interrupted.

"They will, Martin, I am sure of it," he looked his aide in the eyes, an unpleasant grin on his face. "And when they do, you will be watching."

Antunez shifted uneasily on the spot. *So this is what happens when you push Larue into a corner,* he thought. The boss' job was almost certainly on the line; the honourable thing to do was to resign. Instead, Larue was grabbing at fanciful conspiracy theories.

"With the feeds we are getting, we are not very well placed..."

"You will find a way, Martin, I trust you," he said firmly. He sat down at his desk and started flicking through paperwork intently. The small wrist strap he was wearing sent a small impulse to his nerve endings, telling him it was time to curb his enthusiasm and relax. "And one last thing."

"*Monsieur?*"

"I trust you have no engagements this evening? I'm sure you understand that, for obvious reasons, we don't have much time. I want you to get me *anything* you can, as *quickly* as possible. I want you to get everything from the *Clarke* before our control of the nanostations is removed."

Martín left the office quietly, realising the meeting was over. In the corridor outside, he bumped into a young blond woman carrying a wad of paperwork. His face flushed.

"*Excuse-moi, Jacqueline,*" he mumbled.

"Martín," she used the Spanish pronunciation of his name. "You look worried. Can I help?"

He looked at the network programmer for a few seconds before his neurons clicked into place. "*Oui,*" he said. Yes.

Hours had passed.

Martín watched in silence as the American Captain sailed across the Lounge to meet the Chinese Lieutenant. After a brief exchange of words, too quiet to be picked up by the nearby nanostation, the woman left the Captain by the window. He called after her, this time his voice loud enough to come through Martín's headphones, but she did not return. He stayed for three minutes, staring into space, before leaving the Lounge.

He had watched the same recording during a routine run through of the *Clarke*'s activities the day before, but had thought nothing of it. It now stood out as one of the last recordings during which the ESA had been able to control the nanostations. Had he known, and been awake while it had been live and not tucked up in bed with a woman he barely knew and would probably never see again, he would certainly have moved the tiny little nanostation several feet closer.

The *Clarke*'s equipment of nanostations was superb. Over the past weeks, he had been allowed to control some of the little flying machines, sending them this way and that, bumping into walls, getting in the way of the crew. With the number of nanostations active during the day, there were more than enough to go around. He had even seen a feed from a nanostation controlled by someone at JAXA, the Japanese Aerospace Exploration Agency, which had accidentally strayed into a doorway adjacent to the Hygiene Bay. The video had been cut by NASA just as Dr Jane Richardson had entered with her towel, and control mechanisms for restricting movement of nanostations within the Hygiene Bay and personal Pods expanded to include the connecting tunnel from the Lounge.

During Nightmode, most of the stations went to the closest charging pad, ready for another busy shift. Unless there was a fault or something needed to be monitored more closely, at these times there were only eight active nanostations – one for each habitable module. The one that had managed to pick up the meeting between Lieutenant Shi Su Ning and Captain Yves Montreaux the previous day had been on the other side of the room, and although at the time five agencies were able to send basic commands to the lonesome vigil in the Lounge, not one had done so.

He increased the gain on his headphones and flattened the equalizer in the low frequency range; the constant humming of the ship's air circulation units needed to be cancelled out. Pressing play, he watched the video again.

"*I had no idea you did this,*" the Captain's voice boomed through his headphones. He was trying to pick up the quiet sections, and this meant that everything else now sounded incredibly loud.

"*You may be the Captain, Sir, but with respect you don't know everything,*" she replied.

A pause while the Captain went across the Lounge to join her. Martín had already seen the look of surprise in the Captain's face the last time he had watched. But this time he noticed something else; Su Ning had stretched her neck to speak to the Captain. But as soon as she saw his reaction this changed. Martín saw the look in her eyes: she had said too much and knew it. It was a 'blink and you'll miss it' detail, hard to pick up from Earth with the angle of the nanostation; but on *Clarke*, it was obvious that the Captain had not missed a thing.

"*Lieutenant, is everything OK?*" he said.

Up to this part, Martín had always been able to hear everything. The section that he had not been able to decipher was about to begin. He leant forward in his chair, as if being closer to the screen would help. Neither person's lips could be seen, so even if he had been able to lip-read, it would have been useless. Pressing the headphones hard against his ears, he listened intently.

The sound was terrible, but he still managed to get several syllables. He stopped the video and played the section back, writing down the bits he could hear on a piece of paper in front of him. Stopping the video again, he looked down at what he had written:

"I...it...is...an...shoe...Sir....wood...ree...with...thing...less.. was...tain."

It didn't make any sense, but he circled the word '*Sir*', as the only whole word he was sure of; the Chinese Lieutenant was by far the most polite of all the crew members, and always used formal forms of communication.

He was about to play the video again when there was a light tap on his shoulder.

"Still nothing?" Jacqueline asked sympathetically.

He removed the headphones and turned to face her. "Not yet, I'm afraid, but I am getting there, I have half a sentence."

He passed her the piece of paper with the scribbled, fragmented sentence and she took it with interest, reading through it several times before passing it back to him. "My English is not very good, but I'm pretty sure that means nothing at all," she smiled at him. "You look tired, Martín, take a break and let me show you something."

It was raining in the darkness outside, the day's clear skies long forgotten. He checked his watch and saw that he had been sitting at his desk watching various feeds from the *Clarke* for over eight hours. It was ten o'clock in the evening, and it had already been a long night.

"OK," he said standing up reluctantly. "What have you found?"

CHAPTER 17

Montreaux sat in the Command Module and looked at the closed hatch that led to the pod that would take them to the surface of Mars. Stencilled across the hatch in military font were the letters "M.L.P.": Mars Lander Pod. A plan was forming in his mind, but he knew it wasn't a very good one.

Wait until we land on Mars, he thought to himself, *and the nanostations will be left behind.* The little flying stations only functioned in zero gravity, and would therefore not follow the crew down. On-board the MLP there were fixed monitoring stations, dotted around the pod and its exterior, that would send streams of data back to the *Clarke* and Earth, but he could already imagine a situation where he would be alone with the Lieutenant and be able to have a conversation in private; it depended on them both leaving the landing site in protective suits, a normal part of the mission plan, and travelling far enough to be out of range of the MLP's shortwave antenna. With the little power they were able to use on the surface, a handful of kilometres would be amply sufficient. One of the first duties on the surface was to set up signal booster stations at regular intervals, so that they could travel further. He would need to make sure that they were not in the range of one of those, too, or that they had their chat before the boosters were assembled.

As he listed all of the problems facing such a scenario, the thought that the plan was not very good grew, until he was ready to scrap the idea completely.

And what if it's too late? The look on Su Ning's face the previous night had been with him ever since. *What if whatever is worrying her is too big to be left another six weeks?*

His mind was reeling. He had never usually been impressed by conspiracy theories, but the pieces were beginning to fit in an increasingly worrying puzzle. A multinational mission to Mars, the first of its kind, almost at its destination. An ultra-patriotic American scientist intent on planting her flag in new territory. A Russian MIG-34 pilot as second in command. And the youngest member of the crew: a Chinese army Lieutenant. Then out of the blue after over two months in space, the Chinese Lieutenant raises his suspicions. Something is wrong, either with the mission, the crew, both, or something entirely different. Whatever it was, it didn't sound personal. What had she said again? *I am not sure it is an issue and would not worry you with anything unless I was certain.*

And then, as if that cryptic message wasn't enough, the inexplicable behaviour of Mission Control. *Surely if Su Ning has a problem it is as important to them as it is to us?*

He needed space. Space to think, and the Command Module simply wasn't giving it to him; he knew that at that moment, as many as twenty nanostations could be watching his every move, every blink, every bead of sweat. He looked in the air around him and fancied he could make out the movement of a couple of them, like twenty first century mosquitoes, except that they didn't bite. *Or did they?* He laughed to himself, now he felt crazy, and probably looked it too.

He shifted in his seat, running his eyes over the panels of instruments in front of him. *Time to act normally,* he thought to himself. If Mission Control want to keep him in the dark, then it would be best if they think that...

In the dark! Nightmode! With the majority of the nanostations inactive, he only had one per module to avoid.

He unclipped himself and carefully made for the exit. The short tunnel from the Command Module to the Lounge was directly behind the seat he had been using, and he reached it with a single short tug. Emerging into the Lounge, huge by comparison, he could see the back of Dr Richardson's head; she had assembled her laboratory along one wall and was writing some notes on a clipboard.

On the opposite side of the room, Lieutenant Su Ning was sitting on the sofa, playing cards with Captain Marchenko. She looked over her cards at him as he entered the room, her eyes showing candour that he had never before seen.

"I see your twenty and raise you fifty!" Marchenko told her.

The brief moment of understanding between the Chinese woman and Montreaux dissipated instantly as she returned to her game with the Russian.

"I see you for fifty, Captain Marchenko," she said flatly, laying three sixes and two aces on the table.

"Full House? No way!" he complained, before showing his hand. "It's a good thing I had four of these, isn't it?" He laughed at the look of dismay on Su Ning's face as he placed the set of kings on the table carefully. "Do I win?" he asked cheekily.

Su Ning pushed her chips across to him, catching one that had left the table's surface and was now spinning above her hand. "You win, Marchenko, *this* time."

Montreaux pushed across to the sofa and clipped himself in between the Russian and Su Ning.

"Mind if I play?"

CHAPTER 18

Martín gripped the Styrofoam coffee cup in his hand and looked down into the dark swirl of liquid that the machine had given him. It smelt like coffee, but he knew from experience that it carried a bitter metallic aftertaste.

Sitting down in front of him, Jacqueline had been typing and clicking at her computer for five minutes now, in silence. He barely understood half of the functions she was using, and the other half may as well have been in Hebrew for all he knew. Her work was punctuated by short sighs and clicks of the tongue when what she was trying to achieve didn't work. She would then try another method, still without saying a word.

Eventually, she pushed her chair away from the desk and looked up at Martín, who was standing behind her.

"There. What do you think?" she said triumphantly.

He looked up from the depths of his drink and squinted at the screen. He took a step towards her desk. The display was split into two sections, left and right. Running from top to bottom on the left hand side, in green text on black background, were dozens of lines of programming code. Every second or so, a different section would flash bold for a moment, as if to inform the user which part was being used. The right hand side displayed two video feeds, in black and white. Both feeds showed the *Clarke*'s Lounge, but were somehow different. As he watched he saw the top view of the Lounge pan round, until he could see Captain Montreaux, Captain Marchenko and Lieutenant Su Ning sitting at the table playing what looked like poker. Montreaux was collecting the chips from the table, while Marchenko was already dealing another hand.

"Five Card Stud, I think," Jacqueline informed him.

The video feed directly below it showed the same Lounge, but at a different time. As he looked at it, he saw Captain Montreaux enter the room from the Command Module. Martín's mouth dropped open as he watched him cross the room, clip himself down on the sofa, and join the game of poker that he was already playing in the feed above. He moved closer to the screen and studied the code on the left.

"Seventy-five minutes precisely," she told him.

"*Precisely* what?" Martín looked at her.

She looked at him and then tapped the display with the nail of her index finger, first the top feed then the bottom one. "Seventy-five minutes precisely between the feed coming back from the *Clarke* and the feed being sent to us by NASA."

Martín didn't know what was more impressive: that Jacqueline had managed to hack into the original data stream herself within four hours, or that security and encryption at Mission Control eight-thousand kilometres away was so lax as to let such a hack occur.

"So they've added a delay to the feed they're sending us?" he asked.

"Yes, although I don't know when it was introduced, obviously I only know it's effective now." She looked back at the screen and the programming code she had spent hours putting together.

"It doesn't entirely surprise me," he said, despondently. "Our partner status has been downscaled, so they've probably downgraded our feed, too. How long will we have the direct feed?"

"I don't know, I'm amazed it's still there, to be honest."

"And you're recording all of this?" he asked, watching the screen intently. In the delayed feeds, Captain Marchenko had just lost most of his chips, while at the same time in the live one he had already won most of them back again.

She pointed to a little red flashing icon in the bottom left hand corner of her screen and nodded. "Yes," she said. "But it's only useful to you and I as we stand here watching. In an hour and a quarter practically anyone will be able to see this feed, so we don't exactly gain anything."

As she said this, the top feed started to move across the Lounge. He looked at Jacqueline in earnest.

"We can't control anything, sorry. And even if we could, we wouldn't want to. If they haven't realised that we're watching yet, sending commands to a nanostation is a sure-fire way of putting them on the right track."

He nodded in agreement. He hadn't thought of that at all. The nanostation was clearly going to recharge anyway, as it headed for the corner of the Lounge and slowly dropped onto the available induction plate. Just as the screen went blank, Jacqueline sat upright and typed quickly on the keyboard for several seconds.

"What is it?" he urged.

She left him waiting for almost five minutes before replying. When she did, the screen had changed, this time completely full of programming code.

"You say that the delay is because they downgraded our partner status, but I didn't tell you the best bit," she said. She was enjoying her brief spell as a technological spy.

"Yes?"

"Well, while I was searching data streams to tap into, I naturally started by looking for the feeds going from NASA to JAXA, CNSA and the RSA," she said eagerly. "I expected that they would be seeing the same data as NASA, and not the delayed feed NASA is sending us."

The Japanese Aerospace Exploration Agency, JAXA, the China National Space Administration, CNSA, and the Russian Space Agency, RSA he thought to himself. The string of acronyms were unlikely bedfellows among which the ESA should have fitted nicely, had it not been for Larue.

"At first I thought I was going crazy," she continued. "But I ran comparisons several times and I'm absolutely right."

"And?"

She looked him directly in the eyes and said the words slowly and deliberately. "The other agencies are being sent the same feed as us!"

Jacqueline's discovery was still ringing in his ears as he entered his office. The ESA building had been empty for some time now and he checked his watch. Two in the morning. He'd missed the last Metro, and had too much to think about to go home, anyway. He picked up his telephone and dialled Larue's office. It went straight to voicemail, as he had expected.

He had to think carefully about his next move. After the first NASA feed had gone blank, Jacqueline had managed to hack into another nanostation, but her handiwork had been picked up on after about twenty minutes. During this time the feed from NASA to ESA still hadn't caught up with the *actual* live feed they had been watching. Whatever chink in security she had exploited had been resolved, as from that point on she was unable to access anything but the standard, delayed feed. He could picture the situation in America where some programmer had probably been typing frantically for ten minutes before hitting *Enter* and punching the air triumphantly, just like in the movies.

Jacqueline had persevered for almost three hours, trying desperately to hack into another nanostation on board the *Clarke*, but had failed at every attempt. It had been no good. Whatever they had seen was impossible to prove anyway.

She had left shortly afterwards, and he had almost reluctantly declined her offer of a ride home. On any other day, he would have jumped at the opportunity; Jacqueline was beautiful by any standards, single, and he was certainly very attracted to her. But somehow after their discovery, it didn't feel quite right to simply leave.

For Martín, the evening's work had at least served one lasting purpose: having not taken Larue's words regarding NASA seriously that afternoon, he had returned to his desk dreading the task he had been given. Now, however, not only did he believe that Larue's suspicious nature was justified, he was positive beyond a shadow of a doubt that someone at NASA was up to something. And whatever it was, they were prepared to go to great lengths to cover it up.

CHAPTER 19

Lieutenant Su Ning lay on her side and looked across the room at the photo next to the window: a young Chinese man, strong and well groomed with a perfect smile that showed in his eyes as well as his straight, white teeth. His dark green uniform was starched to perfection, and his collar nudged up precisely against the bottom of his chin. His officer's hat was wedged carefully under his upper arm, while his hands shot down in perfect straight lines towards the floor.

They had both grown up in the same small village outside Beijing, and had joined the Academy together. Their relationship had not been spoilt by the fact that only she had been put through for the Mars mission. He had been immensely proud of her and had supported her all of the way. Although he had always dreamed of going into space, he had failed his entrance medical due to a retinal disorder he hadn't even been aware of at the time. Since then, his sight had deteriorated to the extent of being service-affecting, and he was now desk-based.

In the corner of the photo, a neatly written message: *See Mars for me.*

She pulled her eyes away from the picture and looked at her computer screen. *That's where it had all started*, she thought. She pushed gently on the covers of the bed and let herself float several inches above it, enjoying the feeling of zero gravity.

As she lay above her bed, she cleared her mind and thought about what she would tell the Captain. She knew he would be going to the Lounge during the night, she had seen the look on his face and understood immediately what he was thinking: that something was wrong, but that he did not know what. From the behaviour of the others, she was sure she was the only one to have noticed it. Jane had been acting strangely that afternoon, but then again, she so often did.

She would need to tell Montreaux what she knew efficiently. The last thing they needed was a long protracted debate in the middle of the night, which would be a fool-proof way of attracting the unwanted attention of the lone nanostation patrolling the Lounge.

Nanostations. She hated nanostations. They had at first intrigued her, but after a while had brought back memories of her mother's stories of old China, where freedom of speech did not exist and even the birth rate had been rigorously controlled. Even out here, nearly forty million miles away from Earth, they had no privacy. *Especially out here*, she almost said out loud.

Nightmode had become her only way to be alone. She knew there was always one nanostation active in the Lounge, but it was also the biggest room, and she could easily switch windows if she felt like it. Her hearing had become finely tuned to the brief hisses of the nanostation motors, imperceptible during the day, but just audible at night within a foot or two. As soon as she heard it, she would switch window, and after a couple of weeks either the operators had grown bored of the game of cat and mouse, or they had learnt to stay at least a few feet away from her.

She had since spent her evenings undisturbed, giving her time to think about Earth, Beijing, and what waited for her on her return. Sometimes she found herself imagining Mars, and what it would be like to set foot on the Red Planet, but mostly she dreamt of home as she stared out into the twinkling infinity of space.

It had been during one of her Nightmode sessions that she had noticed the change.

She had grown accustomed to checking her watch every now and then, to ensure that she got enough sleep. It was fine staring out to space all night, but she would rather keep it a secret. If she was always yawning at the breakfast table, the others would have quickly started asking questions.

Seeing the Martian time, she had tried to calculate what time it was in Beijing. It was a game she played every now and then, helping not only fight off monotony but also keep her mind sharp.

They had been on Sols rather than days for over a year. *Since midday on July 4th, 2044*, she remembered. It had been the last time they had counted in days.

She knew that every sol was thirty-nine minutes longer than a day. She also knew that the previous day had been the 29th of September, after a video message from her mother. This meant that they had been on Sols for four hundred and fifty two Earth days.

Gaining thirty-nine minutes every day meant that at midday on the

29th September the *Clarke* would have been twelve days, five hours and fifty-nine seconds ahead of Earth. This meant that it would have been 5:59pm on the *Clarke*. She had smiled as she completed the equation in her head, then scratched her chin and looked out of the window, trying to focus the numbers in her mind.

Checking her watch, it was almost exactly 1am, *Clarke* time. So seven hours more or less since midday Earth time, she surmised. Every Martian hour was approximately one minute and thirty-seven seconds longer than every Earth hour. This meant that the seven hours on *Clarke* equated to six hours, forty-eight minutes and thirty seven seconds. More or less.

She grinned. She now knew it was just past 6:48pm, Houston time. With fourteen hours between Houston and Beijing, that meant it was just before 9am back home. Her mother would already be up, and would probably be reading the papers with her second cup of tea of the day.

Su Ning had gone back to her room and fished into her kit bag, pulling out a small, jewel-encrusted time-piece she had been given, "*so you will always know when I am praying for you,*" her mother had said.

Since moving to Martian time there had been a strict mission rule of no Earth-time devices, so she had smuggled the gift onto the *Clarke*, and it only came out at night when the nanostations were kept outside their sleeping quarters. Turning it over in her hands, she had looked at the time and been taken aback.

It wasn't nearly nine in the morning in Beijing: it was barely *seven-thirty*.

She tapped the watch's display and stared at the hands faultlessly ticking away. In the day or two since she had last checked it, could it possibly have come so unstuck? She shook her head, but nonetheless watched it for several minutes to be sure.

Her calculations must be the problem. You only needed to add a few seconds to each day and you could easily be out by an hour after a year or so. But then she had dismissed the thought: she was always accurate. It was a game she often played, and she hadn't been wrong yet, let alone by an hour and a quarter!

Despite this she still double-checked, and after going through the maths several more times, was left with only thought: someone had changed the time on board the *Clarke*.

Why would they do that? Why would they want the time on the ship to be faster than the time being recorded on Earth? This would mean that when people in China thought that it was nine o'clock on the *Clarke*, it was actually past ten o'clock, which meant that what they would be watching would already be over an hour old.

The conclusion had hit her in the face so hard she struggled to breath for a few seconds. *So that what people saw could be controlled.*

As she realised this, more thoughts started to come to her; small throwaway comments that she had read and listened to in her personal messages on her computer screen. Her mother had written to her once, and the letter had seemed disjointed, as if the sentences she was reading were not meant to be read together, and were missing something. One phrase in that particular letter had seemed completely random.

She had quickly found the letter, placing the watch carefully in the bottom of her kit bag. Towards the end, sandwiched between '*It's not raining as much this year*' and '*Good luck*' was a chilling sentence. '*Just like when I was a girl*'.

It had to be deliberate. Her mother had been trying to tell her something, like a code.

She had gone back to the dark space of the Lounge to clear her head and think hard about the phrase. '*Just like when I was a girl*', and then '*Good luck*'. Her mother had been a girl in the twentieth century, before China had given its citizens freedom of speech.

It did not take Su Ning long to work out what her mother had tried to tell her: not only was the feed from the *Clarke* to Earth being censored, so too were messages from Earth to the *Clarke*.

She had been mulling over this when Captain Montreaux had floated through the door.

Su Ning had not been able to tell him then. For a start it had just been a theory. But her mind had been racing and despite herself, she had failed to hide her emotions. It was unlike her. Unlike the controlled, precise Su Ning that the Captain had become accustomed to.

The following day, when their eyes had met in the Lounge, his facial expression had proven to her that, in some way, he was suspicious of something being wrong; he wanted to know more.

She knew she was playing a dangerous game. If her suspicions were correct, then someone had already assumed full control of the *Clarke*. She did not know exactly what their motives were, but the inflamed rhetoric that poured so easily from the American on board, Dr Richardson, gave her a pretty good idea. In her experience, Westerners were usually extremely emotional and headstrong.

However, since the beginning of the Mars mission training Su Ning had grown to like one: Captain Montreaux. With his calm, reflected manner he had always been able to manage difficult situations, and she had been glad that it had been he who had appeared the previous night in the Lounge.

She was certain that he was the right person to confide in.

Captain Yves Montreaux sat in the Lounge and looked at his watch for the fifth time. Still another hour to Nightmode, he noted impatiently.

The poker game had been over for more than two hours, Marchenko finally winning all the chips with a pair of twos. They had then eaten together at the table, before watching the daily news feed on the Lounge's television. As usual, NASA hadn't selected anything particularly interesting for them to see that evening; they were all fully aware that the television broadcasts were carefully screened and selected by a team of psychologists back at Mission Control. This meant that most of what they saw revolved around financials, funny stories and weather. It had been alright for the first few weeks, but by now they all craved something more tangible. It was a sad fact that the news just wasn't exciting if it didn't show you the suffering and plight of others. The psychologists would probably pick up on that fact, so any day now they could expect to see some additional flavour added to the broadcasts.

After dinner, Marchenko and Su Ning had both retired to their quarters, and Dr Richardson had busied herself with disassembling her experiments and returning the laboratory to its compartments inside the walls of the Lounge. He had decided to stay on the sofa to read.

"Waiting for someone?" Dr Richardson said from behind him.

He looked over his shoulder at the scientist, who was looking at him with a grin. "No, Dr Richardson," he said casually. "I was just checking the time."

"What are you reading?" She closed the final compartment and pushed towards the sofa. "Is it good?"

He showed her the cover of the book. "*The Martian Chronicles*, and I don't know yet, because I've only just started it."

"Essential reading for a mission to Mars, I think," she looked at him keenly and cocked her head to one side. "But surely you, Captain Yves

Montreaux, obsessed with Mars, would have read everything there is to know about the planet. How could you get this far without reading Bradbury's classic?"

"I was never as much into Science Fiction as I was into Science," he replied, closing the book and placing it on his lap. "From what I have read so far, Bradbury was the other way around."

Dr Richardson looked at him and smiled. "I am sure that he knew Mars was not as he described it. But the purpose of Science Fiction is not to relate life as it is, but life as it could be. I heard somewhere that Science Fiction is able to tell us about all the possible mistakes we can make in the future, so that with effort, we can avoid them. When you get to the end of that book, you will understand what I mean."

He looked at her with interest. Dr Richardson had always come across to him as hot-headed and impetuous, particularly with her heated debates about flags and national identity. But hearing her talk about Bradbury's book forced a rethink. "I hadn't put you down as a sentimental person," he said lightly.

"As the commanding officer of the *Clarke* you must have read my psych report, so I can only imagine that either you didn't believe it, or that the analyst shared your opinion."

Her reply was good natured, but as always he sensed an edge to her voice, sign enough that to go any further on the subject may take him somewhere he was not keen on going. Just one more question, he told himself, just not about flags. "I prefer to judge people from what I see, not from what somebody with a computer thinks."

She laughed. "I'm screwed then, aren't I?"

The scientist had a cavalier attitude to the conversation, he thought, as if her non-military background excluded her from the formalities of protocol. He chose his words carefully in the front of his mind and then asked her his question. "Dr Richardson, has anything been bothering you recently?" As the commanding officer, he had to ask the difficult questions, but he hated putting people on the spot. Especially Dr Richardson.

"Why do you say that?" She sounded hurt.

The officer in him suddenly took over, changing the tone of the conversation completely. "I have my reasons. Now is there anything you would like to tell me?"

She looked at him in surprise. "Like what?"

"*Anything.*"

"Not really, to be honest."

He sensed that she was holding back on something. "I would rather know, Dr Richardson. Your behaviour lately has been erratic."

She had not yet clipped herself in to the sofa, and had been floating several inches above its cushions. Suddenly, she propelled herself towards the door of the Lounge with a kick. As she reached it, she spun round quickly and stopped herself just inside the mouth of the tunnel.

"If you must know, Captain Montreaux, I'm menstruating, and in zero gravity it's not particularly pleasant." Her voice was bitter and defiant. "Read that book, Captain. I recommend it."

And with that, she was gone, leaving him sitting dumbstruck on the sofa, still holding the book to his lap.

CHAPTER 20

Martín could sense day approaching in Paris. He had left his desk to refill his Styrofoam cup and had been surprised by the crispness of the air. It was still dark outside and he was filled with a sensation that took him back to his days at university; he would typically have been late handing in his assignments, and would regularly have worked all night long in order to hand them in the following morning.

But it had been a long time since his last *nuit blanche*.

Larue had asked for haste, though maybe even he wouldn't have expected such commitment on the first night. But after having witnessed Jacqueline's discovery he didn't need orders. He wanted to find out what NASA were trying to cover up, and find out now.

After more endless hours of watching old feeds from the *Clarke*, the night had started to catch up with him, and as he returned with his hot drink, he felt like he was wading through treacle.

Sitting down at his desk once more, he clicked lazily on his computer screen with his mouse. The feed he was now looking at was also from the previous night, but slightly earlier than the muffled conversation between Su Ning and Montreaux. One part of the video had been bugging him.

Su Ning had been alternating her gaze between her wristwatch and space for about five minutes. At the same time her lips had been moving silently, as if reciting some personal prayer, pausing occasionally to remember a word caught on the tip of the tongue. Eventually, she stopped and looked at her watch one final time, before giving a satisfied nod. Smiling, she turned and disappeared through the door to her quarters.

When she returned she was different, the smile gone, her shoulders dropped. He could not see her face properly in the faint glow of Nightmode, but it was obvious to Martín from nearly forty million miles away that something was deeply wrong.

Something to do with her watch, and the *time*. Maybe the time delay was on *Clarke* as well, maybe they had been *accelerated* by an hour and a quarter, so the time output by the mission was in sync with the delayed transmission from NASA.

But why?

He was too tired to get excited now. The night had begun to overwhelm him. His mouth was pasty and bitter from the coffee, and his head felt like it was being wrapped in foam; the effects of his self-inflicted sleep deprivation. He rocked back and forwards in his chair and put his feet up on his desk, closing his eyes and pulling his collar up to warm his neck.

Su Ning was the key, he thought to himself as his body shut down. Watch Su Ning.

CHAPTER 21

On *Clarke* it was Nightmode once more, and Su Ning was ready.

Two whole Sols had passed since her discovery in the Lounge. Nobody else had noticed the change in time, as far as she could tell, and so she had to tell Captain Montreaux what she knew. Swinging her legs into the void beside her bed, she hung in the air for several moments, listening carefully to make sure the coast was clear.

If someone is up to something, I have to act as normally as possible, she said to herself as she waited.

She was about to push towards the door when something caught her attention: a microscopic movement just at the limits of her senses. And then the sound, to her left and right: the gentle hiss of air passing through dozens of tiny motors. She jerked her head to and fro frantically, trying to sense one of the nanostations in the faint light.

Weeks spent avoiding the lone nanostation in the Lounge had taught Su Ning a great deal about detecting them; the sound they made, the small flurry of air as they moved through the modules, the occasional glint as the light would catch one at just the right angle.

It was Nightmode in Su Ning's quarters, and she was terrified.

Instead of the lone nanostation that would patrol the air at night, making sure everything was safe, she knew she was surrounded by tens of them, shooting past her head as fast as they could go. They had appeared suddenly, as if they had been waiting for her to move.

She turned her eyes to the door connecting her quarters to the Hygiene Bay and tensed. Between her and the door, there was a small flash of light, like a spark shooting from a fire.

Pushing on her arms with all her might, she shot for the opening, ten feet away.

The nanostations were executing their carefully programmed drill, a simple systems test, for safety reasons.

The monitor station sat in the centre of the room, motionless, waiting.

The other stations calculated their vectors with infinite precision, converging with great speed on a point next to the monitor. They came together within a millisecond of each other.

The monitor station, millimetres away, detected the small explosion in its vicinity: a sphere of heat exceeding two hundred degrees Celsius. A fire. No time to evacuate in the oxygen-rich atmosphere.

The door to the Hygiene Bay was sealed in the instant before Su Ning reached it.

Captain Yves Montreaux shot upright in his bed and looked for the lights. A deafening alarm was ringing through the *Clarke*, but its tone told him that his quarters were not in the danger zone. He lunged toward the door.

Poking his head through the short tunnel and into the Hygiene Bay, he saw the faces of Dr Richardson and Captain Marchenko coming out of the modules to his left and right, both with similarly confused expressions. Around all three of their doors were the safe, blue lights indicating the problem was elsewhere.

"Su Ning!" he cried as he pulled out of the tunnel, groping for handholds on the shiny metallic walls of the Hygiene Bay as he struggled to reach her quarters.

The light around her sealed door was flashing red.

A small square control box recessed into the side of the door was also flashing red: *Module Evac*.

Montreaux knew what it meant. They didn't have much time.

"Richardson, get over here!" he barked as he ripped the cover off the control panel. "Open this door!"

The scientist reached his side and saw the warning message. Her jaw dropped. "I can't," she managed to say. "It's flushing the module, all of the air is being sucked into space! Even if I could, opening the door could kill us all!" She looked and sounded helpless.

"Do it!" he screamed. He started banging on the sealed door with his fist and shouting through the metal. Hearing no response he redoubled his efforts with a double fisted blow that sent him cartwheeling backwards. His arms and legs flailed around as he tried to stop himself from spinning, and he finally managed to bring himself back to the door. He had raised his fist for another blow when a firm hand caught his wrist and stopped him.

"Captain, it is too late." Marchenko said, his accent coming through stronger than usual in his voice. "If she was in there, she is gone."

Montreaux turned round in a daze and pushed towards the Lounge. "She may be in here!" he said. "She used to come in here at night!" He looked through into the large spherical room and scanned round it several times before giving up, his body going limp in the connecting tunnel.

He felt a gentle tug at his legs as he was pulled back into the Hygiene Bay. He came to a halt facing Dr Richardson. In the background, the noise of the alarm had stopped.

"Yves," she started.

Behind her, he saw that Marchenko was sliding into Su Ning's quarters: the door was now lit in blue and had opened. Montreaux pushed past Richardson and reached the module, his eyes full of hope.

His face fell when he saw the Russian, cradling Su Ning's limp body.

Chapter 22

Mars filled the window of the Lounge as the *Clarke* completed another orbit. Captain Montreaux looked out over the reddish brown swirl of the Martian atmosphere and sighed.

He could still remember his last private exchange of words with Su Ning, at that very window, overlooking the stars. It was hard to believe that six weeks had passed since the accident.

The official word from Mission Control had been that a group of malfunctioning nanostations had collided inside the Chinese officer's quarters, causing a small fireball that had initiated the isolation procedure. On its own, this would not have been fatal, but a secondary fault in the *Clarke*'s safety protocols had caused it to issue a command to flush the module and put out the fire, despite the fact that no fire could be detected. All the computer had to do to avoid the situation was check the nanostation for a second reading, thereby gaining a measure by which to assess the risk to the spaceship; had it done so, it would have established that the fire had already stopped, and the area was safe.

The faulty programming caused all of the air to be evacuated from the module. The sudden, unexpected drop in atmospheric pressure and temperature killed Su Ning in less than two minutes.

Her body had been stored inside the *Clarke* in an empty refrigeration unit that had once contained food supplies for the outbound journey. The remaining crew members had pasted a photo of the astronaut on the door of the unit, along with a few personal messages. The mourning process had been especially difficult in the depths of space; the melancholic isolation of the had prolonged their silent suffering for well over a week.

In the end, Mission Control had started to play music through the internal communication system on board the *Clarke*. Within two days, the crew had begun socialising and even laughing again. It was amazing the effect music could have on people.

But Montreaux knew that for his part it was all a charade. While Dr Richardson and Captain Marchenko had eventually been satisfied by the explanation of the incident, the commanding officer had seen no accident in Su Ning's death.

Instead, he saw a very clear warning.

They had been orbiting the planet for a week now, waiting for a storm on the surface to let up. It was important that the *Clarke*'s landing module, the MLP, entered the atmosphere in quiet weather if possible, for two reasons.

Firstly, the safety of the crew was of major concern. The MLP was the largest landing craft ever to enter an alien atmosphere, and also the heaviest. Designers had initially toyed with the idea of a winged craft, similar to the old fashioned NASA Space Shuttle. But the lack of sufficiently flat surfaces to land on added to the thin atmosphere made it a far too risky option. A traditional parachute driven approach was therefore quickly adopted. Six chutes would deploy to bring the craft down safely, aided by inflatable cushions on the underside of the MLP. It was therefore vitally important that they did not land in the middle of a storm, as the high winds could easily disrupt the flow of air through the parachutes, and cause the craft to list uncontrollably during its descent. A landing under such conditions could be fatal, and an unfortunate premature ending to the already blighted Mars mission.

The second reason for waiting until the weather subsided was that they wanted to land within accessible distance of a precise point: *Crater Landslide* on the northern edge of Hellas Basin.

ESA's *Beagle 4* rover had already undertaken extensive reconnaissance of the area over the past three years, and proven beyond a shadow of a doubt that frozen water existed in abundance barely two feet beneath the surface. During a particularly impressive piece of footage, *Beagle 4* had arrived on the edge of a cliff barely moments after a mudslide had spilt down into the crater's basin. The video clearly showed rivulets of dirty, viscous liquid pouring slowly down the slopes for several minutes.

NASA had already been in the process of sending supply drops to Mars to supplement the *Clarke* mission, and on seeing this had routed everything to the area. The manned mission was destined to land within close proximity of these supply drops.

"Weather report shows that the storm has almost passed," Marchenko said optimistically from the Lounge's sofa. The storm covered most of the planet, and had been raging for over a month, well before their arrival in orbit. According to the forecast, based on previous planetary storms on Mars, it was due to end soon.

Montreaux looked round at the television screen behind him and studied the chart. He didn't need to fully understand it, that was Mission Control's job, but it was obvious that red was bad and blue was good. Whereas the previous day a three thousand mile long band of red had dominated the screen, it had by now disappeared almost entirely, to be replaced with the soothing tones of light and dark blue.

"Thank God for that. I thought we would be up here forever!" Dr Jane Richardson heaved a sigh of relief. "Everything is ready in the MLP, we're raring to go, all we need now is the green light from Mission Control."

It would take five minutes for her voice to reach Earth, but it seemed that Mission Control had been thinking along the same lines, as within thirty seconds a video message appeared onscreen.

"MLP deployment is good to go in T minus three hours. Please confirm message received and understood, and then report status on T minus two hours and T minus one hour," the nameless American controller read from a printout in front of him. He looked up from the paper, directly into the camera. To the crew of the *Clarke*, it felt as if he was looking at them all individually, straight in the eyes. "*Clarke*, good luck from everyone here at Mission Control, and Godspeed. CAPCOM out."

The television screen went blank.

"OK, you heard the man!" Captain Montreaux shouted after a brief silence. "Last chance for showers and meals in the quiet calm of space before we hit the sands of Mars!"

"At last!" cheered the Russian.

The *Clarke* reverberated with the sounds of a joyful crew as the storm blew over on the planet beneath them.

CHAPTER 23

Larue was sitting at his desk, staring out of the window at the heavy grey sky, when Martín Antunez walked into his office.

His light knocking had been ignored, so he had gripped the handle and entered, intent on putting his report on the boss' desk in his absence. He had been surprised to see him there, and had stopped inside the doorway, waiting for a reaction. None came. It was possible that he hadn't seen him.

"*Monsieur Larue?*" he offered quietly.

Still no response, save for a slight movement of the bottom jaw. He was grinding his teeth.

"I have compiled the monthly CSO reports for you, should I leave them on your desk?" *Commercial Satellite Orbit* reports. Not the most fascinating reads, but essential to the ESA nonetheless.

Larue inclined his head slightly in the opposite direction, as if listening for a noise from the cupboards behind him.

Martín approached the large desk, tidy for the first time since he could remember, and placed the report carefully on its surface, facing Larue. He had turned to leave when the man's voice stopped him.

"Beagle 3 returned some of the most impressive photos of Mars ever seen," he began slowly, playing each word over his tongue as if they were from a vintage red wine to be savoured.

Martín turned to face Larue.

"Robotic missions were clearly the way forward. With *Beagle 4* we proved the existence of liquid and solid water on the surface of the planet, away from the frozen Poles. But for some reason no one cared. In the ten years that separated Beagle 3 from *Beagle 4*, people became so enthralled by the prospect of a manned journey to Mars that they completely forgot to get excited about our rover. If it wasn't about the *Clarke*, it wasn't worth knowing about," Larue spat the words out bitterly. "I made a decision long ago not to let the ESA be a part of the

Clarke mission. Truth be told, I never thought it would be successful."

Martín winced as he heard the words.

Larue looked at the young Spaniard and smiled. "Do you think I was wrong?"

Martín bit his tongue. Larue would not be at the ESA for much longer, six months at most, but he could still not afford to upset him. He may have been powerless against the other space agencies, but inside the ESA he could still fire people. "You had good reason to withdraw from the International consortium, *Monsieur*," he lied. It was no good making him angry.

Larue returned his gaze to the window. "The *Clarke*'s landing craft is to be deployed in the next couple of hours, Martin. Tell me what you know about the mission so far."

He didn't want to know about the mission, Martín thought to himself. He wanted to know what juicy scandals he could leak, to pass the negative press from one agency to another, across the Atlantic.

"It's been a busy six weeks, *Monsieur*. The Chinese Lieutenant is dead, a tragic event caused by faulty programming in the *Clarke*'s nanostations –"

"Made in Japan by JAXA," Larue interrupted.

"Yes. The Chinese are not happy with the explanation given by NASA for the accident. Because the nanostations are Japanese, they are barely on speaking terms with JAXA, too. China has lost a national icon, and although they have not admitted so publicly, I think that they blame either the USA or Japan. For their part, JAXA have stated that it is not possible for the nanostations to fail like they did."

"Their simulations in the ISS did not reproduce the incident, did they?"

"No."

"Interesting." Larue was reading as much as he could into the facts, as usual.

Against Jacqueline's will, Martín had refrained from telling Larue anything about their discovery six weeks earlier. Since the live feed had been shut down and the security loophole Jacqueline had manipulated had been fixed, he felt that they lacked any concrete evidence. Circumstantial evidence, such as Su Ning's concern with her wristwatch, the strange interaction with Captain Montreaux and the disjointed transmissions between Mission Control and *Clarke*, while compelling, amounted to nothing in terms of cold, hard facts.

He was certain that Su Ning had been killed because she had uncovered the time delay, and he had no intention of meeting the same fate.

With Larue's increasingly desperate behaviour, if he had told him everything he knew, he was sure that Larue would have been on the phone to *Le Monde* within minutes. Unless they could prove the time delay existed, which they couldn't, it would just make everything much worse for the ESA.

Larue gestured with his hand for Martín to keep talking.

"NASA continue to supply us with most feeds from the *Clarke*, although the raw data has not been coming our way for over a month now. We get what NASA want us to see." *And over an hour later*, he thought. "Since the incident with Lieutenant Su Ning, there are a maximum of twenty active nanostations at any one time, and none of them can be controlled remotely. We have learnt from sources within the other agencies that Russia, China and Japan have been lobbying NASA for improved access to the nanostations."

Larue moved his hands through his hair slowly. "What do you think of all this?"

"I think that we need to be careful, *Monsieur*. We have no proof that NASA is trying to hide anything, and moreover, we have no reason to believe that they would have a motive for hiding anything in the first place. NASA is a scientific agency, and they do not have a political or ideological agenda." He chewed his bottom lip nervously.

"*Everyone* has an agenda, Martin, even NASA. *Especially* NASA."

"I am still looking, *Monsieur*. There is no smoke without fire, certainly. But this is like looking for a fire without smoke." He sighed. "I will keep looking, though."

Larue stopped looking out of the window and turned his head to his aide. "Martin," he checked his watch. "In one hour and twenty minutes, the MLP will be detaching from *Clarke* and entering the atmosphere of Mars. If they are going to slip up, it will be down there, away from the controlled environment of the spaceship."

Martín looked at his watch quickly. *It was already happening*. "I'll have all my ears to the ground, *Monsieur*."

CHAPTER 24

Richardson, Marchenko and Montreaux reclined in their bucket seats in the MLP, strapped down by four thick belts over their shoulders and round their waists connected by a large metal buckle that nested comfortably on top of their breastbones. Their legs were supported by foam padding that extended from the bottom of each of the chairs. It looked like a busy dentist's surgery, and the patients were nervous.

The single empty chair stood out like a sore thumb.

"It's been good knowing you all," Jane half-joked.

"Let's hope the computer gets it right this time." Marchenko was deadly serious.

"Danny, please!"

"Sorry, Jane. I am sure everything will be fine. The nanostations are not allowed in here."

"Captain Marchenko, please refrain from that subject, it is totally inappropriate," Montreaux warned.

"It's OK Yves, he's only kidding," said Jane.

The Russian bent his head sideways to look at her. "No I am not," he said, before grinning.

"*Ten seconds to launch*," advised the computer.

"Good luck, everyone," Montreaux said, gripping his arm rests tightly. "Good job so far, let's make sure we finish it off well down there and get home in one piece."

Dr Richardson and Captain Marchenko nodded their agreement.

"*Four... Three ... Two ... One ... Launch!*"

They all tensed for the expected jolt that they had experienced in training simulations. It was the moment they had been waiting for ever since they had first floated into the *Clarke* nearly four months earlier.

A light thud was all they heard. The MLP barely moved.

After the initial shock of the anti-climax had worn off, Montreaux checked his instruments carefully. Had the release mechanism failed?

All of a sudden, they heard the lateral boosters of the MLP releasing jets of compressed air into space. The landing craft was now being manoeuvred into a trajectory that would take it into the Martian atmosphere.

"We have left the *Clarke*," Dr Richardson said in disbelief. "I hardly noticed!"

"We are in a declining orbit, entry in twelve more revolutions," Marchenko confirmed.

Montreaux looked at the control panel in front of him. Millions of calculations a second were being performed by the MLP's on board computer, which would control every aspect of the landing.

As their decreasing orbit drew them closer and closer to the planet, there was nothing they could do but watch and hope.

Half an hour later, the MLP shaved the outer reaches of Mars' thin atmosphere and gently forced its way through. The trajectory had been calculated to the last millimetre, to ensure that their entry was successful. A few degrees out either way would have resulted in the craft either disintegrating, a bright shooting star against the Martian sky, or bouncing off the atmosphere and into the depths of space.

The underside of the MLP was coated in ceramic heat resistant tiles that would have been quite happy sitting on the surface of the Sun. As the friction of the air against the tiles grew, they began to glow white hot. The heat caused the passing gas of the atmosphere to combust, shooting yellow and blue flames several metres long up above the leading edge of the MLP as it cut deeper and deeper into the Martian atmosphere.

Inside the landing craft, the tranquillity of space had been brutally cast aside as everything began vibrating wildly, jostling the three astronauts against the bucket-sides of their chairs. A combination of forces assaulted them: the downwards force of returning gravity, a third of Earth's but still a feeling they had not experienced for a long time, coupled with the upwards force of the plummeting craft, pulling them towards the ceiling.

And then that returning sense of direction. There *was* an up, and a down. There was most definitely a *down*.

"Aaaahhhh!" cried Dr Richardson.

"You've done this before on Earth!" Montreaux shouted above the noise.

"I haven't fallen from anywhere for nearly half a year!" she screamed.

Marchenko managed to reach over and put his hand on hers as she gripped her armrest firmly. "We will make it, Jane, trust me." He tried to laugh but the air was being forced out of his lungs, resulting in a strange scoff. "The chutes were designed in Russia!"

She released her grip and took his hand thankfully.

"We're almost through!" Montreaux shouted, reading from the instrument panel.

As suddenly as it had begun, the shaking and roaring of the passing atmosphere outside stopped. It was replaced by a gentle hissing, and the occasional shake.

"We are in the skies of Mars!" Marchenko cheered. "Nearly time for our Russian chutes to deploy."

They sat in silence for several long, anxious moments before Dr Richardson could wait no more.

"How long?" she cried.

"Thirty-six seconds" Marchenko replied instantly.

They all counted it down in their heads.

Montreaux reached zero and continued down well into the minuses. He had reached minus fifteen, and was about to mention that fact, when a sharp jerk crushed him against the padding of his chair. The MLP listed backwards and forwards, so that he had the sensation that his chair was alternating between being on the ceiling and on the floor

"The swinging will stop shortly," Danny reassured them. "It is our momentum carrying us through, we are like a clock's pendulum, hanging from the chutes above us." He was obviously proud that the parachutes had deployed as planned, while the others just looked relieved.

The MLP's on-board computer was already plotting the ground beneath them, mapping every square metre of the surface as it went. As it approached the vicinity of Hellas Basin, it closed in on its homing signal, and small motors began winding in and out the parachutes on each edge of the MLP, guiding it towards its destination.

"Virtually no cross winds," Montreaux marvelled at their timing. "We're sailing down perfectly, with a bit of luck we'll be within a few hundred yards of the target."

A control panel in front of them began to beep repeatedly. Leaning closer, he read the display and tensed.

"Two hundred metres to touchdown," he said matter-of-factly.

The beeping increased in frequency as they descended.

"One Fifty."

"Our Father, who art in Heaven…" Jane began to say under her breath.

"I thought you were a scientist?" Danny joked, squeezing her hand.

She smiled and continued her prayer. "… hallowed be thy name…"

"One Ten."

"…Thy Kingdom come, thy will be done…"

"Ninety."

"…On Earth as it is in Heaven." She stopped. She didn't know the rest of the words from memory. "Shit!" she cursed herself for forgetting.

"Seventy. Give us this day our daily bread, and forgive us our trespasses," continued Montreaux. "Fifty. As we forgive those who trespass against us. And lead us not unto temptation, Thirty, but deliver us from evil." The beeping was now so fast it created a continuous pulsing tone. "For the kingdom, Fifteen, the power and the glory are yours, now and forever, Five –"

The MLP touched the ground and bounced gently like a skipping stone on a pond, its self-inflated underbelly taking the remaining force of their parachuted descent. After the first bounce the bags began to deflate, letting the MLP slide for a few metres along the smooth, sand-covered plain before coming to rest a few centimetres away from a large, round boulder.

Inside, the three astronauts lay in total silence for a whole minute before Captain Danny Marchenko whispered under his breath: "Amen."

They had landed on Mars.

Martín leant back in his chair and closed his eyes, trying to imagine what was happening on Mars, sixty million miles away.

"They will have landed now," Jacqueline said, sipping from her coffee slowly.

And we are the only ones outside NASA who know, he thought.

"It's sickening," she went on. "To think that the world will be watching in over an hour, thinking that they are watching it Live."

He could tell by the tone of her voice that she was dying to tell someone what they knew. "You haven't told anyone, have you?" he checked.

"No! You asked me not to!" She sounded hurt.

He opened his eyes and looked over at her. They were in the coffee room of her floor in the ESA Headquarters, where they had started meeting up during working hours.

"I'm sorry, I know you wouldn't do a thing like that." His voice was soft and apologetic.

She smiled and shrugged it off. "I found something this morning that might help," she said. "The feed we were watching that night, the live feed, I think I know how to get it back."

He sat up and put his hands round his drink on the table, heating them up on the warm Styrofoam surface. "Go on."

"Well, you know that we can't intercept the feed coming from *Clarke* to Earth, and as the feed from Mars is going through *Clarke*, we have no hope. They've put some kind of encryption on the transmission that I can't crack, and since our night of *hacking*," she whispered the word, though the room was empty aside from themselves, "they've clearly upped the security level on everything."

Martín nodded, they'd been over this a thousand times. What they really needed was to capture a feed that NASA then *withheld* from the public; that would be their proof that NASA was screening what the other agencies saw. Unfortunately, during their night's investigations, all of the live data they had recorded had subsequently been aired uncensored. They had been unable to prove a thing.

"OK, so we cannot get a direct feed *that* way." She had a smile on her face as she looked at him. "But can you think of one reason why the Mars mission landed where it did?"

He thought for a second before replying. "It's an interesting geological site?" he said.

"Another reason."

"It's got a temperate climate close to the equator?"

She punched him in the ribs. "One more try!"

He thought for a while longer before it dawned on him. "*Beagle 4.*"

"Exactly. Our lovely little rover proved the existence of liquid and frozen water, in abundance, near the impact crater. It's essential not only for the crew's survival, but also for fuel for taking off from Mars in four months."

"Where is Beagle now?" he asked, suddenly alert.

"Luckily, its current mission plan has it running extended sampling of the Martian soil quite close to the Crater; it's still only a little over thirteen kilometres from the lander site. I've done some calculations; at full speed we can have it within three kilometres of the lander in four days. We will be able to spy on the Mars mission, and send everything back to ESA headquarters directly, via our *own* encryption."

He looked over at Jacqueline and grinned. "You're great!" he exclaimed.

"Calm down," she said trying to hide her blushes. "We still need to get it there. Larue needs to sign this off, and then it needs building in to the Beagle routes."

"Put the request forms in for re-routing Beagle, and I'll make sure they get approval. From there, we just have to hope it gets done sooner rather than later." He got up quickly, throwing his half-finished coffee into the bin and kissing her on the forehead.

As he pulled away from her she caught his cheek with her hand and pulled him closer again, reaching up with her mouth at the same time. Their lips met and Martín's resistance ebbed away as she held him more closely. After several seconds he pushed her away and looked her in the eyes. Her bright-red lips were swollen with passion and she had a playful look in her eyes.

He sat down next to her and put his arm round her waist. Drawing her body against his, he kissed her again, more passionately.

Mars could wait, for a little while at least.

CHAPTER 25

There was more to the Mars Landing Pod than first met the eye. It had been motionless on the surface of Mars for over three hours, and the dust had finally settled in the thin air, when the top half began to move upwards.

Looking like two soup bowls placed one on top of the other, the thirty-foot wide MLP had caught the imagination of the public on Earth as the closest thing yet to a *Flying Saucer*. They had quickly overlooked the fact that it could not possibly fly; floating down to the ground suspended by parachutes was the best it could do. They had also overlooked the fact that it would only look like a flying saucer for a short time once on Mars.

As the top half of the MLP began to separate from the bottom, which remained firmly on the ground, a thin rubber-like membrane extended in the increasing gap in-between. The top continued to lift until the MLP stood fourteen feet high. The flat rubber walls shook for several minutes, and then stopped as they became taught.

Deployment of the MLP had been completed.

Inside, Captain Montreaux wiped the sweat from his forehead. "I don't care what the mission planners say; even at a third of Earth gravity it's still damn heavy!"

"I didn't think the support on this side would click for a moment," Jane laughed. She was standing next to the newly extended rubber wall of the MLP. In the gap between the bottom and top halves they had placed a series of titanium supports, about an inch thick, each slotted neatly into two small holes at the top and bottom. "I haven't had *this* much fun since I last went camping!"

"I agree, it is a bit like a hugely expensive and advanced camper van, isn't it?" Montreaux laughed.

"I think you two should see this," Danny Marchenko said quietly from the other side of the MLP.

Fully deployed, the vastness of the MLP was striking. It was larger than the average one bedroom apartment, at thirty-feet in diameter and with ten feet of internal height. It was difficult to believe that they were on Mars.

They looked over to Danny, who had his head pressed against a transparent segment of the rubber wall. The six windows had been placed at regular twelve feet intervals along the MLP's circumference, and they each went to the closest one.

Outside lay the cool grey dawn of a Martian sol. A slight orange hue from the soil was the only sign that they were on the Red Planet and not in Arizona, USA. On the horizon, light wispy clouds of dust drifted gently from left to right, the tail end of the storm they had been waiting out.

The fantastic reality of their situation hit them simultaneously, affecting them all differently. For his part, while the Russian and the scientist celebrated behind him, Captain Yves Montreaux could not help himself from shedding a silent tear. Despite his excitement, the fulfilment of a life-long dream of visiting Mars, the only thought in his head was of Su Ning, and the secret she had taken with her.

It took them two hours to assemble the airlock. It was in kit form, and they had fun putting it together and arguing over which bits should go where. It had all been good natured arguing, as they were all fully trained in how to assemble the vitally important apparatus.

Despite his initial emotions, it had not taken Montreaux long to be caught up in the moment. They had landed on Mars successfully, and were preparing for their first Extra Vehicular Activity, or EVA.

Their landing had been incredibly well executed by the on-board computer: Jane had already noted that within fifty metres of her window she could see a small metal crate, the deflated airbags that had protected it on its descent just visible in the layer of dust and sand that covered everything around them. Danny commented that being so close to the previous drops could be interpreted as very poor landing; a bit to the left and they would have landed right on top of the metal crates. Not only would it have been inaccessible to them, but the damage to the MLP could have been catastrophic.

Their first directive during their EVA would be to perform an exterior status check of the MLP, followed by a quick reconnaissance of their surrounding area. The crate seemed like a perfect place to start.

"There, all done," Danny declared triumphantly.

The airlock stood six feet tall and five feet wide, to one side of the interior of the MLP. A large round door gave entry to the airtight chamber inside, which could be seen through two small windows. The status of anyone inside the airlock could be visually monitored from there. The sides of the MLP were pre-equipped with three ready-made hatches, one of which the airlock had been placed against. It had been designed so that it could be placed on any side of the MLP, an important contingency in the event that they should incur any damage on landing, or land next to an immovable object, such as a boulder or cliff. The outer door of the airlock lay flush with the rubber wall of the MLP. Opening the door for the first time would pierce that thin membrane and lead on to the Martian surface.

"OK, I think that it needs a road test!" Jane said.

Montreaux was already putting his EVA suit on. "Is everyone alright with the mission plan?" he asked as he zipped and sealed his left boot.

Danny and Jane looked at each other and smiled. "Absolutely, Captain," they said in unison.

The Russian sat down on a small bench next to where his EVA suit had been put, hanging from the wall lifelessly. He unhooked it from the wall and started to unzip the front of the jacket and trouser combination, ready to step into it. "I will follow you once you give the OK."

"And I will stay here like a lemon and make sure that you are both having as much fun as possible!" Jane said, pretending to be hurt.

Montreaux had finished sealing his boots, and the scientist helped him with his gloves. The atmosphere of Mars, and similar pressure to Earth, had meant that their EVA suits could be designed very differently from traditional suits used on the Moon and International Space Station. Consequently, they looked more like divers than astronauts, the skin of the suits hugging their bodies closely. This also improved their effectiveness during EVAs. Although it was not encouraged, it had been possible during testing to run at quite some speed in the suits, and the close-fitting gloves even made it possible to grip certain types of pen or computer stylus and write with a degree of accuracy.

He stood up and walked over to the airlock gingerly. His helmet was sealed, but the inbuilt two-way radio system routed his voice through to the MLP's speakers.

"OK, can you hear me?" he asked.

"Ouch! Way too loud!" she replied.

"At least when *you're* out there, Jane, we will be able to turn you down for once!" Danny joked from behind her as he prepared to fit his head snugly into his helmet.

She shot him a grin and prepared Montreaux for his EVA. She sprayed an aerosol solution over the tight skin of his suit to check for leaks, before turning him around and double checking his regulators.

"You're all set," she gave him the 'OK' signal by making a circle with her index finger and thumb and waving it in front of his visor.

Montreaux returned the gesture and turned towards the door.

Entering the airlock, he looked around. There were two small benches, one on each side. On his left was the door he had just come through, leading into the MLP, on his right, the hatch that led to the never-before-walked-on surface of Mars.

For some reason he didn't feel nervous.

He looked up at the window in the wall and saw Jane looking down at him. Every few seconds she checked a reading in front of her before repeating the OK gesture. Each time he replied in kind. Suddenly, Danny's head appeared in the window next to her, in an EVA helmet. There was a huge grin on his face. Montreaux gave the OK sign with both hands to him, and he waved back.

Inside the airlock, he could see two lights, one red and one green. The red light was on, telling him it was not yet safe to open the hatch.

"How are you doing?" Jane's voice came through the headphones in his helmet.

"Fine, a little cold, but I'm sure it'll get warmer," he replied.

Danny's laugh echoed loudly in his ears. "Oh, yeah, I hear it's real sunbathing weather out there: minus forty degrees Celsius. Get me some ice cream!"

Montreaux was about to reply when the green light came on. He checked his forearm, where a small OLED panel gave him vital statistics on his suit and the surrounding atmosphere. It also let him control heat, airflow, lights and a video camera mounted in his helmet. "How's the video feed?" he asked.

"Crystal clear!" Jane replied.

Looking up at the faces in the window, he gave the OK signal one last time. "Here goes!" he said. Turning towards the hatch, he took a deep breath and reached for the handle, a recessed metal rod that lay vertically at its centre. He gripped it with both hands and turned it a full ninety degrees anticlockwise. He was rewarded with a dull clunk as the locks along all four edges of the hatch disengaged. He pushed gently on the metal and felt the outer wall of the MLP give as the hatch tore through it precisely. The hatch swung open slowly.

He fancied he could feel the cold Martian breeze against his shins as he crouched down to fit through the low opening. Ducking his head, he fixed the small ladder from the inside of the airlock to the outside of the MLP, and stepped out. He descended cautiously, and landed his left foot with a crunch, sinking several centimetres into the dust and grit. His right foot followed, and he was standing outside the landing craft. Turning round, he gently closed the hatch using the external handle. He took a step back.

He was standing on Mars.

He had practised this moment all of his life, in his head. He had always imagined that he would walk on the surface of Mars and say something monumental, something to rival Armstrong's immortal words of 1969, almost a century earlier. An icon for a new generation: a symbol of hope.

He had practised his speech so many times that in that instant, as he took several further steps out onto the Martian plain, he completely forgot to say anything.

After a long minute, he stopped dead in his tracks and looked up at the sky. Not red, as his ancestors had believed, but blue and grey, like a winter's morning on Earth. And then it came back to him, the first words that he knew everyone on Earth had been waiting for.

Over the past couple of weeks, he had played the scene over and over in his mind. Maybe he would use this chance, this opportunity to call for help, to denounce Su Ning's murder. It would be a heroic gesture, for sure, and certainly foolish: he had no way of guaranteeing his words would ever reach Earth. His pre-written walking-on-Mars proclamation, chosen for him by a panel of experts and mission planners, was now long forgotten. He would instead use this one moment to show his defiance by not using NASA's words, but a mixture of his own and those of a twentieth century American writer.

"Earth, this is Captains Yves Montreaux and Dannil Marchenko, and Dr Jane Richardson of the spaceship *Clarke*," he said to the eight billion people he hoped were listening across the gulf of space. His breathing was all over the place with emotion as he spoke from the confines of his suit's helmet. He looked out over the Martian plain before him, and then let his eyes return to the sky, towards home.

"We are calling from Mars, where our wonder has indeed been renewed; space travel has again made children of us all."

CHAPTER 26

Martín reached for the small radio clock on his bedside table and held it a few centimetres from his face. Squinting at the display for a few moments he let his head fall back on the pillow and groaned.

Almost seven o'clock; he was late.

He swung his legs over the edge of the mattress and pushed himself upwards, away from the tempting warmth of the sheets.

"What time is it?"

He jumped and shot a look over his shoulder. Seeing Jacqueline's head emerging from under the duvet on the other side of the bed, the night's events started coming back to him. "Late," he managed to say.

Bringing his hands to his head, he rubbed his face with his palms and tried to piece things together. They had been drinking, he remembered, until the early hours. What had they been celebrating? The Mars landing? Captain Montreaux's unexpected quote? Jacqueline's plan to use *Beagle 4* to spy on the mission? That and a whole lot more.

"Is everything alright?" he heard her say worriedly behind him. He could imagine the look on her face. They were in his flat, after their first night together. It was clear that she liked him. How would he feel in her position? He still hadn't even looked at her properly!

"Martín, are you OK?"

Everything felt alright, aside from the obvious hangover. He'd been here before, with others, but this was different. They would both be late for work, but somehow that didn't matter anymore. He lay back down in bed and brought the duvet up over his shoulder. Turning towards her, he found her arm under the covers, held it with his hand and smiled, looking her directly in the eyes.

"Perfect," he said, relaxing as she melted into his embrace. "Everything is perfect."

After weeks of zero gravity and little activity save for the treadmills and dumbbells, NASA had little requirement to tell the crew of the *Clarke* to start work straight away. The greatest barrier of all had been getting used to the gravity of Mars. Although only a third of that experienced on Earth, it was infinitely more than they had felt for months.

Jane had been a natural adapting to the apparent weightlessness of the *Clarke*, and her two male crew members could only watch in envy as she pranced around the MLP as if she had lived on Mars her entire life. It was the astronaut's version of Jetlag, and as with Jetlag, it only became apparent sometime after landing. Montreaux had been surprised at the weight of a portable computer, which had it not been rugged would almost certainly have smashed as he dropped it on the floor. Danny for his part had already tipped his tray of food over at lunchtime, saved slightly by the fact that they were still eating from food packets from the *Clarke*. As a result, only his peas had fallen, and he had spent an awkward minute on his knees trying to collect them all from the grooves in the metal floor.

Their first Mars-walk had been a resounding success, Danny and Montreaux having gone three hundred metres from the MLP and completed a ninety degree arc before returning to the lander. Their short walk took them less than an hour, but in that time they managed to walk the perimeter of an area of more than a square kilometre. The first robotic Mars rovers had taken weeks to cover similar distances, and even *Beagle 4* would have taken several hours to do the same.

They had also pinpointed six successful drop sites, covering everything from food and hygiene supplies to clothing and scientific equipment. That thirty per cent of the supply drops had been successful and fallen a few hundred metres apart was nothing short of incredible, but what really impressed the astronauts was that the MLP had landed within sight of them.

During this time, Jane had already started to assemble her scientific apparatus inside the MLP, and when her two colleagues returned she was already preparing sample dishes and trays on a long trestle table to one side of the craft.

Now, four hours since the first Mars-walk had taken place, she was getting impatient.

"Right, we only have an hour or so of light left before the end of the sol." She looked across at Montreaux, who was checking the readings on the main control board in the centre of the MLP. "We need to perform one more Mars-walk before sunset, to set up the first perimeter beacons."

"I think that we need to wait until the morning, Jane," Danny said, making Montreaux look up at him in surprise. Catching his candid wink, he sighed and returned to his work.

She glared at the Russian. "Danny, I don't really care what you think. There is no way I am going to spend humankind's first sol on Mars inside the MLP."

"Doing the washing up?" he laughed.

Montreaux tensed and waited for the scientist's response without looking up from the console. Instead of the expected outburst, however, he was surprised to hear her laugh. Straightening up, he turned to face her and saw that it was genuine.

"Danny, if there's one thing that's even more certain than the fact that I am going outside in a minute, it's the fact that today I am so happy, not even you can wind me up!"

He laughed and walked towards the airlock and the protection suits hanging on the wall. "OK, whatever you say."

Minutes later, as she brought down the helmet over her head and fastened the clips to the neck of her suit, she raised her thumbs at him and gave a huge grin.

Danny checked the air regulator on his own suit and returned the OK signal, before winking at her. "Can you hear me?"

"Yes," she confirmed. "As clear as day." She turned to the airlock and opened the inner door.

From the console in the centre of the room, Montreaux caught the look in the Russian's eye and groaned. Danny grinned in return.

"Oh, Jane, don't forget your flag," he said, as matter-of-factly as possible.

She ignored him and got into the airlock all the same. Danny followed and sat opposite her. From where he was sitting, Montreaux could see Jane through the open door, and as it closed behind them her eyes told him she was slightly annoyed by his joke. Smiling to himself, he stood up and walked over to the airlock to perform the safety checks.

If anyone could wind Dr Jane Richardson up, it was always going to be Captain Daniil "Danny" Marchenko.

CHAPTER 27

"My God!" She held the binoculars up to her visor and focused on the metallic object shining on the horizon; one of the supply drops that had arrived on Mars in the last year, it contained some of the vital life-support components for their return launcher, which would take them and the central core of the MLP back into Mars orbit. "We have to go all the way over there?"

"Be thankful we are not salvaging my beloved country's lander, instead. At least we can see this one." Danny said. "But if you do notice any metal objects with red flags on them, please let me know."

The 1972 *Mars 2* lander had been sent by the Soviet Union as part of its ambitious early exploration of the planet. It consisted not only of an orbiter and landing craft, but also a small rover on skis, which would explore the immediate surroundings of the landing site. Like most missions to Mars it had failed, and although the thin Martian air would have slowed it down from the six kilometres per second with which it had hit the atmosphere, its parachutes did not deploy as it hurtled towards the ground. To the best knowledge of the scientific community, it had impacted within a hundred mile radius of where the *Clarke*'s MLP now stood.

Over seventy years later, it was unlikely that much remained of the ill-fated mission.

"OK, no problem, I'll keep my eyes open for it," she replied.

The Russian flipped the lid of a large metal crate and peered inside it. "Besides, we don't have to walk there." He pulled a wheel, forty centimetres in diameter, out of the crate and rolled it towards her, its tread leaving a shallow imprint in the ochre soil. "We can go there in style!"

It took two entire days to assemble the *Clarke*'s manned buggy, affectionately nicknamed 'Herbie' by the media; because of the curved

135

enclosure where the two occupants would sit, it bore more than a slight resemblance to an old VW Beetle car. Its power came from two electric engines, each taking charge of a row of three wheels on either side. Fuel came in the form of eight battery cells, which would be charged using the MLP's generator. In turn, the MLP got its energy from solar sheets, which had been unrolled from the leading edges of the MLP and fastened to the ground. From above, they made the MLP look like some bizarre kind of flower.

In case of emergencies, the MLP had been loaded with three more sheets that could be placed anywhere within a hundred metres. Additionally, Jane was to assemble three wind turbines, especially suited to the thinner atmosphere of Mars, as a secondary source of electricity.

It took another three days to fully charge Herbie, during which time the crew busied themselves collecting the rest of the crates from the surrounding area and setting up four signal boosting beacons around the MLP.

After a short test run, Danny triumphantly declared that Herbie was at last ready to drive.

"He's a better ride than most of the cars I've been in on Earth!" he exclaimed.

"You mean *she*," Montreaux corrected him.

Danny looked at him sideways from the driving seat and shook his head. "No, it is definitely a *he*. *Herbie* is a boy's name."

"All cars are female, Danny, even the ones with boy's names," Jane's voice came over the radio from inside the MLP. "It's just the way it is."

He thought about this for a moment and then laughed. "You are right; in Russian *mashina* is feminine too. I guess it makes sense," he mused, "because –"

"Don't even go there," she warned him.

Montreaux laughed out loud as he loaded four spare compressed air packs onto Herbie's back. Herbie wasn't an airtight craft, the thin cabin was designed only to save the occupants from the worst of the Martian weather, and so they would have to use their suits' air supplies throughout their drives. With just over two hours per pack, they would have a maximum six hours round-trip to where the silvery crates lay on the horizon. They would need to keep a constant eye on the time; it would certainly take more than one trip.

"OK," he said securing the air packs and turning towards the MLP. "Time for dinner. We'll set off first thing tomorrow."

CHAPTER 28

Larue put the phone down and smiled. It was his first for some time.

Sitting back in his chair, he surveyed the view from his office. His smile grew as he took in the sunshine, Paris's first for weeks. The windows of the ESA headquarters let the day's warmth seep in gently, leaving the bitter wind and traffic noise outside. As a young man, he had worked for a short time in the *Tour First*, Paris's tallest skyscraper, and had been impressed at how the sounds of the city were silenced when looking down from the top floors. On his arrival at ESA headquarters years later, it had amazed him even more that the triple glazed windows of his third storey street-facing office were just as effective. Occasionally a siren or beeping horn would make its way through the panes and remind him he was working in a sprawling metropolis of over fifteen million inhabitants.

He opened the top drawer of his desk and pulled out a small wooden box. Opening the lid, he perused the contents for a few moments, inhaling the deep sweet smell of the fine Cuban tobacco before closing it and putting it back in the drawer with a shake of his head. It was a good day, but not yet that good. He brought his gaze back to the blue sky outside, and closed his eyes.

A knock at the door brought him back from his reverie, and he sat up with a start. Looking at his watch, he sighed to himself and tapped the spacebar on his keyboard.

"Come in," he said.

Martín entered the room. He had a huge smile on his face.

"News travels fast, I see," Larue said casually.

Martín frowned in response. "*Monsieur?*"

"I take it from your smile that you have heard the good news?"

"No, I have not heard," Martín said, confused.

Larue eyed him cautiously. "So why the big smile, Martín?"

Martín felt himself blushing; the past week with Jacqueline had been incredible, giving him plenty to grin about. Not that any of it was Larue's business. He cleared his face before continuing. *"Monsieur*, a while ago you asked me to keep my eyes open regarding the *Clarke?"*

"Yes?" he leaned forward in his chair expectantly. He had almost stopped hoping, after so many weeks without any news. "Have you found something?"

"Not yet. But soon, we probably will. For some time now we have been unable to see any direct feeds from the mission. Whilst on board the *Clarke*, this was frustrating, but now that they have landed on the planet, it is even more so." He paused, still unsure of what he was about to say. Telling Larue about the time delay wasn't easy, but something he felt he could do now that they had a chance to *prove* it using the feed from Beagle. Nonetheless, he was still slightly nervous that he would be in trouble for hiding this information from his boss for nearly two months.

"I made a discovery shortly after our feeds were stopped, with the help of Jacqueline from Networks."

"Jacqueline Thomas?" Larue asked, his eyebrow raised.

"Yes, *Monsieur*. She helped me to analyse the information being sent to us by NASA. There is a lot of information, I needed some help interpreting it, and her programming skills are far higher than my own."

Larue smiled. "I did not ask you to justify yourself, Martin, I was merely surprised you would go so far to get help, we have very skilled programmers in this department, too."

Martín shifted his feet uneasily. "She was available at the time, *Monsieur*."

Larue looked up at the young man. He was standing in front of his desk like a schoolboy in front of a headmaster. "Sit down, Martin, make yourself more comfortable," he gestured to a chair opposite him. Martín sat down thankfully and put his hands on his knees. "So, you were saying that you had analysed the feeds from NASA at the time that they stopped relaying direct to ESA. What happened next?"

"We noticed something very strange. So far, we think that we are the first to have noticed it, it certainly hasn't been raised publicly by either the Chinese, Japanese or Russian agencies. A little over a day before Lieutenant Shi Su Ning, the Chinese astronaut, was found dead in her sleeping quarters, we believe that NASA placed a delay of one hour and fifteen minutes in the feed between themselves and ESA. They also placed the same delay in their feed to the other agencies."

Larue stared at him in silence for several seconds. *"Comment?"* he said, eventually.

"NASA have implemented a time delay in the data feed from Mars which allows them to screen everything for over one hour before it is released to any of the other agencies. The other agencies are not aware of this, and as far as we can tell they believe that they are still watching direct feeds." He paused and looked at Larue. Larue's smile had disappeared; his hands were laid flat on his desk, fingers splayed. "To help achieve this, they have also added seventy-five minutes to all of the *Clarke*'s on board clocks and timers. This means that the *Clarke*'s time in the delayed feed on Earth looks correct."

"But," Larue was visibly shocked, "surely it would be easy for everyone to find this out simply by trying to talk to the crew? There would be a huge delay!"

"The change coincided with NASA cutting off our direct feed, which would have sorted us out. As for the others, a serious malfunction of the nanostations caused NASA to stop using them, which forced a policy change on communications. On top of that, the *Clarke* was already so far away by then that we weren't having direct conversations with the crew anymore, it just wasn't practical."

"So how did *you* find out?"

"Jacqueline hacked into the direct feed for a short period, and before she was cut off by NASA, we managed to view the real footage alongside what the other agencies were being sent. The time delay is real, but they've upped their security since, and we haven't been able to get back in."

Larue was taken aback. He looked out of the window and thought carefully about the situation; none of his counterparts at the other agencies had communicated anything to him directly. On top of that, NASA had certainly not lodged a complaint with ESA for the low level hacking of the data feeds. He would leave that issue for another day. For the time being he would concentrate on the facts. "Can we prove this?"

"Unfortunately, we cannot," Martín admitted. "I recorded the nanostation feeds that show the time difference, but since then the *live* footage has also been transmitted normally, so it proves nothing."

"And you haven't been able to access the live feeds since then?"

"No. Whatever encryption they're using, it's impossible to crack."

He looked at Larue, who was now staring at the backs of his hands on the desk. "We've tried several times," he added helpfully.

Larue looked up from his desk and met Martín's eyes, which contrary to his smile had lost none of the joy that they had shown when he had first entered the room several minutes before. "And you said that no one else knows this?"

"As far as we can tell, we are the only ones to have seen this."

Larue looked out of the window again. "How about the Chinese? Their relationship with NASA is very strenuous at the moment, is it possible that they know too?"

"It's very possible, *Monsieur*."

Larue looked across and raised his eyebrow quizzically. "There's something you haven't told me, isn't there?"

Martín hadn't intended to tell Larue any of this, at least not until *Beagle 4* was in place. He had agreed with Jacqueline that it was best to present him with good news rather than speculation. His good mood had certainly helped to break his silence, but he was now finding it a relief to tell his manager everything. "We know of one other person who found out about the time change."

"Yes?"

"We believe that shortly before her death, Su Ning became aware of the difference. Somehow, she must have calculated the time on Earth. This alone wouldn't have helped her, and we've been trawling video footage to find any clues, but the best guess we have is that she must have had access to a watch that showed Earth time with which to verify her calculations," Martín said. He had started the sentence slowly, carefully, but as he had gone on he had found the words pouring out of their own accord. He stopped himself from saying more, and tried to gauge Larue's response.

Larue sat silently for over a minute, before standing up and walking to the window. He looked down at the traffic below, congested behind a bin lorry collecting recyclables from the side of the road. A motorbike weaved its way through the lines of cars, narrowly avoiding a pedestrian reading a newspaper. He looked over at the UNESCO building. The familiar tops of the trees beckoned to him; he would definitely go for a walk today.

Turning round, he looked at Martín and frowned. "You should have told me all of this much sooner, Martín," he said. He walked over to his desk and opened the top drawer again. Beside the small wooden box was a large plastic tub. He pulled it out and popped the lid, carefully pouring one pill into the palm of his hand. He clenched his fist around the pill and replaced the tub in the drawer before picking up a glass of water on his desk. He looked at Martín out of the corner of his eyes and titled his head back, taking the pill and water in one gulp.

He sat down at his desk once more, leaning back slowly and closing his eyes, his arms placed carefully on the armrests.

Martín waited for at least two minutes before speaking. "*Monsieur*," he began, "I am sorry that I didn't tell you this sooner; we wanted to be certain that −"

"I am not concerned with that, Martin," Larue snapped. He did not move from his chair, his eyes remained closed. Of course, he was enraged that his employee had left him in the dark, but now he had to concentrate on what was happening on Mars. If it played out in his favour, this whole situation could be his saving grace. "You did well to find out what you did."

"Then what is wrong?" To Martín, it was simple. The Americans were hiding information from their closest technological allies, and had probably caused Su Ning's death to keep the fact secret. It was more of a conspiracy than even his boss could have hoped for.

Larue half opened his eyes and looked over at Martín. "If I understand you correctly, and you are right in what you say, which I have no doubt you are, then this is more than a simple rivalry between competing space agencies." He paused, shifting his body up in the chair. "NASA would not simply carry out deception on such a scale for the fun of it. Placing this time difference between *Clarke* and Earth suggests that this is bigger than that."

Martín leant forward. "So who could be responsible?"

"I do not know, Martin. But there's one thing that is even more certain than the fact that NASA couldn't be responsible for this."

"Yes?"

"NASA would never intentionally kill an astronaut."

Martín leant back and crossed his arms. "To hide the truth, they might," he said.

Larue sat upright and laughed. "This isn't *Capricorn One*, Martin! This is NASA! This is 2045, and the *Clarke* is a multinational mission to Mars! Why would anyone want to jeopardise our first manned mission?"

Martín had no idea. He looked at his shoes, as if the answer somehow lay in the criss-cross pattern of his laces.

"Which leads me to the most important question. The question that lies at the heart of this whole situation: *what is there to hide?*"

"We have no idea, *Monsieur*. The feeds we have do not show anything revealing."

"And they're never likely to either!" Larue said in frustration. "They slipped up at the beginning, which is how you and Jacqueline were able to see this, and also why poor Su Ning lost her life. They are not likely to slip up again." He looked out of the window again and his frown grew as he noticed dark clouds gathering on the horizon, ready to blot out the sun. "And until we know what they are hiding, or at least have some evidence, there is no way we can say anything to anyone. With what we have, we cannot tell anyone, Martin. Do you understand?"

Martín nodded slowly. "There is one more thing, *Monsieur*," he said, "that may help us, and give us this proof."

"What is that?" Larue had a wry smile on his face, as if he already knew what he was about to say.

Martín sat up straight and looked directly into Larue's eyes. "We still have *Beagle 4*. While whoever it is controls the feed from *Clarke*, we have no hope of them slipping up again. But ESA controls the rover, which is equipped with high resolution cameras and microphones."

"Our maximum resolution being?"

"Beagle can read a book from one kilometre," Martín found himself grinning, "and can travel at roughly two hundred metres per hour. We can follow them pretty closely, and they should always be within sight as long as the atmosphere is clear. All we need is to hope that Beagle is still up to the task."

Larue gave a short laugh. That the people behind the cover up were able to control time and data feeds on the *Clarke* was one thing, but control over Beagle was something else entirely. "I trust you quite a bit, Martin, and based on your recommendation alone I signed off the Beagle mission route changes Jacqueline Thomas put through several days ago."

"And?"

"You know that Beagle mission routes are planned months, even years in advance. It's entirely possible that the route change you requested would only be executed in the middle of next year. *Normally*, that is."

"Normally?"

"I have just been in contact with the Beagle control room in England, who confirm that Beagle is approaching the edge of Hellas Basin once more. I may be old and on my last legs," Larue confided. "But I am not stupid. As soon as the request to change Beagle's route came through I understood why you had recommended it. Putting Beagle in sight of the Mars landing will give us a direct feed, as you say. I had no idea about the time-delay you and Jacqueline Thomas discovered, but with this we will be in a position to prove it conclusively."

"And then?"

Larue thought about this for a second. "Having information like that is a risky business. There are two schools of thought: either keep it and use it to your advantage, or give it away to as many people as possible and spread the benefit. With the former, you gain the most but also run a greater personal risk. With the latter you gain the least, but you also minimise risk."

They sat in silence for at least a minute. The pitter-patter of rain drops began against the triple glazed windows.

"*Risk*," Martín said echoing Larue's intonation "doesn't sound good."

"*Absolument*," Larue said with a raised eyebrow. "If someone's gone to the trouble they have to hide the mission from us, what will they be prepared to do to protect that secrecy?"

CHAPTER 29

Captain Marchenko pressed down on the accelerator with his boot, sending Herbie forwards at walking pace. As they crept away Dr Richardson looked over her shoulder at the open crates they had been cataloguing the contents of.

A little over two thousand meters away, Beagle's mechanical arms seemed to wave goodbye to them as the on-board computer ran through some environmental tests and procedures. It was now standing in the same position in which it had been over a year earlier. Its missions for the last twelve months had been far from linear, and it had frequently crossed its own path on its travels. Each and every time it did it automatically took the opportunity to measure any changes. The Martian weather system had done little to change the terrain, save for few extra coats of fine dust and grit. An examination of the ground proved that, as expected, its past tracks had more or less been erased from the surface of the planet, unlike the eternal footprints of the first men on the Moon.

Beagle's five forward-mounted eyes, consisting of one long range high-resolution video camera and four smaller still image cameras, watched Herbie as it left towards the horizon. After thirty-two minutes and twelve seconds precisely, the two passengers exited the vehicle, which was parked next to the MLP. Re-focusing, the high-resolution camera adjusted its viewing angle by a fraction of a degree, and captured the smile on the man's face through his visor as he gestured for the woman to enter the building first. Zooming out, the camera reported back to the on-board computer that the building was exactly four thousand four hundred and six metres away. It hadn't been there when it had last mapped the terrain, and it duly noted the location and nature of the phenomenon.

Beagle retracted its mechanical arms slowly, folding them against its smooth sides, neatly above the four rows of wheels that had already helped the rover travel over six hundred kilometres on the Martian surface.

The computer had processed and stored the departure of the two people and their vehicle on its internal drives, and had completed its assessment of the surrounding environment.

Its current status and environmental report had already been transmitted to a satellite orbiting Mars, ready for its receipt by the ESA controllers on Earth.

While it waited for their response, Beagle busied itself with some more soil samples. The thin coating of dust that had gathered around it was new and, therefore, interesting.

CHAPTER 30

Remind me again, why did we come here?" Danny complained as he shook the dust from his boots and placed them against the wall of the MLP. A thick layer of light-brown powder covered the floor within several feet of the airlock. "Atchoo!" he pretended to sneeze and shook his head dramatically, before making his way over to the kitchen area where Jane had already joined Montreaux in preparing the evening meal.

"Because for thousands of years, humans have looked up at the heavens and wondered what it would be like to be on the other side, looking back at Earth, and because we won't be happy until we've looked back at Earth from as far away as is humanly possible." Jane said without looking up from the tray of hydrated food she had just pulled out of the processor. "And because the food is so good, of course."

Danny laughed and peered into her tray. "Tell me, Jane: how long until you start providing us with some *real* food?"

"Soon, Danny," she nodded towards her experiments across the MLP. "Everything is set up."

"Thank God for that. Is that really what you think?"

She looked at him strangely. "Of course, my experiments and material are all ready, so –"

"No," he laughed as he interrupted her. "I mean, do you really think that we came here to simply look back at Earth?"

She shrugged. "Why else? Firstly, we are by nature curious creatures, peering into cupboards we're told we can't open, wondering where rivers start and mountains end, when and where we came from. But despite our desire to go into the unknown and explore, we have an overpowering sense of *belonging*, that we come from somewhere and that in a way we are a part of that place. Secondly, as well as being incurably curious, we are constantly trying to better ourselves, I think to improve on what our parents achieved, to perpetuate the advancement of the human race."

"So you don't believe that we came here to find life, or advance science?"

"Of course we did. We have a scientific role to play, a mission that is well defined and thought out, the result of decades of research and theorising by the best minds on Earth. But I believe that is our secondary goal. The underlying reason we came here is to gain a different perspective of our home."

"I don't agree at all!" he exclaimed. "You make it all sound so futile and superficial."

"Captain Marchenko," Montreaux interjected. "When you were a child, did you ever play outside?"

"Of course, everyone does."

"And when you ventured further away from your home than ever before on your own, did you look behind you to see how far you had gone?"

Danny thought for a moment. "Yes, I guess I did. But I wouldn't say I was inherently interested in what my home looked like from the top of a hill, I was probably more nervous about knowing how to get back and wanted to make sure that I didn't go too far."

"Yes, you are right about that, and there's an element of that when we look for Earth in the Martian sky that comforts us when we find it twinkling above the horizon," Jane agreed. "But I am sure that the desire to look back at your house is not just fuelled by concern, but by interest also. When you first visited the United States, did you feel that you had an increased interest in anything to do with Russia, sometimes even in things that you would not normally express an interest in?"

"I found myself reading stories about Russian politics, despite the fact that in Russia I do everything to avoid them," he said.

"I personally find that when I am abroad, I am always listening out for any mention of America. But in the absence of America-related subject matter, I casually introduce trivia into conversations," she admitted. "I don't do it consciously, I just do it. It usually starts with the sentence '*In America…*' and then I'm off. And do you know what I think?" She didn't leave time for an answer, although Danny seemed ready to give one. "I think it's because as humans we constantly act as advertisers for our homes, towns, counties, nations, beliefs. You name it, we advertise it. When we go somewhere, we are obsessed with knowing what people think of where we came from, or what we represent. If we don't receive that input, I'm sure that we are predisposed to plant knowledge, spread the 'good word', so to speak, so that when the next person like us arrives, their curiosity is more satisfied."

He looked down at his plate of unappetising food. "And do you not think we might do this to simply make these foreign places more like home, so that they seem less alien to us, eventually expanding the circle of what our unconscious mind defines as *home* until it includes the location in which we currently find ourselves?"

Captain Montreaux looked at the Russian and smiled. "Like the first settlers in America. They built themselves a little Europe, changing the plants, animals and even soil, until they no longer found themselves in the New World, but in a carbon copy of the old one."

"Which is why Jane would like to plant a nice flag on Mars, isn't it?"

"No!" she said indignantly. "I want to put a flag on this planet to prove our achievement. And I think that whilst there may be some truth in your argument when talking about moving home permanently, the root of our desire to go anywhere is to witness what our homes look like from outside our normal viewpoint. On the smallest scale like a carpenter standing back and admiring his new table, or a builder standing back and looking at the house he has finished, and on the largest scale like a mission to Mars looking back at a reassuring light in an alien sky."

"You said *reassuring*. Does that mean you feel insecure?" Danny smiled.

Captain Montreaux shook his head and decided to concentrate on his meal.

Jane opened her mouth, and Danny saw from the look in her eyes that it was time to get back to his original point. "Anyway," he started, noting the frustration on her face. The word '*anyway*' could at times be the most annoying in the English language, and Danny always used it to great effect. "I think that covers why we came to *Mars*, but why we came *here* precisely. To this exact geographical location on Mars" He gestured vaguely to the outside world behind him. "Dust, rock and more dust, not forgetting the rocks and dust."

"Is there much else on Mars?" Montreaux asked.

"We are here, *precisely*, because of the water, Danny, because *Beagle 4* kindly confirmed the presence of water for us, and because had we landed anywhere else in the hope of finding water and had not actually found any, we would at present be the first human beings likely to die on any planet other than Earth." Dr Richardson said.

"Which wouldn't have been very reassuring," he joked. "I know we came here for the water under our feet, not to mention the gigantic, geologically fascinating impact crater a few kilometres away. I'm just annoyed by all of this dust." He rested his head on the back on his chair and closed his eyes.

Montreaux turned to look at the Russian.

"You're tired, Captain Marchenko, have something to eat and get to sleep."

Danny opened his eyes and looked at him lazily. "I'm mostly tired of the dust. The dust is everywhere! I wear a suit out there, but I feel I have dust and grit in my hair! How can I have grit in my hair?"

"Because over the past two weeks, we have managed to bring the outside world in, despite the airlock." Montreaux said. "I guess we have to be thankful that dust and grit is all that we've brought with us."

Jane scoffed. "And the jury's still out on that one."

They fell into silence at the thought.

If life existed on Mars, it was most likely in bacterial form beneath the surface, which was exactly where they had been extracting their water supply from. Every precaution had been taken to prevent possible contamination, but they all knew that even the smallest amount of the wrong kind of alien bacterium inside their habitable compartment could spell disaster. The headlines were easy to imagine: "*Life on Mars! Kills crew!*"

So their scientist took samples of the dust every day and screened them for any signs of life, and was convinced that it was not a matter of *if* she found something alive rather than *when*.

During the first few days, they had managed to keep the MLP absolutely spotless, using the airlock to clean and decontaminate their suits as it had been designed to do. But slowly, inexorably, as the days went on and the number of EVAs increased, a fine Martian dust had begun to settle inside the craft, for obvious reasons mostly around the airlock.

No matter how many times they cleaned, the dust would continue to appear; Danny's frustration notwithstanding, they had more or less accepted it as part of their lives on Mars, like sand in a beach house.

"Of course," she broke the silence, "if we do find anything harmful out there, or *in here*, the chances are that our bodies would be so totally unprepared for it that we wouldn't stand a chance. And given that we cannot sensibly stop the dust from entering the MLP, we may as well stop worrying about it."

They both looked at her, stunned.

"Great!" Danny said throwing his arms in the air. "The only doctor on board thinks that we're going to die here no matter what! I may as well go out there without my suit next time!"

She laughed, tossing her food tray onto the table and sitting down on a stool. "I would imagine that we're all more likely to die of food poisoning anyway, at least until my experiments bear fruit." She nodded towards a table at the far end of the MLP, covered in small trays with clear plastic lids.

Captain Montreaux reiterated his desire for Captain Marchenko to get some rest, before sitting down in his chair and opening his book. He was on his second read-through of *The Martian Chronicles*, and it was making a lot more sense to him this time round.

The Russian made his way to his bunk and lay down, looking at the ceiling. "So we have to hope for a combination of friendly Martian bacteria and your very successful green-fingers, I see." He shook his head and closed his eyes. "We're doomed."

The next morning, Dr Jane Richardson was alone in the MLP. Strangely, she had never felt more at home than right now. Surrounded by experiments in the middle of the most unexplored environment humans had ever set foot on, she was the first scientist to touch Martian soil outside of a Petri dish, and despite the dangers it presented, she was enjoying every minute of it.

As far as she was concerned, if things stayed as they were and with enough water and food, she could quite happily stay on Mars for the rest of her life.

She prised the lid off a small plastic container and poured the liquid contents into a large, shallow metallic tray. The transparent, clear substance settled evenly at the bottom of the tray, a small bubble bursting on its surface. She tilted her head to one side slightly, as if listening to it, before putting the lid back on the small container from which it had been poured.

Nanoplasma had been the crowning achievement of her work on Earth. The result of five years of her own research and development, she was the first to admit that she stood firmly on the shoulders of giants, and would not have been able to succeed without the hard work of the pioneers of the 'Nano-age', as it had been dubbed by the media back in the 2020s.

The nanoplasma itself was comprised of two main elements: nanocapsules and organic plasma. The minute capsules, each one less than twenty nanometres wide, contained either flavours, colouring, or any other active ingredient that may be needed, and could be opened by stimulating them with very specific subsonic frequencies. By subjecting a capsule-filled solution with carefully controlled frequencies, it was possible to recreate any number of flavours, whilst at the same time filling the solution with vitamins and nutrients as desired. Nanocapsules had been introduced over thirty years earlier to the mass market, and had revolutionised the soft drink industry.

Almost overnight it became possible to buy one drink with multiple flavours that could be switched at will simply by depressing a button on the neck of the bottle. Any capsules that were not required by the consumer would simply pass through the digestive system intact, meaning that a wide variety of flavours could be contained within the same bottle without affecting each other.

Jane had not invented nanocapsules. That achievement had been slightly before her time. Instead, she had successfully combined them with a plasma solution, made from a fibrous breakdown of plant-matter, in an effort to replace what had been a staple food of human beings for thousands of years: meat. Her theory came from the simple fact that if the digestive system of an animal could break down organic matter, for instance grass, and turn what it needed into animal matter, then it must be possible to recreate this process in the laboratory.

Her aim had not been to just provide a substitute for meat; vegetarian products had been doing that for decades. She wanted to literally create a single product that could be transformed into any meat-based product. Indeed, to recreate the texture, taste and nutritional properties of animal meat, with none of the ethical or environmental ramifications.

She picked up a small pen-shaped instrument and placed its pointed end in the metal tray of nanoplasma. Turning a small wheel on the side of the pen, she selected 'Rump Steak' and pressed a red button. Within seconds, the nanoplasma had visibly changed, becoming more viscous and opaque. After about a minute, she pulled the pen out of the tray and looked at her work.

Now looking at a perfectly rectangular rump steak, she picked up a scalpel from the table and made a small incision across the middle. Prying the cut apart to reveal the bloodless cross section, she nodded approvingly and used the scalpel to cut the slab into three equal parts, before stacking them on a plastic plate and placing them in the sample fridge under the table.

"As soon as I make a steak-shaped receptacle, it won't look like I just slaughtered a square cow," she muttered under her breath.

She walked to the MLP's communications console and depressed a button at its centre, before speaking into the microphone stalk.

"Hey guys, while you've been out there playing in the sand, I've been preparing this evening's meal. How does rump steak and mash sound?" she said cheerfully.

There was a short wait, during which the Martian static undulated out over the MLP's speaker system. The Russian replied, fainter than usual.

"That sounds great, Jane. Any way you can make a couple of cold beers using that nano-stuff of yours?"

"I second that," Montreaux laughed.

She smiled and pressed the com button once more.

"Hey, as soon as I develop a nanocapsule that adds a kick, no problem. In the meantime, we're going to have to make do with alcohol-free, if that's alright with you?"

Captains Montreaux and Marchenko had driven Herbie to the very edge of Hellas Basin about two and a half kilometres from the MLP. Exiting the vehicle, they walked to the cliff apprehensively. They instinctively stopped two metres from the edge, and Montreaux let out a gasp.

The view they beheld was simply astonishing.

Hellas Basin was a crater, the largest visible asteroid impact crater in the Solar System, with a diameter of over two thousand three hundred kilometres. It had been created nearly four billion years earlier, and the debris field of the impact covered almost a third of the planet. The main bulk of the debris had formed a sloped rim of rocks and sand more than one hundred kilometres wide around its circumference. The MLP had landed on this rim almost three kilometres from the crater, but it was only when they stood at the very edge and looked back towards their landing site that the gentle slope down to Martian 'sea level' could be fully appreciated.

Looking the other way, towards the centre of the Basin, was a truly terrifying experience. From the very bottom of the crater to where Montreaux and Marchenko now stood was a height difference of almost nine kilometres. If Mount Everest had been placed in the centre, they would be looking down on its peak. As it was, they were looking down a steep slope, and across a wide expansive plain larger than India. The crisp Martian atmosphere gave them near perfect visibility, and only the curve of the horizon prevented them appreciating the crater fully.

In the distance, they could easily see the brilliant white reflection of frost that covered most of the floor of the crater.

Emboldened by curiosity after his initial shock, Montreaux edged closer to the precipice and looked down. Contrary to his initial impression, instead of a sheer drop, the crater sloped away from him, not as gently as the debris field behind him, but certainly not vertical either. He found himself comparing it to a tough ski slope: potentially deadly if he'd had skis on and it was covered in snow, but quite possible to clamber down given the circumstances. What did impress, however, was not the incline of the slope but its scale. Whereas on Earth he would have expected the drop to end after at the most a few hundred metres, the wall of the Hellas Basin did not. It continued on its way down, gradually levelling out as it neared the bottom like the inside of a soup bowl, until he imagined it must merge with the crater floor kilometres below. He had to 'imagine' where it met the bottom for two reasons, he surmised. Firstly, he calculated that with the depth of the crater and gradient of the slope, the intersection of 'floor' and 'wall' of the crater had to be at least fifteen kilometres away from him, and his ability to define accurate shapes at such distances without visual aid was quite low. This was in no way helped by his second reason, which was that as far as the eye could see, all the rocks and debris looked the same.

Looking to his left and right, he saw that from a distance, the crater rim looked like an unbroken ring of mountains, imprisoning the plain below.

The slope was made up of a mixture of varying sizes of rock and Martian soil. Almost everything was the same colour, a pale shade of orangey-brown. Occasionally a particular rock would be slightly darker or lighter, but there were few obvious geological variances, at least to his untrained eyes.

He looked over at Danny, who was kneeling at the edge examining a small spherical rock about the size of a baseball.

"Impressive, isn't it?" he said.

The Russian looked up across the plain and nodded slowly before standing. He wrapped his fingers around the stone and bounced it in his palm a few times, getting a feel for its weight and balance. Without a word he stretched his arm back fully before sweeping it forwards in a flash, releasing the stone mid-swing. They watched the stone fly forwards at least a hundred metres before gravity started to bring it down to the ground.

The low gravity made for an impressive pitch indeed.

Because of the incline, the stone continued to fall for about three hundred metres before finally striking a large flat rock jutting out from the cliff-face. A small cloud of pale orange debris was thrown up from the rock as the stone bounced off and disappeared below.

"See if you can beat that," he grinned and looked at Montreaux.

But Montreaux wasn't listening. He was still looking down at the flat rock that the stone had struck; the dust had now settled and despite its distance, it was obvious that there was a striking difference in colour between the surface dust that had been disturbed and the rock beneath. It was jet black.

"Captain Marchenko, pass me the binoculars, please."

He focussed the electronic device on the stone below. After several long minutes, he passed the binoculars back.

"Look at the flat rock you just hit," he said, seriously.

Danny's first instinct was to be sarcastic. He felt like saying that he was sorry he'd damaged a Martian rock, but that there were billions more identical ones where that came from. Instead, he took the binoculars and steadied the image on the flat rock.

"What do you think it is?" He didn't move his eyes from the binoculars, but instead zoomed in further to examine the small patch of jet black stone that had been uncovered. They had spent days picking up rocks and digging test holes in the soil near their base, and had never seen anything like it.

Montreaux had already been thinking about his answer, and had remembered some basic facts from his early days at school. "Well, on Earth, a black colour in stone often comes from carbon."

Marchenko pulled his eyes away from the binoculars and looked at the American.

"Carbon? From plants and animals?"

"Yes, I think, although I don't know if it can be naturally occurring too." He thought about this for a moment. "In any case, we'll never know until we get down there to look at it. We'll need a sample to take back to Dr Richardson."

"Wow! That was one lucky throw!"

"It certainly was. Now, I propose that we climb down together, but first, we need fresh air, I only have half an hour's worth left."

They climbed down the cliff in parallel, connected by a thin strand of synthetic rope for safety. It was by no means a dangerous climb, and on Earth could certainly have been attempted with barely a second's thought. But on Mars, the combination of reduced gravity and airtight suits made for a nervous descent for both men.

As they came within twenty metres of the flat stone, Montreaux paused and turned his upper body round to face it. He tugged sharply on the safety line to get Danny's attention and pointed down at their goal.

"It's definitely not your standard Martian rock formation, is it?" he said, out of breath.

"There's something out of place about it, definitely. Something –"

"Not natural," Montreaux finished his sentence for him, "I agree."

From where they now sat, the stone betrayed not only its huge dimensions, but also its unexpected shape and orientation. It was about six metres wide and rectangular, protruding at least ten metres from the cliff-face.

Although it was difficult to tell with any accuracy from where they were sitting, the stone looked to be completely flat amidst the chaos of debris deposited around them.

"It looks almost like a," Danny searched for the word. "Like a *jetty*, where you moor a boat on a riverbank."

The two astronauts looked at each other and then continued to descend in silence. Montreaux checked the small LCD display on his forearm to ensure that his suit camera was capturing the whole event.

The Russian reached the stone first. He stood up to his full height and looked at Montreaux, who had continued past the stone and was now investigating below.

"This is incredible," he said. "The stone comes right out of the cliff, it's about a metre and a half thick, below is filled up with soil and other rocks, but apart from that you can clearly see the shape of the stone." His voice was filled with awe. "This stone has to be artificial. The edge is perfectly flat all around, and wait." His gloves had a built in rubber wiper along the seam of the thumb, for his own visor in case of sandstorms. He used it to scrape the stone clean. "Yes, that's incredible! There's a thick coat of dirt and dust, but underneath it's the same jet black stone, and it's so smooth!"

Danny was using his gloves to expand the impact crater that his small projectile had created.

"Same up here; it's perfectly smooth. And whatever it is, it's –"

Montreaux waited for him to finish his sentence, but the words didn't come.

"Yes?" he pressed.

"Oh, my God," Danny said, followed by a short burst of Russian that Montreaux didn't understand. "Yves, get up here and look at this!"

Despite his usual friendly carefree attitude, Marchenko never referred to Montreaux using his Christian name. That was a break in protocol that only Dr Richardson enjoyed. Montreaux almost fell over himself reaching the top of the stone to join the Russian.

"What?" he said, urgently, glancing sideways at the stone.

He pointed to the patch of black surface he had uncovered. His hand was shaking visibly.

Captain Montreaux did not need it spelled out. What had stunned Danny had the same effect on him. His knees grew weak, and he sank down slowly until he could touch the stone. He ran his gloved fingers across it until they slotted neatly into a groove, about two centimetres deep and ten wide that ran in a perfectly straight line from under one edge of the cleaned area, near the wall of the crater out towards its centre. Danny's gloved fingers had left small furrows where he had done his best to clear out most of the sand. After about sixty centimetres, the groove split in two in a perfect V. At the edges of the cleared area, he could make out the lines of two more possible grooves. He stood up and tilted his head as he examined the stone. The grooves made the shape of a V, pointing towards the crater wall, with a line emerging from its apex and disappearing into the cliff.

The grooves had been perfectly, and unmistakably, carved into the stone. And both astronauts immediately interpreted them in the same way: whatever had made the lines had intended them to point towards something that was now buried under the rock and debris of the cliff-wall.

They sat in silence for several minutes before Montreaux regained his composure. He pressed a button on his communicator pad and hailed the MLP.

"Dr Richardson, please confirm that you are getting the data feed from Captain Marchenko's and my helmet cams."

There was a momentary pause.

"Hi there. What am I looking at?" Jane said in a confused voice.

"Please confirm that you are getting this data feed and that it is being stored correctly, Dr Richardson," he said plainly.

"That's affirmative, Captain Montreaux, both feeds coming in, there's a bit of atmospheric interference, a little worse than when we spoke earlier. But what the hell am I looking at?"

"We are out of your line of sight, I imagine that is causing the interference," he explained. "Can you give a quick assessment of the material we are standing on?"

There was a long silence, after which the scientist spoke quite cautiously. "I would say from its colour that it could be an igneous rock, it resembles obsidian."

"Igneous? Obsidian?" Montreaux asked.

She sighed. "Igneous rocks are basically cooled down magma that on Earth forms most of the crust," she elaborated. "Basically, magma leaves the mantle, normally during movement of tectonic plates or during a volcanic eruption, for instance, and solidifies as it becomes part of the crust because it is further from the heated core of the planet. In theory, the closer the magma is to the surface when it hardens, the faster it will do so because the ambient temperature will be lower. If magma cools slowly, the solid crystals that form can easily be bigger than your fist. As the rate of cooling increases, however, so the size of those crystals decreases. If the magma is on the surface, what we would normally call *lava*, and the environmental conditions are *just* right, it can cool so fast that crystals hardly have the opportunity to form, in which case we get obsidian. In these cases, the crystals have to be observed under a microscope."

Danny ran his hand along the smooth surface. "Could obsidian be this smooth, naturally?" he wondered.

"Absolutely. Polished obsidian was even used for mirrors thousands of years ago. I would expect a substance such as obsidian to be that smooth naturally. Danny, can you show me a more *ground level* view, please, from the edge of the stone across it?"

He obliged, climbing down the side of the stone that Captain Montreaux had just emerged from. He scanned the edge of the stone, and then raised his head slightly and tilted it down so that Jane would be able to appreciate how flat and rectangular it was.

"Fascinating," she said eventually. "It looks perfectly flat, and the stills I have taken from the video feed suggest that the angled edges I have seen are all at ninety degrees."

"What do you make of the grooves, Dr Richardson? Could they have been carved or etched into the surface?" Montreaux asked.

"No," she replied. "At least not if the stone is indeed obsidian. Obsidian is very similar to flint, in that it splinters and creates flakes. Fantastic for making arrow heads and knives, but very difficult to craft, and virtually impossible to chisel or strike with any reliability. When used in ornaments nowadays, it is usually polished, so it's relatively easy to create a smooth and accurate edge. However, a groove is entirely different: I don't think you could *polish* a groove into a flat piece of stone, at least not a groove like that."

"Can't you use lasers?" Danny offered.

"Indeed you can. In fact the only useful application of obsidian I can think of right now is surgical knives. The blades of precision instruments can be fashioned using a laser. Because of the compact nature of the crystals that make up the rock, the width of obsidian blades can literally be measured in molecules, so they are hundreds of times more accurate than steel."

"Stone knives?" Montreaux was amazed.

"Even now they're still used in heart surgery, Yves," she confirmed.

Montreaux took a step back and contemplated the stone beneath him. He found his eyes inexorably drawn towards the crater wall by the grooves. He wanted nothing more than an excuse to start digging like crazy, but if this was what he sensed it to be, then things would have to be done properly. "Dr Richardson?"

"Yes?"

He measured his words carefully, not wanting her to infer anything unprofessional. "Having seen the stone we are standing on, its dimensions, shape and," he paused, as if looking for the correct terminology, "other characteristics, what do you think made it?"

"I am not a geologist by trade, Captain," she replied without hesitation. "However, I have seen some incredibly unbelievable rock formations on Earth, particularly where cooling magma is involved. The grooves may have been set as the magma cooled, possibly the imprint of other stones, maybe even by water, which we know at some time existed in abundance in this area. This stone could be a naturally occurring phenomenon. I would need to see a sample." She waited for a response, but none came. "And I would very much like to visit the stone myself," she added.

Danny looked at Montreaux and winked. "Jane, cut the bullshit now, OK? We'll use that last bit as a sound-bite for Earth, you sounded great," he said. "Now tell us what you *really* think."

"Danny, you are standing on a perfectly flat surface, as smooth as a pane of glass, with perfect parallel sides and straight edges, all seemingly at a perfect ninety degrees to each other," she said. "Not only is the stone flat, it also appears to be horizontal, which is why you two aren't slipping off it. It's also jutting straight out of the side of the crater, possibly pointing directly to the centre of said crater. And to top it all off, there is a groove in its surface that is not only aligned with the stone itself, but is also uniformly one-point-eight centimetres deep and ten-point-six centimetres wide – I know because I've checked it from the video feeds you sent. Can any one of these features on their own be produced in the natural world? On Earth, certainly. On Mars? Who knows, but the laws of physics are no different here to back home, we simply have different environmental conditions. I would say that probably yes, too. Now you're left with the big question." She paused. "Is it possible for all of these features to be found together, in the same place, given the context of the stone?"

"Dr Richardson, I appreciate your thorough summation of the situation, but could you just give us a straight answer?" Captain Montreaux was getting uncharacteristically impatient. He knew what the answer was, he just wanted to hear her say it.

"Yves, I am a scientist, and we never say things of any major significance in anything less than five hundred words. But to be blunt, there is no doubt in my mind that what you are standing on was put there. And although I cannot believe I am even saying this, I am sure that you and Danny are not the first beings to have stood on it, either."

There was a very long, weighted silence.

Captain Montreaux couldn't help but remember the journey to Mars, the conversation with Lieutenant Su Ning, the suspicious circumstances of her death. He had known then that something big was going on, and things certainly didn't get any bigger than this. On the one hand he was excited at the magnitude of their discovery, but on the other he knew that people were prepared to kill them to cover it up. His heart sank. He knew deep down that nobody back on Earth of any importance to him would ever find out about their discovery. He also now knew why they had landed on the northern edge of the Hellas Basin rather than any other, and why the pre-planned coordinates of their rover expeditions had been so exact. And now that they had found the Jetty, what next?

If this is going to be part of a cover up, he thought, *how likely is it we'll be allowed to return home alive?*

"What do we do now?" Danny broke the silence.

Montreaux looked over at him, hoping that the reinforced Plexiglas of his helmet did not reveal anything. "I have an hour of air left in this cylinder, how about you?"

"About the same. And we have three hours more in Herbie."

"Dr Richardson," Montreaux hailed her.

"Yes?"

Through the environmental interference on the com system, Montreaux fancied he could detect something odd in her tone, a hint of self-assuredness, of *knowing*, and suddenly an alarming thought materialised: *was she in on it? Were they both?* The dark thoughts crystallised, only making sense now, as he stood on the alien stone with the enormity of the situation staring him right in the face. *Did either of them know of the cover-up because they were involved?* He had a momentary flashback of Dr Richardson and Captain Marchenko the previous day, having one of their friendly arguments. As they did every day, he thought. He swallowed hard. Was he the only one not in on the cover-up? Was he going to be next?

"Captain?"

Danny's voice came through faintly in his earpiece. He cocked his head and looked at the Russian. Suddenly extremely self-conscious, he realised that he must have been looking into space for quite some time.

"Yves, are you alright?" Jane sounded genuinely concerned.

He snapped out of his daydream in an instant. *Nonsensical paranoid delusions,* he concluded.

"Dr Richardson, you'd better put a hold on those steaks, for an hour or so." He gestured towards the wall of the crater, to where the groove in the stone disappeared. "Captain Marchenko, let's get some tools from Herbie and find out where this groove goes."

From its viewpoint two thousand metres further along the edge of the Hellas Basin impact crater, Beagle watched the two figures ascend the crater wall. Using a high-resolution lens, it zoomed in on the black object, three hundred metres below, upon which they had been standing moments earlier.

The rover edged forward slowly, coming to a halt against a small round rock which hid most of its body from the direction of the MLP.

The lens re-focused on the object, picking out the grooves in its surface.

It started taking pictures.

CHAPTER 31

The rain came down in waves, lashing the flat sides of the tall building again and again. Bright halogen beams cut through the darkness from their source along the roofline of the building, reflecting against the drops of falling water on their way to the ground. A simple white door was the only noteworthy feature of the plain white walls. A group of tall palms bowed under the forces of nature, their flexible bodies saving them from the worst of the hurricane. In the distance, the roar of the disturbed sea was hardly perceptible above the sound of the rushing wind.

At the side of the building, a white van sat purring in the darkness, its headlamps dipped, waiting.

"So much for global warming," the driver said, resentfully.

The percussive fall of rain on the van's roof was almost incessant, save for the short bursts of very strong wind, when the water would be whipped back into the air before it had the chance to hit.

His passenger shivered and tucked his hands deeper into his coat pockets. "Warmer for some, though, isn't it? Otherwise where do you think all this would be coming from?"

They both stared into the building's courtyard and contemplated this. Suddenly, as if on cue, the driver turned off the engine and the heating. "Here comes another one, let's get out of here." He switched off the headlamps and rested his hand on the door release.

Outside, the howling wind reached its terrifying crescendo then dulled, the threat of its return lying oppressively in the air.

The men jerked open the van's doors and slammed them shut behind them. As they ran towards the small door in the side of the building, the driver pointed his arm behind him and pressed a button on his keys, rewarded by the quick chirp of the van's central locking system. His passenger had already reached the wall and was pressing the intercom button repeatedly.

The door gave a loud buzz and they pulled it open in unison. They were barely through the opening when the wind made its return, violently slamming the door behind them and making the frame shake. They had been outside for a few short seconds, and yet they were soaked through to the skin. The passenger stood motionless with his legs apart, leaning his body forwards and holding his arms out to his sides, frozen in the posture of a man who has just been punched in the stomach.

"My God!" he exclaimed. The water had already left his hairless scalp and most of it had made its way to his bearded chin, from where it dribbled to the floor with a patter.

They found themselves in a short corridor with another door at the far end, also secured by an intercom.

The driver shook his arms before running his hands through his short hair. "And to think people come here to retire." He stopped in the middle of unzipping his coat. "Your bag?"

The passenger looked in disbelief at his own empty hands. He turned his head back towards the door and the raging storm outside. "Damn."

"You're kidding me, right?" he gaped, still halfway between taking his coat off and reluctantly putting it back on again. "I don't get paid enough for this! Here, take my keys, you can go and get it."

A few moments later, the passenger burst through the small door again, this time holding a satchel against his chest.

"Time for a drink," he said.

"In this place? I think machine coffee is about as good as it gets!"

They walked towards the second door hastily and the passenger pressed the intercom button once.

"Coffee it is then," he said.

Seth Mallus, dressed in an immaculate black suit, crisp white shirt and light blue silk tie, sat in a large executive chair at a large executive desk. In front of him, a letter-size notepad sat exactly perpendicular to the edge of the desk. A Mont Blanc pen lay on the pad, aligned to the margin, in which the day's date had been written neatly and underlined: *November 9th, 2045.*

"Dr Patterson, how are things progressing?" he said to the dishevelled man who sat opposite him in jeans and short-sleeved shirt.

Patterson had been in the facility for barely half an hour, the time to quickly dry off, change and grab a terrible coffee, before their meeting had begun. He brought his hand to his chin and played with his beard briefly. It was well kept, but the silver-grey hue added at least a decade to his fifty-six years.

"Here are the latest transcripts, with the translations." He slid the paper across the table. "They are consistent with the other transcripts; whatever happened to these –" he hesitated before saying the word, "– *people*, there was nothing they could do to stop it." He flicked through his notes. "There is a lifetime of work here," he gestured to the small folder on the table in front of him.

Mallus leaned forward in his chair and fixed his eyes intently on the man. "A lifetime can be long or short, Dr Patterson. You have been studying these texts for years now. How long will it take before you find out what I need to know?"

He swallowed hard and tried to avoid the steely gaze. "Some of the material is very clear as you've seen, but most parts make no sense at all. Context *is* everything, and in this regard I need assistance from someone more specialised in the field." He put his hand on the folder and opened it. "Otherwise, it would take at least another two years for me to decipher it in its entirety, if at all."

"Then I will need to find you some help." Mallus paused and looked across at the transcripts in front of him. "We have experienced some unexpected setbacks that have already subjected this project to a great deal more risk than we anticipated. I need to be sure that you understand how important it is that this work remains secret, Dr Patterson." His cold eyes met the scientist's across the table. "I know how you academics work, and I know that you like to *bounce ideas around the community*. But for this project, the community is comprised of you and me. Do not seek contact from anyone else, I will send someone to you," he ordered.

"Sure," he muttered, "I understand."

Mallus relaxed his gaze. "The cliché tells us that *time is money*, but you will understand more than anyone that in this case, a lot more is at stake. You will get the help you need, and in return you will provide me with the answers I want, quickly." He smiled and leant back in his chair. "And as for getting our hands on more *context*," he continued, "we'll just have to keep our fingers crossed, won't we?"

Dr Patterson nodded his head in agreement as he moved his eyes slowly across the hieroglyphs on the pages in front of him.

"On a positive note," he said happily, "the Mars mission *is* bearing fruit. They have uncovered a jetty of some sort, which I think you'll find interesting and may help you further."

"A *jetty*?" Patterson queried.

"Indeed. I would suggest that you make your way through to Mission Control straight away."

After Patterson had gone, Seth Mallus browsed through a series of résumés on his computer display.

He wasn't happy bringing more help in: keeping things running smoothly was a trial at the best of times, and the last thing he wanted was more questions. For that reason he wasn't about to openly put an advert for the post in the local paper, either.

How on earth had he ended up with Henry Patterson? All that time ago in the corridors of the Peabody Museum it had seemed a good bet. He had certainly delivered what had been asked of him, and in return Mallus had given Patterson the single most important discovery in human history.

But now, enough was enough. *Years* with the texts, and still he had no comprehensive translation. *How hard can hieroglyphs be?* Things had started out well enough: the first leads had been very promising, and had led him to where he was right now. But the time had come for that final push.

Of all the archaeologists, linguists, Egyptologists and anthropologists that Patterson had put forward, one was head and shoulders above the rest because of her Amarna experience. He looked at her photo on-screen; possibly not the most recent snapshot, as the file said she was forty-one years old and the attractive dark-haired woman looking back at him could barely have been a day over thirty. *The same age as me*, he thought wistfully.

She was married, but with no dependents. No known close family. Her academic work involved regular, frequent travel abroad. The husband would be an annoyance, but he'd dealt with worse.

Walker would probably be best suited to the job: reliable, and able to use his head. If things *did* go wrong, he could make any mess-up look like an accident.

Leaning back in his chair, he sent the résumé through to Walker with a quick note attached: *quickly, quietly and in one piece.*

He was looking forward to meeting Dr Gail Turner, and to finally getting the answers he was looking for.

PART FOUR

13TH - 15TH NOVEMBER 2045

CHAPTER 32

Larue looked at the photos that Martín had handed him. His hands were trembling. In his wildest dreams he had not imagined this.

Whilst far less economical and safe, even Larue had to admit that the manned mission had its virtues. It took Beagle half an hour to extract a good geological sample from the soil. In comparison, one of the astronauts could literally bend over and pick up a rock in seconds.

And from the look of the photos, even the versatile rover wouldn't have been able to climb down three hundred metres of cliff.

He placed the pictures carefully on his desk and looked at Martín Antunez and Jacqueline Thomas, sitting in front of him. It was the first time he had seen them both together, and he fancied he could feel the electricity between them. *What it must be*, he thought to himself, *to be in love again*.

"What shall we do with the pictures, *Monsieur*?" Martín said. "They were taken over four days ago, and still nothing has been released by the Americans. The other agencies are still jumping up and down about some of the rock samples that came through yesterday, so I doubt they know either. We have a lead Beagle engineer in Bristol, England on the phone to us every hour or so asking about this data and what it means. They're going crazy over there, and it's only a matter of time before things start leaking out."

Larue opened his drawer and pulled out his cigar box. Now was the right time for one, he thought. Removing one of the *Diplomáticos* from within, he ran it under his nose slowly, before snipping the end off and putting it between his lips. As an afterthought, he offered the box to Martín and Jacqueline.

Martín shook his head. He was amazed that Larue would dare light a cigar inside a place of work, but for some reason he couldn't help feeling that his real indignation came from the fact that he had not offered first before taking one himself.

Jacqueline simply ignored the gesture entirely.

"I think," he said slowly, "that it is time for us to release *Beagle 4*'s newest findings to the press." With this, he took a box of matches from his drawer and lit his cigar. The thick plume of smoke snaked up to the alarm in the ceiling, which remained silent.

"The press, *Monsieur*?" Jacqueline couldn't stop herself from bursting out.

He raised an eyebrow, prompting her to explain herself. Since his conversation with Martín the previous week, and the shocking revelations that had followed, he had found himself full of energy and confidence. The old Larue was back, he thought to himself, and the ridicule that had fallen on him with the ESA's exclusion from the *Clarke* would soon be but a distant memory.

Jacqueline was not accustomed to addressing people of Larue's status. She took a breath and did her best. "*Monsieur* Larue, if you don't mind me saying, the Agency does not normally address the press with this sort of information. This is not a Public Relations exercise. We should release these photos through the appropriate scientific channels."

Larue smiled. "And we shall. But sometimes, you need to point the press in the right direction, so that they find our properly released material. And if they happen to ask for copies of the photos before anyone else has the opportunity, then so be it. The photos will be released across the scientific network before they appear in *Le Monde*, Jacqueline, trust me. Just not by much."

Martín wondered how much Larue would take for the exclusive. If *Le Monde* was able to publish high resolution photographs in its daily edition, it would only have exclusivity for a few hours, half a day at most. But in the world of Journalism, and with the headline that Martín could already see in his mind's eye, sometimes a few hours was all that was needed to sell a few extra million copies.

Larue saw the look on the Spaniard's face and removed the cigar from his mouth. "Martin, the American author Richard Evans once wrote that '*it is in the darkest skies that stars are best seen*'. I think that you will agree that the skies have rarely been darker than most recently. Stars that I had previously never noticed have become visible. You have to pick them out while the skies are still dark, lest the opportunity pass you by."

Jacqueline looked sideways at her partner, but he said nothing to counter his boss.

Instead, he passed Larue the book he had been holding. "I also have this, *Monsieur*. It's my own personal copy. I think that you will find it quite interesting."

Larue took the book and after a quick glance at the cover, opened it. Inside was a dedication. *'Martín – Good Luck – Dr Turner.'* He closed the book and examined the cover again.

"What is this?" he asked.

Martín leant forward and started to explain.

CHAPTER 33

With a kiss goodbye and a cheery smile, Dr Gail Turner left the house, leaving George sitting at the dining room table with his newspaper.

If there was one thing that *had* changed over the years, it was her punctuality.

He cleared breakfast away and placed the dirty things in the dishwasher. He selected the *Quick Wash* option and pushed the door closed.

Picking up his mug of tea he wandered into the living room. The video wall came to life as he picked up the remote control, automatically tuned in to his favourite comedy series. Sitting down on the sofa, he put his legs up on the coffee table and placed his mug on his belly.

There really wasn't much else for him to do on his day off; the house pretty much took care of itself, not that they made it very messy between the two of them anyway. Gail wouldn't be home until late that evening after work and it was Monday, so he didn't need to cook. Monday was always Fish and Chips day.

The traditional British takeaway had almost disappeared at the start of the century, mainly due to dwindling fish stocks in the surrounding seas. But a European-wide restriction on fishing zones had been sufficient to allow the populations of cod in particular to thrive once more. By 2020, whilst fish consumption had fallen drastically, particularly in the Mediterranean states, fish stocks had grown beyond the most optimistic of estimates.

By the time fishing restrictions were relaxed in the mid 2030's, however, fish had mostly been replaced on Europe's menus by organic substitutes. The market leader's product range had been comprised entirely of fish substitutes for over ten years, and they had no plans to change it. This was partly because substitute products were virtually indistinguishable from real fish in terms of taste and texture. Of course, shape didn't matter because most fish products sold were processed anyway. Their landmark advertising campaign twenty years previously had challenged celebrities to tell the difference between a real fish cake and a fish-substitute one. Not only had they been unable to correctly identify the real fish, but most had preferred the substitute. Once consumers knew this, their products were an instant success. The substitute was nutritious, tasty, and ethical.

Rocketing profits sealed the fate of the fishing industry, the final nail in the coffin for an already crippled sector. Processed fish never returned to the supermarkets again.

But there were some things that technology couldn't replace, no matter how hard they tried, the traditional Fish and Chips meal being one of them. With fish stocks higher than ever, most expected the price of Cod to reach all-time lows. Unchallenged, you could literally fish them out of the sea with a bucket. But economics never worked as consumers would like, and the drop in competition allowed the few fishing vessels remaining to inflate the asking price as much as they wanted.

Gail and George always had real Fish and Chips on a Monday; it was one of the many luxuries their lifestyle afforded them.

Gail entered her office and turned her computer on. She glanced at the clock: eight-thirty; *perfect*. Removing her phone from her pocket and placing it on the desk, she pulled the keyboard towards her and opened her email program.

The first email was from George from the previous night. A silly joke as usual, which made her smile and shake her head.

This was followed by half a dozen questions from her students, two of which she answered, the remaining four she flagged to look at later.

Ellie had sent her some pictures the previous day, which she had not had the opportunity to look at yet. She opened the email and scrolled through a series of photos of Ellie, her husband and their two children on holiday in China. The final photo, of her with her grinning youngest son, had the caption *'Come on, don't tell me you don't want one just like this?!'* She hit the reply button and fired off a few short lines, saying how wonderful China looked, how great they looked as a family, and how no, she didn't want one because she knew all too well what they were like the remaining ninety per cent of the time.

She had time for one more email. It was from David Hunt.

Ever since her discovery in Amarna ten years earlier, the now *Professor* David Hunt had been the closest colleague of Gail's at the University. Despite her best assurances to the contrary, he felt that her discovery gave credence to his *alternate histories* theory, blowing wide open all of the dating that had previously been thought to be true about ancient Egypt. In general, Gail disagreed; she saw no reason why Amarna shouldn't fit in the context of ancient Egypt without disrupting known dates, a belief that was gladly shared by the Egyptologist community.

David had always been more radical than most, a position that had caused him problems before. Gail was more than aware of the dangers involved, particularly in Egyptology, if she were to try to oppose established facts as he regularly did: in Cairo, it was the first thing that Professor al-Misri had warned her of as the magnitude of their discovery had unfolded.

She scanned through David's email and grinned. He had something to show her that might change her mind. David always said that, about everything. She switched her display off and stood up, grabbed a pile of notes and books, and left her office.

A few minutes after the door closed her mobile phone, still on the desk, began to ring. Several moments later it stopped, and her office phone rang instead. Then it stopped too.

Seconds later, *both* of her phones started ringing together.

CHAPTER 34

The main lecture theatre of the Faculty of Arts had hardly changed in ten years. She looked around the empty seats and thought of all the lectures and study groups she had stumbled into, late. It had all been different on her return from Egypt.

Her thesis had been a breeze, and her findings then fuelled several published articles and a permanent position within the Department of Archaeology. For the University, she had been one of those most rare accomplishments: a home-grown talent that other Faculties would pay handsomely to attract.

Her crowning achievement to date had been the publication of her book, aided by her friend Professor al-Misri, which had cemented her place on the international lecture circuit.

A new batch of first-year students, now into their third month at university, was about to pile through the double doors to her left, followed some time later by the ones that were enjoying student life a little too much, she imagined. For most, it would hopefully be the first of six optional lectures on Egyptology, spread across the first year of their degrees. An all too significant proportion, however, were likely to drop out of university after the Christmas holidays.

Her job, as she saw it, was to pull them in now, get their attention, spark their enthusiasm, and make sure that they stayed. And her hope for the long-term was that the series of lectures, which she had been running now for the past two years, would ultimately lead to a full-time Egyptology unit.

Gail pushed her memory card into the reader, inset into the side of the touch screen on the lecturer's podium. Quickly navigating the system's menus, she brought up her media set, entitled 'Egyptology - Lecture 1'. The first still slide filled the small preview screen. Turning round, she looked at the projection on the wall behind her.

She used to be embarrassed by such displays of her work, especially in front of an audience of hundreds. But over time her confidence had grown, and she now looked up at the wall with immense pride. On a white background was a picture of her book, placed on top of an old, yellowed map of Egypt. A small mound of sand covered one corner of the map. It was one of her book publisher's marketing shots, but she always used it because she felt it gave the lecture a certain gloss.

The cover of the book showed the title 'Buried Past – The hidden stories of Amarna'. The space underneath was filled with an engraving on a stone lit by an oil lamp; another dramatic effect Gail felt added a sense of adventure to the lecture.

It would be too obvious, she felt, to start the term with a picture of the Great Pyramids, or Karnak, or the Sphinx. But that wasn't the impact she was going for. Her aim was to show that even in the twenty-first century there were still incredible discoveries to make, and there were still huge unknowns. It didn't matter how much research went into Egypt, or for that matter any civilisation, there were *always* unanswered questions, and questions not yet asked

Asking, and answering, those questions was what archaeology was all about.

She focused on the engraving, following its strange lines, remembering what it had felt like to run her hands over the stones for the first time.

Her presentation ready to go, she let her mind wander and remembered that first venture into the Amarna Library.

Professor al-Misri had promised her that she would be one of the first to go into the Library, following the engineers who had to check the integrity of the structure. But first they had to find a way in. After two days studying the stone wall between the ante-chamber and the Library, it had been decided that the only way to access the room was by cutting through the stone itself. To Gail, this had seemed quite destructive, but modern technology and the ingenuity of the engineers had managed to surprise her.

After identifying a section of wall in the corner of the room with no book shelves connected to it on the other side, the engineers had outlined a circle a foot and a half in diameter, about three feet from the floor. Two slots were cut into the centre of the circle, into which the arms of a counterweighted jack were inserted. The counterweight platform was loaded with lead plates and the jack was raised as far as possible. They had then used a large pneumatic drill to sink a series of holes into the wall around the circle's circumference. The goal was to create an entrance to the Library whilst generating as little dust and debris as possible. For this reason, the drill bit stopped a fraction of an inch short of the other side of the wall. It was precision work, and very time consuming.

After three days of drilling, and an enormous amount of dust inside the ante-chamber, the engineers had cut around the entire circle. The jack was then taking most of the weight of the cylinder of stone within, while a thin layer of stone still separated the two rooms.

Gail had wondered what tool the engineers would use to cut the final sliver of stone, without generating dust, and had asked Ben his opinion.

"When you cut, using a drill, or a saw, you always get dust," he had explained. "But when you break, or snap as you say, you get much less. Like cutting a piece of wood."

Which is exactly what the engineers had done; once all of the dust caused by the drill had been cleared away, they had literally pulled the stone outwards and into the ante-chamber using pneumatic pumps, like taking the cork from a bottle of wine. The thin circle of stone connecting it to the surrounding wall had broken easily, leaving a more or less perfectly circular tunnel between the two rooms.

The engineers had then entered the Library, with their black suitcase of equipment, and had spent ten minutes assessing the structure. They had then set up a series of electric flood lights, connected to a generator on the surface.

After they had finished, the Professor had addressed Gail.

"Gail, don't think of the engineers; apart from the strength of the stone in the room, they don't know the first thing about what they have just seen. *You* are to be the first person to set foot in that room for over three thousand years. Savour every moment of it."

She had never forgotten those words. Sliding through the tunnel, she found herself in the room she had dreamt about for days, ever since she had first seen it on the X-ray screen.

The Library was exactly as she had imagined it, with one exception. It was bigger. The Backscatter X-ray, although colour coded for range, simply couldn't give a true sense of scale and depth. On close examination of the Backscatter images, it was obvious that the room was large, and she was certain that the seasoned experts would not have been surprised, but she had been taken aback by the length of the walls, the number of shelves, and the volume of material stacked upon them.

The room was, as the instruments had shown, one hundred and twenty feet long. What the instruments had only barely shown, however, was that it was almost a hundred feet wide and about fifteen feet tall. On the hundreds of shelves were piled thousands of scrolls, and an assortment of bound parchments and clay tablets – they later found there to be three thousand two hundred and twenty-seven of them in total.

The shelves against the walls were made of planks of wood, slotted into each other like jigsaws. However the rows of free-standing shelves lined up along the centre of the room were more like book cases, solidly built with thicker beams comprising their uprights.

A thick layer of dust covered everything, and as she had walked towards the end of the room, she had seen the footprints of the engineers. They had obviously done their jobs very thoroughly, checking in between every set of shelves, and along all of the walls. The sight of recent footprints did put her off slightly, but she tried hard to focus on what the Professor had told her, and soon she was concentrating on the ancient finds, letting her fingers hover millimetres from the surface of the documents, not daring to touch them lest they disappear in piles of fragments and dust.

Eventually, she reached her goal. In front of her stood a stone plinth, like a small altar, on which a book was propped, facing away from her. Her first impression on seeing the X-ray had been that it was like a Bible in a church. That simile felt even more accurate as she had stood before it. She felt like a member of a congregation, waiting for the priest to walk up and start reading.

Now, after many years giving lectures to students, she likened it more to the podium at the front of a lecture theatre.

The stone plinth was simple, unmarked, ending in an angled table surface that projected out an inch or so from plinth. The book was held in place by a stone lip that ran along the bottom edge.

She had walked round the plinth to see the cover, which was when she first laid eyes on the *Stickman*, engraved into the wood.

The symbol was made up of seven straight lines and one circle. Six of the straight lines were connected in pairs to form three upside-down Vs, one on top of the other. A vertical line connected the three Vs, starting at the apex of the bottom V and ending at the apex of the third V. A circle sat on the apex of the topmost upside-down V.

Upon entering the room for the first time, Ben had immediately associated the symbol with a stickman, because quite simply it looked just like one, except that it had a second pair of legs just above the first.

From that moment on, it had been known popularly as the *Amarna Stickman*, previously unheard of and seemingly unique to the Amarna Library. Academically, it remained nameless in the hope that one of the texts in the Library would shed light on its ancient Egyptian pronunciation.

She had not dared to open the book, for fear of it falling apart, and had therefore spent several minutes examining it from every angle. It was about the size of a modern coffee-table book. The covers were a quarter of an inch thick, and the whole thing was bound together, incredibly neatly, with reed. It was in immaculate condition, as if it had only just been placed there.

After a while, she had left the plinth and had walked slowly back to the tunnel, but along the opposite side of the room. It was then that she had noticed that all of the shelf uprights were also engraved with the *Stickman* symbol from the book-cover. As she had walked past the final row of shelves, she had seen for the first time in full the end wall of the Library, through which the tunnel had been drilled. In the centre of the wall was the same symbol again, but about six feet high. Next to it, but roughly half as tall, was Nefertiti's Cartouche. The two symbols were separated by a single vertical line.

It was later confirmed that aside from Nefertiti's cartouche, the strange symbol was the only marking inside the Library. To date, none of the other documents in the Library had been found to contain the symbol.

It was only present on the book from the plinth. And it had never before been seen outside the Library.

She had spent a total of four weeks at the site, longer than she had initially planned, and had returned regularly ever since. In the ten years since the excavation, only a small fraction of the texts from the Library had even been looked at.

Because of the mystery surrounding the Amarna Stickman, she had decided to put it on the cover of her book. Her publisher had readily agreed. For an academic book, it had sold in surprising numbers, nothing short of a best-seller, and beyond her wildest expectations.

CHAPTER 35

The double-doors of the lecture theatre suddenly burst open. She jumped as she was torn from her reminiscing and three hundred students poured inside.

The noise was incredible. There was shouting, laughing, jeering, talking, banging of chair seats as they were flipped down, shuffling of feet, somebody tripping on the stairs and dropping their bag and a particularly deep laugh somewhere near the back which she could only describe as a 'guffaw'.

After about five minutes, Gail looked at her watch and decided it was time to close the doors. As she returned to the podium, she could see students pointing to her slide and whispering comments to their neighbours. *This lot are lively,* she thought to herself with a smile as she prepared to start her lecture.

She dimmed the lights and checked attendance on the podium's console: a better turnout than usual, there were three hundred and fifty-two people seated in the theatre; eighty-six more than the previous year.

Walking out from behind the podium – she briefly thought of the first lecture she had given, when she had literally hidden behind it - she introduced herself and welcomed them to the course, *Introduction to Egyptology.*

Looking around the room, she noted with a certain degree of pride that practically everyone was transfixed by either her or the projection on the wall behind. She had never seen such an eager group.

"Egyptology is the study of Egypt and its antiquities," she began. "It has been practiced in its present form for over two hundred years, and is closely linked both to archaeology *and* history. How many of you here are taking Archaeology and History?"

Approximately half the theatre raised their hands. Some said yes, one person near the back said he wasn't sure, to which everyone laughed.

"Until the turn of the twenty-first century," she continued, "the last royal tomb to be excavated in Egypt was that of Tutankhamen, in 1922. For decades, many people believed that the last tomb in the Valley of the Kings had been discovered. They were very wrong. Since 2006, three more tombs have been discovered and excavated there, two in the last decade alone." She looked around the theatre at her wide-eyed audience. *I must be getting good at this*, she thought to herself. "Over the past fifteen years, Egypt's *Supreme Council of Antiquities* has seen major investment and modernisation; it now has the capability to regulate and oversee three times the number of simultaneous archaeological excavations compared to fifty years ago, particularly in the pharaonic sector. In other words, the Egyptian government, aided by UNESCO, has invested millions in making it easier to go to Egypt and *do* archaeology." She paused and looked behind her at her introduction slide. "And believe me, if you thought two hundred years was enough to find out everything there is to know about Egypt, think again. Egypt is throwing up unexpected find after unexpected find, every day."

She stopped talking and walked back to the podium. Hitting the screen once with her index finger, the slide changed to a photograph of the book that had been on the plinth in the Library at Amarna, with the Stickman carved into its cover.

"Has anyone seen this *Stickman* symbol before?" she asked confidently. She always liked to follow this up with *'don't worry, until about ten years ago, neither had anyone else'*.

Except that this time, not one hand stayed down.

She was used to the normal group, usually near the front, who would raise their hands, sometimes smugly. But since she had started giving the same lecture two years earlier, nothing had come close to this. She was amazed, and was about to say *'Wow!'*, when Professor David Hunt burst through the door at the back of the lecture theatre.

He stumbled down the steps, mumbling apologies to the students, most of whom still had their hands held high. He didn't even say hello to Gail as he rushed over to the podium and closed her presentation. Bringing up an Internet browser, he found the BBC website and expanded the *'Breaking News'* of the day.

"Look!" he said, out of breath, pointing up at the projection on the wall.

Gail turned round, still in shock. She read the words, her eyes widening.

'Evidence of Intelligent Life Revealed on Mars,' the headline claimed, boldly.

"Wow!" she finally said, as if her brain had queued the word she had been about to say before David's entrance, and had to make her say it before more words could be used.

"No," David said with a grin like a Cheshire cat. "*This* is wow!" He scrolled down to the bottom of the page, and clicked on a picture. She saw two people in space suits standing on some sort of platform on the side of a cliff. He clicked to show the next picture: a close up of the platform, which she now saw was like a small stone jetty coming out of the cliff wall. He clicked to show the last picture. It was another close up of the stone, clearly showing the engraving on its surface.

"Is this some kind of joke?" she said, walking towards the screen. She was oblivious to the excited talking going on in the theatre behind her. "Is that *really* Mars?"

"Yes!" he almost shouted.

Gail needed to sit down. She pulled a stool out from under the podium and perched herself on top of it. "How?"

"I have no idea, but I'm going to love finding out," he replied. He was even more enthusiastic than usual, like a small child at a birthday party after too many sweets. "You've got to agree with some of my ideas now, Gail, haven't you? You might even have to revisit some of your Amarna dating," he jabbed.

She was absolutely stunned. "I don't know," was all she could say. "I don't know."

That the news showed proof of extra-terrestrial life was amazing.

That it had been *intelligent* extra-terrestrial life was barely credible.

But that such intelligent life had managed to carve the very same *Amarna Stickman*, in all of its glory, into the surface of a rock a hundred million miles away on Mars left Dr Gail Turner utterly speechless.

CHAPTER 36

Larue's English was certainly good enough to get the general idea of the book Martín had given him, and he had now read enough of it to know what to do next. Nevertheless, he continued to flick through it with increasing interest, dwelling on a series of photos of the archaeological excavation. In one shot, an attractive young lady and a much older, bearded man stood proudly beside a large rectangular stone in the desert. Another picture showed a row of bookshelves covered in scrolls and clay tablets of varying sizes. The picture he was most interested in, however, was of a large engraving on a wall showing the symbol from Mars next to a bunch of hieroglyphs.

He called Martín back in to his office, and when the Spaniard entered he snapped the book shut. He opened his desk drawer and took out a large wallet. "So, you've met Dr Turner before?"

Martín smiled proudly and nodded. "Yes, in London. I was visiting some friends and we went to one of her lectures."

"Why?" Larue was intrigued as to why a young man with a master's degree in physics would be interested in archaeology.

"A friend of mine was studying history, and recommended that we all go to the lecture with him, because we were doing nothing else that afternoon." He looked at the signed copy of the book. "He was also too shy to ask her to sign his copy of the book, so I did it for him. I got confused and she signed it for me instead. My friend was quite upset and told me to keep the book."

Laruc smiled at his little story.

"Martin, I think that this cover-up is not over. I don't believe for a second that whoever is behind it will simply turn over and admit defeat. We will be accused of the same fakery as we are accusing them of."

He opened his drawer and withdrew a credit card. He placed it on the desk in front of him. "This book is very interesting, but from what I can see it doesn't make any reference to Mars. And yet here we are. Dr

Gail Turner will no doubt have made progress in her research in the last few years. Maybe she knows something she wasn't able to publish at the time. While we are unable to get close to the findings on Mars, we should look to this site in Egypt to help explain what is going on.

"Your encounter with her, no matter how brief, does give you an icebreaker of sorts, and she may help us find out more. I want you to find her and get more information." He pulled a piece of paper from the drawer and, along with the credit card, pushed it across the desk. "This is the pin number for the business card, which you may use as required."

"But *Monsieur*, I am not a detective!" he complained.

"You are a researcher in my department. This is your research." Larue closed the drawer and gestured for him to leave.

As the door closed behind him, Martín looked down at the handful of items he was carrying. His assignment was certainly outside the normal remit of the ESA, he thought to himself, shaking his head. But although he was initially apprehensive, he quickly realised he'd just been given a golden opportunity to satisfy his own curiosity, as well as that of his boss.

He strode to his desk and opened up a browser window on his laptop, and started tracking Dr Gail Turner down.

CHAPTER 37

Seth Mallus shut the door and took his seat opposite Dr Patterson at the imposing desk. Bright sunlight poured through the window of the meeting room. Outside, an old man cycled past whistling and in the distance a group of children could be seen playing with a football on the sandy beach. Palm trees swayed gently as seagulls drifted on the warm breeze.

Dr Patterson was looking out of the window with interest.

"It's amazing what can be achieved with modern technology, Doctor," Mallus told him. "When my father was a boy, the most impressive computers could barely play chess. Now, in simulator windows like this they can make us think that we are enjoying a summer's day in California, while in the distance, sitting at a small table, two men who don't even exist are themselves playing chess to the level of the Grandmasters."

One of the boys playing football on the beach was arguing with the others. He was holding the football close to his chest, and shouting at the top of his voice. Dr Patterson could not make out what he was saying, but the outcome was clear. Three of the other boys suddenly jumped on him, trying to wrestle the ball away from his grip. Within a minute, they had seized it and were triumphantly marching off to their friends, where they quickly resumed their game. The first boy picked himself up from the sand, nursing his jaw. Blood was dripping from his nose. He stole a glance at the other boys as he retreated to the promenade by the beach. The three dimensional effect was staggering, to the extent that had he not been assured it was a computer simulation the thought would never have crossed his mind.

"Man will never change, Dr Patterson. Our playground simply gets larger, the footballs more expensive, and the games more deadly." He swung his chair round to look at the scientist. "The strong and powerful continue to make the rules, and there is one absolute certainty: the longer you play, the more likely you are to get hurt."

Patterson wasn't sure what Mallus was alluding to, but his threatening tone was making him nervous. "I see," he lied.

Mallus leant forward and pointed to the scientist's folder, which he had placed on the desk in front of him. "Tell, me; since we last saw each other, has anything enlightening sprung to mind?" he asked.

"I've made some progress, but nothing noteworthy. I was very surprised when -"

"You turned the news on this morning?" Mallus finished the sentence for him.

"I didn't expect them to find it so soon. And I certainly didn't expect to see it on TV."

Mallus looked at him closely then shook his head. "The leaks to the press have caused us to accelerate our project somewhat, but there is still too much that we do not understand regarding *Aniquilus*, too much that you have not been able to tell us, despite your best attempts. This is why, if all goes well, Dr Gail Turner will be joining you tomorrow to start helping."

Patterson looked at him in disbelief. That he was assigned some help from one of the other research teams was one thing, but *Dr Gail Turner...*

"She can read the text, from what the reports say, largely without the aid of a translating device like you, Doctor. And you know everything about Mars and a great deal about *Aniquilus*. Of all the people in the list you provided me with, I believe the two of you will make the best pairing."

There was a shout from the virtual world outside the window, barely audible through the 'glass', and Patterson looked up to see the same fight over the football happening all over again. Following his gaze, Mallus shook his head and snapped a command at the screen, which promptly changed to a sprawling cityscape; Mallus' office had gone from a beach to the topmost floor of a virtual skyscraper.

After a short pause to take the view in, Mallus looked at him intently. "Something has to be done to stop it, Doctor. The book is the key, I'm certain of that. I'm also certain that we don't have much time left."

CHAPTER 38

Gail's phone had not stopped ringing all morning. She had cancelled her remaining lectures and seminars for the day and returned to her office with David Hunt to look at the Mars findings in more detail. Despite speaking to dozens of people, her mobile still had over thirty missed calls, and her desk phone had more voicemails than she dared count.

She held her head in her hands and exhaled loudly.

"Gail, I know this may be hard, but you may have to accept that Amarna and Mars are linked," David said apologetically.

Looking up at him, she scowled before burying her face again. "Easy for you to say," she mumbled. "You're used to people trying to discredit you! This is Egyptology; I'll be hung out to dry!"

Professor David Hunt knew exactly what she meant. Over the years, dozens of weird and wonderful theories had been put forward regarding the pyramids, the Sphinx, and the pharaohs; all of those theories had been ridiculed by Egyptologists. Often, they would simply not bother trying to disprove the theory, but would dismiss it out of hand. Gail was worried about keeping her career intact and away from disrepute.

"Look at the bigger picture, Gail: they've found evidence of intelligent life on Mars!" he said. "And those creatures used the same symbol as your Amarna people. You couldn't have gone to Mars to plant evidence any more than you could have carved the Stickman into all those shelves in Amarna, so they can't possible claim that you made any of this up, can they?"

"That's not the point!" she whined. "The Egyptian authorities are renowned for refusing to authorise archaeological excavations if they believe an unfavourable alternative theory is being developed. They famously stalled excavation of irregularities in Khufu's pyramid because Japanese and French researchers couldn't satisfy their demands that it would significantly advance science. The second I openly admit to a link between Mars and Amarna, I can kiss my access to the Amarna Library goodbye, and there are still over three thousand books that we haven't even opened yet!"

"Not this time: this is science, Gail! You can see as well as I can that those symbols are identical. There is only one possible reason for that isn't there?"

Gail sat holding her head for several minutes as David waited patiently for an answer. She looked up. "There is another possible explanation."

He looked her in the eyes and his face fell. "Gail, don't do this!" he pleaded with her.

"But you have to admit it's possible, don't you? That the Mars photos are faked is a hell of a lot more likely than the alternative, don't you think? Why do you so readily believe that they are genuine?"

"The truth is that regardless of where those images came from, regardless of how authentic they may be you simply don't *want* to accept that there may be some inherent link between the two sites," he told her, firmly. "You're grappling for a conspiracy theory that disproves the relationship between the two, instead of objectively looking at all the evidence and judging it on its own merits." His eyes met hers and softened. "The reason I can still work here, despite all my years trying to prove my unpopular theories, is because I have never forgotten that archaeology is a science, and that scientific method is the foundation of everything that we do.

"I know that there is a twenty-three thousand year old village on the edge of the Caspian Sea because of scientific evidence, not because that's what I wanted to be true. Had it been only four thousand years-old, it would still have been an important find. As it is, it helped fuel my career for the past fifteen years. Look for the evidence to support a link between Amarna and Mars, and you may be surprised. There may be something in the texts that you have already seen that may now make more sense."

"I am absolutely sure that there is nothing in the texts I have looked at that suggests a link. There is no evidence I know of in the archaeology in Amarna, or even in the rest of Egypt – the rest of the world! – that can point to a link with extra-terrestrials." She was angry now, her eyes filled with emotion. Her entire career had been based on the Amarna Library, but the photos from Mars had her looking at a bleak future. "I have two choices," she said as calmly as possible. "Either I support the possibility of E.T., or I refute it completely."

David looked at her and smiled. "You made your choice years ago, Gail, when you accepted your scroll from the Dean. You have to be a scientist."

"There's always a choice to be made. But first, I have to speak to Professor al-Misri."

As if on cue, the desk phone started ringing.

Gail was tempted to let it ring: the sheer volume of calls that morning had left her weary of lecturers, friends, family and even students, all asking her the same questions. But then she recognised the Cairo telephone number on the display.

"Mamdouh, I was just about to call you, how strange!"

David pushed himself up from the armchair in which he had been lounged and gestured to Gail that he was popping into his own office for a while.

Gail nodded and continued speaking to the Professor. "Yes, I saw the news. How couldn't I? I'm fairly certain it's faked, or that –"

He had just reached the door when Gail stopped mid-sentence. Something about the lengthy pause in her telephone conversation made him prolong his stay in her office for a few moments.

"But, how do you know?" she said, the words stumbling out.

David backed away from the door and regained his seat, all the time studying her face for any signs of what the Egyptian could be saying to her on the other end of the line.

Suddenly, she was saying her goodbyes and hanging up. She sat in silence for over a minute, looking into space, before David could bear it no longer.

"Well?" he urged. "Doesn't he think that the photos are faked?"

She looked at him, and shook her head slowly. "No."

"Why not?"

"Because he has seen proof that suggests otherwise."

"What kind of proof?"

"He can't tell me over the phone. I have to see him in Cairo tonight. He's already booked my flight."

There was something about her pale face and expression, telling him that there was more to it than that. "What's wrong, Gail?" he asked softly.

She looked him in the eyes. "He says that there's another book from the Amarna Library, one that I've never seen."

David sighed. "There's more than just one, Gail! There are more than three thousand books in the Library that you've not yet had the time to study, and you know more than *anyone* about that place."

Now she was frantically clicking through folders of images on her computer screen, some that had been used in her book, many thousands more that had not. She finally reached the folder she was looking for.

A rendition of the Backscatter X-ray, from a few days before they had entered the Library for the first time, filled the screen. She zoomed in on the plinth, on which the Stickman book had been found.

She flicked through a pile of papers on her desk and brought out an A3 print of another photo, this one taken from inside the Library, behind the plinth. The Stickman book covered less than half of the plinth's surface.

Comparing the two images, her jaw dropped.

"How did I not notice this before?" she wondered.

"Unbelievable," he whispered.

"My entire career, all my studies, my lectures, my thesis, everything! It's all been based on corrupted evidence!" she wailed.

He looked at her wide-eyed as she broke down in front of him. He was horrified and upset for his colleague. But deep-down inside, part of him thrust a clenched fist in the air and cried victory. All his life he had searched for proof of archaeological and historical cover-ups, and now it looked like he would finally get what he'd been looking for.

For on close inspection, the Backscatter X-ray showed the Stickman book, and right next to it, with barely a gap between, was a second identically-sized tome. The photo from inside the Library, however, showed only one, lonesome book.

Not only had there been a cover-up, but it had happened right in front of her eyes.

CHAPTER 39

Gail subconsciously adjusted her backrest and fastened her seatbelt. She raised her hand and asked the nearby steward for a glass of water. Pulling her tablet computer from her bag, she hit the 'On' switch and waited for the welcome screen before using a stylus to enter her access signature.

A sudden burst of computer graphics brought her to her desktop, where all of her useful applications were waiting to be used. It was the same workspace as at her desk, and on the video wall at home, with all the applications and data synchronising in real time with a farm of University servers, probably deep inside a hill somewhere Gail had never even been. The tablet was never truly 'off' unless its battery was drained, and was constantly performing quick-syncs whenever it had access to WiFi.

The benefits to her and fieldworkers everywhere were enormous. What she saw on her tablet was identical to what she saw on her desktop machine in her office. No matter where she was, she could see the same files, applications and settings, saving her valuable time. In the field, it meant that she could input data and start analysing it on site, and collaborating with colleagues hundreds of miles away, before continuing at her leisure either at home, in the office, or as she was doing at that very moment, on the plane to Cairo. And if ever she lost her tablet, logging on to any new device as herself would synchronise everything once more

She tapped the screen to access her emails and scrolled down the list until she came to a recent one from George.

There was no text, just a picture of a cartoon rabbit looking sheepish. She smiled and checked the time of the mail: half past three in the afternoon. He must have sent it from his phone, as there was no way he could be home yet after having dropped her off at the airport. She saved the picture to her personal files and closed the message.

George didn't pretend to know much about Egyptology, but he wasn't an idiot either. He had known enough to understand that the news from Mars could be both good and bad. Knowing that he would always be with her and supporting her touched her deeply.

When he had learnt about the call from Mamdouh, he had been genuinely shocked. Gail and George had spent numerous holidays in Egypt over the past ten years, and had grown very close to the Professor. That he had never mentioned the missing book, even during one of his after-dinner ramblings, was surprising to say the least, as a great deal of their conversations had tended to centre on Amarna and the Library.

Gail had had time to think about things more now, and on reflection thought that she understood the situation better. In fact, as she deleted a selection of junk emails, she could even accept why the Professor would have hidden the book.

If it had shown any kind of link with Mars, then an unqualified archaeologist discovering it in the desert with no prior study of the area would seem too good to be true: the scientific community would never have believed that the book was genuine. Removing it ensured that the Library as a whole would be accepted without question.

But it did not all fit, she thought as she fired off a quick reply to a student, wondering if the lecture notes from that morning's interrupted lecture would be available on her website. *'Yes'* was all she had written. Not everything made sense to her. For starters, removing one book on the spur of the moment couldn't ensure that no similar evidence was present elsewhere in the Library. No one would have been able to check the thousands of books before she entered. And if you're going to remove a book, then why not the one with the Amarna Stickman engraved on its cover? And why, when all the other books related to politics, economics and demographics, was her book so different, its content almost biblical in comparison? Surely, from what had been seen so far in the Library, her book was unique; *but not enough to be removed?*

Most confusing of all, though, was the fact that Mamdouh couldn't have removed a book from the Library himself. Gail was the first to enter after the engineers, and the book had been sitting on the plinth undisturbed.

How had he made the swap?

She closed the email program and sipped her water. Her emotions had given way to curiosity, and concerns over the future of her career had been replaced by a number of questions she was eager to put to her friend in Cairo. Unfortunately, since their brief phone conversation, he'd not answered any of her calls or emails. *Maybe he's fending off questions left, right and centre, too*, she thought.

She brought another application to the front of the desktop. A simple window, not unlike a word-processor, filled her screen. She dragged George's sheepish rabbit picture over and dropped it in, then tapped a button on the application toolbar. A simple dialogue popped up asking her to enter her keyword.

She smiled to herself and typed *bunny*. A progress bar briefly worked its way along the bottom of the picture, and then a message emerged:

Good Luck Bunny, always with you. Love George xxx

The application she was using had been written by George as a Christmas present for her several years earlier. At first, she had believed it to be a simple viewer for all of her scanned pages of books from the Library. She had thanked him, but had secretly been a little disappointed that the fruit of his labours – three months of programming in the evenings after work – had produced a simple program she could have obtained for free from the Internet.

George had said nothing more of it.

The Christmas holidays had been over for nearly a month before Gail actually *used* the program he had made. She had uploaded her scanned images, and had been idly flipping through them when she noticed the strange icon along the toolbar. She had clicked it, only to be faced with an error: *Please select glyph(s) for translation*. Her heart had literally left her chest.

George had not simply made a *viewer* for her Egyptian texts, he had made a tool that helped her *translate* them. She grinned to herself as she remembered how she had thanked him that evening for his Christmas present.

Closing the message and the picture, she dragged another file into the application and a series of tiny rectangles filled the screen, as if someone had ripped the pages from a book and laid them out in rows on a grey background. She tapped the first page and zoomed in to the wooden cover of the book from the Library plinth, the *Stickman book* as it had become known. The engraved Stickman looked so real she felt she could touch it. Memories of the dry atmosphere of the Library came flooding back to her, memories of the smell of old leather and wood.

The application let you select a hieroglyph or group of hieroglyphs, such as a cartouche, and add custom text, which would serve as the translation. The application would then run through all of the text and suggest the same translation for any matching symbols. It used a simple bitmap comparison algorithm with some additional routines for cleaning up background noise, so it couldn't do anything *too* sophisticated. A common problem was that Egyptian hieroglyphs should be read in the direction in which the characters were facing. This meant that the bitmap analysis would correctly match two sets of glyphs reading from left to right, but would fail to recognise that a third set, reading from top to bottom, was also a match. It was a minor gripe, which George had promised to look into at some point in the future.

Once the analysis was complete, tooltips would appear all over the text. An overview pane would also give a summary of all the available translations in any given selection. By selecting multiple tooltips, it was possible to add further contextual translations too, giving a second or even third meaning to common groups when used in conjunction with each other. Over time, the more she used it the more complete the dictionary became, and while Gail's own grasp of ancient Egyptian had improved to the extent of near-fluency over the past ten years, George's application had evolved such a sophisticated dictionary that it became the envy of her peers. One of her outstanding actions in the Faculty was to wrestle the source code from her husband and hand it over to the Department of Computer Science, so that they could enhance its functionality and distribute it more widely. But before he would let her do *that*, he had to remove his 'love-letter' system, which was what allowed them to hide words in pictures, only to be revealed when a keyword was input.

She highlighted a group of hieroglyphs and read the lines of English text, along with annotations, that appeared in a box below the page.

To conquer | {and} gain dominion {rule?} {wage war?} | leads to no victory {?} | all {we?} shall be judged as one {together?}

She had read the first line of text a thousand times. It was isolated at the top of the page, separated from the rest of the hieroglyphs by the Amarna Stickman.

Gail highlighted the next line of symbols.

A beauty has come {*Nefertiti*} | *with guidance* {*a message?*} *of* | {*???*}

She had never wanted to provide a translation for the Stickman symbol. In her mind, to do so was to admit that they would not find the genuine translation of the glyph and with so many texts from the Library unstudied, she looked forward to the day when she would triumphantly give the application its final translation. In the meantime, it simply returned three question marks whenever it occurred.

The religious undertones of the Stickman book were hard to escape. On every page could be found morals, stories, proverbs, and illustrations, all seemingly pointing to an idyllic way of life, a 'just path' as it had been dubbed, which she had interpreted as being an unsuccessful ideological movement started by Nefertiti under the reign of her husband Akhenaten. It fitted well with the archaeological evidence of the era: a new capital, a changed foreign policy, changing art, all capped by a worship of an old god, the Sun deity *Aten*. The movement had clearly failed, and future pharaohs had done everything possible to eradicate its memory.

To Dr Gail Turner, the evidence was quite clear, and her thesis had brought widespread acclaim. Many of the pieces of the puzzle surrounding Amarna and Nefertiti seemed to fall into place.

But that hadn't stopped other theories cropping up on the Internet. As soon as her research had been published, stories appeared of the *'first coming of the Lord'*, in female form, over twelve centuries before Jesus Christ, passing on his teachings to the most powerful people on Earth. The similes between the Bible and the Stickman book were there if one looked hard, and an increasingly large group of people had made it their sole purpose to look as hard as possible. The *Amarna Adventists* believed that Nefertiti was the true *daughter* of God. They had lifted ancient passages word for word from her book, including some of her own translations, and used them to form their own controversial 'bible.'

Amarna Adventists were not the only people to read more into the Library finds than the Egyptologists. The Internet was full of interpretations of the Stickman figure, from four-legged aliens to strange spaceships. For her part, Gail had felt that the Stickman represented a direction towards the Sun god Aten, its head being the Sun, and the arms, legs and body representing an arrow of some sort. It was an interpretation shared by most serious academics.

Now, however, as Gail read the sentence over to herself, and with the day's revelations in mind, she wondered whether the Internet theorists hadn't been more close to the mark.

The plane shot down the runway and lifted gently into the evening sky, leaving Heathrow and England behind.

And had she known for one second that she would never return, she would have given them more than just a fleeting glance as they disappeared beneath the clouds.

CHAPTER 40

Five hours later, the wheels hit the runway with a screech at Cairo International Airport. She glanced out of the small window and smiled. Arriving in Egypt always brought back memories of her first flight all those years ago, when George had done so well in taking her mind off her irrational fear of landing. By now, after dozens of trips, travelling by plane was as mundane to her as travelling by train or car.

As usual, no one was waiting for her inside the terminal. Instead, she went straight to a line of yellow taxis and quickly negotiated a price with the driver in the first one.

Travelling in Egypt was also something that Gail had grown accustomed to quite fast following that first trip. Their decision to rent a car on that occasion had come from inexperience; certainly the distances looked great enough to warrant renting one. But now, Gail wouldn't have dreamed of driving herself. Taxis were far more convenient, arguably safer and definitely cheaper.

More convenient because parking spaces were virtually non-existent in the city, particularly near the Museum where Gail normally went.

Safer, because the law of the roads in Cairo was survival of the fastest, where even the traffic police had difficulty controlling drivers.

And cheaper because once you knew how to and had built up the guts to do it, bartering with a taxi driver was as natural in Egypt as asking for the time. Within minutes, Gail was sitting in the first taxi, having agreed to half of the first suggested price.

It was already eight o'clock, six in the UK. She tapped the phone link on her earpiece and called her home number. George picked up after one ring.

"Hello?" he said. "Gail, why can't I see you?"

"I'm in a taxi, my phone is in my pocket and it's dark," she replied, holding onto the door handle as the driver negotiating his way past an oncoming lorry.

"Cairo Taxi, eh? Better than Alton Towers. How was the flight?"

"Good, gave me time to think about everything. Thought about you on landing, as always. And thanks for the sheepish rabbit."

He laughed. "Glad I could help, and glad you liked the bunny, Bunny. How about your work? You sound much better."

She felt much better, she thought to herself. "Well, I know Mamdouh pretty well. I trust he would only have done what he thought was best for everyone concerned. I still feel betrayed, like he could have confided in me, but I don't know the ins-and-outs of all this."

"I'm sure everything will be fine. Oh, before I forget. Some guy called Martín *Atony*, or *Antonass*, or something like that, rang for you about half an hour ago. He sounded quite insistent and said he needed to meet up with you. He sounded Spanish or South American or something. He was from the European Space Agency."

"What did he want?" she asked. She had already deflected a dozen reporters wanting her to comment on the Mars finds, but had made a firm decision to say nothing until she knew something. She imagined that this *Martín* was no different.

"He didn't say exactly. I gave him Mamdouh's details so if he hasn't already he'll probably be calling you at the museum."

"Bloody hell, George! You know I don't want to talk to the press or anything like that, and I'm guessing Mamdouh doesn't either."

There was a short silence.

"I'm sorry, Gail, but he didn't sound like he was after a story. I have his number here; I'll give him a call and tell him you're not interested."

"Hang on a second."

Her taxi was apparently racing with another through a junction and despite her experience she couldn't help wincing as her driver swerved in front of the other to cut him up. He was rewarded with three short beeps, and he waved cheerily out of his window in reply.

"No," she said bluntly, her mind back on their conversation. "I'll deal with him when I get there. We're only a few minutes away at this speed, anyway."

"I'm sorry, honey. I love you," he added the last three words almost as an afterthought.

"Me too, George. I'll call you later."

"Oh, and Gail?"

"Yes?" She heard the sound of cutlery on a plate and grinned.

"I've eaten your portion, OK?" He spoke with his mouth full of what she assumed was *her* Fish and Chips.

"Whatever, George." She pressed a button on the earpiece and ended the call.

Five minutes later, the car came to a stop in a street round the back of the museum. The driver turned round to face her with a wide grin.

She wondered briefly if the fact that she always haggled down to half the original price meant the driver always drove at twice the required speed, but then dismissed the thought. The look on this man's face told her he probably drove like that all the time. She paid the agreed fare, added fifty Egyptian pounds of *baksheesh*, and stepped out into the relatively cool Egyptian-winter evening.

Professor Mamdouh al-Misri had always been proud of his office at the Egyptian Museum. It had a decidedly 'Old World' feel about it: dark oak shelves covered every wall from floor to ceiling, while an imposing solid mahogany desk filled the centre of the room. The shelves were mostly stocked with academic publications. The entire bottom shelf, running along three walls of the office, was filled with over a century of National Geographic magazines. A small shelf at head height nearest the Professor's chair contained a selection of old archaeological books from the late nineteenth and early twentieth century. All three volumes of Carter's *The Tomb of Tut-Ankh-Amen* were present in the irreplaceable collection, and were themselves alone insured for over a hundred thousand British pounds.

Of course, in his few years as the General Director of the museum, the Professor had not yet had the time to furnish such a lavish office all by himself. Such a collection of books belonged not to him, but to the museum itself, and had been accumulated over the last century by dozens of General Directors, each one leaving their mark.

Professor al-Misri was more concerned with the safety of the collection, in particular the earlier works, than of adding anything specific to it himself. For that reason, he had been working with the museum planners to modify certain shelves in the office. Soon, for instance, Carter's works would be protected by a thick layer of Plexiglas and steel that could only be opened by entering a six-digit code.

He sat in his chair and looked up at the books. They seemed so old and fragile, their spines mostly bent and frayed at the edges. The dust jackets of some were torn and partially missing. These were books that had been used countless times; thumbed-through by his predecessors, left on bedside tables at night, or lying on a desk under a pile of paperwork for weeks and months on end, and they showed their age with pride.

He thought about the Amarna Library, sealed tight against the elements, its contents immaculately preserved for millennia. Thousands of books and scrolls, more than a man could read in a lifetime, in better condition than the small collection he saw in front of him now.

He shook his head. Books were meant to be *read*, not hidden.

Gail knocked and entered without waiting. She found him sitting at his desk, which had been cleared of all paperwork, revealing in full its leather surface to her for the first time. The Professor looked at her blankly.

"Hello?" she ventured.

His face suddenly lit up. "Gail! Sorry, I was miles away. How was the flight?" He stood up and rounded the desk to welcome her, holding her right hand firmly and kissing her lightly on each cheek – a vestige of his Western education.

"Not bad, thanks," she replied.

They exchanged pleasantries for several minutes after sitting down, before falling silent. The Professor looked down at his desk.

"Why have you cleared up, Mamdouh?" Gail asked.

He gave a deep sigh and looked her in the eyes. "Because I cannot lie to myself any longer. Being in this office reminds me every day of what I have let happen. I will resign in the morning."

She was taken aback by his statement. "No! You –"

"Gail, I have to tell you the truth," he interrupted her. "At least what little I know of it." He fished a piece of paper out of the top drawer and passed it across the desk. "Before I forget, you may want to contact this man later; he called for you earlier."

She read the note. *Martín Antunez, again!* It was followed by a phone number. *Like I don't have more important things to do than talk to him!* She shook her head and put it in her pocket.

"Please let me tell you everything, without interruption, and then we can discuss things," he said.

Gail reluctantly agreed.

"You will certainly remember when you first set foot in the Amarna Library, Gail. That day, you walked into a veritable treasure trove, the single most impressive archaeological find I have ever witnessed.

Certainly on a par with Howard Carter more than a hundred years ago. But I was not entirely honest with you that day." He paused to moisten his lips. "Months before our excavations at Amarna began, I was contacted by an American man; an old friend who studied Anthropology with me at Harvard. His name is Dr Henry Patterson. I hadn't heard from him in years, and we spent a good hour on the phone reminiscing about old times. It turned out he was calling because he had heard of my excavation.

"I was amazed; the excavation wasn't exactly high profile, barely a blip on the Supreme Council of Antiquities' radar. Why would he know of it? He explained to me that he worked for an agency in the States, based near Tampa in Florida. They had reason to believe that certain finds from Amarna could be extremely damaging to the political stability of the region. How they knew of these finds, he could not fully reveal, but he suggested that his agency's investigations pointed to an as-yet undiscovered text, somehow related to Nefertiti. If we were to find the text and reveal it publicly, his agency felt the repercussions would be disastrous.

"Of course, as I listened to him explain all of this I could not stop myself from laughing out loud. It sounded completely preposterous, like a prank call. I accused him of playing such a joke, but he flatly denied it. Instead, he offered me help. On top of providing materials and equipment to aid in our work, his agency would take responsibility for removing the offending finds in the event that we uncovered them, and help 'oil the wheels of bureaucracy' if required. That basically meant *baksheesh*. They would also ensure that no loose ends were left lying around to give anything away. You saw the men from the agency when you were on the dig, Gail."

"The engineers," she whispered.

"Yes, the engineers. They were attached to me from day one. I reported all of the finds to them. From the moment they arrived, I regretted agreeing to work with this agency. I always felt like they were spying on me, on the dig, and on all of my students. There was something dark, something oppressive about their presence that made me want to call him up and tell them they could leave right away. But I never did, and when I found out what they wanted to hide, I was glad I hadn't.

"The engineers pretended to make the Library 'safe' for us to investigate, Gail. In truth, they went in to find what they were looking for and remove it."

"The second book on the plinth."

"Yes. We were left with one volume of a two-book set, Gail. What they took away was removed from the Library as cleanly as possible, they even scattered dust around the plinth so that nobody could guess anything was amiss. I spoke to Patterson by phone shortly before you entered the Library, and demanded that he tell me what they were hiding. What had been so important that the biggest discovery in living memory was to be spoilt by an agency I knew nothing about? I had trusted him because we had been friends, but on seeing the engineers on site with their damned suitcase, I wanted to know everything.

"Patterson calmed me down as best he could over the phone and told me that I could not see the find whilst still on site. However, before it was shipped to its final destination, God knows where, he promised that I would be able to look at it. He was as good as his word, and on his request I journeyed to Cairo the day after you first entered the Library.

"Patterson met me in this very building, in my old office down the hall. One of the engineers was with him, and they had made space for their case on my desk. I had already signed a document stating I would not divulge anything to third parties about our arrangement, but they made me sign another form before they would open the case. They were quite forceful, but to be honest I probably would have signed anything at that point: my curiosity was more powerful than anything. Then the engineer opened the case and Patterson ushered me forwards.

"I will never forget my first sight of the book, Gail, my first glimpse of the cover. It was exactly the same dimensions as the *Stickman* volume, except that it was thicker: it probably contained half as many pages again as your volume. Its cover was also wooden, with a bound spine. On it had been engraved a picture, in the same fashion as the *Stickman*. My God! They would have looked impressive together!"

"Wait," Gail said. "You said that this so-called *agency* wanted to stop information from being spread from Amarna to the outside world, and so went to all this trouble to hide one book. But there were hundreds and hundreds of different books in that room, how did they know for sure that they had removed the only one that mattered? What if *my* book had also contained something important, or what if one of the hundreds of scrolls that we haven't even looked at did?"

Mamdouh shook his head. "I have no idea, Gail. Somehow, they knew that there was only one book to take care of. They certainly didn't have time to read anything whilst in the Library. They couldn't have checked the entire *Stickman* book in that time, and believe me after having read it myself I can assure you that it makes no reference to the content of the book they took away. Their information must have been well sourced, but I'm at a loss from thereon in. And I have not heard from the agency since that day in my office."

"What made this book so special then?" she asked.

"In itself, the cover was interesting enough. The engraving showed a human figure holding a long staff aloft, as if in defiance. But it was upon opening the book that the true surprise came. It was mostly illustrations, accompanied by small segments of text, a mixture of hieroglyphs and hieratic. Full page drawings of people living in vast cities that we would classify, even today, as futuristic; filled with flying machines, vehicles of all descriptions, towering skyscrapers, sprawling forest-parks with fountains and paths. It was like looking at a science-fiction landscape. Then there were pictures of farms rolling over hills to the horizon, seascapes showing fleets of strange vessels. The text below, in the little time I had to read and quickly translate it, simply described the illustrations, like an encyclopaedia, with comments like *Ancient City with administrative centre* or *Agricultural Environment*. And then suddenly, the mood of the illustrations changed. I turned the page, and it was like a vast hand had been swept across the city from the previous pages. Everything was razed to the ground, people were running in all directions in obvious panic. I barely had time to take the scenes in, however, because as soon as I had turned the page the engineer stepped forward and closed the book, quite forcefully moving me aside. I have not seen or heard from it since."

"My God, Mamdouh. Professor Hunt would love to hear about this! But even he would never believe such advanced human civilisations from the past," she said.

The Professor looked her straight in the eyes. "And you think I would? Gail, over the decades I have seen thousands of ancient texts, not just from Egypt but from all over the world. This wasn't some dream-fuelled flight of fantasy, it was a vision of a future world. It was so real, so tangible, so believable that it can only have come from someone who had witnessed it.

"All of the people in the streets of the mysterious city, the pilots in flying machines, the farmers in the fields and sailors on the strange ships *existed*. And from the little I saw, it is clear to me that they were wiped out, erased from history."

Gail could not find the words, her mouth opened and closed slowly like a goldfish.

"When I saw that book I realised what it represented; I *knew* it couldn't be shown to the outside world. I don't pretend to know what wider implications it may have and why the agency would want to cover it up. Whatever religious or political motivations they might have, I simply understood that to reveal it would have been professional suicide. I would have been no better than those who claim that the Great Pyramid of Khufu was built as a landing platform for interstellar spaceships. Here was I, looking at a veritable link between the ancient Egypt I love and something that would destroy everything we think we know about our origins.

"I couldn't let that happen. As a philosopher, I was frustrated that I would never again be able to see the book, to study and translate its text. But as a man who wanted to earn a living and develop my career, I was relieved that it was being taken off my hands. The responsibility was no longer mine.

"Because of this, I never once felt inclined to reveal this to you, or to anyone for that matter. Over time, I made myself believe that the book did in fact represent little more than a fantasy world. I mean, what will people think thousands of years hence when they discover our libraries full of science fiction? Would *they* believe that we had really waged war with Mars, that we genuinely conquered the stars or that we could easily travel through time at will?" He paused and let out a long sigh. "That idea helped reconcile my guilt. The belief that it was a work of fantasy got me through the past ten years in one piece.

"Until this morning. When I saw the photos from Mars, it all came back as real as if I had the book in my hands. The smell of the wood, the texture of the pages, the intricate detail of the alien world; none of it was fantasy, it was authentic. That is why I do not think the *Stickman* on Mars is faked, Gail. I do not believe it is a coincidence. I believe instead that it *belongs* on Mars, as do the people from the book."

He stopped talking and they sat in silence for several minutes. He wanted to urge her to respond, but understood that she was overwhelmed by his story and needed time to digest. Eventually, she looked at him.

"Firstly Mamdouh, let me say I do not judge you for what you did. I would probably have done the same as you, otherwise my career as a result would have been entirely different, and I would probably have had to get my doctorate from the Internet rather than from a good university."

He nodded in reply, as much in gratitude for her understanding as in agreement of her statement.

"Secondly, the photos from Mars prove something else," she continued.

"What?" he asked. He had not expected her to dwell on the photos from Mars.

"The fact that the pictures from Mars reached the media at all can mean only one thing: that whatever the agency you dealt with is doing to cover all this up, they've made a mistake. Somehow, they weren't as thorough as they should have been, and if they were trying to stop 'disastrous repercussions,' then they've failed."

The Professor was about to speak when a noise from outside his office caught his attention. He quickly placed his index finger against his lips. Gail turned round silently to follow his stare.

Two loud knocks on the solid oak door reverberated round the room.

After a moment's hesitation, Mamdouh stood up behind his desk.

"Come in," he said, a slight crackle in his voice.

CHAPTER 41

George woke up to the phone ringing incessantly in the living room. He looked at his watch: six-thirty in the morning.

Bloody hell, Gail, he thought to himself as he stumbled down the stairs. He searched among the empty cans, bottles and food wrappers on the coffee table before finding the remote. One of his friends emerged from the toilet scratching his head.

"What time is it?" he said.

"Six-bloody-thirty, and where did you come from?" he asked as he answered the call.

"Slept in the bath, mate," came the reply as he looked enviously at the couch, where another body lay comfortably, still unconscious.

George wasn't listening. The video wall asked him if he wanted to accept a video-call from a private number in Egypt. He cursed under his breath; the one time that he was home-alone and had friends over for a drink, and Gail had to call him first thing. There was no way he could make the room look even half decent for the camera, so he didn't even bother trying. Instead, he checked his reflection in the preview screen in the corner of the video wall and accepted the call, before focusing his attention on the caller. It wasn't Gail.

"Mr Turner?" a man in uniform asked. He was standing against a plain white background, his navy blue uniform immaculate. He didn't wait for George to confirm his identity, and he didn't look surprised by his attire. To him, all Englishmen looked as scruffy as the half-naked apparition he was talking to. "I am Captain Ahmed Kamal of the Cairo police department. We are looking for your wife, Mrs Gail Turner?" He used a raised inflection at the end of his statement, prompting an answer.

"Well, I assume you're closer to her than I am, Captain; she's in Cairo. I spoke to her yesterday evening, but haven't heard anything since then."

"At what time did you speak to her, Mr Turner?" the Captain demanded.

George crossed his arms defensively. Two of his friends were now sitting on the sofa behind him, looking at the video wall in bemusement. "Am I being interrogated here?" he said. "Why are you asking me about Gail? Is she OK?"

The policeman looked beyond the camera, as if checking something going on in the background where he was calling from. "We just need to speak to her, Mr Turner. Telephone recordings reveal that your wife was meeting a Professor Mamdouh al-Misri yesterday evening at his office in the Egyptian Museum of Cairo. We would very much like to find her so that she can answer some questions relating to our enquiries."

George scratched his head. It was too early for this. "I last spoke to her at about six, that's eight in the evening your time. She was on her way to meet Mamdouh."

"Mamdouh?" the Captain raised an eyebrow. "You knew him well?"

"Absolutely, we spend a lot of time there, we stay with him whenever we go to Egypt."

"That's very interesting." He looked behind the camera again and made a slight nodding of the head. "Do you know of any reason for dispute between him and your wife, Mr Turner?"

George was taken aback; *what a question*. "Not really, no. They were both pretty shocked by the photos from Mars yesterday; Mamdouh called her and arranged her flight to Cairo, he wanted to see her as soon as possible." The policeman was annoying him now, what he really wanted was to call Gail on her mobile to check she was OK. "Anyway, she will be at his house now, they were meeting at the museum but she was going to stay with him as usual. He lives nearby. You'll find her there, Captain" George had a quick rummage on the coffee table before finding his mobile phone. He tried to call her, out of view of the Captain, but the network immediately informed him that her phone was switched off. "Otherwise, I suggest that you ask the Professor where she is."

The Captain looked carefully at George for a few moments. "I'm afraid that won't be possible, Mr Turner. You see, Professor Mamdouh al-Misri was murdered, late last night in his office at the museum. Your wife is missing, and until she is found she is our closest link to the killer."

George's two friends slid out of the room into the kitchen, leaving him alone.

He sank to the sofa and shook his head. The camera embedded into the video wall followed him.

"Mamdouh's dead?" he said in disbelief. "And there's no sign of Gail at all?" he asked more in the direction of the officer.

"I'm afraid not, Mr Turner," came the dispassionate reply. "I understand that this has come as quite a shock to you. To help in our investigation, I would appreciate it if you could try to remember any details about your conversation with your wife yesterday evening."

He shook his head. Now he was extremely concerned about Gail; she usually sent him numerous messages when she was away, to say goodnight, good morning, and to update him on anything interesting in between. His phone and video wall both told him she had done nothing of the sort since twelve hours earlier when she had landed in Cairo. The only other call he had received was from the man from the space agency.

"I had one other call last night," he started slowly. "A man called from the European Space Agency wanting to speak to her. I gave him the Professor's phone number and told him to call there."

The Egyptian didn't look surprised, but instead nodded his head approvingly. "A Mr Martín Antunez, I believe? Yes, he called the museum yesterday evening as you suggest. We found his details written on a note in the Professor's office." He was getting fidgety, as if he felt he would get no further and did not wish to divulge more about his case. "We have already spoken to him, Mr Turner. Anyway, I have sent you my business card, if anything else comes to you, or if you hear from your wife, then please let me know immediately."

He was about to reply when the screen went blank, replaced momentarily by the telephone company logo, which in turn was replaced by the placeholder reel of the video wall, a mountain slope overlooking a wide rain-swept valley through which a river wound its tumultuous path. He stared at the scene for several minutes before standing up and moving towards the kitchen.

Opening the door he interrupted his friends, their sudden silence betraying the subject of their conversation.

"Well?" the one who had slept in the bath said. The look on his face and rasping voice both suggested he had not slept very well. "Is she alright?"

He glanced at them both and reached for the percolator. Sensing its lack of heat, he poured a cup of the thin black liquid and placed it in the microwave. Removing it seconds later, he sipped the piping-hot coffee and looked at them both again.

"I don't know," he said. "But I'm going to Egypt to find out," he added resolutely.

He left the kitchen and his friends in silence as he returned to the video wall to book his flight.

CHAPTER 42

"You did not need to come to Egypt, Mr Turner," Captain Kamal repeated in an unfriendly tone. "Our investigations have been progressing well during the day; your presence is simply not required."

He seemed much smaller in person than on the video wall, which had the annoying tendency of making callers much larger than life. It could be quite intimidating at times, which was why George usually only made voice calls except when speaking to Gail. The added dimension of seeing any other caller was not something he saw much point in, though many people insisted on using the function – in particular for business or official calls.

Standing next to the diminutive officer, he couldn't help thinking that he looked like a much reduced version of Peter Sellers in the Pink Panther films. The fact that his accent was not dissimilar didn't help. Had the whole situation not been so serious and the man so unpleasant, George would have found him more than a bit comical.

"My wife has disappeared in your country, how could I not come here to help you find her?" he asked. "Speaking of which, are *you* any closer to finding her?"

"We will let you know as soon as we find her, Mr Turner. In the meantime, I suggest that you return to your hotel where we can easily find you, should that be necessary."

The Englishman left, albeit reluctantly, and Captain Kamal shook his head in disapproval. Police matters were not to be meddled with by members of the public, he firmly believed. Particularly not *this* police matter.

Why this Englishwoman was so important, he had no idea, but now he had a murder scene and an irate husband to deal with, it seemed that this was all going to be more trouble that it was worth.

A routine murder such as this would be over quickly enough. It was a high profile case, thanks to the murder-victim himself being such a high-profile member of the academic community, but that did not detract from his ultimate goal. Kamal was a focussed and experienced policeman, and he already had three of the four pieces of his murder puzzle handed to him on a plate.

The first piece was the victim: Professor Mamdouh al-Misri, of the Egyptian Museum of Cairo. An Egyptologist with a keen interest in Amarna texts, he had been the General Director of the Museum for nearly four years.

The second piece of the puzzle was the weapon: the sharp corner of the General Director's solid mahogany desk had broken the man's skull at his left temporal bone as he had fallen. This caused an internal haemorrhage that had placed pressure on his brain and killed him within minutes, the autopsy report told him.

The third piece was the motive: a collection of extremely rare texts, dating from the nineteenth and early twentieth centuries, were conspicuous by their absence from the General Director's office. On the black market, they would in total fetch upwards of three million dollars, and he had been reliably informed by other employees at the museum that there would be no lack of willing bidders.

Which left him with one final piece to find: the murderer.

There were three ways this could end. She *could* turn herself in, or be found by the police on the streets. He knew that wasn't going to happen, of course. Or she may never be found, instead disappearing into the ether, never to be seen again. In a city of thirty million people, who would question such an outcome?

But no, now Kamal had met the husband he knew that it wouldn't end that way. He knew people, and he had seen the look in the Englishman's eyes: he wouldn't let this go. If she wasn't found, he would be a thorn in his side.

Which only left one possible outcome: Cairo was a heaving great overweight animal of a city; and overweight animals can have very dirty underbellies. A pretty woman, alone on the streets late at night, on the run after committing a crime, would be simply asking for trouble.

All he needed was a body.

This is all more trouble than it's worth, he thought again as he put his phone to his ear and made all the necessary plans.

George almost ripped the pocket of his shirt as he dug frantically for his ringing phone. His heart sank as he saw the number wasn't Gail's; it was identified generically as *French mobile*.

"Yes?" he said impatiently. He'd been running this way and that for hours, desperately trying to get any scrap of information possible that would lead him to Gail.

"Is that Mr Turner?"

A foreign accent, but it didn't sound French, although George's knowledge of accents was limited to the same old films from which he had characterised the Egyptian policeman.

"Speaking," he said.

"My name is Martín Antunez, from the European Space Agency. I need to meet with you urgently," he continued.

George wasn't surprised at the name. He had expected another call from him sooner or later. "Hello Mr Antunez," he said, still struggling with the name, "I'm afraid I don't know where my wife is. Did you not speak to her last night?"

"No, I'm afraid not, I left a message with a man at the museum."

"Professor al-Misri? He's dead." George added. In his search for Gail he hadn't spent much time thinking about the Professor, and the fact stumbled out, emotionless.

"I heard that; the police told me this morning," he replied, slightly taken aback by the Englishman's bluntness. "Mr Turner, I know that your wife has disappeared, and I believe these circumstances are too coincidental not to be linked."

"What?" George was exasperated, tired of people trying to get hold of Gail, when all he wanted was to get hold of her himself. The last thing he needed was a riddle.

There was a pause, short enough for George not to have to check his phone's signal, but too long to be caused simply by the long distance call bouncing into space and back on its way from France.

"Mr Turner, a massive cover-up is underway at the moment, and what is happening on Mars is somehow linked to your wife, and the finds that she made in Egypt. The reason I needed to speak to her was to talk about this and see where it would lead. I am not the only one who believed that your wife has the answers, Mr Turner, and I am sure that she has been taken."

George bit his bottom lip. "Kidnapped?" The police had said nothing of kidnapping, in fact his impression had been that she was being treated as a suspect rather than as a victim. "Why do you think that? Who would do such a thing?"

KEYSTONE

"I don't want to say more over the phone, we have to meet."

CHAPTER 43

Café du Corail was a French-style affair that, like many in Cairo, harked of a different era. George imagined that it hadn't changed in a hundred years, and by the looks of it neither had its clientele.

Whilst a lot of Cairo seemed to be constantly re-modelling itself with building sites that never seemed to end, many of the older areas still remained.

The great marketplace of Khan el-Khalili was one of the most famous; a sprawling, maze-like network of narrow streets, the awnings of open shop-fronts reaching across the cobbled alleyways, drawing in endless streams of lobster-faced tourists with bum-bags. There, the bartering started three times higher than anywhere else, though few were tempted to shop around too much, lest the tour bus leave without them.

Café du Corail was *not* in Khan el-Khalili. It was on the other side of the busy main street via a dank-looking footbridge, away from the kitsch, in what the tourist-guides referred to as the *local market*. To say it had a different atmosphere was to take understatement to the extreme. It was practically impossible to walk in el-Khalili without being offered something, or if you were a woman, without being propositioned. *Here,* in contrast, if you didn't speak Arabic, or didn't know exactly what you wanted, it was surprisingly difficult to buy anything at all.

On the subject of price, all that needed to be said was that people bought in the local market, and sold on el-Khalili.

But the biggest difference, and the exact reason why George and Gail liked it so much, was that the local market was, indeed, where you found true Cairenes. El-Khalili had its charm, it was bright and colourful and full of happy smiling people who spoke English, Spanish and a dozen other tourist languages. But here, you were actually *in* Cairo, not in a tourist-sustained bubble.

To George, the Café now provided a quiet *shai* served without a smile by a man whose interpersonal skills extended only to waving the flies away from his face. A few minutes later a water-pipe, or shisha, was set down beside him, hot coals were placed above the tinfoil wrap on the top, and the long pipe hooked onto the little lid that covered it. A small plastic packet containing a single-use mouthpiece was placed on the table.

George sat just inside the entrance and waited. He had chosen the café as he was sure no tourists ever went there, and as such he was certain that it would be the last place anyone would look for an Englishman; Martín Antunez had been quite specific that secrecy was highly important.

However, his main reason for choosing the Café du Corail was that he always went there with Gail when they visited Egypt. If she *was* in trouble, she would see him there, he was sure of it.

"Mr Turner?"

He looked up and saw the man in the doorway; he looked exactly as he had imagined, with the exception that his skin was not pale as he expected a Frenchman's to be, but olive-brown instead. Even George would have admitted that he was handsome.

"Good afternoon," he stood up and offered his hand limply. He felt drained, both emotionally and physically.

It was eagerly accepted, and they both sat down at the round table. His guest eyed the tea, and George made a signal to the nonplussed waiter, who brought a second cup, along with a second mouthpiece for the shisha. Martín served himself from the small teapot.

"So you are Mr Antunez?" George said, looking at the man intently.

"Yes, please call me Martín."

"You don't sound French."

"I'm Spanish," he explained.

"And how do you know my wife?" Despite the civilised surroundings, he couldn't help but sound bitter and accusing.

"Mr Turner, I am on your side," Martín defended himself.

"I wasn't aware that there were *sides*?"

"I'm sorry, Mr Turner," he held up his hands. "I forget that while you are coming into this cold, I have already been involved in this for several months now."

George gave a short laugh. "You can say that again. *Cold* is definitely the word."

"I don't really know your wife; we met briefly many years ago at one of her lectures in London." He had a sincere tone that George found quite disarming, despite his bad mood. "I have not spoken to her since I asked her to sign a copy of her book." He placed the book on the table and offered the inscription on the inside of the cover as proof.

George looked at the inscription and recognised his wife's handwriting. It proved nothing; she had probably signed hundreds of books in the last few years. "Why are you looking for her now?"

"As I explained over the phone: because of the finds on Mars. I work for the European Space Agency. We released the pictures to the press."

"And you want to speak to my wife because the Mars finds are like those she found in Egypt, like all the other reporters. All you want is a statement, and when you couldn't find my wife, you thought you'd get hold of me instead. The scoop's almost as good, isn't it? *Egyptologist goes missing – husband has no idea?*" he said scornfully.

Martín shook his head fiercely. "No, I am not a reporter. I am a scientist. And I do not want a story, although I am sure my boss would." He added the last statement almost as an afterthought. "My Agency uncovered the images from Mars and released them to the press because someone involved in the Mars mission was covering them up. Without us, they would never have been seen. We believed that it would be important to speak with your wife to seek more information about the symbols, to understand how they came to be on Mars, to see if she could help unravel the mystery of why this is being covered up."

"Except you were too late?" George asked.

"Unfortunately, yes. It is reasonable to assume that whoever is responsible for the cover up would also want to stop anyone from contacting your wife, and would therefore seek to have her kidnapped."

"Or murdered," George said. The thought had crossed his mind a few times in the past day but he always pushed it away quickly. This time, he felt a huge weight descend on his stomach and his eyes dropped involuntarily.

"No, I don't think so, at least not yet," Martín reassured him. "She knows more about her field than anyone, I expect she is as useful to them as she would be to us."

The man's belief did little to settle him. "And who are these people who are supposed to have kidnapped my wife?"

"We don't know that much, but we do know that they are most

likely to be based in the United States. It's even possible, though I think highly improbable, that they are working from within NASA."

"You're saying NASA kidnapped my wife?" George said in disbelief.

"No, not at all. At the most they may be members of NASA who work for someone else also. NASA is as innocent as the other Space Agencies in this cover up."

George sat in silence for a while before letting out a long sigh.

He hadn't ordered the shisha, but neither had he had the energy nor presence of mind to refuse it. Maybe the owner had assumed from the look of him that he needed it. Now, he found himself unwrapping the mouthpiece and attaching it to the pipe. He looked at it vacantly for some time before lifting it to his lips and sucking on it tentatively, until the water bubbled gently and the glass chamber near his feet filled with thick white smoke. He then took a long, slow inhale, the satisfying crackle of the coals under the lid coming slightly before the thick, warm apple-smoke filled his mouth, throat and lungs. He exhaled slowly, pointing his nostrils towards the ceiling like a curious dragon.

It had been a hellish twenty-four hours. He'd spent the previous evening sick with worry in his hotel room, without a word from the police. In the morning, he'd visited Captain Kamal, who had done his best to outdo himself on the previous day's unpleasantness scale. The afternoon so far had been no better, and now this Spaniard was telling him his wife had been kidnapped by some unknown conspirators.

From what he understood, shisha was simply tobacco soaked in apple; there was nothing *druggy* about it. And yet it made him sink into his chair. Only the fact that he couldn't find Gail remained clear in his mind.

And here, he thought, *is a man who's trying to help find Gail.* He slipped his mouthpiece out and passed the pipe over. Martín accepted it nervously, fumbling the mouthpiece from its wrapper and taking a quick suck of the pipe. He didn't seem to enjoy it, and managed to hook it back on the shisha lid clumsily.

"Did you tell all this to the police?" George asked.

"Not the entire story, no," he said. "But I relayed my fears that many people may want to talk to your wife, and that she may have been taken. The Egyptian police officer seemed very interested in my theory."

At that moment George's phone rang, vibrating its way along the metal table. He picked it up, listened in silence for a long minute, then put it down gently. His fingers were like lead as they released the device and his hand slumped down on the table beside it. He felt his whole body sag like a wet teabag. He'd felt despondent before the shisha, numb during and now, after the call, he didn't know how he felt. Helpless, still. More numb.

Empty.

Now there was nothing. No shisha, no *shai*, no el-Khalili.

No kidnapping.

He closed his eyes and felt his bottom lip begin to tremble.

"Mr Turner?" Martín said, almost whispering.

No kidnapping.

He wanted to get up and leave, but his limbs were unresponsive, dead. He wanted to run, to jump back in time, to stop Gail, to call her, to hold her. To have anything but this.

He could vaguely sense the Spaniard touching his arm, looking at him, asking him something. It didn't matter anymore.

He knew where Gail was, now.

CHAPTER 44

Captain Kamal was waiting when he arrived at the police station in a daze. He didn't accept the Egyptian's outstretched hand and was quickly ushered into the building and immediately down a short flight of stairs.

"Thank you for coming," Kamal said gently.

His attitude was now entirely different, almost as if he felt sorry for the Englishman, possibly even slightly nervous.

George could barely bring himself to grunt unintelligibly in reply.

He was led past an open lift and through a long corridor flanked by half a dozen windowless doors on either side. The passage was well lit, leading to a set of hospital-style double-doors. George did not need to be able to understand the small sign in Arabic; a general sense of foreboding told him he was about to enter the station morgue.

Kamal held the left-hand door open and he walked in.

He stopped in his tracks as he laid eyes on the row of trolleys along one wall. About half were covered by thin sheets, and it was obvious to him that they concealed human bodies. Only one, at the far end of the room, was of a shape that could be his wife. With all his might he told himself that it couldn't possibly be Gail, but deep down inside an overpowering dread informed him that it could be no one but her. His wife was surely under that sheet, but if he didn't get any closer, it somehow made it less real.

Kamal had continued forward into the morgue, and was now standing beside the trolley. He looked back at George, waiting patiently for him to follow.

"Where did you find her?" he said without moving from the doorway. "Gail wouldn't have been far from the Museum or the Professor's house." His voice was monotonous, going through the motions, dodging the fact that lay ahead of him, cold.

"There is a series of canals running to the west of the city. Some are

219

but a trickle of water, as Cairo nowadays gets most of its supply from the purification plants to the north. The canal is used mostly by vagrants. We received an anonymous call some hours ago that a body had been found under a bridge." He looked down at the still-covered body between them. "It's a long way, but still within walking distance of the Museum, Mr Turner. We need you to officially identify the body."

George walked forwards slowly. As he approached the trolley, Captain Kamal gently peeled back the cover to reveal the black hair and white skin of a woman in her late thirties to early forties. Her skin was undamaged and had a frozen, plastic-like quality. Her eyes were closed, but as he looked down at her lifeless corpse, George imagined her looking back at him, her infectious smile lighting his life. What had previously been a weight on his stomach lurched uncontrollable, welling upwards, no longer held back. He stroked her hair, touched his cheek to hers, and as he held her lifeless body tight, wept.

His tears were confirmation enough for Captain Kamal, who after barely a minute moved him away from the table quickly and moved the sheet back across the woman's face.

"How?" George asked eventually, trying to control his voice. It seemed so wrong that Gail should be lying lifelessly in front of him. So wrong because she was such a good person, and could never hurt anyone herself. So wrong because he hadn't had the chance to say goodbye. So wrong because he loved her, because he lived to make her life perfect, and her death only meant that he had failed. Gail *couldn't* be dead.

Kamal hesitated. "It's not easy to explain, Mr Turner. I am very sorry for your loss."

George looked up at the officer. "How did it happen, Captain?" he asked more forcefully.

"She was stabbed several times in the lower abdomen with a knife, probably a switchblade. They are unfortunately very common in the city. We believe that she was robbed," he said.

"What was she doing in the canal in the first place? Why would she want to go anywhere near it?" George raised his voice. Everything seemed to be wrong. Gail was dead, and all because she was wandering around some silly canal? It didn't make sense to him.

"Your wife was found clutching several pages of torn paper." He looked nervously at the grief-stricken man before him. "The book they were ripped from was – and probably still is – extremely valuable. It was part of a collection of similar books that were taken from Professor al-Misri's office yesterday evening."

George felt the hairs rise on his forearms and on the back of his neck. He rose to his full height, towering over the policeman.

"There is no easy way to say this, Mr Turner. However we believe that your wife took these books from the Professor's office."

"Are you're suggesting that she killed him, too?" George challenged him.

"Your wife had a strong motive to take the books: her career was at risk and the books would have offered financial security. We cannot be certain at the moment that it was intentional, as he fell and hit his head on the side of his desk. However shortly after the incident CCTV footage shows your wife running from the museum holding the stolen items."

"You can actually see *Gail* doing that?"

"There were no other women in the museum that night, Mr Turner," he said. "We can only assume that she did not know where to go from there; she probably did not plan the crimes beforehand, and so simply ran in the approximate direction of the airport. She will have stumbled upon the canal around midnight, and been robbed herself shortly afterwards."

George couldn't believe what he was hearing. To find out that his wife had been murdered was bad enough, but to be told moments later that she had robbed and killed one of her closest friends and colleagues was simply ludicrous.

"Are you serious? No, it's not possible. None of what you're saying makes sense!"

The officer gave an uncomfortable smile and tilted his head sympathetically. "I'm afraid that we have all of the evidence we need, Mr Turner. Your identification of the corpse was the final detail, and as far as I am concerned the case is now closed. Of course, we are still looking for your wife's murderer, but that is being handled by a separate department, who have your contact details."

George's mind was a mess of grief, confusion and anger. He looked down at the now covered body of his wife, and then back at Kamal. The forced smile, a dismal attempt at sympathy, was still painted on the Egyptian's face, his head tilted in that patronising manner. His account of the incredible story had left George speechless; there was only one thing he could think to do.

He wasn't a violent man, by any means, but he felt a sudden surge of adrenaline as his fist hit the officer so hard on the chin that the small man literally spun round on his heels and fell over.

By the time Captain Kamal was back on his feet, nursing his chin, George Turner had already left the morgue, with the doors swinging closed behind him.

Kamal fished in his pocket for his phone and toyed with the sheet covering the body as he dialled a number with his free hand. As the phone rang, he pulled the sheet back to reveal the frozen face beneath. He shook his head to himself. Someone answered the phone.

"It's Captain Kamal. Mr Turner has just left."

A short pause.

"Yes, it's done."

He snapped the phone shut and tossed the sheet back over the face before marching quickly out of the morgue.

PART FIVE

16TH - 18TH NOVEMBER 2045

CHAPTER 45

G ail opened her eyes, but could see nothing. She blinked twice, each time chasing away an army of frenzied white dots, like TV static. The darkness in which she found herself was so complete that she had to work out if her eyes were open or not by mentally checking the position of her eyelids.

She blinked half a dozen more times, a reflex of her eyes trying to adjust to the total absence of light, then lifted a hand up to her face, but it was like moving through treacle; eventually her fingers reached her cheek and made their way numbly to her eyes. Her eyelashes brushing against her fingers told her that they were indeed open, and that there was nothing obstructing them.

Her second hand made its way towards the first and together she let them run over her face and body. To her relief, everything was there as it should have been.

Sensation, slowly, began returning and she started to feel a cold, hard surface against her back and head. She was lying down on what her palms told her was a flat, metallic material.

Gail swung her body weight over to the right, ending up on her hands and knees. She craned her neck upwards and peered into nothingness: *where am I?* she wondered.

Placing her hands palms-down, she shifted along the floor for several minutes, first in one direction, then in another, then back again, until she had returned to what her mental map told her was pretty much her starting point. There were no walls, no chairs or tables. No grooves in the floor and no grit or dirt. In her immediate environment, there was nothing.

Somehow her subconscious mind knew it would be pointless standing up in complete darkness, and so she didn't try.

She opened her mouth, but no words came. Closing it, she forced a gulp and tried again.

"Hello?" The word sounded muffled, as if by the darkness that surrounded her. "Hello?" This time she heard herself more clearly. She pushed away from the floor with her hands and rose to a kneeling position and shouted the word out: "HELLO!"

From the darkness, nothing replied.

"Where the hell am I?" she exclaimed.

She let herself fall back onto her bottom. *Where the hell am I?*

She thought back to the evening's events. She had been with the Professor in his office at the Museum; he had just finished telling her about the book. The book! She remembered now: he had lied to her about the Library at Amarna, about the book on the plinth. All these years, he had known the truth and yet he had never told her.

Aliens in Egypt! No wonder he had never said anything: his career would have been in ruins. If what he had told her was true, then everything she thought she knew about Amarna, Nefertiti and Akhenaten had to be false. She tried to imagine the pictures the Professor had described; of towering cities with flying cars. It was like something out of a science-fiction movie.

So how had she ended up here – wherever *here* was? She remembered that there had been a knock at the office door, and then – nothing.

She shook her head in frustration. How could she not remember more?

There was a knock at the door, and then – *the Professor had said something*. What had he said? And then the door had opened. After which she drew a blank. *Nothing*.

"Bloody hell!" she cursed herself for not knowing. "Professor!" she shouted, but there was no reply.

She suddenly remembered her husband. "George!" she exclaimed. She fished around in her pockets and was surprised to find her phone. As it flipped open, the light from the screen almost blinded her, and she blinked several times before she was comfortable with it.

There was no signal. Wherever she was, whoever had put her there, had either no concerns about her contacting the outside world, or they knew that she would not have a signal. To all intents and purposes, her phone was nothing more than a glorified pocket-watch.

She snapped the phone shut and was plunged into darkness again. She blinked several times and banished the static once more; each time her eyes closed she fancied she could still see the screen of the phone, shining brightly in the palm of her hand. Opening the phone again, she was once more bathed in its blue-grey light.

No more than a glorified pocket-watch, *or* a torch.

The phone pushed the darkness back at least three metres, whereupon it started losing intensity. Pointing the screen directly in front of her and at arm's reach, she studied the matt-grey floor. Shifting her body round, she noted its uniformity in all directions; it had seemed metallic to her touch, but she had never seen anything like it. Even the smoothest of floors always tended to have a joint, where two sheets or tiles would meet. Here, there was none of that. It was like a gymnasium floor, but more *perfect*.

Cautiously, she stood up, immediately increasing the draw distance of the light. The absence of any objects in her field of view meant there were also no shadows; judging distance was difficult, and the uniform floor didn't make it any easier.

Almost against her will, her left leg moved forward, followed soon after by her right. Before she could think, she was walking in a straight line, as if the act of standing up had given her purpose, direction.

"Hello?"

Still no response.

Her pace quickened, despite her limited visibility.

"Hello!"

Nothing.

She was almost running now, and still the perfect smooth floor spread out before her. Her voice boomed out into obscurity, again and again, and not one reply came back. In her mind, she knew that if the room she was in had walls, eventually her voice would hit one and return to her as an echo. And yet when she shouted there was no reverberation, as if the darkness was swallowing the sound waves whole.

Slowing to a walk, she stopped to catch her breath. Her phone told her she had been running for just under a minute, and moving forwards for a little over that. In over sixty seconds, she had seen nothing but the flat monotonous floor.

"How bloody big *is* this place?" she wondered out loud. "I mean, for crying out loud! I'm not exactly an Olympic champion, but in a minute I can run a good two hundred metres, easily!" She turned around, pointing the phone in all directions. "And for all I know I'm probably back where I bloody started."

She laughed. "And now I'm talking to myself: first sign of madness."

Exasperated, she dropped to her knees, before lying flat on her back, to stare up at the ceiling of obscurity that pressed down on her. Her phone snapped shut against her chest; its light extinguished, she lay in darkness once more, her eyes shut.

As her breathing evened out she became increasingly aware of a dull ringing in her ears; the kind of ringing that she remembered from years ago would assault her ear-drums after stepping out of a busy nightclub into an otherwise peaceful night-time street. She held her breath for a moment and concentrated on the noise, wishing it away with her mind. Instead, its intensity grew. Sticking her fingers in her ears, she scrunched up her face and begged the ringing to stop. It continued, louder than before, throbbing against the inside of her skull until it was all she could do to press her palms hard against her eyes, her fingers still pushed firmly inside her ears, hoping to force it back. The ringing was now so loud that she could not hear herself breathe.

Rolling onto her knees, she arched her back and pushed her chin upwards. She opened her mouth and felt the rush of air streaming from her windpipe as she screamed. The ringing was now so omnipresent that it drowned her cries before they had even left her throat.

Gail pulled her head down towards her knees and clasped her hands behind her neck, ripping tufts of her hair in the process.

"Stop it!" she moaned. "Stop it, please!"

The ringing persisted, louder than before, louder than any music she had ever heard, more piercing than the sirens of an ambulance. Managing to pull one hand from her head, she felt for the phone, but it wasn't in her pocket any more. With what little faculty still remained for thought, she realised that she had placed it on her chest when lying down. As she had rolled over, it must have fallen to the floor. In a panic, she groped around her with one hand. As she stretched her arm round behind her, her hand struck the phone and sent it flying. Spinning round, she brought her other hand down and scrambled in vain to find it.

"No!" she cried in anguish.

Emotionally exhausted, she didn't even bother bringing her hands up to protect her ears against the constant ringing. Her last drop of energy was used to punch the floor with both fists and shout out into oblivion: "I know! I know! Please stop it: I know!"

As the final word left her lips she collapsed against the floor. *Know what?* She thought briefly, but she was too tired to try and understand what she had said, and why. At the same time, the noise stopped, and the red glow through her closed eyelids told her that the darkness had been replaced by light.

CHAPTER 46

What was the exact opposite of complete and utter darkness? She wondered. *Complete and utter light?*

The last time she had tried to open her eyes, the receptors in her brain had been so confused by the absence of any light that they had forced her to try opening her eyes again, as if the human psyche was not capable of understanding such an environment. Even at night-time, there was always *some* light, some reflected glimmer with which the fully dilated pupil could function.

For some reason, she thought of bats, bouncing sound waves off obstacles and prey within a cave. *Blind as a bat*, the expression went, but even Gail knew that that was a fallacy: bats used sight for many things and rarely relied on sonar alone. She wondered if bat-like ability would have helped her to see earlier.

Earlier. The concept of time struck her suddenly, and her mind shot back to the dark room – could she be sure it was a room? – that she had been in before, and the bright screen of her mobile phone: *Thursday, November 16th 2045 – 2:05pm.* The time flashed repeatedly in her mind's eye, and as she held the thought it changed to *2:06pm.* Her attention moved to the date. *Thursday the 16th?* In a flash the phone display disappeared and she found herself back at Heathrow Airport, standing in front of the automated ticket assistant. She tapped the screen and was rewarded with a pre-punched card that fell from a slot beneath. The date on the boarding-chip jumped up at her: *Monday, November 13th 2045.*

She'd lost more than two entire days.

The Professor was standing beside her now, and she was at the entrance to the Library in Amarna. The hot winter sun bathed the archaeological excavation in bright warm light. Behind her she could feel the eyes of the other students burning into her back. *They must hate me for going in first*, she thought as she descended the steps cut into the bedrock. She ducked as the passageway swallowed her – *surely it's smaller than it used to be?*

From outside, she heard Ben's laugh, joined shortly after by her husband's. *George!* She turned to run back up to see him, but was met by a wall of darkness; the steps leading up were gone. She span round again in a panic, to find that the stairs leading down had also disappeared, replaced by the smooth sandstone of the Library floor.

She was now inside the Library, walking slowly past the rows of bookcases. On the end of each row the engraved symbol of the Stickman drew her eyes from the path ahead, until she had passed the final row and was standing in front of the stone plinth.

Behind it stood a man, shorter than her, and dressed in an off-white robe that fell from his shoulders down to his sandals. His wispy hair was thick with dust and sweat after a long day's work. He was looking at the plinth eagerly, his hands clasped in front of him as if in prayer.

Gail stopped.

"Who are you?" she heard herself say. The sound of her voice surprised her; although she knew what she had wanted to ask, she hadn't spoken in English.

The man behind the plinth looked at her, puzzled. He was about to hazard an answer when she spoke again.

"What is going on?" Still the words were not English, although for some reason she understood them all.

"I am showing you the plinth, where the books will be placed," he said nervously.

Ancient Egyptian, she realised with a start. *But what a strange accent?* The man's hands un-clasped and demonstrated the stone surface in front of him. It was unremarkable, but he seemed proud, as if it was exactly what had been ordered.

"What books?" she asked.

"The book of Aniquilus, and the book of Xynutians," he replied tentatively under the interrogation.

Her ears prickled as the sentence reached them. *Aniquilus* and *Xynutians.* His accent was softer than she had imagined an Egyptian's would be, and she wondered if she had misunderstood the words.

"An-ee-qwe-lous?" She broke the word down into phonemes; she'd worry about writing it later.

The man shifted uneasily. He looked like he was running over the question and its possible answers in his head before offering an answer, like a chess player would mull over possible moves to avoid falling prey to a dangerous rook. After a while, he pointed to the bookcase behind her and repeated the word.

She followed his trembling finger to the edge of the bookcase, where she found the symbol of the Stickman. Looking from the nervous man to the symbol etched into the wood and back again, her eyes widened.

"Aniquilus?" she gasped. *So the Stickman was 'Aniquilus'!*

At this the man looked positively frightened, as if what he thought to be Aniquilus had in fact turned out to be something entirely different, and his engravings inside the Library had all been wrong. Gail reacted quickly, sensing her control over the small man.

"Aniquilus!" she repeated more authoritatively, confirming that the Stickman was indeed known by that name.

A smile broke out on his face as he started breathing once more. "Yes!" he said, bringing his hands together in front of his chest again.

She walked back towards the plinth and looked at it. There were no books on it now. This reminded her of the shelves she had just been looking at; twisting her head round, she noticed that they, too, were empty. She looked at the small man, who avoided her gaze as if his life depended on it.

"And Xy-New-Shuns?" Again, she pronounced it slowly, emphasising each phoneme. In her mind, there was no question that it had to be a person. *"Who* is Xy-New-Shuns?"

"What do you mean?" he replied. His nervousness had returned, and he held his hands together so tightly she could see his knuckles go white.

"Who is Xy-New-Shuns?" She repeated, saying each word individually, in case she had mispronounced them the first time. As she repeated the question she actually saw a bead of sweat run down his forehead, from his hair to the bridge of his nose. He looked left and right, as if trying to spot an escape route, his shadow dancing against the wall of the Library in the flickering light of an oil lamp next to the plinth.

Finding no way to avoid the question, and having exhausted all possible alternative responses in his mind beforehand, he turned his eyes solemnly to the floor and raised his arm. He was pointing straight over her left shoulder.

She turned on her heel, but just as she did the Library disappeared, and she slipped once more into darkness.

CHAPTER 47

D r Patterson entered the Administrator's office, leaving the door
wide open behind him.

"She's been unconscious for almost twenty-four hours now," he
said angrily. "What did your man *Walker* give her?" He stood boldly in
front of the desk with his legs uncharacteristically apart. Realising this,
he shuffled his left leg slightly closer to the other and regained some of
his more reserved self.

Seth Mallus turned round in his chair to face him. "Nothing that will
harm her, Henry. Simply a facilitator for sleep." He stood up and
walked to the video wall dressed as a window. Reaching behind a blind
to the left-hand side of it, he switched it off. "She was very reluctant to
go with Walker, aggressive even. The drug was to protect her, more
than anything else." He ushered Patterson out into the corridor, and
then followed him. "Which is also why she has been restrained," he
continued.

"To stop her hurting anyone?" Patterson asked bitterly.

"You are cynical. To stop her hurting *herself*," he corrected.

Still walking along the same corridor, they arrived at a long window
on their left. Patterson stopped and gestured to the small room beyond
the glass.

"Is *this* really necessary?"

In the middle of the small room was a single hospital bed in which
Gail lay, fast asleep. Nonetheless, thick restraints wrapped round her
body and limbs and held her to the mattress. Set into the headrest of
the bed was a small computer screen, on which a line made its way
from left to right, jerking rhythmically to the woman's pulse. Apart
from this and a small bedside table, the room was bare and sterile.

Mallus nodded slowly. "You seem genuinely upset. And yet Dr Gail
Turner was brought here on your request."

"I did not request her specifically, and I wouldn't have requested anyone had I realised it would have been against their free will!" he retorted.

"I think that you may be forgetting yourself, Doctor," Mallus warned sternly. "Dr Turner will be awake within the hour, sometime after which I will arrange for her to join you in your office." He didn't leave much room for argument, but just as Patterson was about to reply, he continued, more softly. "We would not normally have gone through this process, as you can see for yourself from the perfectly normal way in which I recruited you. However I know you understand that the situation, despite our best efforts, was beyond our control."

Patterson said nothing, but dipped his chin almost imperceptibly.

"Good," he said. "Because together, and with her help, we *have* to find out what Aniquilus is."

CHAPTER 48

Gail awoke, opening her eyes slowly, tentatively, like a child who dare not peek at what was under the Christmas tree for fear that it may all disappear without warning.

Please, not another dream.

The past few hours, days, maybe even weeks, had been the strangest of her life, notwithstanding the fantasy of youth, where as a small person barely four feet high you could walk in a land of giants, dragons and adventure every day.

What the hell? The fact that she was even thinking of dragons and giants raised fears that she was again dreaming, and that she had not woken up after all. Widening her eyes she let the bright white light of her surroundings flood her pupils, which shrank to the size of pin heads as a result. She forced her eyelids to stay open against their will for as long as possible, until eventually they snapped shut and opened again, less wide this time, like the shutter of a high-speed camera.

Instead of bright-white light, she saw a bright-white wall directly in front of her.

"Hello!" she shouted. Immediately, the pressure in her inner ears reported back to her the fact that she was lying on her back. The wall in front of her had to be the ceiling. *This is good*, she thought. The fact that she heard herself perfectly, and understood what she was saying, had to be good. The fact that her sight and ears were now working together as a team, giving her balance and a sense of direction, was even better. *I am awake.* Within milliseconds of this realisation, Gail decided to get up and see where she was.

She struggled with her arms and legs, even wriggling her whole body, for several minutes before admitting defeat. She tried to lift her head but couldn't. Peering along her nose and over her outstretched body, she understood why: thick belts were wrapped around her. She counted at least ten, tightly hugging her body and limbs which underneath were covered by a thin white sheet. Beyond her two wriggling feet, she could see the end of the bed, white-painted metal, with what looked like a flip-chart attached to it. Apart from that, her field of vision was clear – the room seemed empty. To her right, she could just see the top of a door and a window frame, but it was either night time or it was an internal window, because the only light she could see came from two long strips in the ceiling.

Gail had never stayed in hospital herself, but knew exactly what a hospital bed looked like. From what she saw at the foot of the bed, this was definitely one of those. The last time she had seen one had been when she had visited a friend after an operation. The doctors had said that they had got to her appendix just in time, and that another day without surgery may have been fatal. She could still remember the big grin on her face as they had told her she would have to take two weeks off school.

But her friend hadn't been strapped to her bed. Simply thinking about her restriction made her develop an itch in the small of her back. Shortly after that, the back of her left knee started tickling, followed quickly by the sole of her right foot.

Within a minute, she was in mental anguish, writhing within her restraints, trying in vain to rub some cover or strap against the numerous itches that seemed to have attacked from nowhere and everywhere all at once. Arching her back, she pushed her chest tightly against the straps. Lifting herself half an inch from the mattress behind her, she involuntarily let out a long, pained moan. It was quickly followed by a more verbal complaint.

Then, she started screaming her head off; putting to full use the only part of her that had not been restrained.

All of a sudden she heard the door to her right open. A man in a white coat entered and stood at the end of the bed. She looked at him and abruptly stopped screaming, although she consciously kept a few choice words at the ready.

"You're awake," he said, matter-of-factly, as if his job was to go into rooms and make comments on such things.

She hadn't expected him to say that, and had to make a few quick changes to her pre-chosen expletives. Nonetheless, her reply brought a touch of pink to the pale white cheeks of the young man.

"It's good to see that you are feeling better, Dr Turner," he replied, ignoring her verbal assault. "You certainly *look* much better than yesterday."

American, she thought to herself. *Or possibly Canadian?* She widened the scope, not confident enough in her ability to distinguish between the accents of the two countries. He unclipped the flip-chart from the bottom of the bed and looked beyond her towards the bed's headrest. She tried to tilt her head back to see what he was looking at, but gave up quickly, deciding it was probably some kind of medical monitoring equipment.

"I'll let the kitchen know you're able to eat again." He turned and walked towards the door, taking the chart with him.

"Wait!" she exploded, following him with her eyes. "Wait!" It was painful to look down and to the right without being able to move her head, but she forced herself. "How long have I been here? Where am I?"

He stopped and went to the side of the bed. He was now looking down on her face. It was a more comfortable position for her eyes, but with his head silhouetted against the bright light from the ceiling, she felt far less at ease. She was suddenly much more aware of her own helplessness and vulnerability.

"Where am I?" she asked again, this time less defiantly.

He smiled widely, displaying almost all of his perfectly straight, peroxide-white teeth. "You're not in Kansas anymore," he grinned, as if sharing a private joke with her.

What the hell was that supposed to mean? She'd never been to Kansas before anyway, so did he mean to say that since meeting with the Professor she'd been there, *too?* And where did that leave her now?

The man saw the confusion on her face and frowned briefly. "You're like Dorothy, see?" He could see she didn't. "Yellow brick road? Toto? The Munchkins?" After each question he paused eagerly, as if they all held the key to his secret code. "Aw, Jesus," he rolled his eyes. "Have you never seen the Wizard of Oz?"

How could she shake her head with it strapped down? Instead she curled her bottom lip out slightly – which she managed to accompany with a half shrug despite the restraints.

"Really old movie, before World War II," he offered.

"*Before* World War II? You expect me to know quotes from a film that's over a hundred years old?" she laughed bitterly. "Where am I?" she snapped.

His grin faded. "You're in Florida. Flo-ri-da." He broke the word down into syllables slowly, as if her not knowing the Wizard of Oz made it likely that she wouldn't know what *that* was, either. "In the US."

Again he turned and left, but no matter how much she shouted, this time he didn't come back. Instead, the door closed behind him and she found herself alone.

She was still strapped to the bed, and she was supposedly in Florida, and not Egypt. But no matter how strange or unlikely all that seemed she now knew for sure that she wasn't dreaming anymore.

Now she remembered what the Professor had told her in his office in Cairo: *Dr Henry Patterson*. And she also remembered where that Patterson worked: *near Tampa, Florida*. This could only mean that Patterson knew that the Professor had told her, or was going to tell her, the truth about the Amarna books, and was now seeking to 'buy' her silence as well; by abducting her and strapping her to a bed! She gritted her teeth and pulled against her restraints with added passion.

Gail couldn't wait to meet Dr Henry Patterson.

CHAPTER 49

Cairo buzzed and hummed liked a beehive. Cars streamed constantly through the wide avenues, motorcycles flying between them, weaving their ways this way and that with effortless skill. On the pavements pedestrians swarmed, busy with their daily chores, idle gossip and sightseeing. The tourists were easy to tell apart from the locals, and as George made his way calmly across the road with the hundred or so people he had been waiting with for the little green man, he liked to think that he looked more like one of the locals.

For one thing, he didn't have a camera grafted to his hand; most of what was worth photographing in Cairo was already on his computer. And for another, he wasn't wearing insanely conspicuous khaki shorts, shirt and sandals. He shook his head in amusement at the group of visitors in front of him; probably their thinking had been that to visit Egypt, land of the pharaohs, you had to dress like an explorer. To him it was even funnier because that was exactly what the Spaniard Martín had been wearing, and it was exactly what he had been wearing on his first visit to the country, all those years ago. In Egypt, it stood out like a Hawaiian shirt at a wedding.

After crossing the road, he took a left turn and headed down a narrow alley, away from the main flow of the tourist crowd which was probably heading towards the walled compound of Old Cairo.

"*Assif!*" he said as he brushed past a man on a bicycle. George had managed to memorise a few words of Arabic, which he found added to his casual jeans and t-shirt in distancing him from the tourists. He was still unmistakably foreign – his pale skin soon went lobster-red in the sun.

He turned a corner and stopped in front of a small metal gate. He hovered his index finger over the column of buzzers. None were marked, and he suddenly realised that he couldn't for the life of him remember which one he'd pressed on his last visit, a couple of years earlier: too much had happened since then. Each of the ten floors had two buttons, a total of eighteen flats, as the first floor was for maintenance and storage. He finally pressed the left button of the seventh floor; he knew it was at least a couple from the top; seven sounded about right. After a short pause, a man's voice came from the small speaker. George didn't understand any of it.

"*Ma esmouk Ben?*" he said tentatively. He didn't know how to say *Is that Ben*, and *what is your name Ben* was the closest he could come up with.

The reply came thick and fast. *Obviously not, then*, he thought pressing the next one down after a garbled apology.

"*Ma esmouk Ben?*" he repeated his question as the second person answered.

"*La!*"

"*Hal tatakallum Inglesi?*" he stumbled around the sentence. That was it, pretty much the end of his Arabic phrases: it was always suitable to end with *Do you speak English*. There was a shout from the speaker and the man laughed.

"Siix tooo, not waan; tooo," came the heavily accented reply.

"*Shukran!*" *Six-2*, he thought. Even if he'd remembered that, without labels on the buttons it wouldn't have helped him: he had no idea, in a country that spoke Arabic, if 2 would have been the button on the left, or on the right.

He pressed the only other button on the sixth row.

"Ben!" he exclaimed with relief as the familiar voice answered.

"Ha! George, yes it's me! Come up!" Ben sounded ecstatic, and quickly buzzed him through the iron gate.

George remembered that the last time he had visited, the lift had been out of order; Gail and he had stood in it with the door open for a couple of minutes before one of Ben's neighbours had walked past, laughing. This time, however, it seemed to be working, and the door slid closed silently. The lift's soft female voice said something in Arabic as he pressed for the sixth floor.

At their first meeting ten years earlier, Ben and George had immediately clicked. His sense of humour matched George's perfectly, and whilst there were a few years between them, they shared similar hobbies, namely sport, television and computers. Archaeology, it had turned out, wasn't one of Ben's strong points anyway.

Over the years, they had seen each other dozens of times. Ben even visited them in England and worked for a year in London, during which time his English had been perfected, which was more than George could say about his Arabic.

But this time was very different; George had never been to see Ben in Cairo *without Gail*.

When the lift door opened again, he was met by Ben's familiar grin and wide open arms.

"George!" he exclaimed. "It's been a long time!"

"A year or two," George agreed. Instead of a hug, Ben clasped George's outstretched hand, shaking it vigorously while at the same time gripping his shoulder. No matter how good friends they were, it always took George a moment to adjust to his enthusiasm.

"Sorry I missed your calls," he said, leading him towards the door of his flat. "How are things? Did you just get here?"

George hesitated. As soon as he'd been told to go back to his hotel by Captain Kamal of the Cairo police, he had tried to call Ben. Unfortunately, there had been no response on the landline, and either Ben had changed his mobile number or it was turned off in a drawer somewhere.

Since then, he had tried once more, the previous evening, again with no success. It had been on his third attempt, leaving the café that morning, that Ben had picked up. In the briefest of conversations, they had agreed to meet at Ben's flat later that morning.

"Actually, I landed on Tuesday."

Ben stopped in his tracks. "*I* landed? Have you been married that long that you forgot your beautiful wife at home, George?" Ben was grinning, but his eyes betrayed genuine concern. "Where is Gail?"

George had honestly thought that they would have at least made it inside Ben's home before the question came out. As it was, despite several days adjusting to Gail's death, he hadn't fully prepared himself for telling someone face-to-face about it. Telling his parents via the videophone had been hard enough, but somehow this was different. His bottom lip started to quiver and he fought to control it.

"George, what's wrong?" he asked, the long pause too much for him. Before waiting for an answer, he pushed the door to his flat open and ushered his friend through. Closing the door behind them, he took George to the living-room and sat him on a long, black-leather sofa before repeating his question.

In front of the sofa, a large flat-screen television showed four different feeds simultaneously. Ben reached for the remote and turned the screen off.

Apart from the noise of Cairo, which still managed to filter through the closed windows, and the low hum of the air conditioning unit, silence descended on the room. "George, what's wrong?" Ben asked again.

"Gail came here on Monday," he began. It wouldn't be so hard if he just told the story as it was; simply a series of facts. "She came to visit the Professor, because of the finding of the Stickman on Mars." Ben's eyes lit up at this. He was going to interrupt when George asked: "I take it you know about the Professor?"

"How could I not," he gestured towards the television. "Apparently he was murdered by some petty thief on Monday. I kind of assumed that was why you came: to pay your respects." He lifted his head suddenly. "And Gail? If she went to see him on Monday, was she hurt, too? Is she alright?"

The emotional nosedive that George had been in since seeing Gail's body three days earlier had pretty much levelled out. From having been told that his wife was missing, to being confronted by the unwelcome news that she was dead, and then being informed by the police that not only was she the only suspect in the murder of the Professor but that her motive was the theft of a few books, he thought he had reached the end of the week with fairly thick skin. He had even managed to discuss funeral arrangements with Captain Kamal as if the punch in the face had never happened, and had looked into transporting Gail's urn on his return flight. But now he realised that he had not yet fully opened up to anyone; the only person in whom he could normally confide was now gone, and he was a widower.

She was dead.

He was as low as he could get. Meeting face to face with a common friend, someone he had met with Gail and who had only known them as a couple, made it painfully obvious that a large part of him was missing. And now he had to tell this friend that Gail was dead, and that according to the police, she murdered the Professor, another common, if not so close, friend. He looked at Ben and tried to speak, but his lips and throat were too dry for the words to slide out, so instead he croaked.

As if reading his mind, Ben got up and returned seconds later with a glass of ice-cold water. He sat down again sombrely. "She was there, wasn't she?" he asked. "She was with the Professor?"

George gulped down a mouthful of the water and nodded. It was easier like this, he thought briefly; easier for Ben to guess than for him to say the words.

"Was she hurt also?"

He nodded again.

"Is she alright?"

He shook his head slowly; tears welled up in his eyes. He'd shed so many over the last few days; quiet, private tears. But now they were building up in front of Ben, he tried to fight the urge to cry.

This was no easier than just coming out with it. So he told Ben everything. He told him about Gail's cold body in the morgue, about how he'd punched a captain of Cairo's police force on the chin, and about the alleged theft of books from the Professor's office. He told him about the Amarna stickman on Mars, about how it had upset Gail, and how the Professor had asked her to come to Cairo as soon as possible to discuss it.

And he told him about Martín Antunez, the Spanish ESA employee who had been trying to get hold of Gail on Monday, and who on Wednesday had met George in Cairo and had been with him ever since. He even mentioned Martín's short-lived abduction theory. He finished repeating himself, going over in disbelief his identification of Gail's body, and how he had punched Captain Kamal in the head.

When he'd finished he felt drained, his soul empty like a reservoir after the breaking of a dam. He'd let his tears come out in floods, without holding back, for the first time since Gail's death. He could easily have felt quite foolish at his emotional outbreak. Instead, he simply didn't care; what had to come out had come out, and he sat limply on the sofa.

Ben sat rigidly next to him, stunned by the barrage of unwelcome news. After a while, George blew his nose with a tissue from a box that Ben had passed to him sub-consciously during his outburst. As if waking him from his trance, Ben looked up with a look not just of sadness but also bewilderment.

George looked at his friend as he finished wiping his nose.

"What?" he asked, querying Ben's puzzled look.

"George. I am devastated by this news, but I'm also confused. This policeman said Gail murdered the Professor?"

George hesitated. "Yes."

Ben raised both eyebrows and looked to his feet. "I cannot believe that the Gail I know would kill anyone, let alone the Professor, to steal a few books, no matter how valuable." He shook his head slowly. "There is more to this story, George, I am sure of it."

George didn't know what to make of Ben's reaction. What had he expected? Tears, screams, breaking down and beating the floor with his fists? He didn't know, but he was sure it wasn't this. "What are you trying to say?" he said quietly.

"I'm sorry, I know this isn't what you need to hear," Ben said. "But there are parts of your story that don't add up. Firstly, was Gail so upset by the news of the Amarna stickman that she was concerned about your financial security?" George shook his head. "And assuming that she was worried about money, and *did* steal the books, why would she then run across town with them under her arm, aimlessly? Why didn't she get a Taxi? There are hundreds of Taxis on those streets."

"Because she panicked?" George suggested.

"How spontaneous is Gail?" Ben asked. He almost corrected the tense of the verb, but quickly dismissed the thought.

George shrugged. "Sometimes, very. That's why we got to Egypt in the first place."

"But only after she'd been thinking about what to do for her dissertation for several months!" Ben countered. "The Gail I know is very deliberate."

At this, George had to agree.

"Let's ignore the Professor's murder. I am certain Gail would not do that. Let's also ignore the theft. I can't see a reason for it, nor any capability in Gail to go through with something like that. The last part is her running from the Museum, and ending up in a canal, having run *away* from the airport. Imagine for some crazy reason she can't find a taxi. She gets lost. The navigation on her phone is broken. Don't you think she might have called you?"

"Yes," he admitted. He remembered checking his phone on Tuesday morning, and there had been no missed calls. He had been having a bit of a get together with some friends on Monday evening, but he hadn't drunk much; he would have realised if the phone had rung. "She didn't try to call me at all after meeting the Professor."

"And accepting that she did steal the books, and that she did run away randomly, isn't it convenient that she is then robbed herself, and a body is found clutching pages torn from those very books during the struggle?" He stopped suddenly. "I'm sorry, George, I'm getting carried away. This isn't what you need hear."

George, however, continued where his friend had left off. "It does sound a bit convenient, doesn't it? And Kamal seemed only too eager to take it all for face value; he didn't seem interested in there being any alternative explanation."

"And then there is the strangest fact of all," Ben said, encouraged by George's involvement in the debate.

"What?" he asked.

"That the Professor had to speak to Gail in person urgently, and that this Spanish guy, Martín, also needed to speak to her in person. It seems to me this guy was right, and that lots of people wanted to talk to Gail." He looked at George. "He thinks that she was abducted, tells the policeman, and then all of a sudden they find her body, with evidence to prove she murdered the Professor. There are maybe thirty *million* people in Cairo, George. Hundreds of people go missing every day, and no-one even notices. Most bodies aren't even found. And yet Gail's turns up so easily?"

They sat contemplating the facts for about five minutes before Ben broke the silence with a curt laugh. "I can't believe you punched a policeman. And a Captain at that!"

"It was something about the look on his face: so bloody satisfied, so content that he'd rounded up his case." George explained. "I just couldn't help myself. I've never even hit anyone before!"

Ben shook his head as he tried to imagine the scene in the morgue. "So, what did he do?"

"Nothing."

"Surely you got fined, at least, for hitting a police officer? I would imagine that, given your circumstances, and the fact that you are foreign, a simple fine would be enough. Don't tell me you got more than that?"

"Nothing at all," George said quietly. "Not even a mention. I didn't even apologise when I next spoke to him. He was so smug and disrespectful; it's lucky I guess that I only punched him once."

Ben looked at his friend in utter astonishment. "George, I have worked with the police. I have many friends who are still in the police. In Egypt you don't simply punch a policeman and walk away. It doesn't matter if your whole family has just been murdered. It just doesn't happen."

"Well," George shrugged, "it did."

"Then that is, you could say, the *clincher*. The only possible explanation for Kamal not charging you for your offence is that he would rather take that than have more enquiries into the case. He was probably relieved that it was all over; he had Gail's body, and he closed his case. Your punch was like a full stop and he left it at that."

George dried the last of his tears from his face. He felt a new emotion rising in the pit of his stomach; he felt the unmistakable heat of anger rising; anger that there may have been more to the story than he had already been told; anger at Kamal for not doing his job properly, or for doing it *too well*. Mostly, he felt angry with himself for not questioning it more, for letting Kamal get away with this. For failing Gail.

Ben looked at him, his face grim. "Don't worry, George. I'll join you and Martín for lunch, but before that, I am going to make a call."

CHAPTER 50

Gail eyed this new man suspiciously as he entered the room. With his bald head, neatly-trimmed facial hair and thin-rimmed glasses, he looked every bit the James Bond villain. All he needed, she thought, was a white cat to complete the image.

So you're Patterson.

He arrived at the foot of her bed and looked down at what she could only assume was her chart. From the way she was feeling, she guessed the arrow was pointing up: she was now able to move her head from side to side, even though the restraints stopped her from lifting it. He met her gaze briefly before pulling a chair up and sitting down beside the bed. He *was* within spitting distance.

She spat.

Without a word, he wiped his face with a towel taken from the bedside-cabinet, before cleaning his glasses methodically. Replacing them on his nose, he pulled a notepad out of his lab-coat pocket and jotted a few lines down.

Gail laughed out loud. "*Subject spits!*" she mocked.

He turned the notebook round and showed her what he had written.

Don't say anything. I'm sorry for all this. I'm going to do my best to get you out of here.

She looked into his eyes and recognised genuine remorse. Though her blood continued to simmer nonetheless, she bit her tongue. There were so many words she had been playing with in her mind; snappy retorts, sarcastic comments, obscenities. Time had been against her in that respect. Had Patterson walked in an hour or two earlier, while the rage was still burning behind her teeth, he would have been confronted by a verbal barrage as soon as he had entered the room. But through the time lying restrained on her bed, she had whittled away the options, removed all the obscenities and sarcasm. Eliminated dark humour. She was a prisoner, held against her will and drugged-up to boot. There was only one thing she wanted to say.

"Let. Me. Go."

Patterson nodded. After a brief pause, he leant forward and carefully unbuckled her head restraint. One by one he continued to remove the straps that held her down, until she was free.

As the final strap fell clear, Gail fancied she was floating above the bed, as if the will she had been held against was stronger than gravity itself. She felt her body moving up, and wondered at how easily she could lift herself, before realising that Patterson was using the controls of the hospital bed. She was now fully upright, and the sudden return of gravity to her stomach awoke a feeling she had not experienced for an age.

"You must be hungry," he guessed.

She hesitated slightly before nodding. She thought of flight, but she was barely dressed and didn't even know what was out there. There would be, she hoped, better opportunities. And anyway, Patterson appeared to be on her side; maybe she had been wrong about him.

He started to leave, but she called out to him.

"Where's Mamdouh? Where's the Professor?" Her last memory: a knock at the door, Mamdouh had just told her his story, and then she remembered nothing, except for a series of strange and extremely vivid nightmares. "Is he here too?"

Patterson stopped dead, but didn't turn to look back. He stood there for what seemed like an age. "Professor Mamdouh was an old friend of mine."

"*Was?*"

"I understand that there was unfortunately an accident, and he didn't make it."

She froze. "What?"

He tried to explain what had happened, though in truth he barely understood it himself. All he could think was that rather than being collateral damage, the Professor had been silenced. *Seth Mallus finishing off the cover-up he started ten years ago*, he thought. Halfway through his explanations, the *Wizard of Oz* man came back, holding a tray of food.

Dr Patterson thanked him and put the food on a table next to the bed. She barely looked at it, or the other man.

"Mamdouh's dead and I'm being held prisoner because of that

book?" Gail asked, angrily.

He looked at her apologetically. "I'm as upset as you are about what happened to him, Dr Turner. And please, call me Henry."

It didn't matter how nice he was trying to come across, she refused. "I'm being as civil as I can. For all I know you're only being nice to me so that I'll cooperate more readily."

"I had no idea you would be forced to come here, and I have no intention of helping anyone *force* you to cooperate," he said. "But you're right, I do need your help, and even if I had wanted to force you to *come* here, I would want you from now on to cooperate of your own free will."

"What kind of psychological battle are you playing with me?" she exclaimed. "Abducting me, drugging me, then pretending that somehow you're not at all involved in anything that's happened to me? Are you the *Good Cop*?"

He motioned for her to talk less loudly.

"And who the *hell* is the *Bad Cop*?"

"You'll find out in a moment, we're going to see him after you've finished eating."

She looked down at the tray; roast meat and vegetables and some kind of fluorescent dessert. She pushed the table away and it glided softly on its wheels to the foot of her bed

"I've finished eating," she glared defiantly.

Henry Patterson liked Gail Turner; it was something about her defiance. It was ironic that he be attracted to a woman for her attitude, when it was exactly that trait that would make most men think twice.

And attracted he was, from her long dark hair and full lips down to her cute southern English accent that made her pronounce all of her Ts perfectly. He had been smitten before they had met, too, having done a fair bit of research on her profile online since Mallus had advised she would be joining him.

So when he had seen her restrained and drugged in the facility in which he worked, an urge to protect her had overwhelmed him, and even made him have a direct confrontation with Mallus, something he would have been far more cautious about had he been in complete control of his emotions.

It was towards Seth Mallus' office that they now walked. Somehow, despite the fact that he was walking ahead of her, Gail was setting the pace and they moved briskly down the long bleach white corridor. They walked in silence, mainly because Gail didn't seem to want to talk to him, but also because he didn't know what to say to her anyway.

He stopped in front of an inauspicious door set flush with the wall. She positioned herself so that she was standing next to him in front of the door. He caught the look in her eyes, decided against saying anything, then knocked.

"Come in," came the muffled reply from within.

He let Gail enter, though he somehow felt that even if he had moved first she would still have entered before him.

"Ah! Dr Gail Turner!" he heard Mallus say with glee.

"*Ah! Dr Gail Turner* my arse," she exclaimed angrily. "Where the hell am I, who the bloody hell are you and what the bloody hell do you want with me?"

Henry Patterson couldn't resist a wry smile as he closed the door behind them, if not for the vehemence of her assault on the mighty Mallus, then purely for the way that she pronounced *arse*.

CHAPTER 51

B en hadn't liked Captain Kamal from the moment George had described him. It wasn't because he was a policeman: some of his best friends were. It was simply a gut feeling that something was wrong with the situation surrounding Gail's death and that of the Professor.

Kamal had been quick to put forward an unquestionable explanation of the events, which made him suspicious. It also struck him as being odd that he hadn't heard anything about Gail's death in the news. He hadn't even known that there had been another death in Professor Mamdouh al-Misri's murder case!

His first step, however, was not finding out what was being covered up, it was confirming for sure that there was a cover up in the first place. He may have had a gut feeling, but if he was wrong, then he wanted to get that out of the way now so that he, and in particular George, could mourn in peace.

"*Salaam*," he said as the phone answered. "May I speak with Captain Kamal please? It's Farid Limam, from the British Embassy." There was a pause, a brief click and then ringing. He was being put straight through.

Ben loved his country. He was extremely proud to be Egyptian and to come from Egypt, with its vast cultural heritage spanning more than seven thousand years. Coming to his country was, for many, the trip of a lifetime, and an unattainable dream holiday to so many more. There were so many reasons to be a proud Egyptian.

But being Egyptian, Ben was not blind to corruption; for so long it had run so deep it was next to impossible to eradicate.

For the most part, he could understand it. Tourism Police, underpaid, looking for extra money to feed their families by taking people on unofficial 'tours' of areas normally closed to the public; hotels in cahoots with taxi drivers to artificially increase fares from the airport; tour guides charging a hundred times the going rate to take tourists to see pyramids, claiming that taxis are simply too 'dangerous.'

That didn't *really* harm anyone: people needed to make a living somehow, and if you'd travelled halfway round the world to see Egypt, you could probably afford it.

The problem with corruption was that once you accepted it, there was pretty much no stopping it. Embezzlement of funds, rigged elections and conflicts of interest were all commonplace in Egyptian politics. *Everyone* had their price.

That fact notwithstanding, it was no less true that in Egypt bribery and corruption of a member of the police force, especially a Captain of the Cairo Police Department, was illegal. Under recent laws aimed at trying to reduce bribery and corruption, there was technically no cap on what punishment could be levelled by the State if someone was found guilty. More importantly, while in the past there was a tendency to focus on all parties involved, which led to few denouncements, new guidelines were to focus on the corrupt official first and foremost.

Ben knew this. Captain Kamal would too.

"*Salaam,*" Kamal answered the phone.

"Captain Kamal, it's Farid Limam here, from the British Embassy. I work with the Consul on legal situations involving British Citizens in Egypt."

"Yes? How can I help?" Kamal sounded impatient already.

"I have had some concerns brought to me from a British Citizen in Cairo currently. His wife was murdered several days ago, you will certainly remember the case."

"Gail Turner."

"Indeed," Ben paused briefly and shuffled a pile of letters and utility bills on his coffee table. *Office paperwork*, he thought as he flicked through the paper noisily. "There seem to be some irregularities concerning the findings of your case, for instance –"

"What are you talking about?" Kamal interrupted. "This was an open and shut case. Mrs Turner murdered Professor al-Misri, one of Egypt's pre-eminent Egyptologists. If she had not been found dead, she would be facing a possible death sentence, British Citizen or not."

Ben cleared his throat. "Forgive me, Captain, but Mr Turner has highlighted to us some facts that lead us to question this. For instance, she was found in the canals to the west of the city, correct?"

"Yes."

"And you have reason to believe that she ran there from the

Museum after killing the Professor, with a clutch of books?"

"Yes. We have this on CCTV footage."

"How many books were stolen, Captain?"

There was a brief pause. "Eleven. Among them some of the most valuable prints in the Museum."

"And how far, if I may, is the canal her body was found in from the Museum?"

"Roughly two kilometres."

"She ran the whole way? With eleven books in her arms?"

A sigh from Kamal. "She ran at least several hundred metres. We have this on three different cameras outside the Museum."

"Ran?"

"At quite some speed, in fact."

"Filmed at night?"

"It is most certainly her. The cameras are the highest possible quality with night vision: they protect the Egyptian Museum, Mr... Limam is it?"

Ben had his tablet computer open in front of him. "Mr Limam, indeed. Captain Kamal, I do appreciate your assistance in this. Please appreciate that I have a British Citizen here who is quite distressed by what has happened."

"I understand," Kamal softened slightly. "Is there anything else?"

"Well, Captain, there is. You see Mr Turner has a problem with your assessment that Mrs Turner ran nearly two kilometres with eleven books under her arm. I'm afraid I also find it hard to believe."

"She can easily have taken a taxi once out of view of the Museum. Because of the number of un-licenced vehicles operating in Cairo, as I'm sure you are aware, there is simply no way of knowing if that occurred."

"But even, Captain, several hundred yards seems unlikely."

Kamal clicked his tongue. "Now, why exactly would that be unlikely?"

Ben looked at his tablet computer closely. "Because, Captain, Mrs Turner always travelled by Taxi, from door to door. She practically never walked on the open streets in her home town in the United Kingdom, let alone in Cairo."

"On this occasion, she did."

"Captain, I must insist that this was *not* possible."

Kamal's tone had now changed from mildly annoyed to angry. He wanted this conversation over. "Listen, Mr Limam, unless you have some kind of proof that I haven't seen, in which case I recommend you disclose that information now, you are wasting Police time. That is, I remind you, also an offence."

Ben looked up at George and grinned. They'd discussed at length what Ben would say, and how he would try to 'rattle' the Captain into a reaction. They could claim they had CCTV footage of their own, or that they had found voicemail recordings that Gail had left for George while on the run from the Professor's *real* killers.

In the end, all of this sounded too complicated; too likely to be brushed aside by Kamal. He wasn't going to be caught out by some detail like that without seeing or hearing the evidence himself. Instead, they had to demonstrate that his only piece of real evidence, the CCTV footage, was incorrect.

And to do that, Ben came up with a big, fat, incredible lie, which itself was backed up by a quick Wikipedia update to Dr Gail Turner's personal profile article that Ben and George had just made.

If Kamal was hiding nothing, the CCTV footage was genuine and Gail had, unbelievable as it seemed, committed the crimes, then they had lost nothing; Ben had masked his outgoing number on his mobile phone, which in any event was Pay as you Go and could easily be thrown away: they would never trace the call to him.

If, however, Kamal was hiding something and the CCTV footage was in any way fake, then he was sure to find that out.

"Captain Kamal, Mrs Turner *could not* have run from the Museum, for at least a few hundred metres, turned a corner, and continued to run. With or without the books, it would simply be impossible."

"I'm getting tired of this. Explain yourself now, or stop wasting my _"

"Because," Ben cut him off, "Mrs Turner suffered from Usher syndrome."

Kamal said nothing. Ben looked at George intently and continued. "She was born with the condition, which also affected her mother. It means that she had hearing problems, and in the past five years, her sight had deteriorated to the extent that she simply couldn't see further than her hand in front of her face. Even then, she wouldn't have been able to make out the individual fingers, no matter how close. Vision, to Mrs Turner, was simply varying shades of light with no definition whatsoever."

"It's entirely possible she knew the direction of the main road, and ran there," Kamal suggested, though he sounded less confident than before. His bullish attitude had disappeared completely.

"The hearing problems that come with Usher syndrome affect the inner ear, Captain. Mrs Turner had severe problems with balance. She would have needed both arms to steady herself and even then, by Mr Turner's account, she would not have been able to negotiate the corridors of the Museum without sometimes touching the walls and railings. This would have been quite impossible while at the same time carrying eleven books, no matter how much they meant to her, financially."

Kamal, again, was silent.

"Captain? I recommend that we meet to discuss this. Mr Turner is, as I said, incredibly distressed. He has sought legal counsel with the Embassy, which we have agreed to provide."

"Why didn't Mr Turner advise me of Mrs Turner's condition?" Kamal said quietly.

"Because in his own words, he didn't trust you, Captain. From the start you had your own conclusions regarding this case, and you followed those conclusions through with complete disregard for anything he said. You made him feel that he was an *inconvenience* to you." Ben wet his lips and smiled at George. It had all gone better than he had possibly hoped, and he was about to deliver what he considered to be his killer line. "Captain, I have to say that with the evidence I've seen, and your behaviour on this call, *I* do not trust you either."

There was silence on the other end of the phone.

"Captain Kamal?"

After what seemed an age, there was the softest of clicks, followed by a dead tone.

Kamal had not simply been rattled. He had not simply stumbled over a few words. He had been so completely taken by Ben's charade that he had *gone*.

CHAPTER 52

"If Gail didn't steal the books, then she must have been set up," Martín said, setting his knife and fork down on his half-empty plate.

Ben found himself nodding. George simply sat there, looking blankly into space.

"We know that someone is trying to cover up the finds on Mars, and it looks as if they are trying to cover up the finds on Earth too," he continued. "Which means that someone must have known about them, before they were discovered."

Again, Ben found himself nodding. "Which means they must have known about what was on Mars before the mission was sent. But if they worked this out based on the Amarna finds, then Gail would have known about it too." *Which explains why the Professor and Gail are both dead*, he thought.

"But why hide proof of extra-terrestrial life?" George said, breaking his silence. "And even if Gail and the Professor had managed to prove it from the Amarna finds, then so what? The news had already reached the media anyway! That's why she was here in the first place!"

Before either of them could answer, he continued.

"I'll tell you why: because it's not proof of alien life that's being covered up; it's something else. Something bigger. Maybe the Professor knew something, maybe he didn't. But whoever killed them wasn't taking any chances either way," he slammed his fist on the table. Behind them a waiter shot them a disapproving glance.

"What could be bigger than aliens?" Martín and Ben said in unison.

George looked at them both with fire in his eyes. "I don't know, but it killed my wife, and when I find out what it is, I'm going to make sure that somebody pays for that."

Captain Kamal scratched his head and switched off the screen on his desk. There were no two ways around it: Gail Turner just wasn't going to go away as he'd hoped.

At first, he had been concerned that the lack of a body would make her husband a constant pain, a thorn in his side. *Then*, he had been delivered a 'body'.

Back in the morgue, as he'd lifted the sheet that covered her, his heart had skipped a beat. She hadn't looked dead to him. Motionless, yes. But dead? He just had to hope that her husband didn't notice. He'd covered her up as quickly as possible, feeling the game was up, but Mr Turner hadn't suspected a thing, even after being so close to her, *touching* her. If anything, the punch in the face for his lack of compassion had been welcome when compared to the alternative.

And so she had been taken away, and Kamal had staged the cremation of some poor nameless beggar who'd been stabbed in a back alley. Mr Turner had spoken with him briefly the next day to arrange transportation of the ashes back to England, and that had been that.

"*Khara!*" he picked up his terminal's keyboard and slammed it back down on the desk. "*Ibin himaar!*"

Because *that* hadn't been *that* at all. What he'd been promised would be straight forward was now turning out to be anything but. And the worst part was that it wasn't Mr Turner, or indeed anyone else, who had made things difficult.

He only had himself to blame. *He* had been left to cover the details of her 'escape' from the Museum. As far as he knew, she was in perfect physical health. He'd requested the doctored CCTV footage, and hours later it had been delivered to him. Watching it back, he even fancied, for a moment, that it was *her* running from the Museum, and not some computer generated model. It was, he knew, indistinguishable from real life. Even a trained expert couldn't tell it was a fake. He knew, because he'd given it to one in his own department.

Usher syndrome!

How could he not have known, when it was even on her online profile page?

He leant back in his uncomfortable chair and looked at the ceiling. He followed a small crack from where it started next to a hanging light all the way across to where it met the wall. The crack had been repaired barely five years ago. And yet there it was again, as large as ever. Possibly even bigger. It had probably been repaired five years before that, too. He snorted in mild amusement, though it was far from funny.

Even if he managed to get out of his present situation, even if the powers that be accepted the CCTV footage over her husband's testimony and her medical records, five years from now would some crucial piece of evidence be uncovered that would make the string of lies unravel? Would his best efforts barely cover things up, leaving the truth just under the surface, ready for someone to find? Would Mr Turner give it up? What would *he* do if he were in his place?

How long would it be before more people started poking their noses into the investigation? Into his *affairs*?

There was only one certainty: whoever was behind it all wouldn't be there to protect him. He would be on his own. He already *was* on his own.

It hadn't, he decided, been worth it at all.

George stuffed his wash bag into his suitcase and grimaced as he forced the zip shut. Behind him, Ben looked out of the window and shook his head.

"Martín seems to be an OK person. I think he is as genuinely bemused as we are."

George threw his suitcase to the floor and gave the bathroom a quick scan. Satisfied he had gathered everything, he returned to the main room and checked under the bed; socks had a nasty habit of rolling under beds, as he knew from his travelling for work. It was more a force of habit than anything else, though, as socks couldn't be further from his mind.

"But with all this talk of cover ups, I don't know where to begin," Ben continued. "And in any case, it doesn't really help, does it?"

George got to his feet and checked the cupboard for suits, despite the fact that he hadn't brought any suits to Cairo.

"It's actually a shame Martín has to leave so soon. I have enough space in my flat for both of you. We could lock heads and give this some serious thought." He looked at the Englishman, who was now checking every drawer of a chest of drawers he had obviously not used either during his stay. "Besides which, I owe you a drink from last time you were here."

George stopped and looked at him. Last time they'd been in Egypt, he had been with Gail, and they had gotten obscenely drunk in a bar. George knew his friend well enough to understand he didn't lack tact; he knew what he was trying to do. He forced a smile and nodded slowly.

"I'll stay a while," was all he managed to say. Being in Egypt brought back painful memories, but he was dreading returning to their empty house in Southampton even more.

Ben was about to answer when there was a knock at the door.

"Martín?" he asked George.

George looked puzzled. "It shouldn't be, his flight is in an hour, he'll be late if he's still here!" He walked over to the door and opened it.

To his total surprise, Captain Kamal stood in front of him. Looking nervously left and right down the hotel corridors, he forced his way into the room.

"Sorry, Mr Turner," he said in his strongly accented English. "Please close the door." As he said this he closed the door himself, leaving George standing in the entrance with his hand clasping an imaginary door handle.

"What do you want, Captain Kamal?" George said, deliberately saying the Captain's name to identify him, to warn Ben not to speak. If he recognised his voice, who knew what might happen next.

Ben looked startled, but then surprised George completely with a voice he'd never heard before. Heavily accented, he somehow didn't even sound Egyptian. "*Salaam*, Captain. My name is Ahmed Mohammed Naser. I am a family friend of the Mr Turner."

They shook hands, Kamal somewhat reluctantly.

"Mr Turner will be staying with my family for some time while Mrs Turner's murder is investigated. It is much, much, cheaper than the hotel for such a long stay," he smiled weakly.

Kamal pushed past Ben and pulled a chair out from under a small round table in front of the window. Sitting down, he leant forward and placed his elbows on his legs, clasping his hands out in front of him.

"We need to talk," he said, matter-of-factly.

George hesitated. "The Embassy have advised me not to without them being present," he said, thinking on his feet. He and Ben simply hadn't thought of what would happen if they came face to face with Kamal. They hadn't thought that far ahead.

"That's not why I am here," Kamal brushed the matter aside with the back of his left hand and put his right hand inside his pocket. Fishing out a packet of cigarettes he lit one and offered the pack around.

George thought to mention that the hotel, unlike most of Cairo, was non-smoking. He managed to bite his lip instead.

Kamal put the pack of cigarettes back in his pocket and looked around for an ashtray. Ben saw an empty glass beside the bed, but didn't move to pick it up. Following his eyes, Kamal reached for the glass and tapped his cigarette into it anxiously.

"Why are you here then, Captain?" George asked.

Kamal flicked his eyes between the two men before taking a deep drag. "Because I have something very important to tell you, Mr Turner." As he spoke he exhaled, and the thick, pungent smoke filled the room. "Alone," he stared up at Ben.

Ben was about to protest; the last thing he wanted was to leave his friend with this corrupt, possibly dangerous man. But George raised his hand to stop him.

He hesitated, trying to remember the name Ben had made up for himself. *Abdul?* He decided to play it safe. "It doesn't matter if he leaves or not, whatever you tell me, I'll tell him anyway."

Kamal seemed to weigh the options up for a moment, and then shrugged impassively.

"Those aren't your wife's ashes," he said bluntly, nodding towards the urn standing on a desk behind Ben.

George jumped and took a step towards the policeman. "What do you mean they're not Gail's ashes? Where are Gail's ashes?"

"There aren't any. There are no ashes of your wife."

"But I was at the cremation! I was given the urn containing her ashes! How can you dare come here and tell me that this isn't my wife?" George was within a couple of feet of where Kamal was sitting, and the policeman instinctively leant back to defend himself.

"I'm sorry Mr Turner, I really am, but it's true." There was genuine remorse in his voice, and George eased his stance briefly.

"So why are there no ashes of my wife? Who screwed up? The crematorium? You?"

Kamal looked into George's eyes. "There are no ashes of your wife, Mr Turner, because as far as I know she isn't dead."

CHAPTER 53

I'm sorry, Dr Turner, I understand why you would be upset with the way you have been treated," Seth Mallus said. Before she had a chance to respond, he continued. "Dr Patterson has been tasked with making you feel as welcome and as comfortable as possible during your stay."

"Let me speak to my husband," she demanded.

"In due course."

"No!" she shouted, slamming her hand on his desk. "How dare you treat me this way? You abducted me, you murdered a peaceful man, and now I demand to be set free."

He hesitated slightly. "Dr Turner, imagine that what you say is true. Imagine that I did murder a man, and that I did abduct you. That being the case, what sort of position do you think you are in where you can suddenly make demands of me, and expect to get your way?"

"I –" she began, but didn't know how to finish.

"Good. Now I *would* like to spend the next few days gently easing you into your new role, which by the way is of assistant to Dr Henry Patterson, whom you have already met."

"Assistant in *what*?" she demanded.

Mallus looked at her impatiently. "As I said; I *would* ease you in to your role slowly, but unfortunately we simply don't have time. And to be perfectly honest after so many years waiting for Dr Patterson to do this on his own before he asked for help, I don't have the patience either."

Gail looked at Patterson, who looked away uneasily.

"So I'll be quite frank, give you the briefest of briefs, and then it's up to you to decide if you wish to cooperate or not." He leaned forwards and raised an eyebrow. "You may have guessed this already, but *not* cooperating is something I have contingency plans for. Now, I don't like being interrupted, which is something you seem to be in constant threat of doing, so this is your opportunity. Speak."

She stared at him for a moment. He hadn't really given her much of a choice, she conceded. "No," she said bluntly. "*You* speak."

He smiled, as if her attitude was something he'd been expecting. *Feisty*, he thought.

"We need your assistance, and we need you to be able to concentrate fully on what we are doing here. What I am about to disclose is knowledge shared by only a handful of people, all of them within this facility. Its implications are so huge that it cannot be made public. The societal impact of this would be catastrophic." He gestured for Gail and Patterson to be seated.

Her temper simmering, Gail didn't question him, but simply sat down and waited for him to continue. "Some time ago, a discovery was made at an archaeological dig in Amarna, in Egypt. You know it well, Dr Turner, as you made that discovery. By now, I believe you know that the book you focused your attention on was not the only important book in the Amarna Library. Indeed, another book was brought to this facility under a shroud of secrecy." With this he tapped the surface of his desk and the wall lit up behind him with a very high resolution photograph.

Gail instantly knew what she was looking at: the man holding a staff aloft, embossed on the wooden cover of an ancient book. She couldn't help being taken aback; having it described second-hand by Professor al-Misri was no substitute for the real thing, or at the very least a *picture* of the real thing.

"Dr Turner, you devoted your career to studying the *Book of Aniquilus*, what *you* call the *Stickman Book*. What you see behind me is the –"

"*Book of Xynutians*," she interrupted him.

For the briefest of moments, Mallus faltered. He glanced across at Patterson, who looked back, equally as confused. "Indeed, the Xynutians. But how did you know? None of your work indicates that you knew this."

Gail pulled her eyes away from the picture on the wall and looked at the man behind his desk. *I've thrown him* she thought triumphantly. *But how could her dream have told her such a thing?* It took her little time to work out the most likely answer, that when she had been unconscious someone, probably Patterson, must have mentioned the name. Her subconscious mind, still somehow aware of the world around her, incorporated the detail into a vivid dream that was a mishmash of fragments of memory. But she wasn't going to reveal such logic to the man sitting in front of her. "I just knew; I must have read it somewhere. I've never seen it before, but it's been described to me by Professor al-Misri."

"It doesn't really matter how you know," he said dismissively. "But you are correct. The Book of Aniquilus and the Book of Xynutians: two books sealed in the Amarna Library deep underground thousands of years ago. You have studied the former intimately for years, but have never seen the latter. You will shortly get that opportunity, but first I have to fill in some gaps for you, to help you understand how important this is.

"We knew that the books were hidden at Amarna before Professor al-Misri started his dig. In fact, I had been closely monitoring all archaeological excavations in the area before your dig even started. But knowing there are ancient texts hidden in Egypt is like knowing water is wet. Our knowledge was a little more informed: we knew of the existence of the books of Aniquilus and Xynutians, as when they were entombed thousands of years ago, the architect who designed the Library was free to go his own way. At the time, Egypt was in the middle of a short-lived religious revolution. The time of Akhetaten was almost over, and the capital was abandoned within a decade."

"Spare me the history lesson," Gail sneered.

"Indeed, I'm sure you know all this better than I. Nevertheless, please indulge me a little more. Soon, Akhenaten passed away, followed by Nefertiti. The capital was a ghost town, and looting was rife. As you know some of the most prolific looters in ancient Egypt were probably the workers themselves. The very people who created the supposedly hidden and impenetrable tombs knew exactly where they were, and precisely how to get in.

"The Amarna architect however had been a strong believer in the ways of Akhenaten and Nefertiti, and believed that the message sealed in the Library was too important to be lost to thieves, who would throw texts aside in their search for gems, gold and other precious metals that could be hammered flat and resold. Yet he also believed that the message was too valuable to be sealed away forever. Unfortunately for us, whilst he was a competent architect, he was not a great story-teller. The text he left behind, inscribed on a papyrus scroll, only gave the briefest of descriptions of the two important books, and a vague allusion to their location. It did, however, offer some insight into the architecture of the Library, and what he had done to keep its location secret.

"The architect's scroll was found inside a sealed jar in 2015, during some road works just north of Dendera. An art dealer bought the jar from the site foreman; he didn't even want to know what was inside. You will know better than me the dangers of 'rescue archaeology:' a lot of the time, you people are only brought in if the construction company aren't able to hide or destroy the finds first. Of course, in Egypt no groundwork can be undertaken without the presence of an archaeologist. But Egypt is a big country, and there just aren't enough archaeologists. Not only that, but the Egyptians were still getting over a change of regime, and archaeology was lower on the agenda than fixing roads. The scroll was never missed.

"It then came to me by way of a business partner. I made my fortune in nanotech back in the late twenties, and this person had just acquired the jar. He found the scroll inside, itself sealed inside a tube, and realising he couldn't open it was looking for a buyer."

The image of the Book of Xynutians on-screen was replaced with a picture of the scroll. Gail immediately recognised the hieratic text. A stylised, cursive form of hieroglyphs, hieratic looked like a cross between hieroglyphs and modern Arabic. Another similarity with Arabic was that it always read from right to left. Two colours had been used in the text: ochre-red and black. The quality of the papyrus was excellent, and she was amazed at how complete it looked. It would have taken pride of place in any public museum, even in Egypt where such things were so much more common.

"I'm glad you like it," Mallus said. "A couple of years passed with it sitting in storage before I got the chance to try and open the scroll. If I knew what the text was about, you see, I might be able to make more of a profit. And so when I bumped into Dr Patterson during a science convention in Boston, we found we had this mutual interest. His equipment at Harvard helped open the scroll, and as it unfurled so too did the story of our architect."

"So that's how you knew about the texts; fine." Gail interjected. "But while the books and this scroll are priceless to *me*, that value is academic. Even on the black market no one would pay enough to warrant you going to all this trouble."

"Not everyone values life to the same extent, Dr Turner. But anyway, you're right, of course: the books are worth a great deal of money, but it's the message they contain which is their true value. The Book of Aniquilus is like a Bible for the Aten. As you know, it gives clear guidelines on how life should be lived in order to achieve so-called 'celestial magnificence.' But the Book of Xynutians is entirely different. It tells a story of a cataclysm so immense it wiped out an entire civilisation, the same race of Xynutians that you see on the cover of the book. It tells of their ascent to power, and then of their demise. Can you imagine, Dr Turner, such a technologically advanced race, wiped out?"

"I find it difficult enough to accept they existed in the first place, let alone their being wiped out," she said sarcastically.

Until now, Patterson had been quiet. He took this opportunity to cut in.

"I think I felt the same way, Dr Turner, until I saw the book for the first time."

She turned to him. "Then show me the book. Hell, why not show the whole world the book? I'm not stopping you."

"Unfortunately, it's not that simple. This book would cause a major issue in the public domain. You don't appreciate how much: these books are proof of intelligent life pre-dating our own by hundreds of thousands of years. It may seem trivial, but such a thing would turn religion on its head. It de-centralises man's understanding of his position in the Universe."

She sighed. "So you're saying that all this needs to stay hush-hush because you're worried that if it gets out, there'll be trouble?"

"Not quite. Within this story of their destruction comes a clear warning: what happened to them will happen again, to us. We need your help to decipher the last pieces of text that Patterson has been struggling with, so that we can avoid that fate." He seemed almost nervous as he said this, and he looked away from them both, towards the hieroglyphs on the screen.

Patterson cleared his throat. "The Book of Xynutians was written under instruction from Nefertiti. It recounts the fall of the Xynutians more than two hundred and fifty *thousand* years earlier. It claims that the final coming of Nefertiti will signal the beginning of the next cataclysm. The problem is that according to the statement in the book, the final coming of Nefertiti occurred nearly forty years ago."

Gail sat back and looked at them both. Patterson had seemed nice enough, but he also appeared to be as passionate about this story as Seth Mallus, who in every way was coming across as completely insane.

She looked at her options carefully; on the one hand, she could protest, demand to be freed, make a nuisance of herself, and then probably end up dead like Mamdouh. On the other hand, she could cooperate for the time being, play their little game, and wait patiently for her chance to escape.

That option made the most sense to her now. And in any case, she would be lying if she said she wasn't eager to get her hands on the book that had been snatched from under her nose back in Egypt all those years ago.

"Fine," she said. "I'll help you finish interpreting the Book of Xynutians."

CHAPTER 54

"Ridiculous," she muttered as Henry Patterson sat down beside her in what she had been told was her 'room', but which to her only represented her prison cell. "Absolutely absurd. For a start, how would the Egyptians have known anything about these people?"

"Xynutians," Patterson added helpfully.

"Whatever! This so-called *intelligent race* with such advanced technology conveniently leaves no trace at all of its existence. All we're left with is a picture book written long after they were wiped out. *Xynutians* indeed! You'll be telling me Star Trek is a fly-on-the-wall documentary next!" She shook her head and pushed his folder of notes back towards his side of the desk.

Pushing the folder back, he selected one scanned page from the Book of Xynutians. "Look at the detail, Dr Turner," he pointed to a vehicle. "Look at the back: it has what look to be exhaust pipes. Look at the driver: he's holding a joy stick. How can the ancient Egyptians have even imagined such things? They must be based on something!"

"Why? Why must everything have a meaning? Isn't it possible they knew about steam power? That the person who drew this understood what could be done with steam, like the ancient Greek Hero Engine, and that any vehicle propelled in this way would need to expel steam? Isn't it just obvious that in a forward moving vehicle the exhaust goes at the back, so you can see where you're going?"

"I agree in principle, but the Hero engine wouldn't be invented for another twelve hundred years after this book was buried deep underground. And in the case of Hero, it's thought his invention was simply an object of fascination. This picture shows actual *vehicles* being propelled."

"So the Egyptians thought differently. And besides, what does it prove? I've seen films where spaceships battle it out using lasers and death rays. If some other civilisation discover those same films in a hundred thousand years, do they have to assume we actually *had* that technology?"

Patterson sighed. "So you think this is a work of Egyptian science fiction? That the writer was the Asimov of his time?"

"Maybe!"

"What other examples of ancient science fiction are you aware of?"

"How the hell should I know? It's not exactly my domain!"

He flipped through the pages until he arrived at a long manuscript. There were no Egyptian symbols or pictures to be seen. "This story tells of a trip to the Moon, and of a battle between the king of the Sun and the king of the Moon, involving many types of creature, including ants thousands of feet long."

She looked at the text briefly. "So?"

"It was written in the second century AD by Lucian, a Syrian philosopher," he said dramatically. "You're right to question the veracity of the Book of Xynutians, in the same way you would be right to assume that Lucian didn't really sail to the Moon. But the difference is that no one takes Lucian seriously, partly because of his own disclaimer, but also because his story is obviously fake. The hallmark of ancient fiction is exaggeration. It wasn't a lion, because that's too easy to defeat: it was a lion with wings. Or a woman who turned you to stone on sight whose hair was actually made of dozens of snakes. It's not a trip to the Moon, it's a trip to the Moon in a sailing ship after a two hundred mile journey into the sky on the uplift of a tornado. It's clearly imagination.

"The Book of Xynutians has no flaws. No over-enthusiasm on the part of the author. It simply displays a believable advanced civilisation before and after a major cataclysm. And it only requires you to make one leap of faith."

"Which is?"

"That somehow, the ancient Egyptians had an intimate knowledge of something that happened two hundred and fifty thousand years before their time."

Gail scoffed. "That's one hell of a leap of faith. How do you make it believable?"

"Word of mouth?"

"Nonsense! If it was word of mouth, two things would have happened: firstly, the same story would have made its way all over the world, as populations migrated for tens of thousands of years before settling down. We'd get a similar legend in Peru, China, Europe, Siberia, India, Egypt and sub-Saharan Africa. Yet I have never before heard of such a civilisation. Secondly, by the time the story was written down, it would contain embellishment, bits added by the story tellers over the years as they add their own twist to make it their own. You would end up with exactly the kind of exaggerated story you're telling me this isn't."

"Maybe the Egyptians copied the text from something they found?"

"So they found something then hid it again? And since then we've found nothing? Why?" She couldn't feel more negative towards the whole concept.

"Then maybe someone told the story to Nefertiti first-hand."

Gail was about to reply when suddenly something clicked in the back of her mind, like the latch of a door that hadn't quite been pulled-to properly. A faint but recent memory started to surface. Within seconds, she was back in the Library in Amarna, looking at herself talking to the architect. He was pointing to the plinth. She was back in the dream she had experienced while drugged-up and strapped-down to her hospital bed.

"Dr Turner?" It was the first of Patterson's suggestions she had not refuted immediately, and he leant forward eagerly.

She remembered the architect, pointing to the symbol of Aniquilus. He had then pointed to something behind her when she had asked who 'Xynutians' was. She had turned, and then darkness overcame her. Had she caught a fleeting glimpse of the Xynutian behind her?

If Nefertiti recounted the book of Xynutians to the Egyptian scribes, could a Xynutian have told it to *her* directly?

She shook her head: she'd already managed to convince herself that she knew the words 'Xynutian' and 'Aniquilus' from Patterson: somehow he'd probably said the words while she was in a semi-conscious state, and she'd incorporated them into her dream.

So the dream meant nothing. It was simply a dream.

And yet…

She was there against her own free will, but she was not obliged to let them know what she was thinking. She'd keep playing along, waiting for her chance. In the meantime, she needed to have a closer look at the Xynutians.

"Give that here," she said angrily, picking up the folder and standing up. "I need peace and quiet, access to the original text and whatever translations you've already made. And a cup of tea."

CHAPTER 55

Ben and George stared at Captain Kamal in stunned silence for what seemed an age, during which time Kamal, oddly, seemed to relax a little into his chair. Ben was masquerading as Ahmed Mohammed Nasser, a role he was pulling off perfectly.

"What do you mean she isn't dead?" George said, his voice like a whisper.

"You have given me more trouble than I expected, Mr Turner. However, I only have myself to blame. I only hope that in some way the truth does set me free." His eyes moved left and right, as if checking there was nobody in the room that shouldn't be, before leaning forward. "I don't know everything, but I do know enough to have not been able to sleep for the past week," he started.

"I hope you don't expect me to feel sorry for you," George snapped.

"Let me tell you the facts as I know them," Kamal tried to calm him down. "Firstly, your wife was indeed in Professor al-Misri's office the night of his murder, but what I did not tell you is that they were not alone. Approximately twenty minutes after your wife arrived, they were joined by at least two men, and a fight broke out.

"The Professor slipped during a struggle and cracked his skull on the corner of his desk. Gail was alive when she was taken away by the men. Half an hour after this incident, I was contacted by an agency I had never heard of and informed that Dr Gail Turner, whom I had also never heard of, had just murdered Professor Mamdouh al-Misri. I was told to build my case as usual but that the conclusion would be the one that I told you. Some evidence, such as the CCTV footage, would be faked to allow me to make that conclusion.

"They left me a contact mailbox which would allow me to get hold of them indirectly if required. I didn't expect to need to do that, but on meeting you I quickly realised that you would not sit by idly. So I contacted them, and they wrapped the whole thing up. Dr Turner's body would be delivered to the morgue ready for you to identify. Only instead of her dead body, it was your *live* wife; she must have been given some sort of drug that made her appear dead."

"Wait a second," George interrupted. "They told you all of this? They told you that Gail didn't murder the Professor, but was kidnapped instead? They told you that the body I identified wasn't actually a *body*?"

"No, not at all. They told me that I had to lead an investigation that would be solved for me, they told me what to say, but they didn't say anything about your wife being alive, or about what happened in Professor al-Misri's office."

George scoffed. "So how do you know all this?"

"Because I have been investigating crime scenes for many years, Mr Turner, and even though I was unable to publicly announce my findings in this case, you don't just turn off your ability to find evidence, no matter what the price."

"So you were bought?"

"Not so much bought as persuaded. I really had no choice."

Ben wondered what kind of leverage it had taken to buy Kamal; family? Promotion? Whatever the price, it had obviously been eating away at his conscience to the extent that he was willing to throw that away for the sake of the truth.

"How about my wife? How do you know she was alive when I identified her?"

Kamal looked George in the eyes. "How many dead people have you seen, Mr Turner? How many dead people have you stood next to and touched?" George shook his head. "I have lost count," Kamal continued. "Cairo isn't the most dangerous place on the planet, but there are many hundreds of murders every year nonetheless, most of which I investigate, and some of which come with a body. Your wife, Mr Turner, was not dead. She may have looked still, and pale, and it may have appeared that she was not breathing, but I only had to look at her for the briefest of moments to realise that she was as alive as you or I."

There was a moment's silence as they took in what he had just said.

"So where is she now?"

Kamal dove his hand into his breast pocket again and fished out his packet of cigarettes. He placed them purposefully on the small table before standing up and making to leave.

Ben stepped forward in protest. "Wait, you can't leave without telling us where Gail is."

"You can have the cigarettes, Mr Turner, I am giving up," was all he said as he pushed past them and reached the door. Opening it, he turned back towards them briefly. "The agency that is behind all of this is not Egyptian, so I would recommend that you look elsewhere."

Before they could object again, the door closed behind him.

George strode across the room and grabbed the packet of cigarettes. Ripping it apart, he discarded the foil insides and the single remaining cigarette on the table and turned the unfolded card over and over in his hands, looking for some sort of hidden message, before throwing it too onto the table.

"Bastard!" he exclaimed as he made a run for the door. Throwing it open, he launched himself out into the corridor and shot towards the lift.

Ben moved closer to the table and picked up the discarded cigarette. Turning it over in his hands, he checked the make. "George, wait!" he shouted, but the door had already swung closed behind him. He made a wet line along the length of the cigarette with his tongue, before gently peeling it open and emptying the tobacco onto the table.

There was a knock on the door. Ben checked his discovery once more and let George in.

"Bastard's gone already!" he said.

"He left a note," Ben said.

George looked at him in surprise. "I checked the cigarette packet; there was nothing inside but a left over cigarette!"

"Not quite. I looked more closely: why would someone buy a pack of Marlboro and use it to hold a rollup, unless they were using the rollup to hide something?" With this he lifted his hand to show George the small sliver of paper that had been hidden amongst the tobacco. "He left us a note."

George took the piece of paper and turned it over in his hands. On it was a word, written faintly in black pencil:

DEFCOMM

They stared at each other for almost a minute, digesting the information.

"Why tell us so much then leave a secret message?" George asked. "And what's Defcomm?"

"Maybe he wanted to leave a breadcrumb, in case they got to him before he got to us?" Ben said as he tapped the strange word into the browser on his phone. He showed the search results to George. He then asked the single most obvious question:

"What time does Martín's flight leave?"

CHAPTER 56

Gail turned the pages slowly, looking at the symbols one by one and making notes with a pencil in the margin. She'd been given a copy of the Book of Xynutians, with a promise to see the original should her initial investigations be encouraging.

She was now on her tenth page, and was becoming desensitised by the overload of information. She had seen Xynutians in cars, Xynutians in what appeared to be mass-transportation systems, and even Xynutians going up and down in lifts attached to the sides of towering skyscrapers. And then she had seen Xynutians running, Xynutians on fire, skyscrapers broken and twisted and cars and mass transportation systems crumpled and destroyed. The drawings were like no other ancient Egyptian illustrations she had ever seen, though the accompanying text left no doubt that they were contemporary to the Book of Aniquilus.

She scanned through the translations that Patterson, or someone from his team, had made.

Aniquilus cast his gaze over the Xynutians, He eats their pride and ambitions with his swift punishment.

She shook her head. *Eats* made no sense at all in the context of the sentence. Obviously, it hadn't to the Patterson either, who had circled the offending hieroglyphs.

Her tablet would probably tell her what they meant – she knew a lot of Egyptian verbs off the cuff, but she had become maybe a little too reliant on George's application remembering some of the more complex contextual translations for her.

She flicked through a few more pages before stopping at a picture of a group of Xynutians, gathered around what she assumed were houses, looking up at the stars in the sky. Some calculations had been scribbled in pencil below the original hieroglyphs, along with a post-it note: *Nefertiti's return is 3344 years after the writing of the Book of Xynutians. This was in 2007!*

She crossed the date out and scribbled some notes down on her own pad. *Amateurs*, she thought. The ancient Egyptians had followed a three hundred and sixty-five day calendar. Eventually, Roman rulers in the first century BC had imposed an earlier Ptolemaic ruling that every fourth year had to have an extra day, to account for the discrepancy between the solar year and the traditional Egyptian year.

The Book of Xynutians had been written thirteen centuries before this ruling, and at least a thousand years before the Ptolemaic kings had first suggested the change.

Therefore, the calculations in the translation she was looking at were, to the best of her mental arithmetic, about three years out. The 'second coming' of Nefertiti was scheduled to have occurred in 2004, not 2007.

"The year I was born," she said with a wry smile.

She sat back and looked at the next picture carefully. Aniquilus left a trail of destruction behind him, and yet there were a handful of Xynutians, standing outside their homes looking to the stars, according to the translation *waiting for the next coming of Aniquilus*. She scratched her head, and then suddenly gave a satisfied laugh as she snatched the text up from the desk. On her desk was a telephone. It allowed her to dial one number: Patterson's.

He came in with a smile a moment later. "Less than an hour into it and you've already made a discovery?"

She nodded at the paper on her desk. "A few things, I think," she began. "Some odd translations here, I need my tablet to verify them, but the text makes no real sense."

He agreed. "But I probably can't get you access to your equipment. I'll work on that one. What else?"

"The dates. You're about three years out, because of the leap years," she said with more than a hint of triumph.

He looked surprised and nodded. "Well spotted. I had no idea that the ancient Egyptians had no leap years."

"You're obviously not an Egyptologist then, are you? Finally," she pointed to the picture of the surviving Xynutians, "there's this."

He looked at her, puzzled. "What does this prove?"

"Think about it: if Aniquilus somehow punished these mythical Xynutians, but left some alive to pass the message on, then where are they now? Surely such an advanced civilisation would pick itself back up and thrive again. Even in low numbers their technology would be enough to help them survive until their numbers were restored?"

Patterson contemplated the thought for a moment. "But what if there was nothing left? What if all the scientists were dead? Would you know how to make an internal combustion engine, or indeed have the ability to, if no-one was able to assist?"

"Surely not everything would have been destroyed?"

"Maybe not, but who would maintain it all? Once the electricity stops being piped in, or the chip in your computer dies, or the satellite connecting your phone falls out of the sky, how useful is the technology then? How long would it be before a dark age came about, and rival tribes fought among themselves?"

Gail smiled. "Assuming they even existed, they had to live through that once to get to where they were. Surely they could do it again? And the human race has been through its fair share of 'dark-ages', and we always bounce back stronger."

Patterson rubbed his chin pensively. "You do have a point. There is a hole in the story, something the book does not say."

"The book doesn't have a preface indicating it's a work of fiction, but I'm sure that if we look hard enough it'll have a 'Made in Hollywood' stamp somewhere on it."

He ignored the comment. "You need to start looking at this with an aim to helping us, not trying to prove us wrong. I think that you need to see something else, Dr Turner."

Leaving the room, they walked briskly down the corridor, to a part of the facility that Gail had not yet been in. On their left were a series of double doors recessed into the wall. The third set had been left ajar, enough for Gail to glimpse the inside of a huge hanger. Patterson was several yards beyond the door already, and she stopped to peer inside.

Before Patterson backtracked and slammed the door shut in her face she saw an open space that would have been large enough to comfortably house several average-sized passenger jets, of the type that would normally take her to Egypt. Large scaffolds filled three quarters of the space, with rockets or missiles in various stages of completion in each one. The closest scaffold to the door held a complete rocket, the tip of which was roughly twenty yards away and ten above her. From the distance to the floor of the hanger, she fancied she must have been on the third or fourth floor of the building.

Just as the door was shut, she saw a gigantic Stars and Stripes on the opposite wall, flanked by two logos. On its left was the smaller of the two, the familiar logo of NASA. On its right, several times larger, was a name she had not heard of before: DEFCOMM. Written in bold white text across a black background, the *O* was the planet Earth, with the USA dead-centre.

"We're not going in there," Patterson said sternly. He continued down the corridor, keeping her slightly behind him and to his left so he could still see her in his peripheral vision.

A few moments later, they reached a lift. He entered a long sequence of numbers on the keypad and pressed a button marked B3. She could tell because of the momentary weight loss that the lift was descending rapidly. She guessed that the B stood for Basement, so they may have descended six or seven floors, but she was surprised at how quickly. The doors slid open after less than ten seconds.

All thoughts of lifts and their mechanisms left her when she saw what the lift doors had revealed.

"This is the Agency's control centre." Patterson said flatly.

"Are you working for NASA," she asked in awe. Before her were spread out dozens of computer terminals in semi-circles facing a huge screen, like seats of congress facing the leader of the house. On the big screen was a video-feed of two people in space suits leaning over a pile of dirt and rocks.

"No, this is better than NASA, they're a little behind the times. What we're seeing here is the direct feed from the crew of the *Clarke* on the surface of Mars. NASA sees the same picture in seventy-five minutes, which then gets sent to the other space agencies around the world."

"Why do you get to see it earlier?"

He said nothing in reply, so she made the assumption that whatever the reason was, it wasn't legal.

"How can you intercept such data? Surely someone would find out?"

"Someone nearly did, but it's exactly because it's so unthinkable that it became so easy. All of the messages sent to and from *Clarke* are sent via a network of secure satellites stationed around Earth. Breaking through their security model is impossible. Unless you built the satellites in the first place; then you have an advantage – you can get to all the data without anyone ever finding out about it. That way they can then censor out what they don't want people to see, and make up what they do."

"Why would you want to do such a thing?" she asked.

"*They* do it to gain control of information."

Gail noted the correction. Dr Patterson was a mystery to her – he was obviously implicated in Mallus' dealings, but was also distancing himself from him. And then there was the message he had written to her when she had been strapped into her bed.

"Look, Patterson, I get the fact that there are some dodgy things going on here, I get the fact that you didn't want me to be here in the first place, that's obvious. But answer me this: why does the Agency need me here? What can I do or offer that is any different to what is already being done?"

He smiled gently. "Under these circumstances, *I* didn't want you here; but while I have a broader understanding of the Book of Xynutians, you have studied the Book of Aniquilus in infinite detail for ten years. The Agency believes, *I believe*," he corrected himself, "that the book of Aniquilus is a set of rules, without which you get the Book of Xynutians."

"Like the Ten Commandments and Revelations?"

"Not exactly; the Ten Commandments are Old Testament, and Revelations is New, which in that respect is like the two books, yes. But Revelations is something that it was suggested *would* happen regardless at the end of times. I believe that the Xynutians are an actual example of what will happen in our worst case scenario. I had difficulty believing the whole concept, to be honest, until I started looking at the Book of Xynutian pictures in detail. And now, I don't doubt a word of it. Because it looks like we've found Xynutian remains on Mars."

He walked up to a young man seated in front of a computer terminal and spoke to him quietly for a few moments. The operator nodded and started tapping commands into the terminal.

"Watch this," he said.

Gail watched as the main screen of the control room split in half. On the right hand side she could see two astronauts in what looked like a dune buggy, driving through an arid desert. The pale blue-grey sky looked cold and lifeless. The camera filming the scene panned steadily as it followed the vehicle and its occupants from left to right.

The left half of the display was totally different: the camera was jolting from left to right as it made its way through a narrow corridor and under a low archway. The route ahead of it was lit by a torch beam, which brought Gail to the conclusion that the camera must be mounted somewhere near an astronauts visor. She was seeing what he or she was seeing. In front of the camera another astronaut emerged from the darkness holding a shovel. The torch beam bounced off the astronaut's visor, but as it changed direction she glimpsed the excited features of a middle-aged man, his grin taking up half of his face.

"On the right is what the world sees. A computer generated mission to Mars, perfect in every conceivable way: Captain Marchenko and Dr Richardson on a routine outing to drill ice cores from the bed of an ancient frozen river. On the left is what is actually happening on Mars: Dr Richardson has just entered what they have called *The Gallery* for the first time, and Captain Marchenko is coming to greet her."

She looked at the two feeds for a moment. "How do I know it's not the other way round? What if the reality is the dune buggy, and the faked images are the Xynutian remains?"

"Why would we do that?" he asked.

Gail had to admit that she couldn't think of a reason.

"But the world knows that they found the Stickman on Mars. That's why I went to Egypt in the first place. Why would the world accept that they would simply return to drilling ice cores?"

"Because since you have been with us, the images captured by *Beagle 4* and broadcast so readily to the media have been debunked. Dismissed as fakes by the scientific community. They were an attempt by the European Space Agency to cause a sensation, and I believe that attempt is failing."

"No help from you, of course."

He looked at her sideways and raised an eyebrow. "Please pay attention to the video. This was recorded this morning, and should give you all the convincing you need."

As Gail watched, Captain Marchenko led Dr Richardson's helmet camera down the dark corridor until it stopped abruptly at a dead end. Marchenko pointed eagerly towards where the dirt-covered floor met the perfectly smooth walls. As Dr Richardson's camera refocused, Gail began to pick out familiar shapes, and her heart sank. Embossed in the wall, at waist-height, was a small procession of humans. From their clothing it was clear they were Xynutians, but with a difference: these were not Egyptian caricatures as in the Book of Xynutians, but detailed, lifelike renditions. They were being marched towards the dead-end of the corridor, and towering over them, almost squashing them into the dirt-floor, was the *Stickman*, Aniquilus.

Dr Patterson looked at Gail intently, waiting for a reaction. When none came, he broke the silence. "You see, Dr Turner? The Xynutians are not imaginary, they did exist and they were wiped out, in all probability by Aniquilus."

Gail looked at the displays in disbelief. Nothing proved to her that what she was looking at hadn't been made up in an elaborate computer simulation, but there was one absolute certainty: DEFCOMM, and anyone involved with it, was up to no good.

"And now that I've seen all this, all these things that you're hiding so effectively from the entire world, what are my chances of ever being released?" she said as calmly as she could.

"I hope that what you've seen will make you understand how important our cause is, and that you will agree to join us," he replied hesitantly.

It didn't, and she certainly wasn't going to join *anyone*. "And what about the astronauts on Mars? When they get back, how will you keep them quiet?" She asked the question loudly enough for everyone in the room to hear, but her only response was a heavy silence; Dr Patterson looked at his shoes briefly before looking back at the displays. She scanned the control room and her eyes met the fleeting glance of the controller who had reset the displays for them earlier.

Looking back at the video feeds, she could see Captain Marchenko through the eyes of Dr Richardson. His grin was unmoving as he gesticulated excitedly at the Xynutians. Somehow, she had to contact her husband. She had to get out and tell everyone what was really going on. Because now it wasn't just her life at stake; although they may be millions of miles away, she now knew that she could be the astronauts' only real chance of ever getting back to Earth alive.

CHAPTER 57

Captain Danny Marchenko scraped the dirt from his visor excitedly, his hand playing an exaggerated 'hello' as he used the rubber blade set into the seam of his glove. He swore under his breath in Russian, but the suit's sensitive microphone still managed to distinguish between the profanity and his breathing, amplifying it over the control panel speakers of the MLP.

"Keep it clean, Captain Mar – *Danny*," Captain Yves Montreaux corrected himself from his seat in their Martian home. "We don't want Man's immortal words from space to have to be censored, do we?"

He allowed himself a smile as the irony of his last words seeped through. He had told himself, while standing on the precipice of Hellas Basin days earlier, that he had to keep his certainty of their terrible situation to himself. As he had looked down at his excited colleague poring over the engravings – of what he now knew was referred to as the *Amarna Stickman*, whatever *that* meant – it had struck him that while he was certain he'd never set foot on Earth again, at least while they were still useful they were safe where they were.

They. How could he know who was with him, and who was against? He daren't look in the MLP's database, for fear of being monitored. What would Earth think if he suddenly started looking at the crew's personal records? Of course, he had read all of their records several times, but then what he had read then was in blissful ignorance of what had since happened; would he now pick up on some obscure, terrifying detail?

It was a moot point. What would he do about it even if he found that Dr Richardson and Captain Marchenko were involved in a conspiracy, a conspiracy which had killed Lieutenant Shi Su Ning, a Chinese cosmonaut whose family probably thought she had died as a result of a system failure.

If they're in on it, he had thought, *then what difference does it really make?*

He wouldn't confront them, at least not without absolute certainty, and if he believed his life to be in danger, how could he defend himself? Kill them both? *And be left here alone, until I die,* he thought morosely. His only option, he concluded, was to act normally. After all, it may just be his own paranoia, brought on by months in space coupled with his own self-inflicted separation from his other crew-members. *What was left of them*, he couldn't help himself from adding.

Acting normally was difficult on Mars. *Normally* humans walked on Earth, and occasionally in space and on the Moon. Walking on Mars was anything but normal. Captain Montreaux tackled the issues he was faced with in the most logical order he could, and therefore started with the most straightforward: his separation from Dr Richardson and Captain Marchenko. Fixing that started with an impromptu meeting over dinner the night they had discovered the Jetty.

"I've been thinking," he had started, "that as there are only three of us on this planet, it makes perfect sense for us to reduce elements of the formality of our methods of communication, and refer to each other using Christian names only."

"Not exactly the best choice of words if you're planning on that, Yves," Dr Richardson had quipped.

But nonetheless they had taken to the idea like fish to water. *She had taken to it as easily as she had adjusted to walking on Mars* he had thought to himself. Captain Marchenko had grinned and extended his hand to be shaken firmly by the American.

"It's a deal," he said in his best Texan accent, which had taken them all by surprise. It was the first time in many days that they had laughed together, the first in nearly a month since Yves could remember laughing so hard, but as the evening had drawn to a close, he still managed to feel secluded. If anything, the laughter, their jokes, had only served to make him feel more different, as 'Jane' and 'Danny' shared private jokes and candid looks across the MLP's dinner table.

And so it turned out that, despite it being his own idea, he had the most difficulty adjusting to it.

They naturally took to using first names, and for Jane as a scientist this was understandable. But for Danny, with all of his military and academy training, it somehow felt *wrong*.

He told himself he was paranoid. You don't change months of habit and years of indoctrination in the space of a few days. Yet as he sat at the MLP's control panels, listening to Danny's cursing and Jane's whoops of joy, he couldn't help but plan his next comment, designed to spark a reaction, anything that would betray that they were in cahoots with whoever was in control of their mission. *Certainly not me*, he thought sarcastically as he looked at the rows of buttons, dials and touch screen displays.

"Remember people may be watching this live, Danny – we don't want to offend anyone with profanities, do we?"

"No problem, Yves, sorry about that everybody back home, but can you see what I can see?" Danny asked, the pitch of his voice reaching prepubescent levels.

Yves leaned forward and concentrated on the display. "You need to clean your camera a little bit more."

'Cleaning the camera' wasn't technically or physically possible. It was housed within Danny's helmet, protected from the harsh atmosphere of Mars by half an inch of transparent aluminium. Even if one of them, *heaven forbid*, fell down to the bottom of the gigantic crater, the camera would emerge intact. Anything that had not been relayed in real-time to the MLP's processors would be saved to solid-state storage ready for processing at a later date.

Danny swept his glove across the protective housing, wiping clear the layer of dust that had settled during his excavation of the tunnel. "How about now?" he said.

On the display, he could make out a smooth wall of darkened stone. A bold, straight line cut the wall in half vertically from off-screen at the top to where the wall met the equally smooth floor at the bottom. The left-hand half of the wall was unmarked, but on the right, in strokes equally as bold as the vertical line and the Amarna Stickman outside was the picture of a creature, it's long lizard-like form lying prone and its mouth open in a grin, like a komodo dragon celebrating catching its dinner.

It looked so real it could have turned its head and said hello and Yves wouldn't have been more surprised. There was no characterisation, no roughness, and even though he had never seen the creature before, or any of its kind, he was certain its depiction was as true to life as was possible in an engraving on stone, with no artistic licence applied. He said as much to Danny and Jane, whose movements he was tracking on the second display.

"Absolutely!" she said without hesitation. "I've looked at the carvings; they're all over the walls. I don't like to speculate and I'm by no means the authority on such things, but I can't see how they're possible without some kind of laser technology."

"Are you saying that something buried hundreds of thousands of years ago was made with technology as advanced as our own?" he said in disbelief.

"What's the alternative? That primitive man made a spaceship of wood and sailed across space with his bow and arrow and a bucket on his head?" she responded sarcastically.

"Well, that's not exactly…"

"What Jane is saying, Yves," Danny interrupted, "is that we already accept that this find is hundreds of thousands of years old, and that Man did not have the means to do this sort of thing back then. This means we must be looking at artefacts from Mars. Artefacts from *the Martians.*"

Yves was about to answer when a piercing sound came over the speakers. Before he had a chance to turn the volume down, it stopped. Danny said a single word in Russian that Yves didn't understand but was almost certainly rude. "Everything OK?"

Then the sound came back, except this time it was pulsating. With every pulse the video feed from Danny's suit filled with static.

"What's wrong?" Jane said, worried.

"No idea, his cam is all messed up and the audio…"

"I can't hear you Yves! That whining is cutting you off every second word!"

"What?"

"I said *I can't hear*… ah! That's better!" The noise had stopped.

"Shit," Yves said between gritted teeth. "Danny, can you hear us?"

Danny's video, audio and medical feeds had all stopped transmitting. Looking at Jane's screen, he could see the Russian standing in front of the alien engravings. His arms drooped lazily by his sides, his head lolled dangerously. Jane leaped towards him and pulled him back, stopping him from falling head first into the tunnel wall. She lay him down and shone her flashlight through his visor.

His eyes were open, the pupils fully dilated. They didn't respond to the bright light as she moved it frantically from eye to eye.

"Is he breathing?"

She looked at the breastplate of his suit and tapped it twice quickly. A small OLED display flashed briefly. She hit it again several times, but it didn't come back. No battery. Moving to his wrist, she checked his suit controls. The suit should have had enough charge for another week's use, before they would need to be hooked up to the station's power source for two whole days to fill up.

The wrist controls were powered by a kinetic wrist band, as a failsafe redundancy; shake your arm and you'll always be able to check your oxygen. The readout showed twenty-five per cent air. It also confirmed his pulse, faint but still present. He had enough air for a couple of hours breathing, but no power meant that he'd freeze to death before that time was up.

She said as much to Yves, then paused. When she spoke again her voice was grave. "I can't carry him up the cliff on my own. I can't get him out of here without you."

And I can't get to you, he thought to himself. "Have you checked your own suit?" He was going over the readouts himself. "You look fine from here."

"Confirmed. Everything looks good to me. It's just Danny, his suit just suddenly lost all its power. I have to get him warm, somehow!"

"Jane, go back to the Rover. Remove one of the fuel cells, and take it back to Danny."

"Of course!" She was already running.

It only took her five minutes to reach the vehicle, another two to remove the fuel cell. *God Bless mission planners* she thought to herself as she marvelled at the simplicity of the power source's design: completely self-contained like an old fashioned battery. The cable connecting it to the Rover was identical to the cable that emerged from the underside of the suits to charge them up. With a bit of twisting you could even reach it yourself and plug yourself in.

The way back was slightly longer, as she negotiated a couple of rock slides and steep slopes. The cell wasn't excessively heavy, but it offset her centre of balance enough for her to risk falling down the crater if she wasn't careful. She finally entered the tunnel and her flashlight automatically came on.

She reached the dead end just in time to see the stone wall slide back down to meet the floor. And Danny was gone.

CHAPTER 58

A sudden sense of urgency filled the DEFCOMM control room after the Russian cosmonaut's disappearance.

Following that, it took Gail less than an hour to get her tablet back. The hieroglyphic analysis tools would help decipher the engravings on the walls, she had claimed.

She could only thank her lucky stars that she had the tablet in Mahmoud's office back in Cairo, and that her abductors had thought to bring it with them.

Using translation tools was, of course, a decoy. George's application wasn't a translator, and in any case she didn't know of any software on Earth that would help with the alien writing she had seen carved into the tunnel walls on Mars. As much as she would have loved to help solve the mystery of where Captain Marchenko had gone, this was her chance to save herself first.

Save yourself, the thought, *and you stand a chance of saving them*. All that she needed to do now was make sure that no one was looking.

Dr Patterson looked over her shoulder at the screen. "Interesting tool," he said thoughtfully. "It looks a bit out of date, how old is it?"

She grunted and tapped a command into the screen. "There's not a huge demand for this sort of application, in fact I don't know anyone else who uses it. So it'll pretty much do the job until it breaks or something much better comes along." She didn't tell him that George had developed it for her; it was pointless arousing suspicions when she was so close. "Can you get me some coffee?"

"Sure. How do you take it?"

"Julie Andrews," she replied. Seeing the look on his face, she elaborated. "White, none."

He stared at her blankly, then shook his head and made to leave.

"And something to eat!" she shouted after him. *Anything to buy some time!*

Using the interactive pen that slid out of the front edge of the computer, she scanned the first line of symbols from the printout Patterson had given her, and pretended to study the output until she was sure he had gone.

She tilted her head to one side to check for noise from the corridor. Hearing none, she browsed her saved images and found an appropriately-sized photo of some engravings from the Sixth Pylon at Karnak: the texture of the stone and lighting were similar to that of the Library. She tapped an on-screen menu and accessed the application's 'about' pop-up, before holding down a special combination of keys to open a small text-input screen.

It took her less than a minute to write the message, a little under one hundred characters. She knew that any more would be pushing it; she would only get one shot at this, and the smaller the message the easier it would be to hide.

She had known for a while that her tablet would be her best bet of contacting someone on the *outside*. Her first problem had been getting hold of it; something the events on Mars had precipitated.

The next problem was working out what to say so that George could find her, when she didn't even know where she was to start with. For that, however, she'd had a stroke of luck.

Barely an hour earlier she had glimpsed the logos of NASA and DEFCOMM in the large hanger, before Patterson had slammed the door closed. She knew that they weren't at NASA, so DEFCOMM were obviously the culprits, working in partnership with the unwitting space agency.

Later, in the control room, Patterson had let slip another vital clue: that they controlled the satellites and receiver arrays because they *built* them. It didn't take a rocket scientist, and from what she'd seen this place had enough of them, to work out that DEFCOMM probably stood for *Defence Communications*. After what he had told her in the control room, it seemed odd that DEFCOMM should advertise its allegiance to NASA and the USA. But then, what better smokescreen? DEFCOMM was a very American company building American satellites for a government agency, for an American-led first mission to Mars. Who would guess they had their own, hidden, agenda? What scared her more than anything else she had seen was that Seth Mallus had some crazy ideas coupled with huge resources; a dangerous combination. If someone who built rockets, satellites, and who knows what weaponry could be so fanatical about some ancient Egyptian texts, then God help them all.

And, thanks to poor Mamdouh and the *Wizard of Oz* man, she knew that she was definitely in Florida.

With all of this in mind, she barely thought twice about what to write to George.

Her next task was how to hide the message.

When George had first developed the application, he had embedded some basic cryptographic algorithms so that he could send secret love letters to her. Every now and then, he would create a message on his laptop and send it to her to decode.

Now it wasn't for fun: lives depended on it.

There were basically two types of cryptography: overt, in which it's clear you're looking at a code, but you're damned if you know what it means, and covert, in which you have no idea you're looking at a code.

The drawback of overt cryptographies is that once people knew you're hiding something, you have to make it pretty much impenetrable. As a result, some overt encryption techniques are so complex, and require so much to be understood by writer and reader, that they aren't worth the bother for simple love letters.

George had toyed with the one-time cipher, the only truly 'unbreakable' overt code. It involved replacing the letters of the alphabet with numerical values, which would give you a long list of numbers representing your message. These would then be dropped into a completely random string of numbers, which would be used only once. The next code would use a different random string. While the principle of the one-time cipher was sound, it was generally considered to be too much hassle; the random string of numbers had to be shared between sender and recipient, as well as the numerical values and their letter counterparts used to encode the original message.

Because such a cypher *was* generally deemed unbreakable, the hassle of encrypting was reduced by recycling the random string of numbers between messages, rather than always using new ones. As soon as the one-time cypher became the 'more than one-time' cypher, the code was broken.

So for ease of use, he had chosen to build covert ciphers into her translation program. The overwhelming benefit of covert cryptography being that if people didn't realise something was hidden, you didn't need to make such an effort to make it impenetrable.

Covert cryptography, or steganography, involved hiding a message inside a picture, in this case a scan of hieroglyphic text from Karnak. By using the encryption tool, a text-based message would be added to the colour components of the image file: each binary digit, or bit of the encoded message, was taken and added on to the end of the binary code for each individual picture element, or pixel. Adding a one or a nought to a pixel may change the shade of grey slightly, but overall the picture would remain unchanged.

The more code-bits you tried to hide in a picture, the more degraded the original image would appear; as soon as the image became too distorted from the original, the message would become less 'covert'.

Using a specific decryption tool, which would ask for a shared keyword between sender and recipient, the code-bits would be extracted from the image, and the code decrypted for viewing.

Gail made sure the message was as short as possible by deleting a couple of unnecessary words. Satisfied with what she had written, she entered her keyword, and tapped to submit.

Seconds later, the image was ready, her secret message hidden deep inside each individual pixel, undetectable to the human eye and, she hoped, invisible to firewalls. If anyone suspected that there was a hidden message, it wouldn't take them long to break her code; George had used an algorithm readily available on the Internet, and advanced code-breaking programs could unlock keywords within hours. But that was the beauty of George's program: no one need ever know they were exchanging messages, because all you ever saw were pictures.

Now all she needed to worry about was how to send it to him. She leant back in her chair and stared into the screen. The network icon advised her that there were access points in range, but they were all encrypted. The irony didn't escape her.

All the terminals she'd seen in the facility had thumbprint access restriction. No doubt, if they were as security conscious as she believed they should be, the thumbprint scanners would also take a minute sample of tissue to perform a quick DNA analysis. There would probably even be retinal scan software, using the cameras that were embedded into most screens. To back all that up, they might even ask users for a typed password before unlocking the displays, too.

So she wasn't going to get a connection, and she wasn't going to be able to log onto someone else's machine. Despite all the technology she had used to get to this point, it was all going to let her down on the last leg. She had been so caught up in writing the message and hiding it that getting the message to him hadn't even crossed her mind.

She hit the table in frustration. *All I want to do is send a bloody email!* As the word entered her mind, she froze. *Mail!* Tapping the screen quickly, she moved the image file to her memory card and closed the application. She then popped a small flap open and pulled out the thumbnail-sized piece of plastic.

Rummaging through the papers on the desk, she found a few scans inside a brown paper envelope. Removing them, she slipped the tiny drive in and shut the envelope before sliding it into her pocket just as Patterson returned. He was carrying a tray full of cakes, with two mugs of steaming hot coffee. To her relief, he pushed the door open with his rear as he backed into the room, and therefore didn't see the guilty look on her face as she quickly returned both her hands to the laptop.

"Get anywhere?" he asked, casually.

"No," she cleared her throat. "Still a couple of stumbling blocks. Coffee will help though, thanks."

"No problem. I asked the guy in the canteen for coffee 'Julie Andrews' and he knew exactly what I was talking about. Seems you're not so crazy after all!"

"Ha! I think any of you guys calling me crazy when I've seen what you're up to here is a bit out of order."

He looked at her and took his mug from the tray, sipping it cautiously after a short cooling blow. "I'm sorry you're caught up in this," he said sympathetically.

"You should be!" she retorted.

"No, I mean it," he said, obviously hurt.

It suddenly occurred to her that there was something more than just sympathy in his eyes. She still had a big problem to solve: there weren't exactly that many mailboxes around the corridors of the facility, and sending a letter to England was not going to be straightforward. She'd need help. And while she wasn't the kind of person to use someone, Patterson's inability to be an authority on the Book of Xynutians was the main reason for her being kidnapped.

Here was a weak man, who had clearly taken a shine to her. Why, she had no idea; although only forty-one, she felt old and slightly podgy after too many quiet nights in and too little exercise. And she had been anything but nice to Patterson since she'd first laid eyes on him.

I have to get this message to George, she though as she pushed back the feelings of hate towards herself for what she was about to do and painted what she hoped looked like a completely natural, slightly flirty smile on her face.

"I'm sorry," she said, ignoring her morals screaming from deep down inside. "I didn't mean to snap at you. You have been kind to me since I got here." She reached out and brushed her hand against his forearm briefly, before taking her coffee. She hadn't been on the dating scene for over fifteen years now, but she knew that just with that gesture, she was already halfway there.

CHAPTER 59

Jane ran her gloved hands frantically along the edge of the wall, desperately trying to find an opening, a finger-hold, to drag the stone back and get to Danny.

"Shit!" she exclaimed. "I can't get it open!"

"Keep trying, Jane." Yves' voice sounded like he was inside her head, coming through the speakers in her helmet. "I'm going through the footage from his cam immediately before the power surge, to see what happened."

She grunted a reply, moving her attention from the join in the floor to the sides of the walls. There didn't seem to be a gap wider than a fraction of a millimetre around the entire wall. If she hadn't seen it slide down with her own eyes, she would have sworn that it wouldn't be able to, or at least never had.

A few moments later, Yves' voice boomed in her ears again.

"OK, Jane. Turn to your left and down a bit. You see the carving of that lizard thing, going along the floor?"

She looked down and saw the strange creature with its bottom jaw curled into a grotesque smile. Fine, pointy teeth covered the inside of the mouth, and a long thin tongue rasped tentatively against the top lip. She shuddered involuntarily. "Yes."

"The last thing that I got from Danny's cam was when he reached out and ran his fingers along the head of that thing."

She was about to do the same when she froze. "So I'd better not touch it, don't you think?"

There was a pause. "Take the power cell and make your way back here. It'll take me longer to walk there than it will for you to come and get me in Herbie."

An hour later, they both stood in front of the alien engravings. At their feet were three power cells and some reserve oxygen, as well as an

294

emergency decompression bubble, which could be inflated in less than ten seconds, and would provide a temporary reprieve from the thin Martian atmosphere if one of their suits failed. It would be damn cold, but it would keep them alive for a while. Yves had a small backpack filled with emergency rations that could be used inside the bubble. He had no idea what state Danny would be in if they found him, so he had catered for as many emergency scenarios as he could think of.

They went through the plan one final time.

"OK, so I touch the wall, and you stand behind me. If what happened to Danny happens to me, use the power cells to recharge, and if that doesn't work get me into the bubble. OK?"

She nodded and stood back.

Slowly, cautiously, he reached out and brushed his fingers against the stone wall of the corridor.

Nothing happened.

Emboldened, he let them run along the smooth contours of the lizard's head, taking in every detail, making sure that none of the teeth or veins on its skin were left untouched.

Still, nothing happened.

Using both hands, he poured over the engraving. From head to tail he pushed and rubbed against every line, before moving beyond the lizard and on to the strange alien symbols that he assumed had to be writing. He was standing now, looking up and down for any area he could have missed.

"Well, that obviously wasn't it," he said disappointedly. "What do you think?"

There was no reply.

Spinning round, he saw that Jane was laid out on the stone floor, immobile. He rushed to her side and checked her vital signs; she was breathing, and her suit seemed intact. No matter why she had fallen, she must have done so gracefully, without hitting her helmet against the walls. He dragged a power cell towards them and plugged the extension lead into the socket behind her left shoulder.

Very quickly, the lights in her suit returned and he felt the gentle hum as the ventilation system started to move warm air inside. Minutes later, her eyes flickered, then came back to life.

"Can you hear me?" Yves asked.

She nodded. "Yes."

"How do you feel?"

"Groggy. So it was me, eh?" she looked up at him sheepishly. "Didn't see that one coming."

He helped her sit up. "No, me neither. I didn't even see you fall."

"I don't understand, though; surely a loss of power, no matter how it happened, wouldn't make me or Danny blackout?"

"I think we have to assume, given the circumstances, that whatever took the power from your suit may not be something we can understand just yet," he said.

"I guess the door didn't open?"

He shook his head.

She was about to suggest they try again when she noticed the door shift upwards ever so slightly. "Look!" she pointed.

As they watched, the entire wall slipped into the ceiling noiselessly. Where it had once been, a deep groove ran along the floor and the walls, revealing how neatly the door slotted in.

Beyond, the corridor continued for about ten yards before meeting another wall, identical in appearance to the one that had just opened. Along the walls the alien engravings continued, showing people in various poses, all heading towards the far end of the corridor. One of them, a man, was different; he was sitting in a chair which floated above the others, with a long sceptre in his left hand. On the end of the sceptre was the symbol they had seen engraved on the Jetty: the Amarna Stickman.

Yves and Jane crept forwards to take all of this in, and were just about to pass under the door when Jane shouted out. "Wait!"

She ran back to the equipment and dragged the power cells, bubble and spare oxygen pack. He helped her the last few feet, until everything was beyond the doorway. They now stood one on either side of the groove in the corridor.

"The second door must open when this one is closed, like an airlock," Yves said. The sense of urgency was apparent in his voice, and his eyes.

"Wait, what are we about to do? We don't know if we'll ever be able to get back out again." She shook her head slowly. "We can't go in there."

He looked her in the eyes and saw genuine fear. It infected him somewhat and he looked around, as if suddenly realising his own predicament: he was on the wrong side of the door, and it could close at any moment. He'd been caught up in their discovery, so much so that all common sense had gone out of the window.

"OK, you're right." He was about to hand the power cells back to her when he saw the wall sliding back down. It closed so fast he didn't even have time to catch the look of sheer horror on Jane's face.

"Jane!" he shouted. "Can you hear me?"

There was no response.

He spent the next ten minutes banging on the solid rock door with his fists, shouting at the top of his voice and desperately trying to slide it back up, to no avail.

He was alone.

He slowly came to terms with the fact that he wasn't going to move the door, and while it was there, none of his radio signals would be getting out. It also occurred to him that a spacesuit was the loneliest place to die.

Turning round, he examined the corridor. His first assessment of the new engravings from a distance had been pretty accurate. A man, which he assumed to be a leader of some sort, sitting on his floating chair with a big Amarna Stickman staff, seemed to be summoning the others towards the end of the corridor, which Yves hoped would turn out to be a door, beyond which he would find Danny.

On the opposite wall, was an altogether more surprising sight: heading in the same direction as the men were dozens and dozens of animals, of many different species. They weren't quite going in two by two, but Yves easily recognised elephants, giraffes, wolves, lions and several different kinds of birds. The quality of the engravings was exquisite; they looked so realistic he could almost smell them. He scanned the different animals in the procession, picking up on quite a few he had never seen before; a strange dog-like mammal with a long horn on its nose, and what looked like a bear, but with no fur to speak of and very long, pointy ears. Towards the back, the unmistakable form of a bipedal dinosaur, its short arms held close to its chest and mouth open to reveal rows of razor sharp teeth. The respective sizes of the animals he recognized told him the engravings were to scale. This in turn told him that the dinosaur had to be less than two meters tall, although its body was much longer. He realised his mouth was hanging open, and was about to shut it when he saw an even more familiar sight, marching between a lion and a hippopotamus.

The face looked more elongated at the nose and mouth, the slight hunch at the neck, and the squat, solid legs were far shorter in proportion to the rest of the body, causing the arms to hang weirdly close to the ground. But despite these differences, there was without a doubt an early man walking among these animals.

They were all being led deep underground.

Suddenly, the second door opened, sliding into the ceiling effortlessly like the first, and the corridor was bathed in bright light, which picked the engravings out in striking high-contrast relief.

I'm being led underground with them, he thought.

He hesitated briefly, then took a deep breath and put his right foot forwards, into the light.

CHAPTER 60

B en pulled his car up at the entrance of the airport in a space reserved for taxis, of which there were, oddly, none. Seconds later, the muzzle of an assault rifle tapped the window and gestured for it to be opened. He obliged indignantly.

George looked on nervously as Ben proceeded to argue with the armed policeman, who turned out not to be alone. A dozen or so more, all in black uniforms and berets, patrolled the entrance to the airport. Two more detached from a small group inside the main door and walked towards Ben's car.

"Ben?" he tried to get his friend's attention. "Ben, I think we should use the short-stay parking."

The policeman peered down into the car and checked George out, giving him the opportunity in turn to read the badge on the man's uniform; 'Tourism Police'. He had seen many Tourism Police during his years visiting Egypt; they were generally, in his experience, unkempt, corrupt and out of shape guards with out-dated weapons that probably didn't work. They spent most of their time, as was their duty, 'protecting' tourists from terrorists; terrorists who had been absent from Egypt for decades.

Gail in particular had pretty strong views on Tourism Police. Omnipresent at mass tourist attractions and minor sites alike, they sometimes guarded supposedly closed-to-the-public areas, but would lift a metal pole blocking your passage for a discrete *baksheesh*. Invariably, the metal pole would disappear as soon as they did.

These police were different. Not only because they wore black instead of white, but mainly because they seemed well-armed, organised and impeccably presented. Their uniforms were crisp and well-fitted, in contrast to their cousins in white, who sometimes looked like they'd accidentally put on someone else's jacket and trousers.

"You have flight now?" the man asked him in broken English.

George shook his head. "No, later on. We're here to catch a friend before he boards his plane." He suddenly realised he had gesticulated wildly to illustrate what he meant by *board* and *plane*. Saying these words to a member of the Tourism Police outside an airport, it was probably fair to say he didn't need the sign language, so he hid his hands under his legs quickly, a movement which earned him a nervous twitch of the gun from the soldier and a wide-eyed look from Ben.

After a few choice words from the man, the barrel of the gun was lifted from the window sill and Ben put the car into gear, moving away from the taxi rank, leaving it empty save for the patrolling soldiers. Barely five hundred yards later, they joined a long line of traffic waiting to exit the airport, and came to a standstill.

George waited as long as he could before speaking. "What the hell is going on? They didn't look like *Tourism Police*?"

Ben looked round the traffic in frustration; there was no other way to downtown Cairo. They were stuck. "Tourism Police don't have much to do, usually. They used to be everywhere. Before I was born, Egypt had lots of terrorism, religious fanatics, generally people with lots of guns and little sense." A car joined the queue behind them and beeped. Ben turned in his seat and gesticulated. "I haven't seen the black uniform ones for a while. We usually get them in and around monuments and mosques or churches, if something happens somewhere else in the world, though they usually wear white. The only place I know that there are always *black* Tourism Police is on the Sinai Peninsula. It has a border with Israel and is always full of Western and Israeli tourists, so we can never throw too many police at the place to make people feel safe."

"Why are they here now?"

"All flights have been cancelled, except for those leaving in the next hour. That means Martín will be on his way home now, and we won't be able to see him. They're not letting anyone else in the airport. The policeman didn't say why." He shrugged and looked at George.

George fished in the pocket of his shorts and got his phone. Picking through his recent calls he singled out Martín's number and dialled it. They'd hoped to meet in the airport, but traffic had conspired against them. Now, they weren't even going to be let in.

"Hello?" Martín answered on the first ring. "George?"

"Hi Martín," he said. "Are you getting on your flight?"

"Already on board, waiting for the doors to close now. It's crazy here, I don't know how you're going to get back to England!"

He briefly wondered the same thing, but it would have to wait. They had more important things to discuss.

"Martín, what the hell is going on?"

"No idea, it only happened in the last half hour or so; the police came in and then suddenly the whole place went into lockdown. We were hurried onto our plane. I've tried checking the news but I can't see anything there."

George didn't want to dwell on it; as far as he was concerned, terrorism was a million miles from his concerns.

"The reason we wanted to talk, Martín, is that Kamal came to see me in my hotel room," he started. "He says Gail isn't dead, but he can't tell us where she is. She's been taken by someone."

There was a pause. "Sorry, George there must be bad reception. *Taken?*"

"Yes, *taken*," he shouted into the phone. George remembered the first time he had met Martín, the Spaniard had suggested that Gail had been abducted for her knowledge. That had been just before the call from Kamal, asking him to identify her body. It seemed they had come full circle. "All he gave us was a clue as to where she is."

"What was the clue?"

"*DEFCOMM*. Does that make any sense to you?"

"DEFCOMM?" Martín paused for thought. "Are you sure he said DEFCOMM?"

"I have it written down in front of me."

"I'll need to look it up to know precisely, but DEFCOMM are responsible for an array of satellites owned by the US government. They're built by many different people. That's how NASA gets so much funding, by distributing its contracts throughout the States; if all the funding went to one state, then it wouldn't do opinion polls any good, so by sharing the funding and jobs as much as possible, huge amounts of funding can be passed without having such a negative impact on the government's popularity.

"DEFCOMM is more of an umbrella term; no one company is responsible, so it could be any one of three dozen companies in nearly fifty different cities!" Martín said in frustration. "His clue doesn't really narrow it down enough!"

"Well, it must give us something!" George urged. "Why would he go to all the trouble of leaving a clue only to give us a dead-end?"

"To get back at you for punching him in the face?" Ben muttered beside him.

Martín was silent for a few moments. "Did he say anything else?"

"No."

"George, I have to go, but I'll look into this as soon as I land. Call and leave a message if you find out more!"

George closed the phone and looked around.

Their car had been idling, but Ben now decided to turn the engine off, as had many of the other drivers.

A strange kind of calm descended on the queue of traffic; the engine noise had mostly gone, even the pointless horn-beeping had reached a relative lull.

The only pedestrians he could see were carrying guns over their shoulders, with the now familiar black uniform of the Tourism Police. He was about to make a remark about how surreal this was when he heard a loud boom. A fraction of a second later, the car shook from side to side, and somewhere behind them a car alarm was set off.

A couple of policemen ran across the road in the direction of the noise, holding their guns across their chests.

"What the -" George began, but he was interrupted by another explosion.

This time it was on the road they were on, barely two hundred yards ahead of them over a crossroads. A car flipped into the air backwards, landing upside-down on top of the car behind it; blocks of stone and plaster flew into the air and across the road. Their car lurched in the shockwave, and moments later a splattering of small stones and plaster fragments hit their windshield.

Instinctively, Ben turned the wipers on.

They looked at each other in disbelief. "What the hell?" George said.

"Terrorists," Ben said.

"What did they blow up?" he said looking towards the building ahead of them, where dust was now billowing out in a huge cloud, obscuring the scene.

"I have no idea."

Around them the road suddenly filled with activity and in the distance, sirens began wailing. People ran from street to building and back again, cars ignored the queues and mounted the curbs. Debris from the blast littered the road and pavements. Ahead, a tongue of flame darted briefly out of the dust cloud.

Ben checked his mirrors; the car that had stopped behind them had already gone, so he put his car in reverse and retreated back towards the slip road. Turning the car round, he gunned the engine and made for the ring road, back to the airport. As the car hit the dual-carriageway, two more distant explosions reached them, and when the road swooped round in a wide arc to flyover an older district of the city, they glimpsed the scale of the attacks: half a dozen columns of smoke were dotted around the city ahead of them. A couple of helicopters were already circling above, probably filming for the local TV channels.

He was on the wrong side of the dual carriageway, and he hugged the central reservation as he negotiated the oncoming traffic.

"Where are we going?" George said through gritted teeth, his hand firmly gripping the foam of his seat.

"Airport!" Ben said as he dodged a lorry.

"But they wouldn't let us in. It was closed!"

"Different terminal, George. The old one is a little further, but worth trying anyway. The police said there are still flights for the next hour – if Gail's been taken to America then you won't get there from Egypt now that bombs are going off! You have to get back to Europe!" Ben turned on the radio and put the volume on high.

Even in Arabic, George could understand the tone in the reporter's voice: people were panicking. "What's he saying?" he asked.

"Shhh!" Ben listened intently, his head tilted down towards the radio, in spite of the speakers being in the doors. Every now and then he lifted his head to see where he was going, in time to adjust course and speed to avoid crashing.

"He's saying that there are reports of six explosions: the United States Embassy, a couple of hotels, a private American expatriate school – that's the one we just saw – and two Christian churches. Dozens of people, if not hundreds dead." Ben turned the radio down and concentrated on the road. The central barrier disappeared as the dual carriageway went down to single lanes, and he took the opportunity to join the right side of the road.

George gave a sigh of relief. "Which hotels?"

"Not yours. The Hilton and the Sheraton, big tourist places," he replied.

"Who did it? Why?" George asked.

"By the sound of those targets, I'd guess at some fundamentalist group or another."

"Fundamentalists? I didn't think there were any of them left!"

Ben glanced at George and scoffed. "Just because nothing's blown up for a while doesn't mean there aren't any fundamentalists left. Egypt is on a knife-edge between East and West, Africa and Asia, Islam and Christianity. Growing up here, you learn that close by there's always someone crazy enough to blow something up."

"Add to that the findings on Mars," George commented, "and a police chief prepared to kidnap Gail, and there's more crazy here than I think I can take right now."

Ben pulled up to the old airport terminal. Predictably the Tourism Police and their guns were there, too; after the explosions they would probably be twitchier and even less friendly.

They were directed to park the car in front of a policeman, who aimed his gun straight at them.

"Ben?" George asked, apprehensively.

"Don't worry. Just let me do the talking, and we'll have you on a plane in no time."

George's earlier encounter with the police had taught him that where he put his hands was crucial, so he placed them in plain view on the dashboard. As Ben was guided out of the car by the barrel of an automatic weapon, he thought about how lucky it was he had his passport and luggage with him. They were packed and ready to go to Ben's anyway – the airport had originally been a detour.

His door opened and he was escorted to the bonnet of the car, where Ben was already being searched. Two other policemen were going through the car, presumably in search of explosives or some evidence that could link them to the explosions.

As they did their work, his mind wandered to the mysterious *DEFCOMM* and Gail. It had been a horrid week, during which he had lost her forever, and then been given hope from nowhere that she was alive.

But right now, with Cairo airport closed and an armed police officer frisking him, he felt further away from her than ever before, and his heart sank.

CHAPTER 61

I'm glad you're settling in well," said Dr Patterson. "I was afraid you may have resented me because of your situation. But you can see that I didn't want you to be brought here under these horrible circumstances, can't you?"

Gail smiled across the table. "Sure." She put her fork down after toying with the chunk of meat on her plate and looked at her guest across the table in her new quarter's modest dining room-cum-kitchen-cum-living room.

The fact that she'd been moved so quickly from the sterile 'cell' to this almost comfortable apartment worried her; it felt permanent. Ironically, that very feeling made her want to leave more than ever before.

The apartment was divided into the dining area, single bedroom and shower room. There were no windows and she was, presumably, underground, built into the vast complex of corridors and offices belonging to DEFCOMM.

"I know you're one of the good guys, Dr Patterson. Can I call you Henry?"

Henry grinned and nodded approvingly. "Of course, but only if I can call you Gail?" he added cheekily.

Gail grinned back. *Henry*. It would be easy calling him that, she told herself, as she'd gone out with an annoying idiot called Henry many, many years ago.

The only problem was that Henry was turning out to be far less of an annoying idiot than she had expected.

"Tell me," he said. "I've read your research on Amarna and Aniquilus. But everything, including of course my research here, has centred around the main texts from the pedestal in the Library. What else have you found?"

She gave a wry smile. "You haven't read my research very well, then, have you?" He looked down briefly, as if ashamed at not having known more about her. "The Library contained a vast number of texts, indeed thousands, broken down into four categories," she continued. "The tablets, mostly made out of clay, we found stacked on most of the lower shelves. Remember the shelves were made of wood, so the bottom ones were probably the best place to put them. We also found that the shelf space was classified quite carefully: the higher the document in the shelf, the more important it appeared to be. The pedestal is clearly the epitome of this."

"So the tablets were the least important?"

"It appears so. Ironically, they're also the best preserved by a good margin. In a dry environment, the hardened clay doesn't deteriorate visibly. What they showed, almost exclusively, were purchase ledgers for agricultural produce, such as the trade in livestock and the provision of grain to the royal palace. They were written in a mixture of cuneiform, obviously for international trade, and hieratic hieroglyphs. One tablet was different, in that it had a mixture of full hieroglyphs and hieratic; we believe, *I* believe, that it was written by the Library's architect, a sort of 'I did this' note, although there is no signature."

Henry raised an eyebrow. "I wonder if it could be matched to the story that led us to Amarna in the first place."

"You mean your architect's scroll? Well, you could try, but tablets were written on by pressing a stylus into soft clay, whereas scrolls are written with brushstrokes. In my opinion you could probably trace two tablets back to the same stylus, but it would be impossible to link a scroll to a tablet. You may however be able to link the hieratic, which is highly stylised, to the same author. Your main problem would be getting hold of the tablet in Cairo. I would have been happy to help, but then this all happened."

"What other types of text were in the Library?" Henry did his best to ignore her jab.

"The papyrus scrolls. We were pretty excited to find those, because they're exceptionally rare. Because papyrus can't be folded without cracking, it's generally rolled up. This was the principal medium for storing long texts until the time of the Romans, when parchments were chopped into pages and bound into a codex with a wooden cover. Papyrus is really susceptible to pretty moderate conditions. It doesn't like damp, because it rots, and it doesn't like dryness, because it cracks. In fairness, they had nothing better and at the time it was a technological revolution, as papyrus is cheap and easy to use. But for us archaeologists, they couldn't have made a worse choice. Most surviving papyrus scrolls are from the Roman era, so the Library discovery was remarkable." She paused to sip some wine. "Your architect scroll is a unique sample. From what I saw, it may be one of the oldest and best preserved. It belongs in a museum."

"What of the scrolls in the Library?" he tried to change the subject. Ten years ago he had missed his only opportunity to get the scroll in a museum, and it was too late to go back now.

She sighed. "We were spoilt. While a lot of the scrolls were evidently ruined, dried to the extent that they disintegrated on contact, most were solid. Solid evidently means they cannot be unravelled by hand. The reason some were better preserved than others probably goes back to the origin of the papyrus reeds themselves, their age, storage prior to entering the Library, possibly even the ink used to write on them. The surviving ones were boxed up pretty much within a day of the Library being accessed, and over the next few years, robotic 'readers' at the Museum of Cairo opened them, millimetre by millimetre, until their content could be read. The first to be opened revealed a biography of an inhabitant of Amarna. The everyday account of one family's life, who they were, what they did, and why they were there. On its own, that one scroll confirmed the main theory behind Amarna: that it was a religious experiment, a new beginning and a departure from the ways of the previous dynasties. What astounded us more than anything was the way you could really sense the excitement in the text. They were living in an age of religious enlightenment, where the Pharaoh was not so removed from his people; a more 'down to earth' culture. They really had no idea the experiment wouldn't work. Since then, half a dozen scrolls have been accessed, all with the same subject matter, but each focusing on a different family."

"Why did the experiment fail?"

She shrugged. "There are many ideas. It probably became economically unviable, there would have been foreign pressure on a shrinking Egyptian military power, a coup driven by supporters of the traditional polytheistic ways could have ousted them, and so on. Tutankhaten, Akhenaten's son from a marriage with his own sister, Tiye, changed his name to Tutankhamen, becoming the first king to return to the old capital at Thebes and reject the worship of one god, the Aten. He was young and quite unwell, so probably bowed easily under pressures from traditionalists, most notably the priesthood and military leaders."

"What do you believe?" he looked at her intently.

She accepted his offer of a refill and took a gulp of wine. The more she drank, the sweeter it tasted. "I think that someone, Nefertiti to be precise, persuaded her husband, the new King of Egypt, to leave behind Egypt's militaristic, expansionist ways in favour of a simple life in the country. From what I know now, I believe she did this because she believed that the old ways, if continued, could only lead to destruction and suffering for us all. I think she was a pacifist and a humanist. But in the long run, it failed. Professor al-Misri once compared Amarna to the old Soviet Union, because it looked impressive, but was badly built from poor quality materials, and in the end destined to crumble.

"But it also has another parallel to the Soviet Union: it couldn't exist in isolation, and its premise was counter-intuitive to human nature. They were surrounded by other civilizations, all ready to eat away at their weakened state. You have to remember Egypt was a superpower at this time, so it was an attractive target, too. And as if that wasn't enough, Nefertiti's utopian ideal was destroyed from within by greed. To be honest, I'm amazed it lasted as long as it did." She finished talking and emptied her glass. Henry filled it again.

"Sounds like a good theory."

"Hypothesis," she corrected him.

"What else was in the Library?"

"Architectural drawings carved into wooden tablets, some maps, and our famous books. Until the last couple of days, I thought that my Book of Aniquilus was the only surviving Egyptian codex, predating any known Roman effort by more than a thousand years. But now, it has a twin!" She stopped talking for long enough to realise that Henry was looking at her with a smile on his face. She cringed. He was nice enough as a person, but she could see where this was going; the wine, the mood lighting, the meal. *His greasy bald head.*

"Indeed. Do you think there's anything else in the Library, something you might have missed?"

"Why?" She dragged her eyes away from the top of his head, which was reflecting the spotlight above the table.

"Because of what's happening on Mars," he said. "Two of the crew disappeared behind a door, and we haven't heard from them since. There's obviously a link between the two places, and the books don't mention it. So maybe there's something in the Library, something *architectural?* If we found it, it might help us find a way to get them out, or at least find out for ourselves what's behind the door."

Gail thought to herself for a moment. There had been one big puzzle, one that even the Professor had been stumped by. She looked into her wine, as if it would help her decide whether or not she would share this information with Henry.

"What is it?" he asked.

He's not the enemy, she told herself. *He just wants to help those poor people on Mars. And he's always treated you well, hasn't he? And it's not a bad thing that he's obviously attracted to you – if anything you should be flattered. When was the last time George showed this much interest in your work? In you?* She held the stem of the glass and moved it round in circles, the centripetal force causing the wine to rise up the sides of the glass. *Or was it centrifugal? Either way, I have to get out of here, and this is my chance.*

She looked across the table and into his eyes.

"There is something we never solved. The contents of the Library were so incredible that the place itself was overlooked. Over the last few years it has been revisited, but never with the resources it fully deserved. Remember, it's just a big empty room, now. It's not even that interesting to look at, just a hole underground."

Henry urged her to continue.

"Well, I don't know how much you know about the original dig," she explained, "but we pretty much forced our way in using a big drill." He nodded implicitly. "OK, you know that, because the engineers were your guys, weren't they?"

"Well, not mine, but certainly on the same payroll, yes."

"Anyway, they cut a big hole in the wall, which has been used as the door ever since. There was talk of sealing the hole with a submarine-style hinged door, but it was easier to just move everything inside to a better location to preserve it; once the seal was broken, the environment inside the Library became environmentally unstable, open to the changing humidity of the outside world; everything was at risk, whether we closed the door again or not."

"So if you cut a hole in the wall, where was the original, Egyptian door?"

"Exactly." She let the word hang over the table like an unwelcome guest for several moments before continuing. "At first, before we got inside, it was something we had wondered. But inside the antechamber, all the other walls were bedrock. Only the one we drilled through had anything on the other side. Once we got inside, the contents of the Library blew us away, but even so it didn't take long to work out that there was no obvious door."

"So it's never been found?"

"Not just that," she had a sparkle in her eye. "We had so much to study from the Library and so much preservation work to undertake, it would have been scientifically irresponsible to uncover anything else before we had reasonably dealt with the initial finds first."

"*Initial* finds? I thought you said you emptied the Library. What else are you expecting to uncover?"

"Think about it: if we found the Library by digging through the wall, we must have missed the main entrance, and any other rooms in between. Because of its location underground, and our searches above ground, the main entrance has to be some way off. So somewhere down there is something more than *just* a Library. I believe, and so did the Professor, that the Library held the main treasure trove, the hidden secrets of Amarna. But I also believe that once we find the door inside the Library, we'll find something that Egyptologists have been trying to find for over a hundred years."

Henry looked at her blankly, and she groaned. "You *really* don't know much about this, do you?" she said rolling her eyes. "Nefertiti! The Library is part of the tomb complex of Nefertiti!"

"Incredible," he said with genuine surprise. "So the Library is only part of an as yet unexplored tomb at Amarna, and you believe you can get inside?"

"I think that with the correct tools and equipment, we can. Do you think it's worth a try?"

He thought for a few seconds. "I do. There's obviously a massive difference in the two sites, in that one predates the other by a couple of hundred thousand years, and happens to be on another planet," he laughed dryly. "However, they are also strikingly similar: they both contain the only known uses of the Aniquilus symbol, the Stickman, and they're both 'tombs' underground. Finding out the secrets of how to open doors in the Library may help with Mars." He curled his bottom lip and looked down. "And besides, it's all we have to go on, so it's better than sitting here doing nothing."

Now, Gail, ask him now. Her idea to contact George had been darting in and out of her mind for hours, forming and reforming dozens of times from plausible scenarios to preposterous long-shots. Finally, in the last few minutes and moments, it had formulated into what could conceivably be described as a 'plan'. She still had the memory stick in the envelope, but now she had a shot at something far more likely to succeed. She had one opportunity to put it into action.

"We can go to the Library," she started. "But we'll need unrestricted access, with machines and electronic equipment; that kind of thing is controlled by the Tourism and Antiquities Police, in conjunction with the Egyptian Museum in Cairo. It takes weeks, months, sometimes even years to get that granted, with all the necessary paperwork."

"Unfortunately, we don't have that kind of time; and with al-Misri gone, I have no contacts there," Henry said sadly, scratching his chin.

Gail swigged her wine and swallowed hard; deception wasn't her forte, though perhaps the wine would help.

"I have an old friend in Cairo who can get us in, bypassing all of that red tape, for a moderate 'donation.'" She looked over Henry's shoulder as if in thought, before continuing. "If you send him an email, saying you need urgent access to the site and can be as generous as needs be, he should get that sorted. To make it plausible, you'll need to pretend you're doing some research, and need to check an inscription inside the Library."

"Is that all I would need to tell him?" Henry asked.

"I'll give you a picture from my tablet. You can attach that and say it relates to your studies. That should do the trick easily."

He pondered the idea for a few moments, then nodded approvingly. "I don't think we can reasonably wait even several days, so if it could work and he gets us in no questions asked, it's got to be worth trying. Otherwise, I imagine they'll just force their way in. But these guys know the importance of being discrete, so they'll appreciate that. I'll check it with Mallus in the morning, and we'll get the picture on my laptop and send the email."

She almost suggested they send it straight away, but stopped herself in time. *Best not to seem too eager in case it gives me away*, she thought. Instead, she finished her wine, and offered her glass to Henry for another refill.

Filling it up, he caught the twinkle in her eye and smiled, wrongly assuming it was meant for him. "What's his name?"

"I'm sorry?"

"What was his name? This friend of yours in Cairo?"

"Oh! Sorry, I was miles away. His name is Farid Limam."

He repeated the name to himself, as if mentally writing it down.

"Yes, but he doesn't use the *Farid* much, only on official documents and such. His email address uses his nickname."

"Which is?"

She sauntered to the bedroom, leaving the door open behind her as she came back with a pencil and small notebook. "Just like a hotel," she joked as she waved the pencil at him, showing the NASA symbol along its edge. After jotting down the address, she passed it to him and picked up her glass once more, trying to look as relaxed as possible.

"How strange," he said, raising an eyebrow.

Her heart skipped a beat. Had the unofficial-looking email address caused an alarm bell to ring in Henry's mind? "What's that?" she managed to say with a smile before taking a mouthful of wine.

"How on earth does *Farid* give him the nickname *Ben*?" he said with a grin.

She breathed out in relief and swallowed the warm red wine, before returning what she hoped was an amused shrug. Internally, her mind raced as she thought of the complex chain of events that would still have to occur for her escape to be successful: getting the picture to Henry without it being scanned for encrypted messages, Henry sending the email to Ben, Ben reading the email and having the presence of mind to send it to George, George having the common sense to work out what the hell it all meant, and then being there in Amarna at the drop of a hat, armed with hopefully more than just a laptop and a pencil, to rescue her from Henry, Seth Mallus, and however many henchmen they decided to bring with them to protect their investment.

Henry looked across the table at her, the grin still painted on his face. His eyes rested for a fraction of a second too long over her shoulder at the door of her bedroom, which she had forgotten to close on her way back with the pencil and notebook.

Bugger, she thought, coming back to the here-and-now with a thud. Before all of those things could happen, before the picture, the email, the unlikely common sense of her husband and the improbable rescue in Egypt, before all of that came one little thing: making a man wait for the second date.

Suddenly, in comparison, the rescue in Egypt seemed like a walk in the park.

CHAPTER 62

George had never seen such a surreal change in behaviour. Once the police had finished fully searching the car, and both himself and Ben, they lowered their guns and all broke out in smiles. Ben was shaking the hand of a policewoman, the only female in uniform he could see in front of the airport, who pointed to a row of parked cars behind a now-raised barrier.

Looking to his right, he saw the steady line of airport traffic diverted from the drop-off point, people inside their cars looking over at them and the tantalizingly-close entrance to the terminal. It was a miracle they were still alive, and had not been shot on sight.

While Ben parked the car, George was escorted to the entrance. They met at the revolving doors, and Ben gave him a wink before saying goodbye to the woman.

"We go way back," he explained with a laugh. "We did our military service together!" They entered the door and followed it round until they were spat out into the air-conditioned foyer of the airport.

George shook his head. "It didn't look like you went way back before they'd checked us out a bit, though. Doesn't she trust you?"

"I haven't seen her for years, and today is a special day," Ben explained. "We got on well for the short time I was in the army, we keep in touch every now and then."

"Did she just do us a massive favour, by letting us in?"

"Yes and no." Ben looked up at the departures board. "I said we had to get you home, she said the only way was to swim, I said there must be a plane, she said go and check it out for yourself."

George looked at him, then up at the departures. Everything was cancelled, with the exception of an Iberia flight to Madrid, which was boarding: it was the last flight out of Cairo.

"I can get that plane," he said pointing at the departures list. "Then it's easy to get to America!" He started running towards the ticket office, followed closely by Ben.

"I think I've changed my mind, George," he shouted as his friend shot off. "I mean, are you sure you want to get on a plane today?"

Groups of tourists with luggage strewn around them stared as they ran past.

"Sure, why not?" George shouted back.

"Well, because..." Ben hesitated. There were words you just didn't say in airports. "Because of the things that are happening out there."

"You said so yourself: I need to get to the US somehow, and that isn't going to happen if I stay here."

He reached the Iberia ticket desk. Slamming his passport on the desk, he took a few moments to catch his breath before asking for a ticket to Madrid.

Behind the desk, the two clerks looked at each other and shook their heads in unison.

"I'm sorry, sir. There are no seats left. I can sell you a ticket for Monday; we expect full service to resume by the morning but understandably we have a backlog of passengers so all seats for the next two days are already taken. In the meantime, you will have to return to your hotel, or stay in the terminal." She pointed to some seats behind him.

He looked around, and realised that all the seats were taken. There were even people sitting on the floor, some sitting on their luggage, and quite a few leaning against the walls. Almost all of them had looked over at George and Ben, and were now returning to their own little worlds with smiles on their faces, as if to say *idiots, don't they think we would have tried that if there had been any seats left?*

Seeing the mass of people that filled the terminal, George suddenly came back to reality. "OK," he turned to Ben. "Looks like your policewoman-buddy was right. Do you think it's safe to go back to your place?"

"Probably," he ventured.

"First, I need a drink, though."

They found a café in the far corner of the terminal building, nestled between a shop and the outer wall of the airport. It was a small, discreet little outlet, quite some distance from the usual hubbub of Departures and Arrivals. But today was proving to be exceptional in many ways, and it took him ten minutes to get to the front of the queue and order their drinks. He chose a couple of cakes, too, and several minutes later they had settled on a large rectangular flower pot set into the marble floor on which they could sit and contemplate their next move.

"God, I am starving," George said as he munched his way through both of the chocolate muffins he had bought.

Ben was flicking through messages on his phone, sipping the unfamiliarly-sized 'Grande Cappuccino' or whatever it was, when he suddenly gave a confused grunt.

"No way," he said.

George didn't reply, as his mouth was full of chocolate and coffee at the same time. Not wanting to talk with his mouth so grotesquely full, he started chewing faster to offer a reply, but Ben passed him his phone to look at instead.

On screen was an email in English.

Dear Mr Limam,

I understand that you are responsible for archaeological expeditions to the ancient Library of Akhetaten at Tell el-Amarna.

While most research to date has focussed on the texts that were found there, my main area of interest lies in the Library itself. I am particularly interested in the attached inscriptions, and would like to correlate this with the physical evidence on-site.

I would like to be able to access the Library to see some of the evidence first-hand with some special equipment I have developed. I have been led to believe that you may be able to help me with this, without having to go through all of the 'red-tape' of a full excavation. My equipment is extremely experimental, and my fear is that authorisation will not be forthcoming.

It is vital that I am able to present some findings to my sponsors at the end of next week; as you will appreciate, my continued research depends on this.

I will be arriving in Amarna on Saturday afternoon; while I know that this is very short notice, I would be very grateful to you if you can make the necessary arrangements.

Naturally, I will ensure you are more than compensated for any costs you may have in setting this up.

Yours Sincerely

Dr Henry Patterson
Harvard University
Department of Anthropology

George looked up from the phone. Having swallowed his muffin and coffee, he asked Ben. "Do you really do this sort of thing?"

Ben shook his head. "I haven't been near Amarna for years, since just after the dig, in fact. I wouldn't know how to get this guy in there to save my life!"

He took the phone back and clicked on the picture attached to the email. Studying it carefully for a few moments, he turned to George and raised an eyebrow. "And he sent a load of hieroglyphs, too."

George glanced over and shrugged. "He's clearly full of crap. I bet he sent this to everyone who ever went to Amarna. It may even be from the police, trying to trap you." He thought for a second. "Come to think of it, it's probably from that bastard Kamal, trying to get some leverage on you so that you won't talk and spill the beans on him for what he did. He didn't expect you to be there today, so he's probably desperately trying to cover his tracks now."

Ben shook his head slowly as he looked at the ancient writing. "Kamal doesn't know who I am, George. And it seems like a pretty roundabout way of doing things. I'm sure Kamal could just silence me if he wanted to. I mean, I'm just a little guy in a big city, and accidents happen. Besides, if he was looking to cover his tracks, the last thing he would have done is to tell us there had been a cover up, and on top of that leave a clue to help find your wife." He zoomed out on the screen and looked at all of the hieroglyphs at once, then re-read the letter from Dr Henry Patterson.

"That is very strange."

"What?" George asked.

"I'm a bit out of touch with my ancient Egyptian, but that text, I am certain, is not from the Library. Firstly, it refers to the god Amun, and Ipet-Isut."

"Ipet-Isut?"

"The great temple complex at Karnak," Ben explained. "And secondly, it occurs to me now that there are no engravings inside the Library, save for the cartouche of Nefertiti and the Stickman."

George thought for a second then raised an eyebrow. "You're right, come to think of it!"

"So what is this idiot Dr Patterson from America on about? Contacting the wrong person with the wrong hieroglyphs!"

They stared at the screen in silence for almost a minute, before

George's eyes opened wide. "Could it be?" he said under his breath.

"Could it be what?"

"Forward me that email," George said, standing up.

Ben was about to ask why but he had already gone, striding towards a couple of Internet terminals.

"Come on," he said over his shoulder.

Ben jumped up and followed him, bringing his coffee with him.

By the time he reached his friend, the Englishman had already paid for an open session with his credit card, and was connecting to a remote computer through the Internet browser. Seconds later, a boot screen appeared, followed shortly by a whirling logo and a welcome dialogue, asking George to enter his password.

"Is that your home PC?" Ben asked, obviously impressed by the speed with which George used all the shortcuts on the keyboard and touchscreen. "Wow. You're quick."

George grinned. "I have to use this stuff every day; anything that makes it quicker has to be good. Plus, it looks cool," he added with a wink. "Did you send me the picture?"

Ben obliged, forwarding the email from his mobile phone.

Seconds later, George had extracted the image and opened it. "A little app I wrote for Gail; the secret to all her translation skills," he commented, tapping the side of his nose.

Ben had seen enough movies and TV shows to know that tapping the side of your nose implied that they were now sharing a secret; in Egypt, however, it usually meant 'trust me'. The smile also suggested George was probably joking, and that there was no real secret to be shared.

He tapped the screen and a small input dialogue appeared. In it, he entered his usual password, and an error popped up: *'incorrect keyword!'* He entered all the passwords he'd used in the past, in his secret messages with Gail, each time with the same error. He cast his mind back as far as possible, to their first days together. Memorable places, anniversaries, places, people.

"Jesus, Gail, what's the keyword?" he growled in exasperation. In response to Ben's quizzed expression, he explained. "I built a little cryptographic function into this app when I wrote it," he said. "Just a fun little tool to send each other hidden messages. It's called steganography. You can hide pretty much whatever you want in an image, as long as the ratios are correct."

Ben looked at the picture again. "And you think this is one of those?"

"It has to be. Have you ever been sent hieroglyphs by anyone?"

"No," Ben admitted.

"Then why now? Why would anyone send you hieroglyphs now? It has to be Gail trying to get a message to us, using this Dr Patterson and you as proxies to get hold of me." He hit the enter key and slammed the keyboard when the same error popped on the screen for the twentieth time.

"Why do you need a password?"

"It's called a keyword, and I need it to decrypt the message. Without it all I have is a series of zeros and ones in no particular order. I wouldn't know where to start. The keyword is set when the original message is encrypted. It would be a word that Gail would have chosen."

"What have you tried?"

"Everything. Birthday's, our pet names for each other, parents, hometown, university friends, pets, favourite TV shows, films, towns, and I even tried Amarna, just in case."

"I probably would have chosen Amarna first," Ben commented. He thought for a moment. "Have you tried 'Mars'?"

George keyed the four letters in and hit enter. The error popped up. "Yes, I have."

Ben thought for a few more moments then asked George for the keyboard. When he was in front of the keys, he took a second or two to find the letters on the unfamiliar layout, and then hit enter.

After a longer delay, a popup informed them that the decryption had succeeded.

George looked at Ben in wonder. "What did you type?"

"Nefertiti."

George slapped his forehead for not thinking of it. It had to be an archaeologist thing, he told himself. Taking control of the computer screen once more, he tapped the popup to open the secret message.

They both read in silence.

Being held by DEFCOMM, Florida. Dr Henry Patterson. Help. No chance of release. Sorry.

ILY.

G

George could feel the emotion rising in him as Ben squeezed his shoulder. He put his hand on the screen, touched the words, caressed the initial of her name, and pressed the 'ILY' fondly. *She isn't dead*, he thought. *She hasn't been dead.* His mind raced back to the body identification he had been taken through back in the morgue, when he had punched Captain Kamal. Had it been Gail? Had he been so close to his wife, still breathing imperceptibly, and not known the truth?

He punched the screen, liquid crystals changing colour grotesquely as they gave way under his fist. "I could have stopped him!" he blurted out. "Bastard!"

The hand on his shoulder loosened, and Ben re-read the email from Dr Patterson. "We still have a chance to get her back," he said.

"How?" George exclaimed. "She's in Florida, and I can't get out of here until tomorrow at the earliest. And even if I did get there, how am I going to get her out of that place?"

"We know she's with Dr Patterson. And according to his email, he's going to be here tomorrow afternoon, at Amarna. And he expects me to help him get in."

George looked up. "Of course." He brought up the email on the main screen. "He probably doesn't know about this hidden message, and Gail must have tricked him into sending it to you. It was one hell of a gamble," he bit his bottom lip. "She couldn't have known that you would have passed it to me. If we hadn't been sitting together when you received it, you would probably have never shown the picture to me at all!"

"True," Ben accepted. "But we *were* sitting together, and we did get the message. We now know where this Patterson guy is going to be, and when. Even if Gail isn't with him, we'll use him to get to her."

George closed down the terminal session and turned to his friend. "Ben, we're not exactly Batman and Robin, are we? I'm sure he won't be coming on his own. We're going to need some help."

They looked at each other for only a handful of seconds before looking towards the main entrance to the airport in unison.

"Does that friend of yours owe you any more favours?" George asked.

"That's exactly what I was thinking, my friend."

As they burst back through the revolving doors they were hit by the mid-afternoon heat reflecting off the melting tarmac of the road, and they stuck to the shade as they made their way back towards the

Tourism Police. Ben's friend detached from a small group and met them halfway. Her Tourism Police uniform was sharply tucked-in at the waist, accentuating her breasts and hips. A long ponytail of slightly curled, jet-black hair protruded from the back of her cap, which cast a shadow across her strong nose and full lips. She was relatively tall, an inch or so taller than Ben, and George couldn't help but wonder just how close Ben had been to her during their military service.

He shook the thought from his mind as his eyes fell to the machine gun. Slung over her shoulder, she was holding it close to her left hip with one hand, a finger curled near the trigger. Not on it, but close enough.

"You're not flying, then?" she said in heavily accented English, an 'I told you so' look on her face.

"We decided to stay in Egypt for a while," Ben said, matter-of-factly. "Zahra, let me introduce an old friend of mine: this is George Turner, from England."

They shook hands briefly, wondering whether she would have taken her hand off the gun if she'd been holding it on her right-hand side instead. He decided that she probably wouldn't. "It's a pleasure to meet you," he said courteously.

"Me too," she replied awkwardly. She clearly wasn't used to being introduced to English people, her conversational English failing her.

The three of them stood looking at each other for several moments, before Zahra broke the silence. "Farid, what are you doing here?" Through politeness, she continued to test her English. George was surprised to hear Ben's actual name. He had never heard anyone call him that, and it took him more than a couple of seconds to make the association between the name and his friend.

Ben replied in Arabic.

Within less than a minute, George found himself standing back as the two broke into what looked like a full-on argument. He tried to pick up on some key words, and managed to discern 'Tell el-Amarna', but that was it; they were simply speaking far too fast for his basic level of Arabic.

Five minutes later, they stopped their discussion long enough for Zahra to break into a perfect white-toothed grin. Turning to George, she shook his hand again.

"Hopefully, I will see you tomorrow morning, George." And with that, she turned on her heel and returned to the group of policemen, who were pretending to ignore them.

Ben looked sheepishly after her. "She will meet us at Amarna tomorrow at dawn. She'll bring some friends, too. She has the weekend off, so it's a case of extreme taking-your-work-home."

"That seemed easy enough," George commented. "I thought you were going to bite each other's heads off for a minute, but then she's all smiles!"

"It was more difficult than you think, my friend," he replied. "It turns out she didn't owe me any favours at all."

"So why did she agree to help us?"

"Because I decided to take a bullet, as they say in American movies. I promised to take her to one of the most expensive restaurants in Cairo."

George looked at Ben in surprise, and then looked at Zahra joking with her colleagues less than twenty yards away. She glanced over at them casually and smiled.

He wouldn't have called it 'taking a bullet'.

"Is it really that simple?" George said in disbelief. "You've organised our own private militia in less than five minutes?"

Ben smiled and got his mobile phone out of his pocket. "Not quite, George. The next step is to call our friend Kamal and ask for a little favour, which he certainly owes us. We need his authority to clear the area surrounding Amarna. If things get ugly, he won't want Gail Turner showing up anywhere in Egypt, so it's in his interest to lend a hand."

CHAPTER 63

Seth Mallus tapped the screen in front of him and waited for the video feed from the control room to pop up. Of all the scenarios they had gone through over the years of planning, this had not been one of them: one astronaut dead, two disappeared and most likely dead, and the fourth going stir crazy by herself on the surface of Mars.

He spilled a couple of tablets into his palm from a small bottle obtained from the bottom draw of his desk, then reached for a glass of water. Knocking back the pills with several gulps of the cool liquid, he closed his eyes and clenched his teeth; his brain was pulsating against the inside of his skull. With every passing moment his headache worsened, not helped by the flow of bad news that had come his way in the last few days. At least the pills would help his headache, but it would be a few minutes at least until they started to kick in.

In the meantime, he massaged his temples, his eyes still closed, and ran through the facts.

The Mars mission had arrived so close to his dream landing site, he couldn't have planned it better. The Book of Xynutians had pointed directly to a site on Mars. In the Book of Xynutians' own words, *on the shore of an empty ocean*. There were dozens of places that could have fit the description, but within days of comparing the illustrations in the book to satellite photography of the planet, they had found an exact match: *Hellas Basin*.

It was too accurate to be a fluke. Weeks of cross-referencing had revealed no further matches, not even a close-second. How the ancient Egyptians had managed to produce such a drawing was beyond explanation. Barely sixty years ago it would have been practically impossible. Three and a half *thousand* years ago, it was unimaginable.

And then there had been his dream. His dreams had always been very vivid, and surreal. But this one? He could still feel, taste and hear the crater-site on Mars, as it was in the time of the Xynutians. It wasn't

322

just a dream. It felt more like a *recollection*. The image had stuck with him ever since.

Nevertheless, he had certainly not expected the crew to find the Xynutian remains within days of arriving, by simply throwing a stone at them. Either the crew were incredibly lucky, or there were so many remains on Mars that they simply had to stumble upon one sooner or later. More importantly though, his dream, and the book, had been bang-on.

No one could ever find out about their finds, not even NASA, which was where his headache had come from. Influencing the decision to put the mission on the shore of the Hellas Basin had been fairly straight forward: enough of the scientific community thought it would be a good place to land anyway, which reduced the amount of lobbying needed along NASA's corridors. Making sure that no one outside his office knew they had been influenced, and even more importantly, *why* they had been, was infinitely harder.

It had been easy enough to control the nanostations on-board the *Clarke*, and the interception of the communication relay with Earth had been straightforward. DEFCOMM built and maintained the satellites in orbit, the receiver dishes on Earth, and owned the encryption technology that was used to hide the signal from the rest of the world. With five hundred and twelve bit encryption, even an intercepted signal would take over three years to decode using the fastest supercomputer on the planet, barring the use of quantum computers, which remained inaccessible in a practical sense. For all intents and purposes, he was in total control of the Earth's view of the spaceship.

Their first mistake, however, had come after introduction of the time-delay. Sooner or later they would need to be able to edit what was happening to the mission so that if they did eventually stumble upon alien remains on Mars, those facts could remain hidden from Earth. The most obvious solution was one that had been used for decades in reality television: a time lag, which meant that what people were watching was actually minutes or even hours old, giving the show's producers ample time to cut to adverts, bleep out swearwords before the watershed, or change camera to avoid showing certain things that the censors would rather the public didn't see.

Of course on Earth it would become painfully apparent that something was wrong if anyone tried to have a real-time conversation, which was why they had waited for *Clarke* to be far enough away to make any kind of to-and-fro impractical. Earth sent messages out, and the crew replied when it was convenient to do so, and the time delay would never be noticed.

But on *Clarke*, they had not counted on Su Ning, her excellent mental arithmetic and, crucially, her clandestine watch that kept perfect time with Beijing. After she realised the time delay had been introduced, only eliminating her avoided compromising the entire mission.

Shortly after the discovery of the Jetty, and the Xynutian settlement, they had switched to computer generated imagery, to replace almost all external shots on Mars with faked footage generated by their programmers. Shots outside were easy to produce, mainly because everything was either mechanical or alien. Anyone watching would be unable to tell the difference between a fake rock or a real one, and a spacesuit doesn't exactly have a personality. But everything inside the MLP continued to be real footage, edited and modified as little as possible depending on the topic of the astronaut's banter.

But then, disaster.

In the space of a few hours, the two leading astronauts on the project had disappeared inside the Xynutian settlement. That had a double effect: firstly, it was now obvious on all video returning from Mars that Dr Jane Richardson was alone. Secondly, she had been in a near-hysterical state for hours now, and when she wasn't screaming into the cameras, she was sitting down staring into her hands, or shouting into the microphone at the comms panel in a desperate attempt to get hold of her fellow astronauts, whose air had long since run out.

None of the video coming back from Mars could be sent to NASA without him having a lot of explaining to do. He couldn't allow that to happen.

So for a while now, there had been no feed from Mars. NASA had been told there was a technical problem with one of the satellites in the receiver array. At best, it would buy them a month before a new satellite or repair crew could be launched, at worst NASA would demand that video be transmitted via a different satellite. To stop it coming to that, they had provided a steady stream of synthesised voice clips from Mars. These had been much easier to produce, due to the interference that plagued interplanetary communications.

His headache was starting to subside, and he opened his eyes. Looking at the screen, he watched Dr Richardson fetch herself a glass of water from the kitchen unit of the MLP. She was millions of miles away, alone on a dead planet.

He picked up the phone and dialled a secure line. Almost immediately, there was an answer from the other end.

"How long till they reach their target?" he asked.

"Just under an hour, Sir."

"Let me know when you have news." He hung up abruptly and looked at the video from Mars.

Dr Patterson and Dr Turner had come up with a hair-brained scheme, in his opinion. But if the Amarna Library did, miraculously, give them a clue as to how the Xynutian door mechanism would open, then there may be some hope. If the astronauts trapped inside had somehow survived, if there was some improbable source of oxygen inside the ancient settlement, then there was a chance that they could return to the surface of Mars soon, and they could return to normal video feeds before NASA decided to intervene.

That was a lot of ifs, and the odds on the last two were too long for his liking.

From his perspective, the Mars mission had already fulfilled its primary objective: it had proven without a doubt that the book from Amarna had been telling the truth. The Xynutians had indeed existed, hundreds of thousands, *millions* of years before modern humans had crawled from the dirt and started their long journey to civilisation. This in turn meant that they must have been wiped out by Aniquilus, which in turn led to the worst possible conclusion: there was no doubt that mankind was about to meet the same fate.

Which was what was making his head hurt. He had come to terms with the Xynutians, and their advanced civilisation, but what troubled him was Aniquilus. This *thing* that wiped them out just didn't make sense. It came from nowhere.

Unless Aniquilus *was* the Xynutians. And if that turned out to be true, then humans would become their own Aniquilus.

There would be one last roll of the dice, one last chance for Mars to reveal more of the Xynutian's secrets, how the end came about and what could be done to avoid the same fate for the humans. That last chance lay in the mission to Amarna, with Dr Patterson.

And if they don't succeed? In his mind, the Amarna books were clear on one detail: the Xynutians had been erased because they spread too far, they consumed everything and they failed to fit in with their environment. Mankind had achieved the same dominance on Earth, and there was only one way back.

If there was no good news from Amarna, then there would be no choice but to pass to Plan B, before it was too late. All the pieces fit together perfectly.

That he had come across the architect's script and found the texts from Amarna, both could be put down to chance. That he was also able to manipulate a manned mission to Mars, and that half the world's defence systems were in his control could not. There was only one person on Earth who had been placed in such a position, or indeed could have been.

He would therefore follow his instincts, and the prospect of doing so made his skin tingle in anticipation.

He stroked the image of Dr Richardson on the screen.

"Am I Aniquilus?" he whispered.

CHAPTER 64

It was ten years since George had visited Amarna, yet it was as if the whole place was frozen in time. Nothing had changed since 2036, except that the small town on the other side of the Nile seemed slightly more deserted than before, and the ferry had acquired a new pilot.

Even the warm breeze felt the same as he emerged from the air-conditioned confines of Ben's car, which had struggled along the dirt track leading to the bottom of the cliff, on top of which sat the engraved stone marking the entrance to the famous Library his wife had discovered. That is, if sitting on something to catch your breath could really be called 'discovery'.

Ben took the lead as he clambered up the crumbling cliff towards the small plateau.

"Shame we didn't rent a Land Rover," George shouted up to him as he neared the top.

Ben rested against the cliff top and looked out over the sandy-plain below, towards the Nile. "Not really," he said shaking his head. "It's much quicker this way, as the other route takes you round the whole place to approach from the back."

George reached his level, and they both took the final steps up to the plateau. Less than ten yards from where they stood was a small gatehouse made of breeze-blocks, no larger than a typical garden shed. It had no windows, and the metal door was locked with a large Yale padlock. A few yards away was the stone that had sealed the Library.

"Welcome to the finest archaeological find of the twenty-first century," Ben mused as he handled the padlock, turning it over as if looking for weaknesses. "The most important site in Egypt is closed by a single lock, with no guard. And thanks to Kamal, the closest police are over five kilometres away." He took off his rucksack and opened it, removing a foot-long crowbar. Inserting it into the ring of the padlock, he wedged one end of the bar against the frame of the door, and pulled back. The leverage applied to the padlock was insufficient to break the hardened steel, but the bolt the lock was fastened to buckled almost immediately. After re-adjusting the angle of the crowbar, he pulled back again in a single, jerking motion, and the lock fell away from the door, leaving it to swing freely on its hinges.

George looked at his friend in surprise. "Have you done this before?" he asked.

Ben opened the door and shrugged. "No. But when you've watched as much TV as I have, you pick up a few useful tricks."

They were about to step inside when there was a shout from behind them.

"Stop!" a female voice barked authoritatively.

Ben turned round with a grin on his face, and George did his best to fight the urge to run away; the natural response programmed into him was to get as far away from the scene of the crime as possible, whether that crime was stealing cookies between meals as a child or breaking into one of the most highly regarded historical sites in Egypt. The dilemma facing him must have been obvious to his audience, because Zahra laughed out loud, and Ben slapped him on the shoulder.

"Sorry, George," he said. "I lied to you, there are some police here." He nodded towards Zahra and her four friends, three men and a woman, who followed her out from behind an outcrop of rocks twenty yards away. George thought he recognised one of the men from the patrol outside the airport in Cairo the previous afternoon. Though none of them were in uniform, they all carried weapons, which George assumed to be AK-47s. They were certainly not the sleek, modern-looking guns from the day before.

Zahra caught him looking at her rifle, and she winked at him knowingly. "So they do not know it is us," she said.

"The police weapons are all traceable to the individual," Ben explained, "based on biometric authentication built into the grips. Each bullet can be traced back to the gun that fired it, which can in turn identify who fired the shot and when the gun was fired."

George looked at him in wonder. "You really do watch a lot of TV, don't you?" Turning back to Zahra, he smiled and offered his hand. "Thank you for helping us, I hope you aren't taking too much of a risk?"

She laughed freely, shaking his hand and then nudging Ben in the ribs. "No risk, don't worry. It's like old times, eh Farid?"

Ben looked sheepish, like a schoolboy being told off for getting his uniform muddy playing football, but knowing that he's not in too much trouble and that it was absolutely worth it. Looking at George, he shrugged.

"I don't know what she's talking about," he said.

Zahra brushed away his denial with a movement of her free hand. Choosing to move on to more important things, she proceeded to introduce her friends by first names only.

Manu and Haji waved as she gestured towards them and they heard their names; it was quickly apparent that neither of them spoke a word of English. It still came as a surprise to George to meet people who didn't speak any English at all, which said a lot for the frequency with which he left the beaten track and ventured into the heart of any foreign country. Their lack of English also highlighted his own deficiencies in Arabic; usually, he would be able to meet anyone half way with a mix of English and Arabic, bastardised into some unofficial 'Arabish,' but when it relied solely on him, it was another story entirely. While they had obviously not been chosen for their linguistic or interpersonal skills, it was clear why Zahra had decided to bring them along: Manu was over six feet tall, had arms as thick as George's thighs, no neck and a nasty scar running down the left cheek of his otherwise attractive, angular features. Haji, despite being a good six inches shorter, had a stocky physique and wouldn't have looked out of place in a boxing ring.

Without weapons, they would have been a fearsome sight. With them, they were truly terrifying, and George was glad to have them on his side.

The third man, Tariq, had indeed been at the airport the day before, and he shook George's hand enthusiastically. There was obvious excitement in his eyes, and while his English was worse than Zahra's, which itself was far from perfect, his willingness to understand more than made up for it. Despite his less imposing physique when stood alongside Haji and Manu, Tariq carried his AK-47 rifle with an ease and comfort that demonstrated years of experience handling weapons.

The final addition to their septet was Leena. Almost as striking as Zahra, she was slightly taller, and had a crop of short bleach-blond hair covered with a Yankees baseball cap she wore back to front. Her English, though heavily accented, was close to perfect, which she explained as being down to her university education in Ireland. As soon as she mentioned it, George couldn't help but pick up on a hint of

329

Gaelic melody in her voice.

On top of the Kalashnikov assault rifles, the small company each had a holstered pistol and rucksacks, which George guessed held everything they would need for a small war. Zahra explained that they each carried ammunition, food and water as well as flashlights and encrypted walkie-talkies. They were all dressed casually except for their jackets, which were the type of flack-jacket the press would wear while reporting from a war-zone.

Tariq had a large spear-point knife in a sheath buckled to his lower right leg. It was a foot long, and had a hanger attachment on its wood-covered handle, indicating it was a bayonet. George couldn't imagine how lethal the man would be holding an AK-47 with ten inches of carbon-steel sticking out of the end.

Again, Zahra caught him staring at the weapons, and she broke into another perfect smile. "The bayonet is a real history item," she said. "Over eighty years old."

He raised an eyebrow, impressed, and Tariq gladly pulled the slender blade from its metal sheath and passed it to him. It weighed as much as a bag of sugar, and he marvelled at how the ancient weapon, which felt more like a sword, looked as good as new.

"Amazing," he said, passing the bayonet back to Tariq. "I really hope you don't have to use it today!" He truly meant it.

"Don't worry, George," Ben reassured him. "We'll do our best to get Gail back without bloodshed. But don't forget, we're not starting this; they took her away. And because they left a body in her place, we know that they have no plans of ever releasing her. They're going to kill Gail if we don't rescue her first, George."

He nodded slowly, looking from face to face as he summed the situation up. He felt that they were waiting for his approval before moving forwards with their plans; *my wife - my call*, he thought grimly. There were seven of them in total; five well-armed and, he assumed, well-trained people, alongside Ben, whom he was sure would be getting a gun from somewhere before Patterson arrived. And then there was him, the odd one out, with no previous experience, he'd never even been in a fight, save for punching Captain Kamal and the odd bust-up at school, let alone fired a weapon. When he had held the bayonet, the one thought that occurred to him was how much heavier than his bread knife it was. This alone told him he was better off out of the combat zone.

But his emotional side was in conflict with this calm analysis. Gail was being held by Patterson, who would be in Amarna in a matter of hours. Would he be happy to simply stand by and watch as people he barely knew did all the work? *Like hell I will*, he thought. For the past few days, she had been officially dead. Now the man responsible for that was going to be handed to him on a plate.

He looked at Zahra sternly. All trace of a smile vanished from her face as she waited to hear his assessment of the situation.

Ben leaned forwards. "George, this may be our only chance to get close to these people. Once they leave Egypt, they're untouchable," he urged. "What do you say?"

"Do you have a spare gun?"

CHAPTER 65

Squatting in the shade of the gatehouse, they went over the plan once more, with Ben and Leena translating into English, to make sure George was comfortable with it.

"I will greet Patterson at the foot of the cliff, with Zahra's Toyota, on my own. I will be unarmed, and carry with me the fake excavation permits that we made last night back in Cairo," Ben said.

"And if he realises they are fake?" George asked.

Ben shook his head. "He won't. Zahra was completely taken in by them at first, so an American will be fooled for sure. Besides, he has no reason not to trust me." He looked at his watch and realised they had little more than an hour until Patterson's scheduled arrival time. They had all agreed that they should be in position with three quarters of an hour to spare, in case he was early. Otherwise they would all be clearly visible from a distance, standing on the small plateau. "I will then lead him round the road to approach the plateau from the rear. Zahra, you will observe from the ridge. This then gives you five minutes to prepare before we arrive at the Library entrance, and to make sure we are not followed by anyone. We then have one of three options." He gestured to Leena to explain.

"Option one, this Patterson man is alone: we meet him at the top with guns. Option two, he is not alone, but there are more of us: we meet him at the top with guns. Option three, he is not alone, but there are more of them." She pointed to a narrow gulley, at the bottom of which a rough trail led up towards the Library entrance. "There, if there is more than one car, we attack the rear one when it passes through. This makes a trap."

"So if there are two cars, the front one has nowhere to go," George agreed.

"We attack first," Ben added. "If they outnumber us, then we have one chance only to take advantage. Once we lose the element of surprise, it'll be impossible to win. If he brings people with him, I have no doubt that they will be well trained."

George nodded in understanding. "What do we do to the trapped car?"

"Hopefully, the trapped one will be the Toyota with me in it." Ben replied.

"And Gail?"

Ben looked at Zahra. "You have the photo of her, so you know what she looks like. If she is here, I will make sure that she gets in the Toyota with me and Patterson. Just in case she doesn't though, you will need to make sure everyone knows which car she is in."

George mused this for a few moments, scratching his chin. "What if she's in the last car?"

"Then I let them go ahead of me on the way up. They go through, and I block the exit," Ben replied simply.

The three of them thought this through in silence for over a minute, before Zahra stood up, stretched her legs and picked up her AK-47. "Good plan," she said with a yawn. They'd all been there for over three hours now, and had been over the plan several times in Arabic already.

Ben started to stand up as well, but George put his hand on his shoulder. "Ben, what is the worst case scenario? What don't we want?"

"That they get inside the Library, especially if they have Gail. If they get her down there, they have her as a hostage, and it gets complicated." He looked back at him and put his hand on George's comfortingly. "But don't worry, we won't let that happen.

George looked at the door hanging loose on its hinges, the padlock and bolt mechanism, now useless, sat in a heap in the sand. "If you hadn't broken the lock, it would be a lot harder for them to do that, you know?" he said sarcastically.

Ben shrugged and picked the padlock up as he made it to his feet. "True, but if they have guns, and they live that long, then they'll have bullets to open the door anyway."

George brushed out the attack plan diagrams they had made in the sand with his foot, and picked up his own AK-47 that had been leaning against the breeze-block wall. The first time he had held a weapon had been an hour ago, when they had passed him the rifle from the back of the Toyota. It was heavier than he had imagined it would be, more so than a six-pint container of milk. He shook his head as he thought of the comparison; it was odd to find that the only things he could compare weapons to had so far been things found in the kitchen.

Tariq had walked him through the basics of holding, arming and firing the rifle, which seemed simple enough that even a child could do it. He thought of news stories from the Middle East and central Africa, and realised that children *did* do it.

The AK-47 had two firing modes. The first of these was semi-automatic, where one bullet, or *round* as Ben kept reminding him, was fired every time the trigger was fully depressed. To fire another round, the trigger needed to be fully released and then pressed again. The second mode was full-automatic, which everyone seemed to refer to as *full*. This meant that when the trigger was depressed, rounds would continue to fire until either the trigger was released, or the magazine was empty. You chose which mode to fire by operating a selector on the right-hand side of the rifle to the lowest position for semi-automatic and middle position for full. In its topmost position, the selector acted as the safety catch, and stopped the rifle from firing. "The most important thing," Leena had reminded him, "is to make sure you turn the safety off before firing, and when you hear *click*, let go of the trigger and reload."

While firing seemed pretty straight forward, reloading was something he was less comfortable with. Although it seemed simple in theory, he was sure that in the thick of things, he would forget to do something crucial and the magazine would simply fall out of the bottom in a slapstick fashion, leaving him with an empty weapon and a stupid grin on his face. As he stood in the shade on his own, Zahra and Ben having gone to meet up with the others to confirm their plans, George decided to run through the reload a few more times.

He turned the AK-47 on its side and found the magazine catch, which was underneath the trigger assembly, behind the magazine itself. *I can just see myself pressing that by mistake*, he thought nervously. Pressing it, he pulled the magazine out, and placed it at his feet. He then put the selector on the right of the rifle from *safety* to *semi-automatic*. Grasping the bolt catch, also on the right side of the AK-47, he pulled it back firmly and the single round that had been in the chamber of the rifle popped out of the side. It fell to the floor, and he picked it up cautiously, feeling the weight of the bullet in the palm of his hand before sliding it into his pocket.

Picking up the magazine, he slotted it back into the bottom of the rifle, and pulled the bolt catch back; this time it slid back and forwards again effortlessly. He then very carefully moved the selector into its topmost position and onto safety.

To ensure he'd done it properly, he gave a quick tug on the magazine. Satisfied that it was firmly secured, he release it again, and repeated the whole process twice, on the last attempt managing to catch the chambered bullet as it popped from the side of the rifle.

Happy that he had put in enough practice to remember how to do it in a rush, he ensured the safety was on and shouldered the rifle.

"How are you doing?" Ben said as he strode across the sand towards him, a grim smile on his face.

"Not bad," he admitted. "I think I have the hang of reloading now, it's easier than I first thought!"

Ben patted him on the back and went to lead him to the rest of the group, who were starting their climbs towards their elevated positions on either side of the gulley, above the track. Suddenly, he stopped and pointed towards George's clenched fist.

"What's that?"

George opened his hand, revealing the round he had caught moments earlier. His hand dived into his pocket, and came back out with two more identical rounds. Looking up at Ben, his face dropped.

Ben laughed and took the rounds from him. "Easy, eh? If you'd practised reloading much longer, you'd have run out of bullets!"

They both laughed as Ben removed the magazine, un-chambered a fourth round, and then proceeded to demonstrate how they could be reloaded into the magazine by pressing them down against the other bullets. The spring loaded mechanism would carry the rounds down into the magazine until the last round sat neatly between the lips of the magazine at the top. He then reloaded the AK-47, reset the safety and passed the rifle back to George. "You shouldn't need to do that again, because there are three of these fully loaded magazines in your backpack anyway. You won't need to fire any more than that."

"And if I do?"

"You won't."

Just then, Zahra shouted over at them.

He looked at his watch and cursed in Arabic. "Time, George!"

They were late to their positions, and Patterson was due to arrive in less than forty minutes. Looking up at his friend, he put his hand on the Englishman's arm and smiled. "Do not worry, my friend. You will be fine. We will also be fine, and we will rescue Gail. In less than an hour, we'll all be standing here laughing about it, wondering what all the fuss was about."

George watched as he walked towards the cliff and disappeared over the edge, on his way down to where Zahra had parked the Toyota in preparation. Ben's car was safely hidden behind an outcrop of rocks further down the track.

He turned towards Zahra, in time to see her taking up position, lying down just behind the cliff's edge, giving her a perfect view of Ben and the track that led back to the Nile. Leena and Tariq were settling behind some rocks on the left hand side of the gulley, while Manu and Haji had already disappeared on the right.

He stood on the plateau, alone, surveying the scene for more than a minute before Zahra barked an order at him to hide. Doing as he was told, he ran towards the left side of the gulley, and as he climbed up the smooth stones, thought about Ben's parting comment: *In less than an hour, we'll all be standing here laughing about it, wondering what all the fuss was about.*

George had no idea how wrong this would turn out to be.

PART SIX
18TH NOVEMBER 2045

CHAPTER 66

Seth Mallus checked his watch impatiently. He then barked a single command and looked at the virtual window behind his desk.

The news channel logo sprung into the centre of the screen, wobbling slightly as if to emphasise the speed of its arrival. In doing so, introductory movies of the latest news stories slid out in all directions, filling the screen. The logo then spun round to reveal the disembodied head of a young lady, with thin librarian-style glasses and hair tied up in a short ponytail.

"Would you like a news roundup, or a specific story?" she said smilingly, her head cocked to one side and an eyebrow lifted in anticipation.

"Give me a summary of everything major," he mumbled.

"Thought so," she smirked. She turned round as if to look at the introduction videos behind her, and the camera shifted to her point of view. The videos that had been looping their short introductions in the background fizzled out, to be replaced by a tapestry of a dozen or so smaller videos. One by one they were brought forward, as the avatar gave a running commentary.

"There's been widespread flooding in Eastern Europe, they're now in the fourth consecutive day of non-stop deluge in the Carpathian Mountains, which has swollen many of the rivers in the region. Bratislava and Budapest on the Danube are currently the worst affected large cities, while large areas of countryside in Romania and Slovakia are completely underwater." The video moved from raging torrents of swollen rivers to swathes of people wading knee-deep through murky-brown water, carrying bundles of belongings, children, the elderly and the exhausted. The standing water stretched as far as the eye could see, and power boats littered the countryside, picking up passengers here and there. "A humanitarian crisis is being predicted by the Red Cross and Medecins Sans Frontières, with thousands of refugees fleeing the

339

worst hit parts, while Austria has closed its border with the Slovak Republic. Vienna is on heightened alert for fears the rainfall will move west in the coming days and the Austrian government is making preparations for large scale evacuations of the city. More than a thousand people are thought to have died already, with that number set to rise as conditions for refugees deteriorate."

The video dissolved, to be replaced by several bodyguards clearing a way through a heaving throng of reporters and protesters; then emerged an attractive woman in a red dress-suit, smiling and waving as she followed the bodyguards towards a waiting car. "Jane Getty was today cleared of all charges in the Oil-Aid scandal, by a High Court ruling in Canberra. The Australian far-left politician, who made headlines in July last year for her strong support of the Central African Republic's communist uprising, had been accused of embezzling several billion dollars of funding from the World Bank targeted towards developing infrastructure in Africa. The aid, designed to facilitate the increase in oil production for the region and help meet global energy demands, has so far been very effective in Nigeria, more than doubling its crude oil output to make it the fourth largest oil producing country in the world, behind the United States, Russia and China."

The video switched to a view of a desolate African town. Burnt out cars littered the sides of the road, barely a dusty track between rows of dilapidated shacks. "Jane Getty, a former advisor to OPEC following Australia's accession to full membership in 2042, has fought back at her recent critics, who say that her position in Australian politics is untenable, by attacking Prime Minister Humphries directly. In an interview after her court hearing, Ms Getty called Humphries a *Puppet of Westminster* and a *Slave to nineteenth century Imperialism and the Old World*, who didn't have the strength to break away from Europe and forge new alliances in the Southern Hemisphere to help make Australia a truly great nation." The video cut to a three dimensional pie-chart. "Polls taken directly after the interview showed Getty's Populist party taking a slight lead over the Australian Labour Party, sparking fears in London that dissolution of the constitutional monarchy, in effect since 1901, could be a real possibility when votes are cast in the New Year."

Mallus checked his watch again and then returned his gaze to the screen.

The video disappeared, and another story came forwards.

"Diplomatic relationships between China and the United States worsened this afternoon, as four Chinese warships moved into defensive positions in International Waters off the Pacific coast of America. The ships, Lanzhou class destroyers, form part of the country's recently formed Fourth Fleet, the first Chinese fleet to undertake exercises in so-called *blue water*, beyond the traditional coastal and pacific island range of the Chinese Navy. The public display of strength, a first for typically well-guarded China, comes after talks between the two countries broke down regarding the US military presence in South Korea. In an attempt to play down fears that the situation will escalate further, the President of the United States stated in a press conference that talks would resume soon, and that the diplomatic process would prevail." A flying camera took in miles of border fences, lookout towers and barracks, mirrored on the other side of an empty band of grass a couple of miles wide. "The United States continues to have a significant military presence in South Korea, in particular along the one hundred and fifty mile long Demilitarised Zone, with over forty thousand active personnel stationed there. A recent peace treaty between North and South Korea has been brokered mainly by China, though the former has refused to sign the accord while the United States maintains a presence in the region. Despite significant external pressure, the US has refused to leave its defensive positions, a move largely resented by South and North Koreans alike."

The next video showed the unmistakable backdrop of the Pyramids of Giza, in front of which the sprawl of Cairo shimmered in the baking sun. Plumes of smoke emanated from half a dozen locations across the Egyptian capital. "No one has yet claimed responsibility for yesterday's terrorist bombings in Cairo, which left dozens dead and hundreds more injured. The attacks, against mainly Western targets, are believed to have been carried out by one of a number of Islamic fundamentalist cells in the country, who have been calling for the creation of an Islamic State, the introduction of Sharia Law and an end to the democracy that many Egyptians believe has favoured Western influence over traditional values."

The video of Cairo vanished, to be replaced by a deserted factory, its gates padlocked. "Production at the Chicago Assembly manufacturing plant ended for the last time this morning. The factory, Ford's oldest remaining manufacturing plant, first built the famous Model T Ford in 1924, and in the subsequent century saw production of the characteristic Taurus, Mercury and Centauri models. Analysts see the closure of the Chicago plant as the final nail in the coffin for the American automobile industry, following –"

"OK, stop," Mallus held his hand up, giving a quick glance to his watch as he did so. "Floods, terrorists, diplomatic tension over Korea, political scandals, factories closing, I get the picture." He looked into the eyes of the lady on screen, who had turned round to face him as the screen zoomed away from the news. "No mention of Mars in all that, was there?"

She shook her head. "Nothing new. But everyone knows the real tension between the US and China is because of the cover up on Mars and the suspicion over the Taikonaut's death in transit to Mars. The Korean situation is a good excuse for China to really pull its weight, and thanks to the Mars story, there is considerable public support behind the action."

"And Cairo? The fundamentalists?"

She looked to the top left of the screen pensively for a few seconds, as if trying to remember something, then faced him again. "The online community is largely of the opinion that Islam sees the West as being weakened by the Mars findings. Christianity, which is the main religious belief system in the West, is reeling from the discoveries, and is not dealing with it very well. The existence of intelligent life on Mars seriously puts into question the Book of Genesis, which is the fundament for most of Christianity. So far, the only defensible position that has been put forward is that the Martian findings are human artefacts, but that still contradicts the timelines put forward by the Bible. No official body has commented on the Mars findings yet. Until they do, and in particular until the Vatican does, news agencies remain cautious. One consideration is that with a lack of follow-up evidence from Mars, there is a hope that the story will simply blow over and be judged a fake. This is something the Islamic fundamentalists don't want to happen, so they're taking advantage of it while it's still a hot topic among the general public."

He looked at the lady and shook his head. "Screen off," he said bluntly, and she dissolved into the background looking slightly offended to be switched off.

In her place, a busy cityscape emerged, giving the impression that his office was actually at the top of a tall skyscraper overlooking a large coastal metropolis. The illusion was impressive, one of the more satisfying virtual landscapes that had been programmed in to the office's window to add colour to an otherwise bland underground setting. He afforded it a half-interested gaze for several moments, following a small airship with minor enjoyment as it wound its way round the towering buildings advertising a popular beer. The attention to detail in the simulation was truly stunning, although he knew full well that if he sat there watching for long enough, the very same airship would wind its way inexorably back along the exact same route, *ad infinitum*. The one touch that was unpredictable was the weather, and its effect on the sky. In fact, in spite of the basic algorithms that governed the 'actors' in the scene, the way in which the light played off every surface, even bending round and through individual drops of water as they ran in rivulets down the window panes on a rainy day, meant that it never looked the same twice.

He kept the scene going for a few more moments, until a dark cloud finally slumbered its way in front of the morning sun, before bringing himself from the reverie into which he had so easily fallen. He checked his watch.

It was time, and he didn't want to miss it.

With a couple of concise spoken commands, the window scene disappeared, to be replaced by a split screen. In the top left hand corner he saw Mars; Dr Jane Richardson was sitting at the communication panel of the MLP. Her left hand rested on the joystick controller of a remotely operated camera, while her right hand fidgeted with her unkempt hair. She was staring endlessly at the video output of the remote camera. In the bottom left hand corner, the camera, stationed inside the underground tunnel into which the other two members of the Mars mission had disappeared, panned slowly from left to right, then back again. On the floor, Dr Richardson had set up a spotlight, which was focussed on the stone door that now remained tightly shut.

The bottom right hand corner of his display was blank.

In the top right hand corner of the screen, a CCTV camera showed three utility vehicles reversing into DEFCOMM's main hanger through a large sliding door, which closed as soon as they were safely inside. The drivers, wearing blue overalls and baseball caps, got out and almost as one opened wide the split rear doors of the vans. Three identical teams of six people, wearing white lab coats, wheeled three identical devices, roughly the same dimensions and shape as an average household refrigerator placed on its side, up to the open doors.

Quick checks by the drivers were followed by the devices being loaded carefully and smoothly, until they had disappeared inside the vehicles. The doors were closed, the drivers got back behind their wheels, and the large sliding door of the hanger opened once more. Seconds later, the three vans were gone, the hanger closed, and the men in lab coats had returned to what looked like normal duties: overlooking the final assembly of a thirty foot long missile, checking visual readouts or supervising a large winch assembly that brought segments of a second missile from deep within the DEFCOMM complex.

He checked his watch again: a blink-and-miss-it ninety seconds had passed. Carefully planned, expertly executed. He shook his head in wonderment; there literally was no substitute for getting the right people for the job.

And in that time, on the left hand side of the screen, Dr Richardson had panned the remotely operated camera from left to right and then back again, half a dozen times. Her posture remained unchanged, and she was still fidgeting with her hair.

While hope remained that a solution to the Mars problem would be found, his instincts told him that Dr Richardson, regardless of whether they found the other crew members alive or not, would not fully recover from this ordeal, and replacing her with a simulation was simply out of the question.

Cityscapes indistinguishable from the real thing, busy playgrounds, even Martian exploration; you could fake them all and no one would suspect a thing. But there was no substitute for genuine human behaviour. A real human could tell a fake human's face. Oh, there was no doubt you could play a trick for a while: advanced textures, hair, lighting effects, frame-perfect animation, cartilage-elasticity algorithms and detailed muscular modelling could all come together to create a truly believable person.

But eventually, and unavoidably, the truth would be apparent to the human eye. The news reader was a case in point. She was attractive, had girlish combed-back hair in a cute little ponytail, a nice smile, a couple of freckles here and there, and even had a cheeky little personality. Take a still photo and you could make someone believe she was real. But you only needed to watch one newsfeed to recognise that she wasn't the product of a fruitful human relationship, but rather the output of a skilled development team, the illusion broken by the one thing that cannot be programmed: *Life*.

This to Seth Mallus, at this very moment, was the crux of the whole matter. The paradox with which he had battled internally since the Book of Xynutians had first been presented to him.

How can the propagation of intelligent life, the success of a species, be met with annihilation? How can an advanced species such as the Xynutians be wiped clear from the face of the planet with little or no trace?

The philosopher inside him told him that this was not a paradox. The logical culmination of all life is eventual death. But the logic inside him disagreed. While death was a certainty for some, why should this affect the species as a whole, and not simply the individuals concerned?

He had eventually drawn his conclusions based purely on gut feeling. The action plan he had devised had been put into place almost immediately. There had been no public debate. His position afforded him such executive luxuries, while the lavish defence budgets put forward by the United States government over successive years had been easily diverted to fund the plan. No one had ever sought to question expenditure on a line-item basis, and many of the initiatives had cost relatively little, being simple divergence from original, legitimate projects, the truth of which was divulged to a select, well paid few.

And after years of careful planning and research, tonight he had reached a crossroads, although it vexed him slightly that his hand was being forced. The timing wasn't of his choosing, and he would have enjoyed more freedom to study the Mars findings more.

Of course, there was still a chance that Dr Patterson would make a discovery, that the crew on Mars would be recovered safe and sound, and that the elaborate charade could once again resume. The 'alien findings' would gladly be accepted as impressive hoaxes, the 'issues' communicating with the Mars team put down to computer viruses initiated by the hoaxsters. The whole debacle would be given a suitably inflammatory 'cyber-terrorism' headline in the daily news, and undoubtedly a government agency previously unknown to the general public would suddenly receive billions of dollars of funding to combat this terrifying threat.

But just one look at Dr Richardson, alone in her little world on Mars, told him differently.

He was at a crossroads.

To the left, unfortunately made inaccessible by a big red 'No Entry' sign, the Mars team turn up safe and sound and everything goes back to normal.

Carry straight on, and DEFCOMM is investigated for its part in the biggest cover-up in history. He is arrested on suspicion of murdering a member of the *Clarke*'s crew and the head of a museum in Cairo, and also for abducting a respected British scientist and faking her death, in doing so making it abundantly clear that he had no intention of ever letting her go. Not to mention the lesser charge of misappropriating millions of dollars for personal research, and misusing government-owned equipment and defence systems, for which treason and piracy would probably be mentioned. He would be tried in Florida, where there would be no avoiding a certain death penalty.

Of course, he had always known this to be the case. All of the risks he had taken had been well calculated and very deliberate, which is why he still had one more direction to take.

A ninety-degree turn to the right. The answer to Aniquilus' Paradox was not that life resulted in death, but that death allowed life. Just as modern Man had benefitted from the demise of the Xynutians before them.

Am I Aniquilus? he mused.

With the vans safely on their way to despatching their deadly cargos, he turned his attention to Dr Patterson's expedition to Egypt, the final hope for plan A, before plan B was executed. It was due diligence, he told himself, to give them a fair shot.

He barked a command and the final quarter of the screen lit up: a satellite view of a barren, desert scene. Seven hours ahead of his current time-zone, it was mid-afternoon, and by the dark shadows moving along the rock and sand he could make out a trio of all-terrain vehicles labouring their way along what could barely be called a dirt track. Their target lay a few hundred yards away, round a couple more bends and through a gap in a small ridge: a small plateau, in the middle of which stood a small building.

It was a live-satellite feed from above Egypt, one of the perks of distributing hardware and software for United States defence satellites, and the display was grid marked for easy referencing.

"Full screen," he snapped. As the image filled the window, he caught a glimpse of movement along the narrow gap in the ridge, through which the small convoy would shortly be passing.

"Magnify C7," followed by "Magnify range D3 to F6."

Now filling the screen was a man in khaki cargo pants and a short sleeved shirt. Held across his knees was the unmistakable form of an AK-47. He zoomed the display back one level, and panned across the gap to the other side of the ridge. Within seconds he had located two further men with guns. While these were far better hidden than the first, they clearly hadn't been expecting to be seen from above.

Seth Mallus shook his head slowly before picking up the phone and calling Walker.

CHAPTER 67

George shifted uneasily between the two rocks he hoped offered him cover from the track below. He was uncomfortable, primarily because of the unfamiliar AK-47 laid across his knees and the approaching 4x4s he imagined were full of men with guns, but also because no matter how hard he tried there always seemed to be a sharp rock nestled somewhere it shouldn't be.

To make matters worse, his nerves were making his stomach churn more than any fairground ride he had been on.

He raised his head over the boulder and sneaked a peak across to the other side of the gulley. Although he knew more or less where Haji and Manu had taken up their positions, he couldn't see them at all. Certainly anyone approaching from below wouldn't stand a chance.

A few yards to his left, Tariq was going over his weapon one last time, calmly, methodically, making sure that it would fire when he needed it. The routine reminded George of the crazy man in boot camp in *Full Metal Jacket*, though he daren't say that out loud to Tariq, no matter how friendly he seemed.

Somewhere to his right, and slightly below him, he imagined that Leena would be going through a similar routine.

Ten minutes earlier, Zahra had disappeared from her position on the plateau overlooking the track below. Before she had done so, she had waved twice then held up three fingers, followed by one finger of the other hand, signalling that there were three cars in total, and that Ben was in the first one. There were no warning signals, meaning one of two things: either Gail was also in the first car, or she simply wasn't there.

After an hour spent shifting uncomfortably among the stones and rocks, it suddenly occurred to him that these men and women, dotted around the gulley and plateau with their Kalashnikov rifles and deadly bayonets, really were risking their lives for a man and woman they barely knew.

The 'date' that Ben had agreed to with Zahra was small payment indeed for such a massive gesture, and George suddenly felt overcome with nerves.

His stomach lurched uncontrollably as he tried to fight back the flow he knew was about to follow.

He retched, and his cheeks bulged out as he tried to keep the contents of his stomach inside. Instead, they filled his sinuses and he impulsively opened his mouth, spraying the rock in front of him. The acrid smell that followed caused him to retch again, and this time he didn't try to stop it.

Within seconds a pool of vomit had gathered in the dust between his legs. Looking down he noticed that the AK-47 had taken a battering. He wiped his sick covered hands against the legs of his khaki shorts and shook the dripping rifle.

George looked in despair towards Tariq, who urged him to be quiet. He was about to apologise when the unmistakable noise of diesel engines bounced off the rocks above their heads.

He kept his head down, tried to breathe through his mouth, and closed his eyes.

And for the first time since his childhood, without even knowing where the words came from, he prayed.

Dr Henry Patterson leaned forward and tapped the man in the passenger seat on the shoulder.

"What was that all about, Walker?" he asked. Walker had just come off the phone, and it didn't sound good.

Walker twisted round and stared directly into Ben's eyes. "Turns out there might be some company ahead," he grunted, putting his phone away. "Little welcome party you've prepared for us?"

Patterson shot an accusing glance at Ben, before switching his gaze to Gail. "You knew about this?" he said, sounding hurt.

She didn't answer, instead probing Ben's expressionless face for any sign of what was to come, her heart swelling in anticipation of the rescue attempt that was about to unfold.

Walker pulled a walkie-talkie from his breast pocket, all the while staring fixedly at Ben. Holding the walkie-talkie to his mouth he ordered the last car in the convoy to turn round and approach the plateau from below, from where the Toyota van was still parked. That had been where Mallus had suggested they approach from over the phone.

He then ordered the second car to overtake them and wait before the last corner while the last car's occupants took up their flanking positions.

Patterson leaned forward again, as if wanting to have a private word, but Walker pushed him back. He then replaced the walkie-talkie with a pistol, which he pointed directly at Ben.

"I don't want to have to kill anyone today," he said matter-of-factly. "But believe me I will if I have to. You make one move," he waved the gun across the back seats of the 4x4, taking in Gail, Patterson and Ben. "In fact, if any of you make a move, you're all dead."

Patterson sat back, his jaw dropped. "Me?" he said indignantly. "What have I done?"

The man grinned. "Not only have you dragged me and my men out here to this shithole, surrounded by Arabs," he gestured with the gun towards Ben, "but it looks like you've dropped us all into a trap, too." His grin disappeared, replaced with what could only be described as a snarl. "And if the purpose of that trap is to catch or save or whatever either of you two, then believe you me one way or another, it's going to fail."

George sneaked a peak as the 4x4 lumbered slowly through the gulley and came to a stop on the plateau, next to the entrance to the Library. He couldn't see any sign of Gail or Ben getting out, and so switched his attention to the second 4x4 which drove slowly along the tracks of its predecessor and pulled to a stop slightly beyond it.

The two cars were side-on to their position in the gully; the doors on the far side of the lead car opened and several men got out. They waited outside the entrance to the Library, without leaving the cover of their vehicles. George felt that they were eyeing the exact place in which he was hiding, and he shrank back behind the boulder.

Anticipation rose inside him as he prepared himself for the third and final 4x4, which was their target. Zahra would cover the other vehicles while the third was immobilised, and then they would call for the surrender of the remaining people.

After a long pause, it became obvious that the third 4x4 wasn't coming. George looked at Tariq nervously, who returned a worried glance. Had they misread Zahra's signal? Had there been only two cars? Had they completely messed up their chance?

Unlikely, George told himself. Maybe one person could make a mistake, but all five of them?

"Tariq," he whispered. "What's going on?"

"I don't know," he replied. "Something is wrong."

He was about to ask what they were to do when Manu and Haji made the decision for them. Shots rattled across the bonnet of the second 4x4, eruptions of sand in the ground evidence of several stray bullets that missed entirely.

George instinctively ducked his head as low as possible between his shoulders and sank down between the rocks. In the gully, the echo of the AK-47 fire was deafening.

Moments later, a reply sounded from near the 4x4s. Not the explosive crackling of the Kalashnikov, but a muffled whump, like flat stones slicing into a mill-pond.

Like a conversation, the Kalashnikovs and their opponents exchanged volleys, though the overwhelming sound of AK-47 fire from all around him made it difficult to judge exactly how much reply they were receiving.

Suddenly Tariq was beside him, holding his collar and dragging him along.

"Come!" he shouted.

George's legs somehow managed to comply, and he scrambled for his rifle and followed Tariq down through the rocks towards the gulley. Moments later, the hiding place they had been occupying erupted violently as dozens of rounds pounded into the rocks.

Tariq dragged George round the corner of the gulley, until they were standing on the trail along which the 4x4s had driven to reach the plateau. A quick glance in all directions confirmed the absence of the third 4x4.

"Leena?" George said, gasping for breath after their dash from hiding. She had been on their side of the gully, shortly before it had been sprayed with bullets.

Tariq shook his head. "Don't know."

"How many of them are there?" he asked. "How many?"

Tariq held up two hands full of fingers, his thumbs curled inwards.

"Eight?" George said, amazed.

Tariq grinned grimly and shook his head, curling three fingers of his left hand inwards.

Three dead! George was surprised; the enemy had clearly known about their intended ambush, and had brought possibly better weapons and more people. *Against six of us!* He stood upright and held the AK-47 firmly with both hands, positioning his index finger very deliberately on the trigger mechanism. He made to go back towards the gulley, but Tariq stopped him.

Using hand gestures and broken English, George got the principles of Tariq's plan. They had been outmanoeuvred by the Americans, who had climbed the cliff onto the plateau from the third 4x4. From that position, they could lie low and pick Zahra's company off at will, and they had effectively reached a stalemate.

"The best way to fight fire is with fire," George agreed as they started running along the track. "So we out-flank the out-flankers."

They rounded a corner and broke into a faster pace, Tariq taking the lead, George trying not to trip on any large stones as he followed several yards behind.

He felt bad leaving Zahra, Manu, Leena and Haji behind. He felt even worse thinking what might have happened to Ben. He couldn't bear to think where Gail may be and if she was OK. He just hoped that he could fight through the pain and drag his unfit body round the mountain in time to do something about it.

CHAPTER 68

Gail screamed as Ben shoved her head down behind the passenger seat of the 4x4. Dr Patterson did his best to follow suit.

Walker had ordered the driver to move the car in front of the small building in the middle of the plateau. The other 4x4 followed, parking at an angle behind them. Their new position formed a triangle, the bumpers of the 4x4s meeting at the apex, with the gatehouse to the Library at the base. This provided them with cover from the gulley, and direct access to the cliff edge, where Walker's men had positioned themselves.

As soon as the shooting had begun, Walker jumped out and fired a quick volley over the bonnet of the car.

"Out!" he yelled at Patterson, yanking the rear door open. He gestured for Ben and Gail to follow. The driver of the other vehicle opened his passenger door and dragged another out. By the way he fell to the floor, it was clear he was either dead, or close to it. Only one soldier got out of the back.

They sat down along the edge of the vehicle, while Walker barked orders into his walkie-talkie. Gail could see the odd head peak over the cliff-edge: Walker's men from the third 4x4. It reminded her of their initial discovery of the Library all those years ago, when Ben had awkwardly popped his head above the cliff during her phone call to George.

Except these men were dressed in black and were carrying the strangest guns she had ever seen. *Not that you've seen many*, she reminded herself.

The man who had been driving their car loaded a new clip of ammunition into his gun. Standing sideways, he fired half a dozen shots straight through the windows of the 4x4 and into the rocks beyond.

A single shot was returned.

As he came down from his firing stance, his gun arm fell limply and his weapon crashed into the dust. He managed to get to one knee as his legs crumpled under his weight, and then toppled sideways in front of Gail, Ben and Patterson.

It was then that Gail saw the bloody mess where his right eye should have been. Looking away in horror, she saw the look on Ben's face: he was staring at the strange weapon that had fallen almost into his lap.

He was about to reach for it when Walker intervened.

"One, you're too slow. I saw that coming a mile away." He took the fallen gun and removed the magazine with a click. Dropping the empty magazine from his own, he reloaded with the dead man's ammunition then looked Ben in the eyes. "Two, you wouldn't even be able to fire it." He nodded at the small indentations on the grip of the handle. "Unless of course you took his hand with it," he grinned viciously before turning back to the two remaining soldiers in their improvised fortress.

"Fucking prick," Gail managed to say under her breath before anyone else got a word in.

Ben looked at her in surprise. "I've not heard you swear like that before."

"I've never met such a prick before," she replied, this time elevating her voice slightly as she swore. Walker gave the faintest of reactions, in the form of a wry smile as he patted the side of his gun.

The three soldiers took it in turns to fire over the top and from underneath the cars, changing position frequently. On a few occasions, as they ducked down after firing, they exchanged tips on where to fire next. Of the three heads that had been popping up from the cliff edge, only two appeared to be firing now.

The opposing gunshots also seemed to be decreasing, with longer gaps between bursts and fewer impacts around them.

Walker dropped down to a crouch after firing a particularly long volley, a wild grin on his face. "Got the Arab bastard!" he exclaimed "Ripped him apart!"

Gail looked at Ben; it was obvious he was fighting to keep down a torrent of emotions. She put her hand on his knee and squeezed hard. She opened her mouth, but couldn't put a suitable sentence together, so closed it without saying a word.

He put his hand on hers and squeezed back.

Dr Patterson nodded towards the gatehouse, its unlocked door swinging freely on its hinges. The top third of brickwork was covered in bullet holes, though he could see none in the bottom portion. "Bit odd," he whispered to them both.

"I'm no expert," Gail said, "but if they're hidden in an elevated position above us, then they should have an advantage shouldn't they? And yet I get the feeling they're the ones taking the most hits."

Ben took a moment to think about it. "They're aiming high; they know we're still here." He nudged the corpse in front of them with his foot. "Unless they have a clear shot, and then they'll aim to kill. The problem is, these guys have figured that out."

Gail looked at the soldiers. With the rhythm they had entered into, it was difficult to see how any attacker could take a good aim at any one of them. Despite there being only five of them left, practically all the gunshots now came from their side, and the louder crackling fire from the gulley had practically stopped, save for the odd burst every twenty seconds or so.

Walker shouted a couple of concise orders, followed by some jerky hand signals, which Gail didn't get the meaning of.

"They're moving in," Ben whispered quickly through gritted teeth. "Gail, George is up there."

Her heart stopped beating for a fraction of a second. She looked at him in despair. "What?"

"We have to stop them moving in, otherwise it's over," he said.

One of the soldiers was crouched down at the back of the 4x4 furthest from the gulley, his gun held against his chest. Walker nodded at him, and then he and the driver who had dragged the corpse from the car levelled their weapons towards the gulley and began firing, while the soldier ran from cover and darted towards the enemy defences.

"Now!" Ben hissed.

He got up and ran towards the doorway, pulling Gail with him. As they ran, he shouted something in Arabic at the top of his voice.

Patterson followed, and they all piled into the building and practically fell down the stone-cut stairway the ancient Egyptians had made thousands of years earlier. On their way, Gail managed to punch the light switch, and the LED bulbs in the stairway and entrance hall beneath lit up.

When they reached the bottom of the stairs, Gail gathered her senses and looked around, immediately spotting the circular hole cut into the wall of the chamber a decade earlier, beyond which lay the Library itself.

"We made it!" Patterson exclaimed, searching himself for bullet wounds.

Ben was listening intently at the bottom of the steps, a worried look on his face.

"Ben?" Gail asked.

He hushed her with his hand and craned his ear upwards.

After a moment of silence the muffled sound of Walker and his men's automatic rifles echoed down the stairs. But this time, instead of being followed by the odd return shot, a salvo of gunshots and ricochets came back. Even from underground they could hear glass windows breaking, metal being punctured and the thuds of bullets hitting the dirt.

"Yes!" Ben shouted, punching the air. "There must be at least three of them left." He slapped Gail on the back, grinning. "We'll be –"

The rest of his sentence was cut off by a massive explosion which made the whole room shake. Dust fell from the ceiling and poured down the steps into the chamber. Seconds later another explosion shook the room, followed almost instantly by another, final blast.

Gail instinctively clasped her hands over her ears and crouched down, closing her eyes. The rumbling from above continued for a while, eventually replaced by a loud, painful ringing. She opened her eyes cautiously and in the dust-filled air saw a pair of army boots on the floor in front of her. As the dust began to clear she could make out the uniformed legs they were attached to, then the utility belt with empty holster and spare clips of ammunition, followed by the shirt with the walkie-talkie in the breast pocket, and finally the bloodied face of Walker.

He was lying on the floor, his back and head propped up against the last three steps. His eyes were open and he looked disoriented, blinking heavily and lolling his head from side to side.

Ben was standing over him with Walker's pistol in his hand, pointed directly at the soldier's head.

"I knew I should've killed you," Walker shouted, slurring his words. "Should've put a bullet in you when I had the chance."

"Yes, you should have," Ben replied. "What was that explosion?"

"Did the cars blow up?" Gail asked.

Ben shook his head. "Maybe afterwards, yes, but that first explosion sounded too big to just be cars blowing up."

Walker grinned, his teeth and gums full of blood. It bubbled out of his mouth as he talked. "Not heard one of those before, tough guy?" His eyes had steadied now as he trained his eyes on the Egyptian. His head still bobbed up and down slightly, but it looked like he was regaining his strength. He shifted his position and grunted, holding his ribcage as he pulled away from the steps to sit forwards.

Ben took a step back and brought his other hand up to steady the pistol on the man's head. "What was it?"

"Goddamn it," he grimaced as he removed his shirt and started to unfasten the body armour he was wearing underneath. "It was a HICUP Grenade."

"Hiccup?" Gail mused.

He looked at her sarcastically. "Yeah, sweetheart. High Impact Concussion grenade. The UP stands for Under Pressure, or pressurized. When it explodes, it's like you packed a ton of TNT into a baseball."

Ben looked at him with a confused look on his face. "We don't have anything like that to throw at you, so where did it come from?"

Walker held up his body armour to display three star-shaped impacts across the chest. "Me," he said simply. "I pulled the pin, reached back to throw it, and then got shot. The impact of the bullets threw me back and I dropped the little bastard. Once you've lit a firework, you just don't go back to it, so I had to jump for cover." He looked at them one by one, and shook his head. "Which is how I ended up joining your little party you've got going on down here."

"OK, enough of the story. Get up," Ben gestured with the pistol and Walker followed him to the other corner of the room. Standing a couple of metres away from him, he called over his shoulder, "Peterson, check what's going on up there, it's gone very quiet."

"Patterson," he corrected. "Call me Henry."

"Oh aren't you all just best of buddies now," Walker said.

They ignored him.

Patterson left the room and Ben called over to Gail. "Don't worry about George, Gail. I'm sure he's fine. I left him in very good hands."

"Thanks, Ben," she managed to say.

Patterson came back down the steps with a grim look on his face. "We have a problem," he said.

Gail's face dropped even further. "Are they still fighting?"

He shook his head. "I don't think so, can't hear anything, that's for sure."

"So?"

357

"The entrance is blocked with rock and sand in the first flight of steps and I couldn't make it more than ten steps up. It's a job for proper mechanical diggers, we're not getting out of here in a hurry."

They stood in silence for a few moments before Patterson continued.

"I'm sorry, Gail, but it looks like we're going to *have* to find the other entrance to the Library now, because it might be our only exit before the oxygen runs out."

Gail cursed under her breath.

Ben raised an eyebrow. Looking from the steps to Gail, and then across to the hole in the wall that led to the Amarna Library, his gaze fell on Patterson, who was beating the dust from his shorts and tucking his sweat-stained shirt back under the beltline. "What other way in?"

CHAPTER 69

George sucked air into his lungs in short wheezing breaths as he slowed to a walk before finally stopping completely and bending over, his hands pressed against the insides of his thighs. It didn't help with the rifle he'd slung awkwardly over his shoulder banging against his ribcage with every step.

Pain seared through his chest, and he winced as he looked up to see Tariq stopping some twenty yards ahead, seemingly unaffected by the gruelling pace that he had set down the rocky terrain.

It took all of his effort to lift an arm and motion him to wait. Tariq squatted down and used the spring in his legs to bounce impatiently up and down as he waited for the Englishman to catch his breath, never once taking his eyes off the road ahead for any sign of danger.

From having accompanied Gail on trips back to Egypt since the discovery of the Library, George knew that they were only one turn away from the foot of the cliff. It wouldn't do him any good to turn up for what he assumed would be a fierce gun fight if he could hardly breathe. He grunted in amusement as the mental image of him turning up to a battle and having to ask for a quick timeout popped up. It was quickly replaced by fear at the realisation that he *was* about to turn up to a battle.

The pain in his ribcage had subsided, only to be replaced by a heavy ache that seemed to fill his legs, from the calf up to the thigh, spreading across his groin. He remembered the feeling from school many years earlier, when the PE teacher had forced them to run cross-country in the middle of winter. He had never been a sporty person, and he had always found himself among the stragglers who walked the final couple of miles back to the changing rooms. Arriving late had its drawbacks, especially when it meant missing the first half of the next lesson and being reprimanded by the teacher.

He shook his head and looked up at Tariq. From behind the

coloured spots that filled his vision, he could just about make out the Egyptian, who was looking over his weapon, occasionally glancing back at him, while always keeping an eye out for the road ahead.

They couldn't have been running for more than five minutes, but the relentless pace of the man had been too much for George, and he fought the almost overwhelming desire to topple onto his back and close his eyes. He'd stopped in the shade of the rocky slope to his right, the gentle incline to his left dropping off to what looked like a dried up river bed a dozen or so yards wide before rising up on the other side, creating a U-shaped valley his secondary education told him was formed by glacial displacement, not rivers.

But he couldn't imagine glaciers round here; maybe the school's textbook rule didn't apply to this hot, arid place.

Straightening up, he pulled the AK-47 against his chest with both arms and let his legs propel him gently down the slope until he was standing next to Tariq.

"One more corner," he said, gesturing towards the track ahead.

Tariq nodded and started walking forwards, covering the final yards at a more cautious pace.

The sound of the gunfight got louder as they neared the bend, and George noted that the predominant sound was the muffled popping of the American weapons, not the harsh crackle of their own AK-47s. His heart sank noticeably, and he stood expectantly a few feet back from Tariq, who took barely two seconds to look round the corner, take stock of the situation, and return to cover.

"Three," he said with his fingers. He then held up just the index finger. "One of them looks dead, or dying."

George followed Tariq's jerky hand signals accompanied by the odd word of English, and understood what they were about to do; Tariq would dart from cover towards the Toyota truck, which was a mere fifteen yards away. George would offer covering fire from his hiding place if required, but if they didn't turn around, Tariq would fire a warning shot into the rocks when he reached the vehicle. Finally, all being well, George would use his command of the English language to demand and then accept the American surrender.

It seemed like a good enough idea, so he nodded his approval. He particularly liked the fact that if all went according to the plan, he wouldn't need to fire a single shot. He still didn't know if his earlier vomiting had damaged the firing mechanism, so he offered the gun to

Tariq to check over.

The Egyptian glanced at it briefly and gave a quick thumbs-up.

He checked round the corner one last time, then gave a brief nod towards George and made for the Toyota. George brought his AK-47 up and swung it round the rocks.

They were much higher up than he had imagined, despite Tariq's best efforts to explain the layout. The two men who were firing over the cliff's edge were about thirty feet above him, and the third lay motionless on a small ledge a few feet further away. In his peripheral vision, he saw Tariq slide behind the front end of Ben's Toyota. He regained his footing and took aim at the men, who were still unaware of what was going on behind them.

George could feel the adrenaline coursing through his veins as Tariq completed the outflanking manoeuvre. Without a shot fired, they were now in a winning position behind enemy lines, and he waited for Tariq to fire his warning shot before announcing their demands for surrender.

When the shot didn't come, he looked quizzically towards Tariq and saw him grappling with his gun. George could only imagine it was jammed, and so making sure he kept Tariq in his line of sight, moved back under cover while he waited for him to un-jam it. As he watched him feverishly taking his rifle apart, it suddenly occurred to him that he was dangerously exposed to the Americans. Despite the cover of the Toyota, he would still be visible if any of the men on the cliff happened to turn round to face the car, due to their elevated position.

Which meant that he would have to provide cover for him.

He felt an odd reluctance to emerge from his hiding place; while he realised it was clearly the right thing to do, the wall of rocks he was leaning against offered him some protection against the raging battle. The internal debate was short lived, and he sucked his gut in before swinging out and aiming directly at the Americans.

"Hey!" he tried to say as he pointed the barrel of the gun at the two men. Unfortunately, his having not said anything loudly for some time together with the effects of the dry atmosphere made the word come out as a croak, like a teetotaller knocking back a shot of whisky. Somehow his voice failed to carry far enough to be heard above the noise of the battle, so he summed up his courage, cleared his throat and tried again.

"Hey, hands –" he was about to say *up* when the thundering sound of an explosion tore through the air. Moments later, a couple more loud bangs came from the plateau, and he saw a cloud of dust and grit pour over the cliff's edge and fall down towards him. "Don't move!" he shouted to the two Americans, who had turned to face him more to shield their eyes from the fallout of the explosion than to question his 'Hey, hands -' challenge. "Throw down your weapons!" he added, his voice shaking as he realised the fragility of his position: two heavily armed professionals against him – a quiet Englishman with an antiquated rifle he hadn't even fired a shot in anger from yet.

The look of surprise on the men's faces was evident. Standing on the track below was what looked like a tourist, covered in dust. It was only after a second take that they realised he was carrying a weapon, and that it was being pointed straight at them.

"You wanna think real hard about what you're doing," the man on the left said. He sported a thick moustache, and an even thicker Texan accent. To show what he thought about George's 'ambush', he levelled his gun at him, and very deliberately took aim. The second man nodded to his colleague before returning to the fight over the top of the cliff, effectively ignoring them both.

Oddly, it wasn't the thought of Gail needing to be rescued that made him see red, but the wonton disregard for what should have been an unassailable position of authority: him pointing a loaded weapon at two men should have been met by humble resignation, when instead it had been met by pure indifference.

He snarled, aimed for the chest of the Texan, and squeezed his trigger finger to let out a volley of bullets.

But none came. The trigger didn't budge.

The Texan grinned.

George fumbled for the safety. *Surely it had been off!*

The Texan pulled his trigger.

A loud crackle came from the Toyota, and the Texan thumped into the cliff wall, spraying bullets as his gun-arm flew sideways. The second man turned just in time to see the barrel of his buddy's gun pointing into his face, and a fraction of a second later the man's trigger finger went limp.

He slumped against the cliff, motionless, while his shooting partner cart-wheeled from the ledge and rolled down to the ground, leaving behind a trail of blood and brains.

George clicked the safety off in time to see the two corpses settle into the dust.

And then, almost serenely after what seemed like hours of shooting, the final echo of gunfire dissipated. His hands and forearms were numb from having held the AK-47 upright for so long, and he pulled them down till the rifle was pointing at his feet. His gaze fell on the man who had tumbled to the ground.

The top half of his head was missing.

Of the part that remained, only his bottom lip and chin were recognisable, the rest was covered in blood and fleshy fragments.

He didn't think there'd be much sick left in him after his earlier episode, but then the human body always had the capacity to catch you by surprise. After he had finished throwing up, he turned and faced the dusty plains that led to the green-belt of vegetation bordering the Nile. A cool breeze came to meet him, bringing with it the smell of the river. The smell of vegetation and oxygen. The smell of life.

Tariq placed a hand gently on his shoulder. For a brief moment, the language barrier between them seemed to dissolve. George looked up at the Egyptian and saw complete understanding in his eyes; understanding that George had seen more death today than ever before, and understanding that for one heart-stopping moment, he had seen his own, too.

Had it not been for the soft click of the magazine loading perfectly into Tariq's un-jammed AK-47, the Texan would have certainly killed George.

"Hello!" came a shout from the cliff top behind them. They turned in unison and saw Zahra waving down at them, a grim smile on her face. "Thanks for that!" She gestured for them both to come up the cliff, and Tariq helped George to his feet.

They gathered near the smouldering remains of the two 4x4s and a pile of rubble which used to be the gatehouse. Leena had her arm around Manu, whose red eyes came not from the dust but the death of Haji. Tariq stood guard over the one surviving American who sat bound and motionless in the dirt, staring fixedly ahead. According to Zahra, he had run from cover moments before the explosions in an effort to outflank them. Ironically, the daring move had saved his life.

"George," Zahra said apologetically. "Your wife was with them, and so was Ben. They ran down the stairs just before the explosion destroyed the entrance."

George looked at the pile of rubble, and instead of replying started to move some of the smaller stones and fragments of breezeblock from the entrance of the Library. It looked a hopeless task.

"George," Zahra was about to tell him as much, but she was interrupted by a burst of Arabic from Tariq.

Then Tariq was at George's side, helping him lift a beam that had once been part of the tiled roof. Leena and Manu also joined in, and before long the four of them were fervently clearing rubble in search of survivors.

Zahra took up Tariq's place guarding the American, who looked on, unmoved.

CHAPTER 70

Mallus ordered the display off, and the satellite image of Tell el-Amarna vanished. A virtual aquarium appeared in its place, making it look like his office was underwater in some tropical paradise; colourful corals and exotic fish shimmered perfectly under the sunlight that shone down from the virtual surface above.

He gave another command and the cityscape that had soothed his thoughts before Patterson and his men had launched their assault returned.

The assault had failed.

A plane soared silently through the evening sky. He'd seen it all before. He almost whispered at the screen and it switched off completely, blending seamlessly into the wall.

The assault has failed, he thought to himself.

He had no need to launch Plan B, as it was already in motion. On the contrary, while one word from him would call off the vans, no such communication was needed to carry on as planned. Such an act would potentially leave a trail back to him, and for Plan B to work, what was about to happen had to look like it came from outside the United States of America.

"Has it ever really been Plan B?" he mumbled to himself as he shuffled in his seat nervously. He didn't think so. Deep down inside, he had wanted to see Plan B in action and now, while it was being carried out, he felt a surge of excitement. Another, conflicting part of his mind cried megalomaniac, which he chose to ignore. "This was always meant to be," he soothed himself. "The Book of Xynutians showed me the way, it's no coincidence that it fell into my lap!" he started to raise his voice. "What would be the point of me having all of this if it didn't have a purpose?"

He stood up and started pacing around his desk. The search for answers to the ancient riddles and a possible way of avoiding the wrath of Aniquilus had certainly been fascinating, but ultimately it had done little more than confirm what he already knew.

"I *am* Aniquilus," his face lit up as he said the words out loud for the first time, as if some internal flood barrier had finally been breached. Years of pent up emotion started to pour out. "I am Aniquilus," he laughed. "I am Aniquilus," he roared, sweeping his arms over his desk sending paper and pen and telephone flying. "And I will rain down fire on this world!"

He barked orders at the computer and the screen lit up, filling with video feeds and streams of text.

For him, secretly having complete control of the country's defence satellites had more than one advantage. Not only could you spy on whatever you wanted to, such as a covert operation in Egypt, you could also make the Department of Defence *see* things that simply weren't there, like unauthorised fighter jets entering US airspace, or a build-up of foreign troops on a disputed border.

You could even make it look like three nuclear Inter-Continental Ballistic Missiles had launched from deep inside Asia towards densely populated targets within the United States of America.

And while the powers that be scrambled to verify and counter the imaginary attack, three very real unmarked utility vans with nuclear bombs inside them would arrive unchallenged in Los Angeles, Chicago and New York.

And so the Apocalypse would begin.

He rounded the desk and made for the door. As he slammed it behind him the lights automatically shut off, and the screen went dark.

CHAPTER 71

Wait, no!" Gail exclaimed as Ben approached one of the ancient wooden shelves inside the Library, intent on upending it to examine what lay beneath.

He paused briefly, the time to turn and offer a brief apology; it was more for Gail than for the archaeological world as a whole. Taking hold of the middle shelf, he tentatively rocked it from side to side, to get a feel for its weight and structural integrity. After thousands of years, it was surprisingly solid, offering little give.

Applying more force, he managed to obtain a groan from the thick timber. He stepped back and took in the room as a whole, before turning to the rest of the group.

"What do you think? If we lean on it together it will budge quite easily."

"And then topple into all the other shelves like dominos!" Gail cried. "Thousands of years perfectly preserved, then destroyed in seconds by us. We have to look for another way."

"And die in here, for the sake of a few bookcases?" Ben said. "I understand how hard this must be for you, Gail, but if there's another way out of this place, we have to find it very soon."

Patterson approached the shelves and gave them a quick nudge. "Bear in mind that even if we do find another way out, the air inside whatever tunnel or room we uncover may be toxic," he shook his head soberly. "It'll quickly mix with the little air we have left, and we may simply pass out and die within a few minutes."

There was a long silence as they digested what he had said. There was no denying the fact that air trapped for thousands of years wasn't going to be fresh, and there was a strong chance that it would be quite toxic. The air inside the Library was finite, and wouldn't last them for long if the area it had to fill suddenly became a lot larger.

Eventually it was Walker who broke the silence.

367

"Not wanting to use up any of your precious air by talking," he began patronisingly. "But tipping the bookcases over will make a lot of mess, and it won't uncover your hidden door."

They turned to him in surprise.

"Oh, and how would you know?" Patterson said sarcastically.

Walker got to his feet, waving away their protests and Ben's raised gun barrel with the back of his hand. He sauntered over to the circular entrance to the Library.

"You made me climb through a tunnel carved into solid rock to get in here," he began. "The Ancient Egyptians make that?" Gail shook her head. "No, I guessed not. You lot cut your way in because you couldn't find the door in the first place. Did you find any bodies in here?" Gail didn't need to shake her head, she could already see where he was going with his argument. "Not even a dead fly. So the entrance to this damn place remains to be found. But it ain't just the entrance is it? It's the exit too." He turned on his heel and waved his arms around him. "Millions of years ago —"

"Thousands," Gail cut in.

"Whatever! It don't matter if it was yesterday, personally, I don't give a damn. *Thousands* of years ago some guy closed the door on this place for the last time. Are you suggesting," he pointed at Ben, "that when he closed it, he somehow managed to build a bookshelf on top of it?" he flapped his arms and jutted his jaw out at him. "And you can stop pointing my own gun at me for a start. You think I'm gonna try and stop you escaping from here? This is my funeral too."

Ben looked back at him, but was reluctant to lower the pistol. Somehow, he didn't believe Walker was harmless at all, even if they were in the same boat.

"He's right, of course," Gail said matter-of-factly. "If there's a door, it won't be under the shelves. They were stacked with parchments and scrolls when we came in here. Even if they did somehow slide into place when the Egyptians left, it would have been difficult not to drop something on the floor."

"So where is it then?" Ben said desperately. "There's nothing else in here! No gaps or grooves in the wall we can prise open, the only other feature in the whole place is the plinth."

They all looked to where he was pointing. It was the structure that Gail had originally seen on the x-ray screen all those years ago. It protruded from the floor, its top tilted with a lip at the bottom edge, in which had sat the books of Aniquilus and Xynutians. Roughly three feet wide and two feet deep at its base, it sat in an alcove at one end of the rectangular room, the bookcases lined up in front of it like pews in a church.

Walker was already there, inspecting the base of the plinth. Gail joined him, despite Ben's best efforts to stop her from going near the man who barely half an hour earlier wouldn't have hesitated in shooting them all.

"It's a separate stone from the floor," she told him. "We know that much already."

He grunted in reply, then looked up at her. "No drawings of Egyptian things and cats and shit? I've seen all the adventure movies, there's always some writing somewhere that someone leans on, then the secret passage opens up; hey sesame."

"This isn't a movie," she said bitterly. "Yes, there are usually inscriptions inside Egyptian tombs and monuments, but not in this one. The only recurring symbol is the stickman – Aniquilus."

"*Aniqui* who?" Ben asked, surprised at hearing the name for the first time.

"It's a long story," she said dismissively. "Anyway, there are *no* other hieroglyphs in here. We've always focussed our research on the literature that we found, the contents of the bookcases rather than the structure itself. I mean, how many times do you check the walls out when you go to your local library?"

"My local *what*?" Walker joked. He stood up laboriously and looked at Ben. "If there's one thing we should try knocking over, it's this."

No one disagreed, and soon they were pushing with all their might to try and topple it sideways.

It remained solidly in place.

They tried again from the other side, with the same results. After a few minutes, even Walker conceded that the plinth wasn't going anywhere.

"Could we lift it?" Patterson suggested.

"Bit of a heavy trapdoor isn't it? How would they have dropped it in place behind them?" Ben commented.

"Fill the space underneath with sand and then take the sand away slowly from below," Walker said, as if it was the simplest thing in the world. "But then we have the same problem: how'd the last person get out?"

They stood looking at the plinth for several long minutes.

"In any case," Patterson said finally, "whether it was dropped in behind them or slid across, I don't see how they could have done it. It's too heavy and it would have left marks all over the floor if it was dragged, and there are no signs of anything like that."

Gail sat down and leant against the back of the alcove, exasperated. Letting her head thud against the cold stone, she buried her face in her hands and groaned. "What's the use? We've been down here nearly an hour, and we're already running out of air. Our only hope is that someone up there digs us out."

Ben got up onto the plinth, so that he was leaning against the book holder, his backside wedged into the lip that originally stopped the books from falling to the floor.

Gail gave him a disapproving look, then shook her head and closed her eyes.

"What?" he said. "I'm sorry Gail, but we're going to die down here, the last of my worries is damaging the –"

"Ben, shut up!" she said suddenly, sitting bolt upright, her eyes wide open.

"Oh great! First I'm not allowed to –"

"No seriously, Ben, *shhh*!" she put her finger to her lips and everyone listened: somewhere beneath the floor, a rumbling had started, like the rolling of a bowling ball making its journey down to the pins.

Then there was the muffled sound of something clicking into place, followed by silence.

After waiting a few seconds longer, Gail got to her feet and pressed her ear against the back wall of the alcove.

"Whatever it was, it didn't do much," she said, disappointed. "When you sat on the plinth you must have set off the first part of some mechanism, but over the centuries whatever function it had has probably rotted away."

They all returned their attention to the plinth, but despite Walker, Patterson and Ben pressing down on it together as hard as possible, nothing further happened.

Gail turned and kicked the wall hard, swearing both out of frustration and pain for having kicked the stone with soft shoes. As she crouched down to nurse her toes, the distinctive grating of stone against stone filled the room, and before her eyes the entire back wall of the alcove slid downwards, revealing a long corridor, the end of which was so far away the lights in the Library left it in darkness.

The air from both spaces mixed in a cloud of dust where they stood, causing more than one of them to cough. But despite their original concerns, the air remained breathable. Walker took a couple of steps forwards, crossing the threshold of the corridor by stepping over the half-foot of door still protruding from the floor.

"How the hell would that work? That stone is over a foot thick, and must weigh tons," he said, amazed.

"You said it yourself," Patterson answered. "Put the stone on a load of sand. When the mechanism is activated, in this case probably a ball or roller of some description taking a series of pins or plugs with it as it goes, sand pours out of holes, and the door slides down."

"But instead it got stuck and didn't budge, while the sand poured out underneath it," Gail continued. "That kick was all it needed to start falling down. It was a pretty tight fit!" She was inspecting the gap between the wall and the groove into which it had been placed.

They all walked into the passage, with the exception of Gail, who continued to examine the doorway.

"Wait, this raises more questions than it answers."

"Who cares?" Walker said, striding forwards into the tunnel. "It's not like we have all the time in the world, is it?"

"No, seriously, this is important," she insisted. "If this door opened from *inside* the Library, then whatever lies beyond this door must be *further* away from the original entrance. We've found a way to get deeper into the tomb, or whatever this is, but we haven't found the original way *into* the Library." They were all staring at her, even Walker. She tried to put it as simply as she could: "If we go down there, we're getting further away from the outside world."

Ben broke first, visibly agitated. "So what do we do, ignore this entrance and keep looking for another one? And what if we do find the original way in to the Library, and it actually just takes us back to the stairs that are filled with rubble? What if that *was* the original entrance, but we simply didn't take the time to find the original door?"

"Makes sense to me," Walker nodded.

"Oh, and now you're the archaeologist are you?" she targeted him vehemently. "A little while ago you were killing people and threatening to kill us too, but now you want to go down there like Indiana Jones and find some hidden treasure while we wait to be rescued, or worse, wait to die?"

Patterson and Ben took a step away from Walker, as if Gail's comments had suddenly reminded them who he was.

"No," he replied calmly. "But we're not getting out through the stairs, and there ain't no books to read in this so called *library* of yours, so I thought it'd be best to have a look round and see what else there was to do. And while I'm at it, if I come across another exit, I'll let you use it too," he said with mock gallantry.

Before she could say anything, he had turned on his heels and was striding down the corridor into the gloom. Before he was completely in the dark, they saw him rummaging in his chest pocket, and a light came on in front of him. As they watched, the light grew smaller and smaller.

Patterson coughed. "Well, he has a torch, and we don't. So I vote we go with him."

Gail held back, and Ben looked at her in earnest.

"Gail, I hate to say it, but he's right; there's no reason to stay here, and besides, we shouldn't let him out of our sight. He could still be planning something."

She thought about this for a moment before conceding. "Alright, but I'm only going with you because I want to make sure that whatever we find gets treated with respect. This is now officially an archaeological dig, so I'm in charge."

They walked along in silence for a few yards.

"Do you kick all of your archaeological digs?" Patterson said quietly.

Ben suppressed a laugh and while Gail pretended to ignore him, the darkness made it much easier for her to hide a smile.

CHAPTER 72

They met Walker coming back up the corridor. He shone the torch directly in their eyes as he moved the light between each of their faces.

"I think you're gonna love what's up ahead," he said blinding Gail with the narrow beam of light.

"Don't mess with that light, Walker," Ben said. "I still have the gun, remember?"

"Oh yeah, I'd forgotten. How silly of me to forget that you have my sidearm. Jesus, what kind of soldier do you think I am?"

"One of fortune?" Gail suggested.

He turned without a word and carried on back down the tunnel at a faster pace than they could comfortably follow in the dark.

"Might be an idea *not* to upset the man with the light," Patterson said.

The tunnel sloped downwards in a smooth curve, so that the doorway they had come from was now hidden from view. After twenty more yards Walker's light disappeared, and they heard him shout back up the tunnel.

"Left turn!"

Now completely in the dark, they fumbled their way forwards.

"Walker! We can't see!" Gail shouted back. "Come back here!"

They continued to shout and complain until he returned; they had managed to proceed barely five yards in the darkness.

"Well, what are you all waiting for? Didn't you bring torches?" They glared at him as one, and he gave them a wide grin back. "OK, game's over, come and look at this."

Despite the anger they all felt towards the man, there was an excited tinge to the way he was talking, and they found it hard not to be caught up in the thrill of discovery.

They followed him more closely this time, and as they rounded the corner, he made a quick adjustment to his torch, going from narrow to wide beam. Suddenly the area around them lit up and even Walker, who had already seen it, was speechless.

The corridor ended abruptly and opened up onto a landing at the top of some stone steps, which descended to the floor of a huge hall. Walker bounced the light off two rows of stone columns; they were at least fifty feet high, connecting the floor to the ceiling. While it was difficult to make out the opposite wall, the room had to be at least the length of a football pitch. From the top of the stairs, they felt like spectators looking from end to end.

Gail started walking down the steps, and Walker followed. Patterson joined them as they made their way down to the floor. Ben hesitated for a while, as he tried desperately to focus on the far end of the hall. Then, shaking his head and rubbing his eyes, he went down after them.

The staircase led down to a central avenue. Walker scanned the hall with the torch, and as far as the light would reach on either side they could see row after row of identical columns.

"My God," Gail whispered. "It's like Karnak, the Hypostyle hall."

Walker continued to scan between the columns with the torch.

He let out a long whistle as he slowly moved the beam of the torch from row to row, for while the central avenue was empty, the rows immediately adjacent to it were completely filled with an assortment of crates, wooden boxes, cabinets, large pots and cloth bags.

"Oh my God!" Gail said in shock. She let out a series of yelps and whoops like an excited puppy as Walker and Patterson tried to keep up and follow her round the piles of artefacts.

"Good?" Patterson asked.

"Good?" she turned on him, the glee in her face was infectious. "Good? This is better than good, this is unimaginable! That Library was one of the most amazing archaeological finds of all time, but *this*, this is even better!" She leapt from one pile of boxes to a stack of sacks. "Why worry about reading a book on how much grain they stored, when we have it all here?" She stopped just short of plunging her hand into the open-topped bag, as God only knew what toxins and fungi had grown in there. She moved on. "And a box full of tools, so we know how they farmed, a box of cooking utensils, and…" she hesitated before a third box, "and a box of sheets or clothes or something."

Patterson had been as enthusiastic as her, but as they examined more and more boxes, he started to slow down, until finally he stood still looking at a collection of wooden blades that would have been used to till soil.

"Gail," he said softly. "Do you realise what this is?"

She stopped in her tracks and looked at him. Walker swung the torch round and pointed it in his face.

"It reminds me of the scenes engraved into the walls of Ptah-hotep's mastaba at Saqqara, from the Old Kingdom. They show really detailed scenes of people bringing offerings to him, including grain, ducks, milk, there are even scenes showing the taming of wild animals and farmers bringing a bull to mate with a cow. The offerings lead to the burial chamber, where Ptah-hotep himself was laid to rest. My guess is that this, instead of showing what the offerings were like, actually *is* the offerings."

Patterson shook his head. "You are the expert on these sorts of things, but to me it looks like something else."

"What do you think it is?"

They hadn't drunk any water for some time, and in the dry atmosphere he swallowed painfully before continuing.

"Remember in the book of Aniquilus, it talks of how humans should lead their lives to avoid the wrath of Aniquilus, and in the book of Xynutians it shows what the potential punishment was?"

She nodded and hushed Ben's inevitable question.

"Well, *this*," he showed the room with his hands, "is the Ancient Egyptian equivalent of an insurance policy. Despite their best efforts, they must have known they couldn't change the whole of humanity, so they left a message for future generations, inside the Library. They then left supplies in here, just in case the worst did happen, so the survivors would have a good enough start."

"There's a problem to your theory, in that the timings make no sense. If the book of Xynutians states that the next event would happen close to our time, why would the Egyptians nearly three thousand years ago start stocking up on grain?"

"That one's easy," Ben said. "If I tell you that you'll die in fifty years if you don't start eating fish, you probably won't care. But if I tell you that you'll die tomorrow if you don't eat any fish, you'll probably catch one yourself. If Nefertiti and Akhenaten knew that they needed to bring about change, then telling people that it would only matter for their descendants over a hundred generations down the line wouldn't make much sense."

Gail made an approving sound. "So they instead state that *The End of the World is Nigh*, but simply refrain from saying how nigh it actually is. In the meantime, locking the Xynutians and Aniquilus books up for safe keeping, so that future generations will know why they did it."

"What the hell are you guys talking about?" Walker snapped. "Zynusense and Anoushka? Who the hell are they?"

"Xynutians and Aniquilus," Gail corrected. "It's a long story, but in short, Henry is saying that this is the three thousand year old equivalent of a nuclear bunker with enough stores to start building the new world again after the apocalypse they feared might descend on them."

Walker let out a long whistle.

Ben was in the central avenue, in the dark. He laughed out loud. "It's funny how we found the entrance to the Library all those years ago because we sat on a stone, and now we find this because I sat on another stone. I hope one of us sits on the exit to this place!"

She laughed back, but quickly stopped when she realised Ben had fallen silent. He was staring ahead, towards the far end of the immense hall. His face was frozen in a look of utter terror.

"Ben, what's wrong?" she asked. "What is it?"

"Turn the torch off," was all he managed to say as he continued to stare fixedly into the darkness.

Walker snorted. "Why the hell would I switch the flashlight off, what —"

"Do it!" Ben almost screamed.

He obeyed, and they all followed Ben's gaze. Now in pitch black, it took a few moments for their eyes to adjust.

And realise that they weren't in complete darkness.

For right in the centre of the wall at the other end of the hall was a pinprick red glow.

It was the kind of light that you would normally find on an electronic device on standby; it wasn't the kind you would expect to find in an ancient tomb in the middle of the desert.

And as they all stood there holding their collective breath, the red light turned green.

CHAPTER 73

On the count of three, George and Manu heaved with all their might to lift one end of a large stone slab while Leena inserted the broken beam from the ruined roof underneath it.

As it slid into place, they let the slab drop, exhausted, and staggered back.

There were now two large piles of rubble and debris on either side of the old entrance to the Library, which had mostly been cleared. All of the rocks that they could carry had already been removed, and they had reached several large blocks that until a couple of hours ago had formed part of the ancient staircase's ceiling.

"If we can remove these," George said between breaths, "then we might be able to make a hole big enough to crawl through." He was bent over, hands on knees, and his face was covered in dust streaked with rivulets of sweat; the late afternoon sun was still appreciably warmer than a hot British summer.

Zahra, having passed the gun back to Tariq before making good the job of tying up their prisoner, had returned from Ben's Toyota with a five litre container of water, which she offered to them.

George drank last. The warm liquid mixed with dust as he swilled the first mouthful around, spitting it out with distaste. He then drank thirstily, gulping down rapidly until his stomach complained by contracting, and he suddenly felt an strong urge to go to the toilet. Passing the container back to Zahra, he suppressed the desire to urinate and went back to their excavation of the stairs.

After a further thirty minutes of persistent leverage from Leena using the beam, their combined strength pulling against the only exposed edge, and several failed attempts at lifting it fully, the first stone slab finally rose up on its end and they toppled it over triumphantly, exposing the two stones it had been pinning down.

Getting down on his hands and knees, George clawed at the mixture of sand and rubble that filled every hole in the heap, keeping the Library beneath them airtight.

"Lift this one," he said pointing to a large slab the general dimensions of a kitchen table, "and we should be there."

They wasted no time attacking the second stone, and their eventual success and experience gained in lifting the first stone, despite this one being larger and heavier, meant that within twenty minutes they had upended it. The ground shuddered as it fell away onto its side with a thump.

George dived into the dirt, and seconds later he was rewarded with a small hole, big enough to fit his arm through. He pushed his face against it and started shouting.

"Hello!" He listened as his voice echoed down the stairs, past the corner and into the ante-chamber of the Library. When no reply came, he cupped his hands against the sides of his head and tried to peer through. The build-up of dust coupled with the bright daylight behind him made it almost impossible to see anything, but he was almost certain he could detect artificial light. "Hello! Gail?" he shouted again, to no avail.

Zahra pulled at his shoulder. "George, they may be too weak to talk, or injured, unconscious, we don't know. We need to make the hole bigger, so we can get to them and help."

He shouted one last time through the opening. "We're going to make the entrance bigger, we'll be with you soon…" he hesitated, before adding, "I love you Gail!" Standing up, he looked down at the stones they still had to move; they had uncovered one even bigger than the first two, and he could see that the deeper they got the more difficult it would be to use leverage on the stones. Nonetheless, in his mind's eye it was simply a matter of time and effort to clear everything that stood between him and Gail, no matter how heavy and unyielding it might first seem.

He wiped his face with the back of his hand, clearing away the sweat and tears that were making it difficult to see. He then turned away from the others for a moment to take a couple of deep breaths, before returning to work with renewed vigour and passion.

I'm coming Gail, he thought as he threw a couple of small rocks behind him blindly with both hands. *I'm coming.*

CHAPTER 74

It was a long time before anyone said anything. They stayed completely motionless, in the darkness of the hall, staring at the solitary green light; and despite the fact that it lit up nothing, it seemed to them as bright as the Sun in the centre of the Solar System.

Eventually, and predictably, it came to Walker to break the silence.

"Something just turned itself on," was all he said. He turned the torch on and pointed it directly at the green light, promptly rendering it invisible.

It took only a few seconds for them to reach the bottom of another steep staircase. The mirror image of the one they had descended on their arrival, at the other end of the hall. Looking up, they could see no doorway, though as they started to ascend the stairs the green light became easier to make out inside the warm glow of the torch's beam.

"Inscriptions!" Gail said in wonder.

They reached a platform roughly ten feet deep and double that across, and Walker ran the beam across the whole of the wall in front of them. It was covered in symbols and pictures engraved into the stone.

"They're not Egyptian, and I think that this might be one of your friends, Henry," Gail said, pointing to a man in strange clothing reaching for the skies. He was wearing a triple-pointed crown, his face lifted skywards, his staff held aloft.

"Xynutians!" Patterson exclaimed.

Walker was examining a small indentation in the wall, from which the green light continued to glow. "It may look just like an LED from over there," he said. "But it isn't."

"Don't touch it!" Patterson warned.

Ben stood back as far as he dared in the darkness without getting too close to the edge of the platform.

"What's going on here, Gail?" he asked suspiciously. "Who are the Xynutians, why is this not Egyptian writing, and why is there an electronic LED in a tomb that's been sealed for thousands of years?"

She poured her hands over the engravings, trying to feel for their meaning and significance.

"This place," she began, "is proof that Nefertiti and Akhenaten started this city, the Royal city of Akhetaten, because they had received a warning. They passed that warning on to us in the book of Aniquilus, the book that we found in the Library. It tells people how to live their lives peacefully and how to interact with the world around them. The fact that they built this underground storage area shows how seriously they took not only the warning, but also the threat.

"Why they chose this geographic location was never clear. The stone quality was poor and they rushed the building of houses, monuments and palaces, which is one reason why so little remains above the original foundation layer. But now we know why." She pointed to the LED that Walker was still groping around. "Because the Xynutians chose this place before them; the Xynutians received the same warning, and didn't heed it. In time, they were wiped out by Aniquilus."

Patterson looked up from the engravings for a moment. "So now you believe it?"

"In the past few minutes, I've come to believe three things. Firstly, that the LED Walker is trying to break over there wasn't made by Ancient Egyptians. Secondly that these engravings are not Ancient Egyptian. And thirdly, that somewhere on this wall is the mechanism that will make a door open. And whatever is behind that door, it's not going to be Egyptian."

Ben clicked his tongue. "That's a lot to take in right now. You're saying that these Xynutians are behind this wall? Couldn't this staff guy be Egyptian? Could this writing just be a dialect we haven't discovered yet?"

"No," she said simply.

He chuckled nervously. "I hate it when academics do that, discount what you say without even bothering to say why."

Walker stood back from the LED and scanned the wall with his torch, letting it rest on the area that Patterson and Gail were studying.

"So if there is a door, is it a good thing that the light turned from red to green?"

Patterson shook his head. "For all we know, it might do that on a timer every thousand years. And we have no idea if red is off or on, or if it has any meaning at all to the Xynutians. What we do know is that this isn't the first door we've seen like this. Minus the LED, which may have been there and we just didn't see it, this is strikingly similar to the wall that they found on Mars."

Walker moved the torch to Patterson's face. "What?"

Patterson sighed, cursing himself for his loose tongue. "I can't really say any more," he said. "It's kind of a 'need to know' thing."

"Well let me just summarise our little situation here: we're God knows how many feet underground, without much air, no food or water save for a few ancient loaves of bread down there, and we're stuck at a door that we don't know how to open, which for all we know may just be our way out of here. If it's a need to know thing, then I need to fucking know. Where have you seen this door before, and how did it open?"

Walker had visibly used all his mental strength to keep his voice down, but the fire in his eyes was enough to scare Patterson into talking. He explained everything, as briefly as possible, from the time delay in the Mars mission video feeds down to the secret archaeological dig that had uncovered the Jetty and Xynutian passageway, ending in the mysterious doorway that had swallowed Captains Yves Montreaux and Daniil Marchenko. Throughout the story, Walker flicked the light between Gail, Patterson and Ben, realising that only he and Ben were hearing this for the first time.

"So the door simply slid open, and they went in," he said when Patterson had finished.

He nodded.

"And they didn't press any buttons or anything?" He groped the engravings, pressing down hard on anything his fingers encountered. "No idea how it worked?"

"There seemed to be some power drain from anything that was near the door before it opened, almost like it was using up the electricity from around it to power itself. The first time it took out Captain Marchenko's suit battery, almost killing him, and the second time it knocked Jane Richardson's suit out, but luckily they'd been expecting it. The thing is, it doesn't matter what we press, we don't have a power source."

Gail looked at Walker's torch, and they followed her gaze.

"No way!" he exclaimed. We lose the battery, we lose our way out! There's no way we can find our way back without this, we're literally in the dark here without it."

She turned round and examined the wall once more. The Xynutian writing was unlike any she had ever seen, like a crazed cross between Arabic and Chinese. She knew from experience – learning the hieroglyphs, and then later on hieratic Egyptian scripts – that she was not a natural when it came to learning another language, particularly one that you couldn't have conversations in every day. She also knew from history that no matter how good she'd been, there was no way that anyone would understand this writing without possibly a combination of supercomputers, super intelligence, and as much time as was needed.

Even with the famous Rosetta Stone, ancient Egyptian hieroglyphs had taken over twenty years to decode, and it wasn't until more than fifty years of the stone's discovery that the full text engraved on it was actually translated.

Basically, she didn't stand a chance of understanding what the Xynutians had written, and she knew it. Worse still, there were fewer pictures on this wall, and more writing, than in the passageway on Mars.

"Give me the torch," she said, yanking it out of Walkers hands. He tried to protest, but didn't offer much resistance. Whatever plans of killing them he may have had, he was saving them for when they were free.

She scanned the wall, from the base of the landing they were standing on, to the ceiling thirty feet above them. Concentrating on the join between the floor and the wall, she let out a satisfied *hmph* and stood up. "The stairs were added later, probably by the Egyptians."

They all looked around the landing on which they stood. It was completely featureless.

"Which begs the question, if the Egyptians built this staircase to get to the LED and the writing, then how did the Xynutians get to the door?" Patterson asked.

"By walking up to it, from down there," Gail answered as she made her way down the stairs with them in tow. "Somewhere down there is another door."

Under the stairs, missed in their eagerness to get to the green LED at the top, they found an arch just taller than a normal doorway and half as wide. Inside, a small room six feet square housed two small statues of a man and a woman, both about three feet high.

"Nefertiti and Akhenaten," she gasped. "Incredible. I've never seen anything like it. Engravings of them together are more or less common, often appearing in private homes from Amarna, but a statue of them together like this is unique."

She crouched down in front of the statues and studied their faces. Akhenaten was unmistakable, his elongated, almost caricatured face smiling serenely through large, inflated lips. The statue was still painted, and Gail marvelled at the tone of his skin, only a shade or two lighter than the deep black of the Nubians. His eyes were set in jet black obsidian.

His left arm ended in a clenched fist pointing directly at the floor, while his right arm wrapped around Nefertiti's back, pulling her close at the waist.

"They were equals, here," she commented. "Often the kings of Egypt would scale themselves far larger than their wives or concubines, who would commonly be shown at their feet. I've seen one notable exception, in Luxor where Ramses II is seated next to Nefertari. Ironically, a couple of miles away in Karnak there's a huge statue of them again, but this time she's a few feet high and barely reaches his knees."

"I know the statue you mean, in Luxor," Ben said. "I remember we went there together with George, on your second visit to Egypt. Except the one in Luxor has two differences. Firstly, here Akhenaten and Nefertiti are standing up, not sitting down," he said.

"And secondly, in Luxor only Nefertari is holding Ramses II, while his hands are on his knees," Patterson finished. "I've been there too, many years ago as a tourist, funnily enough." He chuckled to himself, amused by the odd twist of fate.

"Almost," Gail said. "His hands would be on his knees, if his arms weren't cut off above the elbows. There's another small statue of Nefertiti and Akhenaten I can remember, in the Louvre in Paris, of them both holding hands. They were quite a caring couple, even seen in contemporary artwork playing with their children, which is quite uncommon."

Nefertiti's face was a far cry from the famous bust in the Berlin Museum, instead sharing the same stylised approach as had been applied to her king. Gail remembered her first visit to Egypt, and asked herself if she would have been so fascinated in the woman and her story had it not been for the beauty of that bust.

Looking into the statue's eyes, the intense blue of Lapis Lazuli against her pale olive-brown complexion, she knew without a doubt that the answer was yes; bust or no bust, she felt an irresistible connection with the enigmatic queen.

Nefertiti's statue in turn pulled Akhenaten towards her with her left arm, so that their bare bodies touched. Both their hips were pronounced and feminine and their stomachs bulged slightly at the waistline, but not so much so in Akhenaten's case as in the huge statue Gail had gazed at for hours in the Egyptian Museum of Cairo's Amarna exhibit. Their stance didn't follow traditional regal symbolism, either, with left foot forwards to represent their existence as both divine and mortal; instead they both stood with their feet together.

"Is it normal that they're naked and bald?" Walker said pensively.

Gail clucked for a moment, playing with her thumbs. "No," she said finally. "Semi-naked isn't so uncommon, there are many statues of both Nefertiti and Akhenaten without clothes, but they always have crowns or headdresses, or have some form of accessory, such as a staff or amulet, even a loose fitting sarong. But for both of them to be completely naked is unique." She paused for a moment. "The baldness is less strange, in fact it's quite likely that one or even both of them were bald anyway, and that any hair they would have had, particularly Nefertiti's, would have been a wig. It's even possible that these statues had wigs, or were carved with the intention of having such an accessory."

She inspected the statues more closely for several minutes while the others watched in silence. She was looking for any signs of wear on the paintwork, any scratches or markings that might betray the presence of some missing clothing or jewellery. She found none. It was possible that any clothing used on the statues failed to leave a mark, but somehow she doubted it. She was pretty sure the couple had always stood here, humbly.

"Small statues like this are fairly common. Like votive statues, inviting offerings from people visiting a temple. But as far as I know this one is absolutely unique. It's obvious from first glance, but when you look more closely the peculiarities are stunning. They're not like temple statues, designed to show the power and strength of a king during their own lifetime; these are normally made after the subject's death, and by someone who probably never saw the person alive. Caricatured features like this are typical only of Amarna, and yet I wouldn't have expected to see that here.

"And what's more," Gail continued, "they're not showing any royal symbolism. They're just a couple, standing naked, exposed, even their legs are together, almost rejecting their own divinity."

"This is all very well," Walker broke the silence that followed her monologue, "and we're all learning a lot about history and all that, but this ain't getting us out of here."

Gail shone the torch around as Ben and Patterson reluctantly agreed that they should focus on looking for a way out. The small room under the staircase was completely bare save for the statues.

"There's nothing in there," he continued impatiently. "Give me the torch and let's look around this place." He made a grab for it but she twisted away just before his fingers closed around the black metal shaft.

"Wait!" she exclaimed. She looked down at the statue, and drew a line in the air with the beam of the torch, to the blank featureless wall where Nefertiti and Akhenaten had been staring for over three thousand years.

Except it wasn't just a wall. Thin strips of wooden beading ran along the walls, floor and ceiling, almost invisible at first glance and in the poor lighting. She walked to the end of the room and carefully placed her hand against the wall. Instead of the hard coolness of stone, she encountered the soft-warm touch of finely woven cloth. She could feel the hardness of the surface it hid.

"A fake wall!" Patterson gasped.

Walker strode to Gail's side and placed his palms on the material. Looking up and down at the beading holding it in place, he slowly curled his fingers inwards, letting his nails run along the weave, testing its strength.

"You can't just rip it down," Gail protested, reading his mind.

The look he gave her stopped any further complaints, and he dug his fingers into the cloth, taking the few millimetres of slack up and ripping downwards. After several long rips, the entire wall was uncovered, and the remains of the cloth lay scattered at his feet.

Still recovering from the initial shock of Walker's lack of respect, Gail moved the torchlight from side to side on the now uncovered wall; it was crammed with inscriptions and drawings from the book of Xynutians; Xynutian cities with flying vehicles and towering buildings followed by the chaos and destruction of the wrath of Aniquilus. There was no need here to understand the Xynutian language. This was the story of the destruction of a civilisation, a story that had survived the millennia to warn the ancient Egyptians, who stood here in humility before it.

On top of the engravings, it's four legs and two arms covering the width of the walls and its round head rising above the ruins of the Xynutian world, the Stickman of Amarna, the symbol that Gail had chased the meaning of for a decade. *Aniquilus* stood before them.

Seeing it like this, the final pieces of her jigsaw were starting to fall into place.

Akhenaten and Nefertiti, laid bare, abandoning the old gods, were accepting the higher power of Aniquilus, who it was shown had destroyed a more advanced civilisation than their own. But how would they break with thousands of years of tradition and present the truth of Aniquilus to the Egyptian people? By taking Aniquilus and linking it with the old god Aten, the sun disk with outstretched rays touching the people below, and then moving the capital of Egypt to Amarna, away from Thebes and Memphis, away from the old way of life.

And then, finally, by renouncing their own pharaonic link with divinity, by showing that they were mere mortals, and that they would all face the judgement of Aniquilus, from the people who worked the fields right up to the kings and queens.

Gail fell to her knees.

"So this is it," she whispered. "This is what it was all about. I saw it in the books, I saw the finds on Mars. But this," she nodded to the statues facing Aniquilus, "is what *this* is all about."

Patterson resisted the urge to say 'I told you so', and patted her shoulder. But he could little understand what this meant to Gail. After so many years of studying the texts from the Library, without the missing pieces of the puzzle, to finally see everything in context so clearly was at the same time immensely exciting and unbelievably demoralising.

"Before I saw the Book of Xynutians this week, I only had ideas. Now, I have the actual truth," she said, deflated. Up until now she had been denying the evidence fed to her by Patterson and Mallus, but now there could be no mistaking the message in the small room under the staircase.

Suddenly, the torch switched itself off; a heartbeat later it came back on again. The momentary darkness made everyone jump.

Walker seized the torch and inspected it. "There's enough battery left for another eight hours," he claimed, after checking the charge. But no sooner had he finished his sentence than they were again plunged into darkness for good.

"Shit!" he exclaimed among the cries of the others.

In the pandemonium, Gail had a vivid recollection of her dream when she was kidnapped, of being helplessly stuck in the darkness. She felt a tingle down her spine, as if the lack of light had taken all warmth from the air.

After what seemed like an age, but what could in reality barely have been a few minutes, a thin blade of blinding white light appeared at the bottom of the wall. Within seconds the wall had disappeared into the ceiling, and they were shielding their eyes as they tried to see what had been revealed.

Gail, still on her knees where she'd been facing the Xynutian engravings, squinted into the light. At first all she could make out was a straight corridor, the light coming from strips along the ceiling and walls. As her eyes became more comfortable, the strips split up into single points, and she saw that the corridor was illuminated with thousands of small dots of very bright white light, like the solitary LED at the top of the stairs. They led down the corridor, deeper underground; to a dead end that she guessed must also be a door.

Walker recovered first, and strode into the corridor towards it. Ben hesitated, pistol in hand, on the threshold. Gail looked up at Patterson.

"Henry, this is all very familiar," she said slowly, thinking of the astronauts trapped behind the door on Mars.

He nodded and started walking into the corridor. "It is, and I know what you're thinking, but we don't really have a choice: the air in here is turning stale and the flashlight has gone out."

As he said it, she became all too aware of the acrid taste on her tongue from the low quality air they'd all been sharing. The hall they had entered was massive, but she knew that its oxygen content had been poor to start with.

"Feels fresher in here," Walker said with an approving nod. "Just need to work out how this other door opens, but we've been doing well so far," he joked.

Gail paused for a moment as she got to her feet. George was somewhere behind her, *above* her, and yet ahead and further down was the only possible route. The lack of torch and dwindling air supply made further exploration or even retreat impossible.

It was the only way forwards, and yet she couldn't shake the feeling that there was something very final about going down the corridor. Nonetheless, she accepted Ben's outstretched hand and joined him and

Patterson inside. She was barely a few steps down the corridor, moving towards Walker, when she thought to look back at Akhenaten and Nefertiti.

What she saw terrified her.

The white light from the corridor had picked out the polished stone of their eyes. But instead of reflecting in the black of obsidian and blue of Lapis Lazuli, Akhenaten and Nefertiti were fixing her with blood-red eyes. Their peaceful smiles took on a whole new sinister dimension, and as Gail stared incredulously at their evil gaze, the door that led back to the Hall, back to the Library and back to George, slid closed, leaving them trapped in the corridor.

CHAPTER 75

During the mid-1980s, more than seventy thousand nuclear weapons existed in stockpiles maintained by the Americans and Russians. It is often quoted that the yield of those nuclear weapons was sufficient to destroy the world several times over, but that is poor imagery to help describe how such a cataclysmic event would take place.

In reality, a mere fraction of those nuclear arsenals would ever be deployed. After the first few hundred ICBMs had landed on foreign soil, there would be precious few people left alive who could even launch the remainder, and even fewer of whom would want to.

In 1991, the Cold War ended; on both sides of the border, no one had ever truly wanted to use the weapons they had created. The understood devastation of nuclear holocaust, the indiscriminate killing of millions of innocent people and the no-win situation that would arise from its aftermath ultimately spelled the end of the stand-off between East and West.

Nonetheless, in the post-Cold War era nuclear disarmament was both slow and unenthusiastic. The Russians, reeling from their own economic implosion, were unable to maintain their existing weapons, let alone decommission them. For its part, the West was particularly loath to take a large proportion of its nuclear arsenal off hair-trigger alert. Despite numerous attempts to pass resolutions through the United Nations, the United States of America, France and the United Kingdom persistently voted against the action.

This meant that several decades after the end of the Cold War, the old West maintained an arsenal of hundreds of nuclear weapons pointed at targets in the East that could effectively be launched in less than five minutes.

Then, on 28th July 2015, the Islamic Republic of Iran announced to the world that it had officially joined the elite club of nations in possession of nuclear weapons.

The announcement came not via the state media, nor from the network of foreign intelligence agents and informants who risked their lives on a daily basis to provide up-to-date reports on the country's machinations, although the very existence of such networks did mean that few were surprised when the announcement finally came.

Instead, it came from the vaporisation of fifty square miles of desert and arid shrub-land in the South Khorasan region of the country, less than a hundred miles from Afghanistan. It was confirmed by satellite imagery, but such technology was not needed for the majority Kurdish population along the Afghan border, who saw the mushroom cloud hit the Earth's stratosphere around about the same time the ground started to shake.

The show of strength caused international relations in the already volatile region to heat up considerably; particularly damaging was the face-off that ensued between Iran and its pro-West neighbours Pakistan and Afghanistan, with many skirmishes along Iran's heavily fortified border causing tensions to rise dramatically within the UN.

India was critical of the militant stance taken by Pakistan in particular, and terrorist activity in the two countries increased. The governments blamed each other, but nonetheless decided to increase investment in their own already substantial nuclear deterrents.

While Pyongyang sent congratulations to Tehran, Moscow urged prudence on behalf of the world's largest nuclear power. Israel was up in arms, stepping up air patrols and angering Iraq and Iran for infringing airspace with spy drones.

The announcement meant it was now theoretically possible, although practically less so, to travel by land from the Mediterranean to the Bay of Bengal or even the East China Sea without once having to set foot in a country that did not possess or have access to nuclear weapons.

The United States of America quietly slowed down existing disarmament programs, continuing to decommission warheads and delivery systems (that would in any case have belonged in museums) while installing ever more effective systems to support the warheads that would remain active.

At the same time, the President issued a stark warning to Tehran: "Nuclear Proliferation will not be tolerated," he said with his hands firmly rooted to the podium at a press conference. "In cooperation with our international partners, the United States of America will strive to uphold the values that saw the end of the Cold War; the end of the nuclear arms race."

In Tehran, they could read between the lines: *Welcome to the club.*

In 2045, nuclear weapons were still a deterrent; one that earned the owner greater respect, and made it far less likely you would ever be attacked. Everyone understood the destructive power of the technology and where it could lead the world.

And it would still take a complete maniac to actually use them.

The white utility vehicle turned left into a side alley connecting Franklin Street and White Street, a block away from Broadway, and came to a stop. The enticing smell from the Lafayette Grill kitchens made the driver's mouth fill with saliva, but there was no time to pop in for a bite to eat. He'd have to grab a McDonald's or a Burger King on his way out of New York by train.

He couldn't remember which would be available at Penn Station, probably both. He would have half an hour or so before he hopped on the train to DC to make up his mind, as long as he could hail a cab and they didn't get stuck in traffic.

Having already changed out of his overalls and into jeans and a shirt, he shouldered his gym bag and locked the doors. He also checked thoroughly for parking restrictions, and peered into the windscreen of another car parked on the same street to check for parking permits. He'd stopped where he'd planned to, of course, but he didn't want to leave anything to chance. That's why he'd been chosen for this job; not just that he understood the importance of getting it right, more importantly the consequences of getting it wrong. He also knew there were no surveillance cameras in this street, and the narrow alley made it very unlikely that any decent satellite imagery would be obtainable.

A police van drove slowly along White Street as he emerged into the sunlight. He carried on walking nonchalantly, ignoring the look from the officer riding shotgun. It was a long time since he'd been in New York, but it was pretty much like any big city in America: mind your own business, and everything'll be just fine.

He jumped in a yellow cab and pointed up Broadway. "Penn Station, please."

The driver grunted in reply and they seamlessly joined the lunchtime traffic.

Fifteen minutes later, he was sitting on a bench in the station, enjoying an early lunch of Triple Whopper, large fries and Coke. The slices of tomato slid out from under the bun as he tried to hold the burger together, biting small chunks from around the edges to get it somewhere near a manageable size. It was a pain to eat and surely a sorry substitute for the Lafayette Grill, but he made a promise to himself to get some proper food as soon as he got back to Florida.

Ketchup and juice dripping down his fingers, he finally popped the last morsel in his mouth and washed it down with a mouthful of Coke. He left most of the fries and cleaned himself up, chucking the ball of rubbish into a nearby waste basket. Grabbing the still three-quarters-full Coke, he strode across the platform and boarded the train.

A few minutes later, he was watching the station slip away.

He flipped open his cell phone and called the voicemail box hosted in an anonymous business park somewhere in a nameless warehouse in Central America. After one ring, the auto-attendant picked up and asked him in a sweet southern accent how he wished her to direct his call. He input his six digit pin and snapped the phone shut.

Closing his eyes he bid a silent, eternal farewell to the City of New York. *So nice they named it twice*, he thought. He settled down into his seat and opened his eyes, curious to see the city rush past.

He was more of a country man, and he wouldn't be missing it. He wouldn't be missing it at all.

Seth Mallus put the handset down and smiled quietly. The third device was in place.

Los Angeles, Chicago and New York had all been planted within ten minutes of each other. A perfectly coordinated attack, despite Los Angeles being over fifteen hundred miles further to drive than the other two, they had managed to leave at the same time and arrive at the same time.

He applauded the drivers' organisational skills, as the finer points of their journeys had been left to them. They had strict instructions to arrive and be out of the cities by a certain time, but other than that no communication could be traced back to DEFCOMM in Florida.

It was vital that when the bombs went off, nothing could cause the authorities to look inside their own borders for the perpetrators. For a start the fissionable material could only be traced back to the ex-Soviet block, namely Georgia. And of course, compromised defence systems would ensure that military advisors thought the threat was external, but there was always a chance a meddling FBI agent or rogue cop could sniff a rat.

The last thing he wanted was to be assigned his own personal Hollywood Action Hero.

CHAPTER 76

Captain Tan Ling Kai looked out across the bow of the *DDG Hangzhou*, towards the horizon. *Beyond which lies America*, he mused.

Barely fifty years earlier China had been little more than a thorn in the United States' side; a hugely populous nation, full of promise for the future but no real threat to the global dominance of the world's only superpower.

In the decades since, power had shifted inexorably towards Asia, with China taking up the lion's share. China's dominance in the economic arena was symbolised in many things, not least of which was the surge in Mandarin language courses in the West. The greatest compliment to pay to another culture was to learn its language and customs, and China was more fashionable now than ever before. It was a sign of the resurgent East.

But becoming a superpower wasn't simply a matter of cultural and economic influence; Captain Tan Ling Kai was part of the blunt edge of China's hammer blow to end three hundred years of Western dominance: military might.

The flotilla, or *zhidui*, was laid out before him, pointing East towards America. They'd been misrepresented by the world media, he had heard. *Misclassified as 'Lanzhou' class destroyers, a forty year old relic with outdated stealth technology and diesel propulsion systems*, he scoffed. But the Lanzhou was a Type 052C ship, whereas Hangzhou was the first of two Type 056B destroyers, with nuclear propulsion, advanced stealth and semi-submersible defence systems.

The other Type 056B was in position three miles off *Hangzhou*'s port bow.

Along with two Jianghu V class frigates, off the starboard bow, they formed the main bulk of the Fourth Fleet, a *zhidui* put together to show America that they could no longer expect to rule the world unchallenged. The situation in Korea was an ideal opportunity to demonstrate that China was ready to do that. And thanks to an effective government-run media campaign, the incidental death of Lieutenant Shi Su Ning in space had swayed public opinion against the Americans, which had made it far easier for the State Council to approve the Fourth Fleet's first active deployment.

Their command currently came from a nuclear submarine, the *Houjian*, which lurked somewhere below them in the depths of the Pacific. Their latest orders had been to weigh anchor and sail at a rate of 15 knots to the limit of US territorial waters.

Captain Tan Ling Kai was proud of his command. As the water was pumped out of her ballast tanks, the *Hangzhou* rose from her semi-submerged 'cruise' state, where the sea covered the main deck and visibility was primarily from the bridge and observation deck.

Along with the satellite dish and radar arrays, in cruise they were the only non-submerged parts of the vessel. As the water ran off *Hangzhou*'s angular surfaces, he ordered a weapons systems test – standard procedure following any submerged state for the new destroyers.

In rapid succession, sections of the ship slid open, revealing the full range of weaponry on board. The first compartments, running parallel to each other along the flanks of the ship, exposed sixteen banks of four vertical launching system cells for a combination of cold-launch surface-to-air, surface-to-surface and surface-to-submarine missiles. Capable of undertaking up to eighteen simultaneous engagements, the brand new Chinese-built VLS was a quantum leap from the antiquated revolver-style favoured by the outgoing 052C class destroyers. Next, two compact gattling gun turrets emerged from either side of the bridge, their deadly barrels springing to attention as they each circled through two hundred and twenty degrees in a full protective sweep of the *Hagzhou*'s deck. The *sea-whiz* defence system could fire nearly six thousand rounds-per-minute, up to a range of over three kilometres.

Finally, the top of the deck midway between bridge and bow folded back and a single domed turret emerged from below. After rotating through three hundred and sixty degrees and pivoting the 120mm gun barrel from horizon to zenith, it disappeared into the bowels of the ship, helping it regain the quasi-zero radar profile that made it one of the most advanced warships afloat.

China was ready.

CHAPTER 77

Gail stood, frozen to the spot, as the corridor sealed itself behind them. The memory of Akhenaten and Nefertiti's piercing red gaze was still fresh in her mind.

Patterson ran back to the door, reaching it the moment it closed, and slammed his palms against it. "No!" he exclaimed.

Ben started towards him but was caught off balance by Walker, who slammed him against the floor and easily prised the pistol from his hand.

"Fucking Arab," he muttered as he stood up and kicked Ben in the stomach. He pointed the gun at his heart and started to squeeze the trigger.

"Wait!" Patterson shouted. "Don't shoot!"

Walker hesitated long enough for Patterson to explain his objection.

"We may still need him," Patterson struggled to come up with a valid reason quickly enough. "What if we find something heavy that needs lifting, what if we need to force this door open?" He knew it was a tragic excuse, and he almost winced as he gave it.

Walker weighed up his options briefly. As far as he was concerned, he'd waited long enough already. He'd played the nice guy long enough to get out of the crumbling tomb he'd woken up in following the explosion. Now he was in a corridor lit by electricity, with increasingly fresh air being pumped in from somewhere. He was in no doubt that from hereon in he could fend for himself. He couldn't rule out the possibility that there may be a need for more manpower, but on the other hand he didn't consider the Arab to be particularly strong anyway.

"I doubt it," he surmised.

Gail was going from turmoil to anguish. In the last five minutes she'd had her academic beliefs finally shattered, and now she was faced with one of her dearest friends being brutally executed.

"If you kill him, then I won't get you out of here. I would die with him rather than help you." She was amazed at how calm her own voice sounded; it was like hearing someone else speak.

"You'll help me if I point this gun at you," he threatened.

Gail shook her head simply, a wry smile appearing on her face. "You kill him, and we all die down here."

After a moment or two, he lowered the gun and stepped away from Ben. "Your lucky day, Mohammed," he jeered.

Ben stood up, helped by Gail and Patterson.

"Thanks," he whispered to them both, with a nod to Gail.

For the first time, Walker was in control. "You," he said pointing the pistol at Gail, "find out how to open this door."

She knew now that Ben was only alive because there was a chance she could still be useful. Thinking hard, she desperately tried to live up to that promise. The corridor they were in was very similar to the airlock found on Mars. The Russian, Captain Marchenko, had entered it first, and when the airlock opened for a second time, to let the other crew members in, he was gone. That meant that Marchenko had passed through the airlock successfully. *And he must have been groggy, with hardly any air and no power to his suit*, she thought.

Looking around, she noticed for the first time the engravings on the walls. Processions of Xynutians, along with dozens of different species of animals, heading towards the door that Walker was standing by.

She breathed in deeply, and noted that the air was almost fresh now, and at a pleasant temperature, rather than the chill of the hall behind them.

It's just an automatic airlock, she realised suddenly. How else was it possible for an astronaut to make his way through while suffering from a lack of oxygen, which would have impaired his thought processes?

She walked towards the door and pushed past Walker. *No time to lose, this thing could open any second now!* She moved her hands over the inscriptions on either side of the door and settled for the head of one of the Xynutians, who was wearing a particularly elaborate headdress and holding another staff, this one double-headed, aloft. Pressing hard twice, she stood back and observed the door anxiously.

"Well –" Walker began, but before he could continue his sentence the door slid open silently, and what was revealed instantly made him forget what he'd been about to say.

For staring right back at them, its staff held aloft and its teeth bared in a gruesome sneer, was a Xynutian.

CHAPTER 78

George sat down, exhausted. Tariq and Manu were gulping down the last of their own water, while Leena had descended to Ben's Toyota to fetch more.

He looked across at Zahra guarding the American, who was shifting uncomfortably against the hand and ankle ties that made sure he wasn't going to try and escape.

"We need some help," he said. "We need medical help."

After an hour or so of excavating, he had been able to squeeze his entire arm and head into the hole they had created, but despite all of their cries and shouting, no one had responded from beneath the rubble. If there was still a chance that Gail was alive, or Ben for that matter, the fact that they weren't answering meant that they probably needed urgent medical assistance.

Zahra nodded her head. "On their way," she answered. "But by car, and from al-Minya. They'll be here as soon as they can."

George did the sums in his head and worked out that they were still at least twenty minutes away. Zahra had only called for backup when there had been no response from inside the Library.

It was easy enough to explain what five members of the Tourism Police were doing in Amarna, as it was still fairly common for tourists to request armed escorts into the lesser travelled parts of the country, and Egypt had more Tourism Police than it sensibly knew what to do with.

And the fact that they'd been involved in a battle with an unknown terrorist organisation would probably help.

But Haji was dead, and she was dreading having to explain that. The shock of losing Ben had dissipated now, and she was only left with the harsh reality of her situation. What she had thought would be a fairly simple operation had turned into a bit of a nightmare.

Leena returned with the water, a large five litre plastic container with a handle, and they all refilled their bottles.

"Torches?" George made what he hoped was the international hand signal for 'torch', and not something deeply offensive.

She nodded and put them down on the ground. It made sense to pack a torch if you were going anywhere away from the beaten track, and Ben had packed two large Maglites before setting off from Cairo.

George gulped some more water down thirstily. The Sun had already set, sinking into the Sahara almost half an hour earlier. In the twilight, it was clear that the batteries running the lights inside the Library had run out, as no light emerged from the hole in the rubble.

Tariq, Manu, Leena and George stood in a small circle over the hole in the ground. Only one more stone. They had needed the rest, but now he felt a resurgence of energy, a desire to reach Gail, whatever her condition, and be with her.

It felt like years since they'd last held each other, since he'd said goodbye to her in England, although it had been barely a week. However long, it had been *too* long.

The four of them took up their positions around the block of stone, which was almost the size of an average man. On three, they heaved upwards, and managed to lift one end about a foot from its resting place. Rubble and sand streamed through the new hole and fell down onto the steps below; the hollow rattling noise the stones made as they fell caused a pang of emotion in George: they were so close now he could have let go and slipped through with them.

"Come on!" he yelled at the top of his voice as they heaved at the mass of sandstone. "Come on!" As the outburst left his lungs they fell back and the stone crashed down on its side. Tariq fell on top of Leena, and they cheered triumphantly, seeing the stone well and truly clear of the hole.

Tariq got up and stretched over to slap George on the back, but his hand swiped thin air as George grabbed a torch and launched himself down the hole, landing on the bottom steps of the ancient staircase with a thud.

Sweeping the ante-chamber of the Library with the torch, and ignoring the shooting pain that ran across the top of his foot following his spontaneous dive down the stairs, he quickly moved on to the hole in the wall and the Library beyond. He searched between the empty bookcases, and in every corner of the room, but there was no one to be found.

"Gail!" he shouted. "Gail, where are you?" Tears were streaming down his face as desperation made him lose all self-control. "It's me!" he sobbed.

The torch beam fell on the podium that had held the Stickman book. Wiping the tears from his eyes, he blinked several times before understanding what lay before him. Beyond the podium, where previously there had been a stone wall, there was a corridor, plunging down into the depths of the Earth.

Zahra arrived at his side and handed him his borrowed AK-47, which was still fully loaded. It reminded him that two of the Americans were still down here with Gail and Ben, and he checked the position of the safety.

"Where are they?" she asked.

George collected himself and took a deep breath. "Down there," he said pointing down the corridor. Before she could answer he'd left her behind and was half running, half limping down into the unknown, the AK-47 in one hand, the torch in the other, and with renewed hope in his heart.

CHAPTER 79

Walker was the first to take a step towards the Xynutian, who hadn't moved since the door had opened. Its steadfast gaze, although very lifelike, was utterly lifeless.

The statue was in the centre of a large hall, about thirty feet on each side. Directly opposite was another doorway, towards which Walker now marched.

Gail entered the hall slowly. When she reached the Xynutian, she turned and looked back down the corridor.

"They're looking at each other," she said in wonderment. "They're acknowledging each other across the millennia."

Walker hurried her up. "No time for history lessons now, sweetheart. You promised to get us out of here, and part of that means you going first."

The entrance hall gave onto a larger room, as brightly-lit as the first but almost twice as large. Along the middle of the room were three benches with glass tops. The opposite end of the room housed three doors.

It seemed that each door corresponded with one of the benches.

"It's a worktop," Patterson said. "They must have worked almost lying down, though." He looked back through the door at the statue, and tried to imagine the Xynutian using the knee-high displays.

"Or they used their feet," Ben joked.

Gail knelt down and touched the glass on the middle one. Immediately, shapes sprang to life in mid-air, hovering several feet above the worktop. Three concentric circles rotated at different speeds in front of her. The largest of them was also the slowest, barely moving at all, while the smallest rotated fastest, completing two revolutions in the time it took the middle ring to rotate only once.

Gail touched the two remaining screens and they sprang to life in a similar fashion. Soon, they all showed what looked like three clocks, with varying symbols and colours.

Examining the doors, she noticed three symbols etched into the floor of the room, one in front of each. The middle door was the outline of a Xynutian; the left hand that of a bear, while the one on the right showed a tree.

She went back to the right hand console. Whatever this place was, trees sounded less scary than Xynutians and bears.

Moving her hands over the display, she touched all of the symbols in turn, hoping for some response. Occasionally, the symbols would reconfigure, bringing incomprehensible charts and graphs to the foreground, before automatically fading them away to return to the spinning concentric circles.

"There's something we're missing here," she concluded. "The ancient Egyptians were able to write a whole book on this place, showing what happened to the Xynutians in some detail, and also, correct me if I'm wrong, Henry," she gestured at him, "they spoke of Mars, hence the Mars mission and what's going on up there."

Patterson didn't disagree.

"Unless they made it all up from the pictures and writing they saw back in the main hall, there's no way they could have written so much from what we see here. And more importantly, we know they're called *Xynutians* from the cartouches in the book. By the same token, *Aniquilus* too. So where did the Egyptians hear those names, unless they could interpret the Xynutian writing on the walls in the hall?"

She didn't have time for hypotheses; instead she strode back to the previous room and searched for any hidden symbols.

The room was bare, the walls perfectly smooth and featureless. Running her fingers along the surfaces, she had a sudden flashback to the vivid dream she had experienced just before waking inside DEFCOMM. It was that same seamless floor, almost *too* perfect. There, she had been in the dark save for the glow of her mobile phone; but here light was coming from recesses in the ceiling about six feet above the tip of the Xynutian's raised staff.

She gave the statue her full attention. From the nails of its toes to the pupils of its frozen eyes, it was absolutely perfect. Like a waxwork model of a celebrity, she could almost feel it breathing down her neck as she studied the intricate needlework on its tunic, which fell between its legs, leaving the powerful thighs exposed.

If this were a prime example, she was certain it would have been able to use those legs to run faster than any human athlete, and she could only imagine how strong it was.

It was human in every way, and yet somehow different.

Curiosity getting the better of her, she carefully lifted the tunic and peered underneath; there was no doubt this Xynutian was a man. Suddenly realising that she was staring at the Xynutian's private parts, she quickly dropped the tunic, her cheeks reddened. Whatever its culture, their gender had been private enough to cover.

She wondered for a moment about Nefertiti and Akhenaten, at the opposite end of the corridor, completely naked. There was some definite symbolism in the use of clothing going on here, she realised. Perhaps some form of submission to the Xynutians, as she had first suspected; but instead of submission to Aniquilus, this suggested it was submission to the Xynutians.

She shook her head and cursed herself for not having at the very least a notebook and pencil.

She stood back and stared at the creature head on. The Xynutian was huge, about two feet taller than her, its raised staff reaching a good three to four feet above her head.

The staff itself was a rod of what looked like solid gold. Certainly there was no tainting of the metal after so many years, and she could think of few other metals that possessed that property. It culminated in a clear-stone ball, perfectly spherical and, it occurred to her, as near as damn it in the exact centre of the room.

"Is that a switch?" Patterson asked, pointing up to where the Xynutian gripped the staff.

Ben and Walker had been staring at each other in the other room, but at Patterson's question, Walker pushed the Egyptian through the door and they joined them next to the statue.

"Too high for me to reach," Gail said. "Walker, you're the tallest, you press it."

He laughed. "Nice try. No, you press it, I'll be waiting over here, keeping an eye on you." He retreated into the corner and kept the pistol pointed in their direction.

After a brief discussion, Gail agreed to be lifted up on Ben's and Patterson's shoulders. With the added height, she easily reached where the Xynutian was holding the staff, and fumbled around for the switch. She felt it move under her fingers, and pressed it fully until it was flush with the shaft.

She had barely been returned to the floor when the lights went out.

A faint glow emanated from the stone ball on the end of the staff, and the walls, ceiling and floor of the room dissolved into nothingness.

She was in the depths of space; the spirals and warm glows of distant galaxies and nebulae beckoned. She soon found herself shooting up through wispy gaseous clouds. Leaving the plane of the Universe behind, she soared upwards: below her was everything that ever was.

The experience had taken her by surprise, but the visual effect was so intense that Gail felt herself lift from her physical self, her extremities numb. This was a voyage of the mind, like a dream, yet at the same time very real and tangible. She would have asked the others how they felt, what they could see, but she was on her own. They were still in the same room, yet at the same time millions of light years apart.

The galaxies swam beneath her, like small whirlpools, swells and ripples in a turbulent river. Gail had seen the Nile behave like that. She found herself inexorably drawn towards one galaxy, its tentacles wrapping round each other like an octopus in a spin. She recognised it as the Milky Way. As the galaxy enveloped her, she saw a single star ahead. She entered the solar system, and the gas giants flew past at breakneck speed as if their mere existence was inconsequential. Asteroids and debris from ancient collisions during the system's formative years littered her trajectory, but somehow she made it through and before long Mars appeared and expanded from a small red dot until it filled her field of vision. It was beautiful, the outline of continents and dead rivers on the planet's surface top and tailed by the frozen poles; memories of a more active past.

She hovered briefly by the shore of a vast empty ocean; a jetty thrust out towards a strange ship, hovering in mid-air.

But before she had time to focus in on the details of what was happening, she shot back up into space again, towards Earth.

Her heart filled with warmth as she saw the blue planet and its moon, dancing in the dawn like illicit lovers, their faces lit up by the familiar Sun as they whirled round and round to their own private rhythm.

Gail passed the Moon, and skimmed the atmosphere of the Earth. But something below her was different. She couldn't see the familiar continents and oceans. Instead, there was one massive continent in the centre of one hemisphere, while the rest of the planet was a vast expanse of ocean.

Pangaea; she could remember this from history at school. All present day continents had emerged from a single landmass many millions of years ago.

Somehow, in this immersive simulation that was playing out around her, she could sense from different perspectives at the same time. It was as if she was in two or three, or maybe a dozen different places at once, and could see, hear and smell all of them seamlessly. She continued to orbit the Earth, but the black space around her turned to forests and she found herself deep inside an ancient jungle. Rain was falling in drops the size of her thumbnails, beating the blades of fan-like leaves into submission and creating rivers in the mud.

The rains ended, and below her the landmass on Earth started to change shape; at the same time, small dinosaurs started to move around the forest, eating foliage. The continents became more distinct, and she could easily recognise North and South America drifting away from Africa and Eurasia.

All around her the dinosaurs grew to monstrous proportions, the familiar long-necked herbivores and ferocious meat-eaters only a tiny fraction of the thousands of species she was now looking at.

Most of the landmass remained on one hemisphere, the Atlantic and Indian oceans far smaller than she was used to on modern maps. With the exception of Europe and Asia, the continents looked correct. Central America still didn't exist, and though on each orbit she searched for them, Britain and Ireland also refused to emerge.

She was completing another orbit when an object hurtled past her and landed next to where Mexico would be. The debris thrown skywards hit the top of the atmosphere and flattened against the roof of the world like an umbrella, covering the continents below. Gail tried desperately to see through the haze, but it was impossible.

She knew without a doubt that she was looking at an event 65 million years ago: the extinction event that wiped out the dinosaurs.

The air remained murky as she orbited several more times, slowly clearing to reveal the ravaged earth beneath. Notably, Central America had risen from the sea.

To her surprise, dinosaurs still roamed the Earth, though in lesser numbers and variety than before, and the great giants of the Jurassic had gone.

Somewhere in a small forest, a small rodent emerged from a hole in a riverbank and shot up a tree. It started dangling from branches to reach nuts and fruit in the forest canopy and as it did so its limbs stretched. The tail, at first a long, straight point, started to curl round and balance the animal as it grew larger, reaching bigger fruits and insects, and eventually other small animals.

Suddenly it dropped from the trees and emerged from the forest into a grassy plain. It balanced on its hind legs to see above the long grass. Seeing it was safe to do so, it walked into the grass and away from the forest. As it did, its limbs elongated, giving it higher standing and allowing it to stride with greater comfort and speed through the fields.

It picked up a branch, and within one step it had become a spear. A step later the creature was wearing rough clothes, and within a few more Gail was looking at a fully developed human, only much stronger; a Xynutian.

Had she been able to feel her arms, she would have pinched herself. It was the Xynutian version of her first biology class on evolution at school.

The long grass turned to farmland and holes in the earth on the banks of the river turned into elaborate dwellings rising into the sky. Industry became apparent, smoke churning out of small round buildings away from the river, and in a matter of minutes the first vehicles emerged. Roads connected the rapidly growing city to its neighbours up and down the river, and the first lights came on.

She looked down at the planet beneath her and saw that all the continents were now in place, although they appeared somehow bloated, fatter versions of their modern selves, due to lower sea-levels. Europe still touched Africa along parts of the Mediterranean, Britain and Ireland, while now recognisable for the first time, were still part of the continental landmass, and Scandinavia was simply a blob near the Arctic circle.

In the Atlantic, connected to Spain and Morocco, she noticed part of Europe that didn't seem familiar. It only took a few seconds for her to realise that she may be looking at the mythical Atlantis. The Xynutians had obviously lived with Atlantis, so to them it probably had little or no significance, but thousands of years later it still sparked the imagination of humans who had never known it and had no proof it had ever existed.

And then she noticed the rivers.

Not just the ancient forebears of the Nile and Amazon and

Mississippi, but in the bloated landmass that had since sunk into the sea there were complex deltas and marshlands, while upriver water seemed to find its way into every crease of the world.

And as she orbited the planet slowly, on the night-side of the Earth she saw the lights of thousands of Xynutian cities, and she understood why they had slipped under the radar of human science for so long. Their cities mainly occupied the lowlands that were now in her time under the oceans and seas.

A small flare of light shot from one of the cities and flew towards her, and she knew the Xynutians had reached their space age. In the moments that followed, hundreds of rockets left the planet on various voyages of discovery, and she already knew that for some, that voyage would end on Mars. She wondered what other planets and stars had been touched by the ancient beings.

In the African Savannah, she gasped as she saw more early hominids walking upright through the long brown grass, with spears in their hands. *So we evolved separately,* she thought in wonder. This new knowledge would shatter everything they knew about human evolution. What were the chances of humanity evolving twice? She watched as the hominids fought against the Xynutians along rivers, though the Xynutians easily pushed them back into the forests and plains, and she found herself caught in an emotional tug of war between these fascinating Xynutians and her ancestors that they were killing, like a man might kill a beast. *That's all we were to them,* she shook her head.

Before she could give it any more thought, a shadow in the shape of the Amarna Stickman, Aniquilus, covered the Earth and the hominids disappeared from view. In their place she saw fire and death spreading through the Xynutian cities. The towering buildings collapsed into the water of the rivers and seas, and Xynutians lay dying in the dust of the fields.

One final armada of spaceships blasted off. As they reached orbit they paused, as if to say their last, silent, goodbyes, before pointing to the depths of space and vanishing in a flash of light.

Below her, the fires from the cities extinguished one by one, and the seas rose, swallowing Xynutian civilisation forever. Sadness overwhelmed her as she saw the last of the Xynutians slip beneath the waves.

The shadow of Aniquilus went. The age of Man had arrived.

In the room, darkness followed.

The wind whistled in her ears, and gradually dawn broke over the ridges of mountains she instantly recognised: Amarna, before humans. Though the vegetation was different, with lush forests and green plains all the way down to the Nile, the shape of Amarna was unchanged. A small doorway on the plateau above the plains of Amarna led to a spiral ramp with shallow steps every meter or so that descended into the ground.

She found herself walking and instantly knew where she was going. At the end of a long corridor, she reached the inscriptions on the wall that had been at the top of the stairs in the Egyptian hall. The red light was there, and as she watched it flicked to green.

As she descended another spiral staircase she thought of the coincidence that red and green had similar meaning for both humans and Xynutians, and wondered whether there was something universal about the two colours and what they represented. She reached the airlock, noting the absence of Nefertiti and Akhenaten.

On the other side of the airlock, she passed the statue with the staff in its hand, and entered the room with the three doors. The doors with the tree and bear were already closed, but the Xynutian door was open. She entered.

The vault within was as deep as the tallest skyscraper on Earth was tall, and just as wide again. She was standing on a small ledge, jutting out into space, and facing a wall of small drawers, like millions of filing cabinets stacked on top of each other. The drawer in front of her was open, and looking back at her from within was the frozen face of a Xynutian, completely naked inside a glass bubble.

The drawer closed and she exited the vault. The door shut behind her and she found herself at the control benches in the middle of the room. She didn't understand any of the symbols or concentric circles that hovered before her, but somehow their meaning seeped into her mind.

She had no time to digest the significance of this information, however, as all the lights suddenly went out.

When they came back on, her body and senses abruptly came into focus. She was back in the room with Ben, Henry and Walker, facing the Xynutian statue.

They stood there in silence for at least a minute before Ben reacted. Walker had caught him off balance in the airlock, and he had been waiting to return the favour.

Diving towards the American, Ben slammed his upturned palm into his chin and reached out with his other hand to grab the pistol. His knee found the other man's groin, and Walker let out a yelp of pain.

The Egyptian's advantage only lasted a few moments, however, and it quickly became apparent that the American would overpower him. Ben was focusing most of his strength on obtaining the pistol, which had left Walkers left hand free to try and gouge one of Ben's eyes out.

Reacting instinctively, Gail jumped into the air and grabbed the Xynutian's staff. Hanging from it for a few seconds, it suddenly gave and ripped out of the statue's hand. She ran up behind Walker and struck him across the back of the head with all of her might.

He shuddered under the impact and fell into Ben, sending them both crashing to the floor, the pistol held in between them. A shot, muffled by their bodies, echoed in the ante-chamber.

Patterson ran to pull the two of them apart, and as he did so Walker pulled the pistol barrel round and fired a second shot, hitting Patterson in the chest.

As Ben lay motionless on the floor and Patterson gasped for air, his back against the wall, Walker stood up and faced Gail.

"Just you and me now," he grimaced, nursing the back of his head. "And from what I've just seen in that little mind-fuck back there, those people didn't make this place with an exit. So we're stuck down here after all."

Gail brandished the Xynutian staff defensively and took a step away from him. She looked down at Ben and tried to see if he was still breathing or not. He blinked at her slowly, his face pale. Patterson was gasping for air and reaching out to her.

"You bastard," she said between clenched teeth.

He took two steps towards her. "Sorry you feel that way, sweetheart, because I was kind of hoping you'd make the stay down here more interesting."

She cringed at the thought of it, and took another step back, moving past the Xynutian statue. "You're crazy," she said. "After all this all you can think about is raping me!"

"Rape!" he laughed. "I'm not that kind of guy." He levelled the gun at her chest and his smile disappeared. "But I don't see why you need to be here any longer taking my air."

She closed her eyes and raised her arms defensively in front of her.

The cacophony of gunshots that followed made her eardrums feel like they were exploding, and she fell backwards. The Xynutian staff clattered to the floor beside her.

But the pain she had been expecting never came.

She waited for a moment before opening her eyes to see Walker lying on the floor in front of her; blood covered his face and the wall behind him. The angle of his head told her instantly that he was dead. She looked beyond the Xynutian statue and her whole body started to tremble. Her heart pounded in her chest and her breath shortened. Tears streamed down her face, and while she was still unable to hear following the gunshots, she knew she was uncontrollably repeating his name over and over out loud.

Because there, standing in the airlock with a gun held to his shoulder like the last action hero, was George.

CHAPTER 80

George lifted Gail up and spun her around the room, and as her feet finally touched the ground they kissed, melting into each other with unrestrained abandon.

"Gail, I –" George didn't know where to begin, as he broke from their embrace and looked her in the eyes. "I thought I'd lost you, I –"

Gail cut him off, wiping the tears from her cheeks. "I know, George, me too. But first we need to see to Ben and Henry."

He was about to ask who Henry was when Zahra pushed past him and made her way to Ben's side. She knelt down beside him and located the entry point of the bullet in his left shoulder through a hole in his shirt. She asked him a series of short questions in Arabic, and after each response nodded matter-of-factly. Finally, she repositioned herself so that she was kneeling behind his head and propped him up against her.

"I need some saline," she told George. "And blood for him," she nodded at Patterson, whose breathing had turned into a pant. Gail had gone to his side, and was trying to comfort him as best she could.

Tariq had followed them in through the airlock, and Zahra quickly gave him his orders in Arabic. Gail panicked for a moment as she wondered whether the airlock would let them out as easily as it let them in, but as soon as Tariq entered the brightly lit corridor the door closed behind him.

Probing the back of Ben's shoulder, Zahra found the exit hole directly opposite the entry point on his front. It looked like a clean pass through the shoulder, and some tentative movement of the arm suggested that none of the bones or joints had been hit on the way through.

Using her knife, she cut his shirt open and cleaned the small hole with water from a plastic bottle she got from her backpack. Her medical training in the Army reminded her that there was one major artery and a major vein in the left shoulder, which supplied the left arm and the top of the neck. But the slow rate at which this wound was bleeding and the colour of the blood told her instantly that the bullet hadn't severed either of them.

"Get me some bandages," she asked George.

George ferreted in her backpack and came out with two rolls, which he ripped the cellophane from and passed to her one by one. She held the first roll over the hole in his front and used the second bandage to wrap over his shoulder and under his arm. Within a few moments the dressing was secure. She lay him back down on the floor and, standing at his feet, lifted his legs up so they rested against her groin.

"He's a bit light headed, but the wound itself is not serious," she said. "This will push some blood back to his head. But he still needs a saline drip to be sure – he could go into shock if we don't treat him."

When the colour started to return to Ben's face and he smiled at her, she put his legs back down on the floor and got him to bend them at the knees.

She moved on to Patterson, and her face dropped. He had started to splutter drops of blood. She gave him a quick inspection and shook her head at Gail and George.

Patterson was drowning in his own blood. He needed emergency treatment, blood, saline and invasive surgery now to stand a chance of living, and they were capable of delivering none of it.

Gail mopped his brow with her sleeve.

"It'll be fine, Henry," she said comfortingly. He started to say something, but she hushed him. "No, don't try to talk."

He shook his head as best he could, spitting out a mouthful of blood and saliva. "No," he insisted. "We failed; Mallus thinks he's Aniquilus. He's going to plan B."

"Who's Aniquilus? What's plan B?" George asked.

Patterson looked him in the eyes. "Nuclear war," he coughed and held his chest as he gasped desperately for air. His eyes widened as he realised he was unable to breath.

"Today." he managed to say as the last breath left his body. He sagged limply against the wall and his chin fell to his chest.

They reached the surface carrying Ben between them, emerging into the evening chill to the welcoming arms of the al-Minya emergency services. George wasted no time in taking advantage of his phone, which had been useless underground.

Martín answered after the fourth ring. "George?"

"Martín, it's me, we're OK, and Gail is safe," George summarised. He cut Martín's joyous reply off. "DEFCOMM are launching an attack, Martín. They're going to try and start World War III!" On their way to the surface, Gail had told him about DEFCOMM's hangers full of missiles being assembled. There was no doubt that if Seth Mallus wanted to kick things off, he had the muscle to do so.

He said as much to Martín, and after wishing him luck, hung up.

They could only hope that Martín was able to get the message through to the Americans quickly enough, and that they would take it seriously.

As Ben was being looked over by two paramedics, Gail slipped her hand round George's waist, pulled him close and kissed him softly on the lips.

CHAPTER 81

Martín was immediately on the phone to Larue, as Jacqueline tried to figure out what had got him out of bed in such a hurry: it was barely seven o'clock in the evening. They were still in the earliest stages of their relationship, where love had no timetable and the world revolved around the bedroom. Plus, he'd been away in Egypt for days and they had spent most of Saturday making up for lost time.

She clung to his neck passionately, and he managed to untangle himself tactfully in order to concentrate on the conversation with Larue. Once she heard his tone of voice, all thoughts of love-making left her head, and she pulled a pillow to her chest for comfort.

Martín explained the situation in Egypt and what Patterson had told Gail and George before dying. He'd expected to make a full report to his boss after the weekend, but this new information couldn't wait that long.

Jacqueline got dressed while he listened to Larue's response.

"I've already told you," he said desperately, cutting him off mid-sentence. "DEFCOMM, in Florida. Yes I know it sounds crazy, but think about it: they control the defence satellites for the United States, which includes all of the early warning systems for nuclear attack. If they want to, they can simulate an attack on the United States from anywhere on Earth. We need to warn the Americans!"

By the time he put the phone down Jacqueline had been to heat up some coffee. She passed him his mug.

"What did he say?"

He looked her in the eyes. "I've done what I can. I'm not sure he really believes it, but he's going to talk to his counterpart at NASA."

"Do you think it's true, what they said about them wanting to start a nuclear war?"

He looked into the thick-black liquid. To Martín, coffee was one of the world's great paradoxes; it would certainly put him on edge and make him nervous later, but when he was actually drinking it he felt a smooth calm descend on his mind. Its heat and bitterness could lift any doubt and confusion, allowing him to focus effectively.

"Think about it," he said eventually, "remember what they did to the crew of the *Clarke*? What did we think at the time? That there must be something pretty incredible worth hiding to go to all the trouble of disrupting *all* transmissions from the spaceship, and then from Mars, too. And now, God only knows what's happened up there, since we haven't had any news from the planet for days.

"Not since Apollo 11 have the eyes of the world been so firmly rooted on a space mission, and never in the course of history has technology made it so easy for people to follow it. And yet they tried. Imagine the *risk*!" He took a gulp of coffee. "If they were prepared to do that, then they either had a lot to gain, or nothing to lose. It's inevitable that they would be found out eventually, because –"

He froze. Jacqueline stared at him wide-eyed, and pushed him to talk. "Because what?"

"Because the mission was *never* coming home. That's the only way they would have been able to ensure that no-one found out. But Gail Turner's free now, she's talked."

He didn't know half the story, didn't know where Gail had been for the past week or even what she had seen, but he was convinced that DEFCOMM was about to do exactly what George had said.

CHAPTER 82

Seth Mallus went over the final lines of the programming script on his computer display and inserted a missing semi-colon. It was horribly manual work, no high-level software had ever been written to do what he was about to do. The thousands of lines of code had been tested and re-tested several dozen times on his simulator; now, with this final adjustment, it would run perfectly.

He hit a key and the code executed, running through the simulation one last time. It really took him back, seeing the scripts run, right back to the early days of the nanotech boom, when he would still get involved in the programming; before the money, the empire, the power. It was an old-fashioned and usually unnecessary way of doing things. The only reason he had used the arcane method was that it was only in this way, by communicating directly with the machine, that all of the ghosts introduced by decades of amended programming sitting between the user and the processors could be eradicated. The last thing he wanted was some obscure security protocol getting in the way at the last minute and ruining so much hard work.

It was the language that the DEFCOMM Satellite Defence Network, or SDN, talked, and its beauty was that almost no human being alive was able to interpret it. Above ground level, outside the hermetically-sealed bunker in which he was now placed, the team of primary coders lay dead, gassed in their labs by the new air-conditioning system. It would be at least an hour before they were discovered, but by that time it would already be too late to stop him.

He finished running the simulation and checked the logs: no errors and the output was perfect. The paranoia of the world in trying to defend itself from an enemy that didn't exist would now be exploited to the maximum by a simple computer program.

The code was packaged, uploaded to the SDN mainframe, and executed.

416

The United States of America was about to come under attack.

Twelve hundred miles away in New York, Frank Bartolini kicked open the side-door to the Lafayette Grill kitchen and strode out, a leaking garbage bag held at arm's length and a disgusted look on his face.

"Jesus, Harry, how many times have I told you not to throw drinks in the waste?" he shouted over his shoulder.

He'd just thrown the bag into the dumpster and was wiping his hand on his apron when the white utility vehicle caught his attention. It was worthy of his attention because it was parked in the chief's spot, and the chief was due to arrive any minute now.

He went back in, cursing. "Anyone know what idiot's parked here?" he shouted through the swing doors and into the bar area; the restaurant was emptying after the lunchtime rush, but the bar was always held up by a handful of regulars.

A quick roll call established that nobody within was responsible, and Frank cursed some more as he dialled the tow company. It was free parking by law, but in practice, it was the chief's spot, and even the tow company knew that, the owner being the chief's brother.

Better still, he'd go out and make sure that on top of the tow fine, it would never occur to the utility vehicle's owner to park there again. Armed with a rolling pin, he quickly checked that nobody was passing by before attacking the van's headlamps. He then broke the tail lights, and took a final swing at the rear window. After two hits, the glass shattered, leaving a gaping hole in one half of the split rear doors.

He was about to leave it at that when curiosity overcame him. The van had blacked out windows, so maybe there was something inside worth hiding. He peered in.

A tarpaulin covered something about the size and shape of a fridge lying on its back. On one corner the tarpaulin had slipped off, and he bent his head round through the broken window to get a better look.

Whatever the object was, it was smooth and painted glossy white.

It looked just like his fridge at home.

He pulled his head out, no longer interested in the contents of the van, and was about to go back to the kitchen when he heard a click behind him.

"Stop!" the female voice cried. "Stop right there, or I fire!" He stopped. "Now, turn around, slowly, and drop the weapon on the floor!"

He obeyed, the rolling-pin bouncing on the pavement and into the gutter, and he found himself facing a female cop, a good foot shorter than him, holding her Taser up with both hands and pointed directly at his chest.

CHAPTER 83

One of my researchers is convinced," Larue breathed in deeply, he couldn't believe he was actually going to say it, "that DEFCOMM is planning to start World War III this afternoon by simulating an attack on the United States of America."

There was silence at the other end of the line. Larue decided it was best not to interrupt it.

"DEFCOMM?" the reply came, incredulous. "The guys who design and make our defence satellites?"

"And are also responsible for the video feeds from the Mars missions." The story was still wafer thin.

More silence, but somehow this time more pensive. "How?"

Larue didn't know; neither had Martín, nor his source. All they had was speculation. They could speculate that they could somehow override the USA's missile launch codes and start the war automatically, but that was incredibly unlikely – if anything could be less likely! – given the safeguards in place. The best theory was that the attack would be a ghost, fabricated by the network of sensors placed in orbit and around the country, in the hope that the USA would respond in kind.

"But we will know it's a fake," the reply came, "it's happened before, both here and in Russia! Once a visual confirmation cannot be made, the assumption is that there is a bug somewhere. That's why we retain human control."

A reply he'd been expecting.

"Remember that DEFCOMM don't only make defence satellites," he said. "But also a large part of your next generation nuclear weapon deployment systems,"

A short pause. "But, why would they want to do such a thing?"

To this question, Larue didn't know what to say. If it were all true, if it was all about to begin and they had so little time left, then finding a motive could wait.

419

He'd made the call thinking he would be laughed at, and had only picked up the courage to do so because of Martín's insistence. That, and a niggle in the back of his mind that there might actually be something to the crazy story.

But by the time he'd put the phone back on the hook he hadn't been laughed at. They hadn't hung up on him, and they had even thanked him, *sincerely*, for his information. This meant that there were people on the other side of the Atlantic who at least half-believed him.

And he found that deeply unsettling. Because the odds of Martín being right had just dramatically shortened.

CHAPTER 84

Martín looked sideways at Jacqueline, who forced a smile. The lights of the city flickered across her face as the TGV picked up speed on its way out of Paris. He was awestruck by her beauty, which almost made him forget why they had run to get the train.

And yet his mind did stray back to that rush, and also to the young family they had bumped into in the *Gare de Montparnasse*. The couple, with two small children aged no more than one and three, were just off the train from northern Spain and had been looking at their Metro guide. They had stopped Martín in his tracks, asking for directions in broken French.

He had greeted them in Spanish, and they had laughed enthusiastically; the eldest of the two children was tired but excited on this adventure to a foreign country, while her young brother slept in a sling on the father's chest. The mother had turned to share her map with him, pointing to where they intended to go.

Martín had looked across at Jacqueline in despair; what could he tell them that would possibly help? If someone had stopped him in the street a week ago with the same information he had now, how would he have reacted? If he told them to flee Paris, they would think he was mad, and yet if he told them how to get to their hotel, he may live to regret it for the rest of his life. He'd sent messages to any family member or friend he could think of: simple and short, it had advised them to get away from any large cities. To people you knew that was an easy thing to do. It was something else entirely to stop random people on the streets and spread panic.

He remembered looking down at the little girl, twisting on her heels and humming a tune to herself as she gazed around the brightly-lit train station, her eyes wide with anticipation.

And so he had told them to flee.

Maybe it was the look of earnest in his eyes, the tone in his voice, possibly even having Jacqueline with him; after all, madmen rarely had accomplices, did they? In any case their ESA identity cards had definitely helped. And it was as he had explained to them: if he was wrong, they could get off at St Jean de Luz, and return the following day. *He* would pay their hotel, and even phone ahead to book a room just in case. Just as long as they passed Bordeaux; that was all he had asked.

Back on the train, he looked along the aisle to the other end of the carriage, where he could see the young girl was now jumping on her father's lap. Their eyes met and they nodded at each other solemnly.

In the end it was a simple matter of planting that seed of doubt in a parent's mind. And then their instinct to protect, combined with Martín's powers of persuasion, meant that they only had one real option, and that was to get back on the train and leave Paris.

If Martín was wrong, then it was a ten hour round trip with two hyperactive children. On the other hand, that was a small price to pay if he was right.

They all hoped that wouldn't be the case; and if he *was* wrong, he was due some holiday, anyway. Despite it being early days for their relationship, he thought it was an ideal opportunity for Jacqueline to meet his family.

The TGV would take them direct to San Sebastián, where they would hop on a relatively slow train to the family home in Asturias, sandwiched on a cliff-top between the snow-capped *Picos de Europa* and the rolling waves of the Bay of Biscay.

And so Martín closed his eyes and thought of home, his family and of Jacqueline as the last remnants of Parisian *banlieue* disappeared into the darkness.

CHAPTER 85

Mallus looked at the computer display: the warnings told him they were coming for him. Sooner than he had expected; but nonetheless, it *had* been expected.

Warnings were flashing all over the place, showing breaches on all sides *and* on the roof of DEFCOMM headquarters. Of course, he couldn't *see* the soldiers enter the building – their light-bending body armour saw to that – but he knew the sensors never lied.

He had well-armed ex-military security personnel in the building – it wasn't all sensors and alarms – but he decided not to send them in; it really didn't matter anymore, because nothing could stop his code from executing in the SDN. He looked at his watch; only seconds to go.

He heard the footsteps before he saw the tell-tale warping of air in front of him. In case either of those details passed him by, the computer's soft female voice told him someone else was in the room. It was interrupted by a gritty, military voice.

"Sir, you are under arrest. Step away from the keyboard and do not attempt any sudden movements." The voice attached itself to a fully-suited soldier as the cloaking device was disabled halfway through the statement.

Mallus got to his feet slowly and took a step back, his hands in the air. The soldier was joined by two more who de-cloaked near the door. He was sure there were many more in the underground bunker. They would certainly find his stores and living compartments, the staff and guards who he had allowed into his circle of trust, and all the rest of the evidence needed to justify his arrest.

But that didn't matter. With billions of taxpayer's dollars invested in DEFCOMM over the years, many millions had been diverted into personal projects.

These included automated security systems: as the soldiers had walked round the building looking for him, they had already ingested hundreds, if not thousands, of microscopic capsules, which now circulated their bloodstream, waiting for the ultrasonic command that would unleash their deadly poison, targeting the victims' central nervous systems. The capsules were contained in controlled bursts of vapour, fired from tiny concealed turrets along the main entrances and corridors of the building into the path of any intruders, which the system automatically identified as anyone without a valid ID chip in their forearm; you would need a spacesuit to get through unaffected, and he noted with satisfaction that these soldiers, while fully kitted-up, were not wearing full self-contained breathing apparatus. Instead, they wore the more comfortable and practical full-face respirators.

The respirator's particulate filter was designed to remove any particles from air larger than a third of a micron. This represented over three hundred times smaller than the width of the average human hair, and was just sufficient to get rid of spores and bacteria such as anthrax. The capsules transmitted in the spray were little more than a quarter of a micron wide, and he knew from testing that his defence solution would have sailed straight through the filters, as if they hadn't even been there.

The respirator's second line of defence was, he knew, an activated charcoal filter; it would absorb impurities in the air, which would bind to the carbon, letting the treated air pass through. Nevertheless, even chemically treated charcoal, capable of extracting Sarin and any number of other known nerve agents, would let the silicone-based capsules through unhindered.

There was, he knew, no defence. Which was why to-date the experimental capsules had still not been certified for active use: if you couldn't defend your own forces against it, you couldn't use it in the field.

So, with one carefully selected voice-command from him to his computer, an ultrasonic wave would run through the building, killing all of the soldiers almost instantly.

He smiled as he looked the soldier in the eyes.

Seth Mallus, *Aniquilus*, would lead the New World that would rise from the ashes of the old. The loss of life was a shame, and the fallout would take time to disperse, but he would be there to see it through. His would be a different world, a more *just* world, safe from the out-of-control population explosions, energy crises, food shortages and petty wars and conflicts.

Sometimes, you had to start afresh, and only Aniquilus could make that happen. The ends *would* justify the means, he was sure of that. He looked down at his screen and saw the SDN's display fill with missile trajectories as the war to end all wars finally began.

Looking into the soldier's eyes coldly, he cocked his head slightly. He showed no fear, but saw only opportunity. This man, with his advanced training and high-tech weaponry, would be useful in the dark years to come.

"You're too late," he said simply. And as he explained the situation to the soldier, he made his proposition, taking great care not to mention that he was entirely responsible for the global devastation that was unfolding on the screen before them.

The phantom missiles crossed the Arctic Ocean and passed over the vastness of Canada. Their trajectories parted, and they homed in on their targets. Somewhere deep in the Satellite Defence Network, the sub-routine sent its alerts and confirmation codes.

Shock and confusion reigned as the blips took form. Screens filled with satellite images, trajectories, possible targets, probable origins, and weapon descriptions.

Calls were made, procedures followed.

The President was eventually interrupted in the middle of an interview.

CHAPTER 86

While Officer Sandra Peele called for a pickup, Frank Ancelotti eyed her up. For a cop, she was pretty cute, and just his type.

He told her as much.

"You've heard your rights," she said. "Anything else you say will be taken as evidence."

"Oh for Christ's sake," he moaned. "All this for a fridge."

She cocked her head. "What?"

"Yeah, a fridge. Some dumbass parks in the chief's spot with a fridge in the back, then leaves the car there. I'm the guy who's gonna get beat because of this. The guy parks there without even asking."

She looked at the white utility vehicle suspiciously. *A fridge?*

"I'll show you," he offered, making a move to the van door, but she brought the Taser back up to point at him and he stopped.

Minutes later, backup arrived and he was safely in the back of a squad car. She and another officer approached the van from the rear.

"A fridge, apparently," she explained.

New York was always on some form of alert; it just never publically displayed it unless it was absolutely necessary. As for the van, it was suspicious, but the last thing she wanted was to cordon off Broadway without at least having a look first. There were plenty of unmarked vehicles parked in back alleys, and people *did* sometimes move fridges around in New York. It was acceptable that the driver may have left it in the van rather than taken it with him.

She peered through the broken window and saw the tarpaulin. She agreed it did look like a normal fridge. Using her baton, she reached in and carefully lifted the cover until it slid completely from the object.

That's no fridge, she thought. And in the split second when she realised what it was, she didn't even have time to scream.

Nanoseconds after Sandra Peele died, the Lafayette Grill was flattened. The alley between Franklin Street and White Street, Broadway, and all of Manhattan beyond would have ceased to be in the blink of an eye, had any eyes not been vaporised instantly to witness it.

The shockwave rippled across the Hudson, pulling boats from their moorings and flipping passenger ferries over like leaves in the wind. A flat-bottomed boat rode the expanding sphere of energy, flying high into the air before disintegrating in the heat.

The Statue of Liberty was whipped-up from its pedestal, leaving just the toes behind, which quickly melted. The statue itself buckled and broke apart in mid-air, what little remained raining down onto Hudson Bay and sinking into the water.

Manhattan was completely flattened. Everything above ground level had either been ripped apart, melted or if it was small enough been blown so far into the sky that it would be deposited in a debris field over one hundred miles in diameter.

For five miles in each direction from the Lafayette Grill, from Newark in the west to Queens in the east and as far north as the Bronx, not a single human survived the explosion above ground. Underground, several thousand people survived in the parts of the New York Subway system that hadn't collapsed or been filled with water from the river. With no lighting, fresh air or indeed any understanding of what had happened, most perished where their trains had come to a stop, in the vain hope that someone would come looking for them. The few who braved the cave-ins and flooded tunnels to reach the surface faced a bleak few days. Within a week the last survivor of ground zero, who had been in the Subway thirty metres from the epicentre of the blast, suddenly collapsed and died of internal bleeding.

He had managed to travel more than twenty miles from Manhattan by foot when he started seeing people walking in the opposite direction, towards New York, looking just as bad as he did.

CHAPTER 87

The President of the United States of America had been advised on the best course of action. Several hundred targets were being tracked by the SDN, which thank God was still helping defend the Nation.

Alongside New York, which had been the first, both Chicago and Los Angeles had been wiped from the map.

It wasn't even possible to know for sure how many had died, but even the most conservative of estimates put the total at two million. The most pessimistic of reports suggested nearly ten times that figure.

Russia was probably responsible, no doubt in cahoots with China; as he sat near his military chiefs in the Presidential cavalcade barging its way through the heavy DC traffic, a dozen more blips appeared on the car's SDN display.

They were attacking from the western seaboard. Smaller tactical weapons, heading for military installations along the West Coast.

The United States of America was about to fall.

Nuclear weapons had always been a deterrent. There was no genuinely effective counter measure. The only defence was offence.

He stared at the screen and clenched his fists till the knuckles were white. He remembered what one Senator had once told him, when he had been starting out in his political career; *'in a nuclear war, the only winning move is not to play.'* He had no idea where the saying had come from, but he wasn't prepared to simply stand by and watch the Russians and Chinese destroy his country with impunity. That was what had differentiated him from that Senator. Some people were born to lead; when it was time to make a hard decision, they had the backbone to act. That was why he had been elected.

That was why he was still, halfway through his second term, the President of the United States of America.

And that was why without hesitation and with full, devastating force, he gave the order to retaliate, starting with the Chinese warships out in the Pacific.

CHAPTER 88

Captain Tan Ling Kai had barely ten minutes to react. He reached the bridge of the *DDG Hangzhou* seconds after the alarm had sounded, and by then a second satellite had confirmed that they were under attack.

This was most unexpected. They were still in international waters, and had made no ultimatum to the United States. This was meant to be a show of strength and nothing more.

And yet the nature of the threat came in loud and clear from the communications officer. The Captain digested the information. He told himself that it was merely the swell of the Pacific and not nerves and weak knees that made him need to hold on to the computer console in front of him.

The first threat was from six incoming cruise missiles, Tomahawks. A defensive salvo of surface-to-air missiles from the *Hangzhou*'s vertical launch system dispatched the first five, with the *sea-whizz* turrets finishing off the sixth in a long burst of fire as it closed in, well within sight of the crew on the bridge. No sooner had the sound of the explosion reached them than reports of more incoming targets came through, this time double that of the first wave.

This was a sustained attack with only one aim: sink the Chinese fleet.

He made up his mind of what to do.

His second-in-command by his side, he pushed his hand down on an incredulous weapons officer's shoulder. "We shall launch a counter-attack."

At this distance their cruise missiles were at the limits of their effective range, but he entered the confirmation codes nonetheless and waited for approval from Beijing.

Approval from Beijing, along with confirmed targets, arrived as the *sea-whizz* were obliterating the last of the second wave of incoming missiles. This time, they had been within one kilometre of the *Hangzhou*, and five had slipped through the longer range surface-to-air missile defences.

China's counter-attack, eighteen surface-to-surface missiles, aimed at military targets along the west coast of the United States, left its silos less than sixty seconds before the final American weapon arrived out of nowhere, completely undetected by the fleet's early warning systems. It missed the ships entirely and detonated underwater, causing a thousand-foot swell to engulf anything within its reach. This included the two older frigates of the *zhidui*, leaving the modern destroyers untouched. Captain Tan Ling Kai looked out of the bridge at the explosion a kilometre away, aghast at the destruction yet optimistic for the survival of his command.

The swell broke and fell back into the sea, leaving no sign of the frigates. They were gone. He stared out at the site of the explosion and saw a small wave coming towards the *Hangzhou*. As it approached he began to realise its true scale, and within a second the roar of the incoming tidal wave had reached their ears. His jaw dropped as he watched, unsure of the kind of weapon capable of such an attack; it had clearly not missed the ships, relying instead of the destructive power of water to do most of the work.

He looked down at the silos on the deck, still open after the departure of their cruise missiles. The water from the wave would undoubtedly fill them, and from there, possibly enter the bulkheads and flood the ship. He issued the command to close them.

As the wave grew, so too did the noise of the surging water.

"Close the silos!" he repeated his order at the top of his voice.

The panicked weapons officer reset the command switch and pulled it down twice, to no avail. Some minor glitch was telling his console that the vertical launch system's silos were already closed. He looked at his Captain helplessly, and the Captain looked back, with a fleeting thought that the older, less advanced revolver-style VLS would never have malfunctioned so catastrophically.

By the time the wave reached the ship it towered fifty feet above the antenna array, and the men and women on the bridge instinctively covered their faces with their arms and braced for impact as the water crashed into the windows.

The ship lurched sideways and plunged down into the water as the wave forced its way over.

There had been no time to issue the order to abandon ship – in any case it would have been pointless – he told himself as he fell against the computer console. The *Hangzhou*, listing at forty-five degrees, was sliding down into the depths of the ocean, gathering speed as the lower decks filled with ice-cold water. The bridge was watertight, a natural design feature of the semi-submersible defence systems, but it wouldn't withstand the pressure from the water outside. He nursed a cut on his forehead and held on to the console. The emergency lighting came on, and in the eerie-red glow he saw the faces of his terrified crew.

All were looking to the main window of the bridge, to the toughened glass that kept the water out, and the spidery cracks that were dancing their ways from the edges towards the centre. When they joined up, the cracks paused as if not knowing where else to go.

There was a terrifying groan as the pressure increased on the outer hull of the ship. In the split second before the window finally gave, the only sound from the bridge was a collective intake of breath.

CHAPTER 89

A ir Force One left the runway and climbed quickly through the low-lying clouds. Within minutes it was cruising close to the speed of sound at sixty thousand feet, at the limit of enemy interceptor operating ceiling. Two US Navy F35 escorts trailed on either side of the supersonic stealth liner that carried, as well as several score of supporting personnel and crew, the head of state and his Joint Chiefs of Staff.

They watched the horror unfold from the screen built into the wall of the President's office.

"Mr President, Sir," an aide entered the office bearing a clipboard and a grave face. She didn't bother with further formalities, striding to the screen and tapping it abruptly. The mash-up of video feeds from surveillance satellites and various computer programs gave way to the video conference setup.

"Neither Russia nor China are taking responsibility for the attacks on New York, Chicago and Los Angeles." She passed the clipboard to the President. On it were some simple bullet-points in large bold font. The President took one look at the notes and discarded the clipboard on his desk.

"They think we made it up? We tracked those missiles from their silos all the way here, and then bang!" he slapped his fist into his palm. "Three American cities wiped off the map."

"Mr President, there have been some reports coming to us from NASA. There were allegations made that one of the Satellite Defence Network contractors was planning an attack this afternoon."

"Any reason why we should believe them? This wasn't mentioned earlier, so I'm guessing none of the Federal agencies knew anything about it?"

"Well," the aide looked straight into his eyes, "a counter terrorist unit was sent in as a matter of course, but we've not heard anything from them since. All communications with the team were lost shortly after they entered the contractor's headquarters."

The President stared fixedly at the young aide. There was something cocky about the way she addressed him. A lack of respect of his judgement, he was sure. Right now ICBMs, the American counter-attack, were racing through the stratosphere on their parabolic trajectories that would take them to their targets on the other side of the planet. At the same time, the SDN was tracking dozens of similar weapons coming the other way.

The Chief of Staff of the United States Army stepped forward and voiced what the President was thinking. He was a large man with deep-set, cold eyes and a lack of compassion she had always disliked.

"Don't doubt for one second that these attacks are real," he pointed at the screen dramatically. "What do you think our enemy wants most of all? Do you think they want global destruction? Of course not!" he threw his arms in the air. "They want us to recall our weapons, while theirs head towards us *as we speak*. They want to take us out of the picture, while at the same time minimising any damage to themselves."

She looked around the room. These *dinosaurs*, she thought with contempt. She struggled hard to fight back her emotions. Her beloved Nation, at its knees, was about to wipe out half of Asia, and she was certain that it was a mistake.

For even if the attack on the United States was real, the only just course of action was to *not* respond in kind. In the same way she abhorred the death penalty, she could not understand the basic premise that mutual destruction was in any way justifiable.

"Mr President, Sir," she said, taking great care to ignore the Chief of Staff. "I do thank you for your patience." Humility was the best way to subtly get what you want, she had decided years ago when first faced with the egos of men. "Our counter attack will destroy China and Russia almost completely. If we are wrong, and NASA is correct, then *we* will have performed the first strike.

"The Chinese are enraged by our destruction of their Pacific fleet, but at the same time they accept that the fleet's counter-attack, authorised by Beijing, has caused considerable damage to military targets along the West Coast. They are willing to talk to avoid this escalating any further."

The President looked down at the clipboard on his desk; a bullet-point list of events, one by one, leading up to the *now*. He rubbed his chin pensively.

Seeing the hesitation the Army Chief of Staff tried to interject but the aide quickly capitalised on her short advantage.

"Our ICBMs are still in disarm range," she said quickly. "We have less than two minutes to destroy them harmlessly in the upper atmosphere."

"And if their attack is real, and destroys us?" the Army Chief sneered.

She didn't take her eyes off the President. "Then if you still decide that a counter-attack is appropriate, the combined strength of our deployed nuclear submarine fleet and remaining domestic silos is still enough to destroy both China and Russia."

"Damn you," the President muttered under his breath. *Damn her,* he thought, *for sowing this seed of doubt.* Counter-attack was justifiable, he knew that, but only with enough evidence on their side to make it clear-cut. "When will we have visual confirmation of the ICBMs launched against us?"

"No sooner than five minutes, Mr President," she replied. It was simple maths: they couldn't confirm that the next wave of attack against them was real until their own counter attack was three minutes beyond the point of no return. In effect, the President had launched his nuclear weapons too soon, and based on too little evidence.

"General," he said addressing his Army Chief of Staff, "can you confirm we will still be in a position to launch a counter offensive should the weapons we believe to have been fired against us prove to be real?" He stared his aide in the eyes as he addressed the Chief of Staff, and she stared right back.

There was a pause, followed by a frustrated intake of breath from the Chief of Staff. "Mr President, that scenario is not my recommendation. We will have a reduced capability to respond."

"Is *reduced* still enough?"

"Yes," the General eventually conceded.

"Then cancel our attack," he replied.

"Sir, I must insist that –"

"General, your orders are to stop the attack, now!" the President barked.

Reluctantly, the General returned to his computer and tapped in the command sequence. Looking up briefly at the President and his aide, he shook his head in disgust.

They then both entered the codes that would destroy their counter-attack in mid-air.

The SDN received the command from Air Force One.

A loop in the security protocol detected that this command had initiated a previously unused, new, function.

The SDN was intelligent enough to know this function was new. It had been received during the latest update, which it had accepted. But it hadn't yet been tested or proven. That wasn't so unusual; as an advanced defence system, many of the SDN's commands and events had yet to be exercised for real.

Basic logic tests confirmed the validity of the commands, and ensured that the parameters received did not exceed the specified data types. A simulation of the function call was tried, and completed with success.

The SDN was an array of independent devices positioned in Geostationary orbit above the United States of America. Covertly, of course, some dozen or so other satellites in lower non-geostationary orbits were also part of the SDN, allowing for surveillance of other parts of the world to be linked in to the defence network.

Each independent satellite's processing and memory contributed to the network's 'brain', which could be thought of as self-aware insofar as it knew of its own component parts, what it was designed to do, and had an understanding of the importance of that role in the defence of the United States of America, which to it was simply a geographical location that contained a number of potential military and civilian targets.

The SDN's brain had proven the validity of the command it had received. It did not understand the *logic* of the command, as it was not part of the brain's known scenarios. But human logic was still tantalisingly out of its reach, as for all its intelligence it was still simply a machine.

Taking its attention away for a nanosecond from the highly classified simulation exercise it was still running, the brain executed the strange new function.

"In an effort to achieve peaceful resolution of the current situation, we have issued the command to destroy our counter-attack until the nature of the threat to the United States of America is more clear."

The President addressed the video wall. His aide stood nervously behind him. She had made a potentially dangerous enemy in the Chief of Staff, who stood threateningly behind her left shoulder.

The video wall was split between the Russian and Chinese leaders.

"We are still tracking your missiles." The Russian President didn't try to hide his anger. "You must recall them *now*."

"A delay in your satellite feed, surely," the President's voice wavered.

"You bluff!" cried the Chinese head of state. "You seek to destroy us and avoid us destroying you!"

The President turned to his aide. "Can you confirm our offensive has been recalled?" he asked.

She stooped over the computer screen on the desk and tapped a few commands. The results popped up. She typed the commands in again and the same result returned.

"The command was received and confirmed. However," she swallowed hard, not knowing where to look, "our offensive has *not* been recalled. It's too late to recall them now."

"Mr President," the Chinese President said with disdain, "Your acts of unprovoked aggression towards the People's Democratic Republic of China and our friend and ally Russia have left me with little choice but to launch full counter offensives against the United States of America before we are left completely defenceless."

The video wall blanked out, and a stunned silence fell on the office.

"So what command did you actually send?" The President turned on the Chief of Staff.

"The command to self-destruct all of our missiles," he said defensively. "I cannot understand why the command failed, when we can clearly see it was received and confirmed by the SDN."

"Unless NASA is right," the aide said slowly. She turned the screen towards the men, showing the Russian and Chinese weapons finally reaching their targets around the United States. Seconds after each one hit, the live text feed below updated: *RUS010:Negative Impact... RUS018:Negative Impact... RUS006:Negative Impact...*

One by one, the weapons reached their targets. One by one, the ground reports confirmed that no impact had occurred.

"The SDN *was* compromised." She let the fact sink in. "Our attack on Russia and China has not been recalled, and therefore we can probably expect a real attack from them to reach us in the next half hour."

The Army Chief of Staff looked at her screen and double checked on his own. His silence confirmed what she had said.

"So, we have been deliberately provided with false information by our own defence systems, on top of the real nukes that blew up this afternoon. Whoever planned this knew we would possibly try to recall our own weapons, so made sure that wouldn't work," the President said, astonished.

"God help us," the aide whispered.

Air Force One's alarm system broke the long silence that followed. The Captain's stern voice came over the speakers in the office.

"Get the President to the evac' pods, we are under attack!"

Guards ran in to the office and bundled the President down a staircase that had opened up in the floor, leaving the Joint Chiefs and the aide above. Moments later, through the small window, they saw the starboard engine of the aircraft explode, severing the wing a third of the way along its length.

The plane lurched to the right, inexorably falling into a downwards spiral in slow motion as the pilots valiantly battled with the one-and-a-third remaining wings to keep Air Force One as steady as possible while the President was evacuated.

"Laser!" the Army Chief of Staff shouted. "The SDN has a built-in network of lasers designed to bring down ICBMs. Only they're not as effective as we hoped – the power draw is too great and ICBMs move too quickly. We, on the other hand, are an easy target."

"Why did the SDN never try to use those lasers against the nukes that hit New York, Chicago and Los Angeles?" the aide asked in disbelief.

They were being ushered down another flight of stairs to the secondary evac' pods. The President's pod was now clear, and the pilots had confirmed that Air Force One was going down.

"They're not active," he said shaking his head. "Not technically allowed by international treaty. They're not even supposed to be up there. But we still have them in case we need them."

"And you didn't think that would be now?"

Each evac' pod took five occupants. She was relieved when she and the General were each herded into separate capsules opposite each other.

"Like stopping the holes of a sieve with your fingers," he shouted over to her as the door closed.

The door to her own pod closed. She found herself sat next to a cook, two stewards, a man in a dark suit and a marine. The rockets on the evac' pod fired and the negative G force pushed her against the restraints towards the ceiling. The cook's harness was badly fastened and he knocked his head against the side of the cabin, losing consciousness instantly.

She caught a glimpse of the crippled Air Force One through the small window in front of her, but any hope of seeing its fate was swallowed up by a blanket of clouds.

The pod jerked sharply as the parachutes deployed to control its descent, and they floated gently down towards an already different world.

PART SEVEN

EGYPT - WINTER 2063

CHAPTER 90

Gail woke with a start, her dream replaced in an instant by the cold, grey ceiling above.

The short paralysis that accompanied her frequent abrupt-awakenings no longer scared her; she had grown used to the effect long ago. George had explained to her that when dreaming, muscles were deliberately disabled by the brain, allowing free movement in dreams without endangering the body at rest. Sleep walking was the result of an error in this process. Conversely, and as was her case, when you woke suddenly you sometimes found yourself conscious in a still-paralysed body. He'd sounded so knowledgeable about it all until a little questioning revealed everything he knew came from a BBC documentary he'd watched over thirty years ago.

In any case, Gail was used to the phenomenon now because her sleep pattern was completely messed up, and she almost always woke with a start.

Her husband put it down to the added responsibility of parenthood; there was simply so much more to be worried about now that she was a mother.

But she knew that was only part of the story.

The fact was that the world was very different now. It was colder, bigger, and much more dangerous. They had lost so much many years before, and what little remained was that much more important to them all.

And in the post-Chaos world, there was often little to distinguish the nightmares from reality.

She was greeted by the chill southerly wind as she stepped out of the tent and into the dull morning. The faint circular glow of the sun barely managed to make its way through the clouds on the horizon, and she knew that would be all they would see of it until sunset when it might peek under the sheets of grey, if they were lucky.

George beckoned her over to the fire, which was crackling soberly in the centre of the small clearing around which six tents had been pitched. There were three similar arrangements of tents in the clearing, which with their sixty-three inhabitants made up their nomadic village. The tents were far from the usual run-of-the-mill camping affair. Instead, they were Bedouin-style, like small beige houses with short walls and long sloping roofs. Inside, the bare minimum of furniture and rugs ensured that they were comfortable, yet mobile. They had been in their present location for several months now; since Spring.

Spring, she thought. *Now there's a word that doesn't mean anything anymore.*

She leant in to kiss her husband on the cheek and grab the tin mug of something they still referred to as coffee, but which bore little relation to its ancient cousin. If farmers still produced the beans in Africa, they were keeping it to themselves; as a rule, anything you couldn't eat was a waste of land and effort, and trade had more or less stopped happening on any large scale. Gail had stopped caring what went into her coffee many years ago, and certainly wasn't about to ask what was in her mug on such a cold day.

After taking a short sip of the acrid black liquid, she huddled up to the fire and used the heat of the mug to warm her hands.

"It's not that cold this morning," George said, distantly.

She shivered and leaned in closer to the short flames licking round the dry branches that had been bundled onto the fire. It was generating more smoke than heat, but to her it provided immeasurable warmth.

"Where is everyone?" she asked. They were alone by the fire, which was unusual insofar as there weren't that many other places for everyone to be.

"Jake's asleep, Ben's out hunting with the others."

"You didn't go with him?" she said, surprised.

He shook his head and gave her a sympathetic smile.

She hugged him back. "You and Jake should go along next time; he needs to be more active and you need to spend more time with him."

Even after the end of the world, it seemed, seventeen-year-olds were still teenagers, and their son was a prime example.

"Agreed," George nodded and poured some more coffee from the pot sitting next to the fire. "But we'll be moving on soon, we'll have plenty of time to stretch our legs then."

It wasn't long before the twenty tents that made up their village were packed and bundled up as tightly as possible, then lashed to the sides of their six remaining donkeys. They were then weighed down with two twenty-litre tubs of drinking water each. As much as possible was carried by the sixty-three nomads, who led the animals back to the relative warmth of the north. The water would last them a couple of days, by which time they would have completed a third of their journey.

Ben caught up with Gail and George, who were near the front of the caravan. Jake, as usual, was straggling somewhere near the rear.

"Have you thought of what I said?" he asked them, nervously.

They exchanged a quick look. "Yes," Gail said after a while.

The ground beneath her feet was hard and unforgiving. She hadn't walked far in months, and was already weary after barely a couple of hours.

"We need to go, leave this place," Ben pressed. "Zahra and I have been talking about it with the others, and we all agree. This land is dead. It was already dying centuries ago, but now the river is so unpredictable, there is nothing left here for us."

"That's what we're doing, Ben. We're moving, like we always do. There is still food," George commented dryly. "We simply need to follow it. And the water is *mostly* clean."

"Every time we go hunting, we bring less back than the time before. And each river and inlet we pass flows stronger in my memories." Ben held Gail back by the shoulder and looked her in the eyes. "Jake has no future here, Gail. We need to move on. We need to leave Egypt."

George stopped walking and looked back at them. "What do you suggest, Ben? We go north, and we need to find a way to cross the sea. And we don't know what we're heading to. We head south, and we die in the desert, unless we're unlucky and manage to reach the warlords of Sudan. We go west, and we die in the desert, for sure. As for going east, well, we know there's nothing left there."

Gail looked along the line of people and donkeys idling past them. Towards the back, she saw Jake, sharing a joke with Fatima, one of the young girls from the Tek family, and Saïd, her brother. The three of them were the only teenagers in their village, and along with two smaller children, the only non-adults.

Ben followed her gaze. "We need to find more people like us, Gail. Our people are dying, and there will be nothing left for them. Jake and

Fatima get on well enough, but how about Saïd? Is there anyone he could be interested in?"

"So, what do you suggest?" she asked. Having children had been difficult for their village; even Gail and George had never been able to add to their family after Jake's unexpected arrival, in the first year of the Chaos. She had fallen pregnant shortly after their reunion in Amarna, following her kidnapping by DEFCOMM.

After that, it had taken years to settle into the relative safety of their nomadic lifestyle, with its migrations between middle-Egypt and the south. By the time they were ready to start trying to make their family bigger again, her body was already too old. She was only fifty-nine now, and yet almost two decades of surviving had been unrelenting; she and George both looked, and for her part certainly felt, at least seventy.

"Europe," he said calmly. "We leave Africa, and head for Europe, through Italy."

By now the last of the village had walked past them. Zahra had held back, and the group of four stood in the middle of the dusty road. Gail kicked at the layers of sand and dirt till her toe scraped the tarmac beneath. It had been a poor road even then, but the years of neglect and disuse were rapidly turning it into little more than a scar running across the arid landscape.

"Europe, Asia and the Americas were worst hit by the war," she said reflecting on the few news reports that had reached them during those early months. "Africa escaped the worst of it; we should stay here."

"But Africa is dying, Gail," Zahra said, almost in earnest. "You can see that for yourself. Every year we pass fewer people on the road. And what little remains is still at war with itself."

"Europe may already be dead, for all we know."

"But the climate will be better, there may be more food, we might find something left apart from slum and disease. This place was a mess even before the climate changed; it has so much further to go to be a good place to live again."

George put his hand on his wife's forearm. "We're old, now. And tired. Who knows how many more migrations we'll be able to make."

She looked up at him and saw the love in his eyes, stronger now than ever before. She also saw a glint that she had not seen for a long time. They had not been apart for longer than a day since her kidnapping all those years ago. Looking in his eyes now, she could see that he wanted to go. But he would never leave her behind.

She looked to her son, who was still at the rear of the group that had overtaken them. He was carrying Fatima's rucksack on his chest as well as his own on his back, and they were walking hand in hand. It was the first time she'd seen them that close.

"Alright, I agree we should at least try," she said after a deep breath. "But we need to plan this properly; I don't want to go into any danger we don't need to face."

Ben's face opened up with the first grin she'd seen from him in days; George wrapped his arm around her shoulder and pulled her in tight, and they resumed their trek.

CHAPTER 91

On the third day of travelling north, they passed what little remained of the modern Egyptian town of Tell el-Amarna.

They enjoyed the hospitality of a local farmer and his wife for an evening, sleeping mostly in abandoned houses by the main road, although several of the travelling families decided to pitch their tents instead. The hospitality consisted in a few bottles of harsh, homebrewed liquor, along with a dozen rock-hard loaves of bread. In exchange, the farmer and his wife were given news of the growing strength of the Sudanese clans, and the lack of good hunting to the south. It wasn't a fair trade; the information had been true every year for as long as they could remember, but it was gratefully received nonetheless.

The old couple had hosted their party many times over the years, and simply enjoying the company of people you knew was enough for them.

They didn't share their plans to migrate to Europe, and the old couple neither asked nor seemed to care about where they were all heading. Travellers, though few and far between, were frequent enough not to warrant any special questioning. The only thing the farmer and his wife knew was that they either went north or south, and that sometimes they came past again in the opposite direction. Sometimes.

Gail toyed with the idea, as she always did, of staying in Amarna. She had a strong emotional attachment to the place, and on the surface there seemed to be plenty of room for their entire village to move in and live.

But the same drought and famine that affected the region they were leaving had already blighted Amarna. With the exception of the farmer and his wife, who were too old to move on and had resigned themselves to their fate, Tell el-Amarna had already been abandoned. This last couple would wait for their time to come, and then they would probably decide to leave this world together, rather than risk being left alone.

As they left Amarna on the fourth day, Gail felt drawn towards the cliffs where she had made her discovery all those years ago. She couldn't be sure what it was, but something new, something powerful deep down inside her, was pulling her towards the Amarna Library.

Even so, as Tell el-Amarna disappeared behind them, she managed to shake the feeling off and march on.

What little still passed for government and authority bumped into them on the sixth day.

The lone horseman, an ancient firearm slung across his back, rested with them for the evening, gladly swapping some strands of sorry-looking jerky for a refill of clean, unpolluted water from one of the donkeys' containers.

There could be few stories of worth to tell from the shambles that was Cairo and 'government,' though to hear the horseman's rhetoric one could only assume that the city had risen from its embers and had taken over the world.

His audience knew better than to believe such propaganda, though it played along willingly, for the sake of old times.

The truth was that the sprawling, brightly-lit metropolis that Gail and George remembered so vividly since their first visits to the country no longer existed. Pestilence and famine were destroying what war had not, though the process was infinitely more drawn out and painful.

Slowly, what had for decades been the largest city in Africa had torn itself apart. Fires, started by the inhabitants to stem the flow of death and disease to new quarters, razed whole neighbourhoods, leaving black scars across Cairo. For the hundreds of thousands of Cairenes who had not either fled to the countryside or died in the years that followed the Chaos, the city was an unforgiving place, and the population shrank each year as tens of thousands more succumbed to this harsh new existence.

Egypt had played a key role in the Middle-East part of the global conflict. With the United States, Russia and China out of the picture and the United Nations and NATO effectively disbanded, the religious powder-keg had finally blown. Israel had found itself set-upon by Syria and Iran, in all-out, relentless war.

However, Egypt successfully mediated between the states, staving off the use of nuclear weapons for months.

By remaining impartial when history made vengeance so attractive, Egypt's role in those stages was decisive in the closing chapter of the Chaos.

So when the last nuclear weapons were finally deployed, annihilating cities and stripping the very earth itself of life, Egypt alone in the Middle East, on the fringes of a world gone mad, was spared.

CHAPTER 92

On the tenth day they saw the smoke of the city, several kilometres before they saw the ruined capital itself. Fires raged to the west. Towards the centre and east, minarets and spires could still be seen rising from Old Cairo, reminders of a rich cultural past.

"Why is it burning?" Jake asked in wonder. He had never known a city, and this was the closest he had ever come to Cairo. He spoke in fluent Arabic, though his parents insisted on always speaking to him in English, which he understood perfectly well but very rarely used.

Gail pulled her son closer. He was more man than child now, but she could still remember when it was his head tucked under hers, and not the other way round. Sometimes, she longed for those days to return, when he would run to her and wrap his arms around her legs in the biggest hugs. Such moments were rare now. This was his world and it no longer scared him, but instead filled him with a sense of adventure that she desperately wanted to control and contain.

"Because there's no one there to put out the flames," she replied. "So when a fire starts for whatever reason, it just burns and burns. Eventually, all of Cairo will burn away." She drew a short breath. "There's only death in Cairo, which is why we should always avoid it."

"Actually," George said pensively, "they're probably trying to get rid of areas that they no longer want, because of disease. It shows there must be some kind of organisation there, even if it's only localised in one or two areas."

Gail shot him a nasty look, and he shrugged. Of the two of them, Gail had always been the more adventurous. But motherhood had an uncanny way of changing that, and since Jake's birth their roles had naturally reversed.

Jake kissed his mother softly on the top of her head and released himself from her grasp.

She watched, fighting back a tear, as he walked slowly away, towards the rest of the village who were assembling further down the road.

"He's not a child anymore, he has to learn this stuff for himself," George started.

"You're wrong!" she cut him off, barely able to keep her voice down. "You tell him stupid things like that, and you make him believe that there's hope in that hell-hole!"

"There might be hope."

"There's no hope in Cairo, and you know it. We've seen it. We saw what it was like years ago, and we barely escaped it. He's here because we got out of places like that and learnt to survive, so don't you throw all that away by inviting him to go in there because there *must be some kind of organisation*," she pulled a face and waggled her head from side to side mockingly.

"I'm sorry, I just –"

"You should be," she turned her back on him and crossed her arms. She stood rigid for several minutes, but softened as he wrapped his arms around her from behind and held her tight.

"I'm too tired for this," she sighed. "The only reason I'm going along with this exodus of yours is because of Jake. Him and Fatima, and Saïd, and anyone else who still has some life left in them and deserves a better go at it than we've had here."

"I know," George whispered gently, kissing her on the cheek. "And so does he."

She turned and pulled him in closer, burying her head in his chest. She listened to his heart beating for almost a minute before looking up into his eyes. Big, silent tears had started to roll down his face and his bottom lip had curled outwards in that ugly way she somehow found so attractive.

"What's wrong?" she asked, wiping his tears away with her thumbs.

He nodded towards Cairo. "If we hadn't landed there, twenty-seven years ago, do you think things would have been different?" he asked, swallowing any further tears.

"What happened was always going to happen," she dug her chin into his chest and smiled. "But because we landed there all those years ago, and because of everything that happened from that point on, we both found ourselves hundreds of miles away from the nearest explosion when it did. Because of all that, we're here, and so is Jake. And that's all that matters."

They walked hand in hand to the assembled villagers, who had already started to plan their route past Cairo.

"The biggest danger is that we have no speed," Zahra said. If anyone tries to stop us, for any reason, we have no way of escaping. I can guarantee you that they will have horses that are faster than our donkeys."

Their migrations over the years had never taken them past Cairo. It had always been an un-passable barrier to the north of their world. For the younger generation, life in the countryside was all they knew or remembered.

"Why would anyone want to stop us? What do we have that they could possibly want?" Fatima spoke clearly and with an indignant tone.

"Places like this are different," Zahra explained. "It doesn't matter what you have, you can still be shot just because you walk into the wrong street, or look at someone the wrong way."

"So what is the right way to look at people?" Jake asked. No one answered.

Of all the villagers, Ben and Zahra knew Cairo best, and they had started to draw a map in the dust on the side of the road.

"This used to be the road, up from Saqqara and Dashur towards Giza," Zahra explained. "We're about here, and up ahead the pyramids will be visible on our left."

The Pyramids of Giza, Gail thought suddenly. *Jake's never seen them!* She envied the fact that he was going to see them for the first time, and wondered how much time, if at all, she would have to show them to him. When he was very young he'd seen other pyramids, like the Step Pyramid at Saqqara, and the Red Pyramid and Bent Pyramid slightly further north. But *never* Khufu's Great Pyramid.

"Giza was still there ten years ago, and our visitor a few nights ago confirmed that it was still there now, though there's not much left. Hopefully we should be able to go through relatively quietly." Zahra saw the look in Gail's eyes and laughed. "We probably won't have time for a history tour Gail, I'm sorry."

Gail shrugged it off and smiled, though inside she clung to the hope of an unexpected detour.

Zahra's biggest fear was that they would lose their donkeys. The animals had been with them for so long, and had been indispensable throughout their travels; no human could carry enough water to last that many days between refills. Camels and horses would certainly have to be handed over to whatever militia controlled the Saqqara road. Who knew how desperate they'd be for six tired donkeys?

"Then we should reach the sea in two days by following the road to Alexandria," Ben finished the plan off.

"And as for how you look at people," Gail said to Jake with a smile, "don't."

CHAPTER 93

Gail was shocked at how little their party took notice of the pyramids. Admittedly, from where the road lay it was impossible to get a good view. They took a right angle turn off the main road and onto the principle crossing of the canal, which with its stagnant waters and years of detritus could probably be walked across without getting a toe wet.

They turned their backs on Cairo as they crossed the flat bridge, and got their first decent glimpse. Khafre's pyramid, though half a mile away and partly hidden by the encroaching sand-dunes, stood proud, the smooth limestone casing still clinging to its upper reaches. The Giza plateau was a dozen or so metres higher in elevation compared to the bridge, exaggerating the monument's scale, but her scientific mind ignored that for the time being. She'd never walked across this bridge, never stood there, looking at it as an ancient Egyptian would have: from water-level.

George stopped and gave her time to reflect, but hurried her along as soon as the last of their group had passed them. She looked at Jake, who had paused on the other side. He was looking past her, at the ruins of Cairo.

She could sense Jake's eagerness to explore, and the realisation that he was more intrigued by what remained of Cairo than the ancient Egyptian pyramids upset her. She would later acknowledge that they were both fascinated by a lost culture, just not the same one.

They gathered on the other side of the canal. The pyramids were now all but hidden behind the wall of sand that had practically invaded Giza, and in the years to come would no doubt cross the canal and eventually reach the Nile itself.

She looked back, towards Cairo.

An impenetrable concrete barrier ten feet high cut across all four lanes of the main road into the city, joining two large buildings on opposite sides of the road and sealing off the outside world. A hundred-metre wide band of scorched-earth had been created between the wall and the rest of Giza. Rubble, the remains of all the buildings that had been demolished to create the flat-zone, had been piled up in a neat border on the side nearest them. Cairo was a fortress.

"I don't think they want visitors," Jake said.

"It's a good thing we don't want to visit then, isn't it?" Gail commented, turning back to their path and patting him on the shoulder.

Her protective nature towards her son, and everything she had said the day before about Jake and Cairo, still stood. But the main reason she didn't want to give him the time of day to look at Cairo was the most non-maternal instinct of them all: spite. To her the pyramids, along with countless other sites in the country, epitomized what had been great, and what was to this day still so intriguing, about the ancient Egyptians. That her own son had failed to recognise that, or even vaguely share her interest, to look at the pyramids in all their glory and *gasp*, made the anger well up in the pit of her stomach.

Only three steps on and the anger subsided. As emotions went, it was one of the short-lived ones, mainly because of the overwhelming guilt she felt at being spiteful towards her son.

She turned round and looked at him.

"One day, Jake," she began, then sighed in that tired sort of way only a mother can. "One day, you'll come back. When things are better, when things have had more time to settle down."

He caught up with her in one stride and put his arm round her. He glanced over his shoulder at where the pyramids hid behind the sand. "They look amazing, Mum," he said in English with a glint in his eye.

They walked on for several minutes, George falling into step beside them.

"You mean *we*," Jake said, breaking the silence.

"Sorry?"

"You mean *we*. *We'll* come back and see Cairo, and the pyramids, when things have settled down a bit."

They pushed on in silence.

They carried on along the road to Alexandria, towards the sea, until nightfall. Along the way, they were challenged once by a group of old boys sitting atop a broken down tractor, who quickly gestured for them to keep going on their way after looking the donkeys up and down a couple of times.

How sorry must we all look Gail thought, *that even the robbers and brigands don't want us!*

The campfire talk, as usual, was of the road ahead.

"A day's walk along this road and we should be able to find any number of fishing villages along the coast," Ben said eagerly. "Diesel will be a problem, of course, so sail boats are our first target. The smaller the boat, the more we need; nothing less than twenty feet for crossing the sea."

A large number of the party had sailing experience, but mostly from the river. Even George, who had sailed along the coast of Britain throughout his youth, had no real sea-skills, save for a quick trip across the Channel. In comparison to that, the Mediterranean was an ocean.

Gail looked across at her husband as the plans were drawn out, for the twentieth time, in the dirt around the campfires. Their eyes met across the flames. *He understands*, she thought with relief. She didn't want to have the conversation with him or anyone just yet, the argument, the tears. There would be plenty of that when the time came.

A twenty-foot sailing boat might carry four people comfortably enough to Italy. Six at a squeeze. Any more, with the great distances involved, would be uncomfortable indeed, and probably dangerous. She didn't even dare to imagine the lack of water and food that such cramped conditions might create, should the weather turn out to be anything but favourable.

Maybe she was misjudging the type of boat they might find. Maybe they would find a yacht capable of taking them all in luxury, like some modern-day Noah's Ark, donkeys and all.

But she doubted it.

CHAPTER 94

Shortly after passing the pyramids of Giza, Gail had made her decision to stay in Egypt. George, of course, would stay behind with her.

But Gail had known her husband now for the better part of forty years, and there was little he could feel that she wasn't aware of; she knew he had an overwhelming desire to go back to Britain, to see his home and the country he loved, to see if anyone or anything from their old life was left standing. Yet he would sacrifice all of that to be with her. She only wished that she had something left to give him in return.

After two more days of marching along the dusty road north-west, towards the sea, she was starting to have second thoughts. She was on the verge of having a let's-wait-till-we-see-what-kind-of-boats-we-find conversation with George.

"We will stay behind with you," Ben suddenly said out of the blue. Along with Zahra, he'd fallen into step with them, behind the main group of travellers. Gail and George now tended to make up the rear of their human caravan; because of their age, certainly, but also because it made her see the community as 'us' and 'them'. The self-detachment would make it easier to say goodbye when the time came, particularly to their son. Plus, they enjoyed watching him with his friends from a distance.

Gail tried to feign ignorance. "Thanks, Ben," she smiled after a brief hesitation, "but you don't need to worry about us, we're happy to walk at the back."

He looked across at her, and then at George.

"No, that's not what I mean," he said in English. Of the entire group, the four of them spoke the language better than anyone, with Jake coming in a close fifth. To his credit he sometimes made efforts to talk with them in their native language, even though it was next to useless in their community. "Zahra and I have decided to stay behind with you, in Egypt."

They walked on in silence for a dozen or so steps.

"Why?" George asked. They had tried to be discreet, to hide their plan from the rest of the group, in particular from Jake. Clearly they hadn't fooled their friends.

"Because if we cannot persuade you to come with us, then we will stay with you. This is my country, and while you are here, you are still my guests."

Gail giggled at Ben's mock bow. "You don't need to worry about us, we'll be fine. We've lived here long enough now, and besides you and Zahra are the heart of the community, you belong with them."

Ben looked across at Zahra, walking next to George; one of those looks that only a couple completely in tune with each other can exchange, like an unspoken conversation.

"Gail, you are funny," he said without a hint of humour. "There's always been something funny about you." George was about to make a joke, but stopped when Ben raised his hand. "You came to Egypt on a whim, arrived at a well organised archaeological dig and within hours instinctively found what had eluded the best Egyptologists in the world for more than a century." He accentuated the *instinctively*. They stopped walking, and Ben faced her. "Professor al-Misri knew there was something different about you. Somehow, even before you arrived in Egypt, he was genuinely excited to see you, like you were the most reputable archaeologist in the world, come to inspect his work, instead of a struggling post-grad student," he put his hand on her shoulder. "And now, instead of going back to your home country, instead of taking *that* opportunity, you are going to walk all the way back to Amarna, aren't you?"

She nodded quietly.

"Then you know the rules in Egypt, Dr Turner," he said with a grin. "You can't visit any archaeological sites without the authorisation and accompaniment of the Tourism Police," he gestured to Zahra, who smiled in return, though she couldn't hide the apprehension she felt.

But not one of them was as nervous as Gail. The reasons she had built up for staying behind meant nothing. The size of the boat, her age, how tired she felt, were all excuses to hide her real motivation. Something was drawing her back to Amarna. Back to the Library, and to the Xynutian vaults beneath it.

And the fear inside her was growing.

CHAPTER 95

Even eighteen years after the beginning of the Chaos, the Nile Delta remained the most densely populated area of what had been, what some insisted still was, Egypt.

But rather than this concentration of people making the area livelier, it served only to make its desolation all the more pronounced.

What little remained of infrastructure was patchy at best; freshwater canals were mostly blocked and stagnant, roads were broken and littered with the carcasses of obsolete vehicles, and power cables were strewn across the landscape like a gigantic collapsed spider web, where one by one the high tension electricity grid had collapsed after years of neglect and unpredictable weather.

People lived among all these remains, mostly in squalor. Some, as some always will, had managed to climb to the top of the heap and make the very most of a bad situation.

It was people like this they did their best to avoid as they weaved their way up the road towards Alexandria, keeping themselves to themselves and walking mostly in silence through any built up area.

About twenty miles from Alexandria, they turned towards the sea port of Abu Qir.

"It's where we're most likely to find a large boat," Ben explained. "If people are to be believed, there may even be some international trade there, we might be able to get on board a ship heading for Europe."

The fact that the four of them would remain in Egypt had not been shared with the others yet, on Gail's request. She didn't want her last days with Jake to be fraught with arguments.

"You may be interested to know," Ben turned to George and Gail, "that Abu Qir is where your Admiral Nelson and the Royal Navy fought against the French in the Battle of the Nile."

George nodded in interest. Although he had heard of it, he knew nothing of the battle itself; but the mention of the Royal Navy caused a lump to form in his throat. It might have been a male thing, for Gail didn't seem that affected, but to him in that very moment the Royal Navy *was* the United Kingdom. Knowing that in all probability neither existed anymore, and that on top of that he wasn't going to return to see the remains, was hard to take.

"Let's hope the place is a little more peaceful, nowadays," Gail said bitterly. History was a sequence of battles, wars and conflicts, punctuated by periods of peace. The lull they found themselves in now would barely have been described as peaceful thirty years ago. *Peace*, Gail had decided, was a distinctly relative term.

It was shortly after thinking this that they were stopped by a man brandishing an AK-47, pointed straight at them.

He wore a white thawb, the traditional long tunic worn by most Arab men, including most of the people travelling with Gail. What made this man's thawb special was its brilliant whiteness, crisp and clean even in the dull evening light. His long, flowing black hair and carefully trimmed beard framed a hook nose and thick-set eyes that looked at them impassively.

Despite the half dozen weapons the group of travellers pointed at him in return, he didn't flinch or lower the barrel of his rifle.

It didn't take them long to realise that they had in fact been surrounded by men with AK-47s, and that they had been both outgunned and out-manoeuvred.

Their luck had run out.

CHAPTER 96

Over the years, Zahra's connections with the military and police in Egypt had been beneficial in almost every incident that the group had been involved in. Though the Tourism Police had famously been disorganised and generally poorly-lead before the Chaos, in the post-war period people had craved some form of authority and sign of governance.

Everyone, that is, except *al-Gama'a al-Islamiyya*. Literally *the Islamist Group*, *al-Gama'a al-Islamiyya* had been famous in the twentieth century for violence towards any form of authority in democratic Egypt, and were responsible for the killings of dozens of government officials and countless policemen, policewomen and civilians, during the latter part of the century. Their long-term goal had been for an Islamic state, an enforcement of Sharia Law, and the expulsion of foreigners from Egypt.

Now, a power vacuum had clearly given them authority over their own little part of the country.

After some brief questioning, during which Zahra and Gail struggled to keep themselves quiet as the men negotiated, their captors escorted them to the Abu Qir dockyards, where they were locked in an empty warehouse, with no food and little water.

On the third day of captivity, they were provided with a thin meat stew of what they suspected was some of their own donkey, though it could just as easily have been sick cow.

On the fifth day, the man who had stopped them on the road appeared on a walkway running along the end-wall of the warehouse, several metres above their makeshift camping area. This time he wore a black thawb, and he looked as impeccable as before. They, in contrast, had done their best to stay clean but the lack of facilities for such a large group of people had taken its toll. He peered down at them and curled his lips in disgust.

"As you can see," he said in Arabic, showing the empty expanse of the warehouse in a flowing gesture, "we do not have much to offer. We, like most, are a poor people, though we are infinitely richer than you in both culture and pride."

George held Gail's arm tightly, both for comfort and to attempt to quell any rebellious leanings she may have been feeling. She patted his hand reassuringly and he released his grip slightly.

"We have considered your request for a vessel to leave Egypt. It has been rejected. Our boats are too valuable, and your old, stringy donkeys are not sufficient compensation. I must add on a personal note that we would not have been sorry to see you leave. You are rabble. Only a few of your people are strong enough to be a part of our country, though I suspect all of your minds have already been infected by blasphemous liberalism," he spat the words out in disgust. "And at what cost such liberalism?" he threw his arms up in the air. "The end of your world! Fire and devastation! Death!" Pacing up and down the walkway, he stopped above Gail and Zahra. Their faces and hair were uncovered, and he looked down his nose at them. "And now you want to leave the last place on Earth where order and law remain?"

Zahra looked to the floor, not wanting to exacerbate the situation. But Gail kept her eyes fixed on the man on the walkway. George's grip tightened once more, but she didn't waver. The seconds drew out into minutes, until eventually the man swore and drew a pistol from inside the folds of his thawb.

He pointed the gun directly at Gail's head. "You dare to stare at me, you whore?" he exclaimed, his pistol arm trembling. George was about to act when Jake stepped between his mother and the man with the gun.

In Arabic he apologised for his mother's indiscretion, and in English he pleaded with her to swallow her pride and look to the floor.

"You are British?" the man asked in surprise.

George nodded. Gail dropped her chin to the floor but kept her eyes on the man as much as possible. "Yes," she said, defiantly. "My name is Dr Gail Turner, and I worked with the Supreme Council of Antiquities in Cairo."

The man lowered his pistol and leaned over the railing to get a better look at the dirty, dishevelled elderly woman who had defied him. He raised his eyebrows and a wide grin played across his face, exposing his perfect, straight, white teeth.

He dug inside his thawb and brought out a small book. On its cover was an emblem looking rather like a green rose flower with writing across the centre.

"Do you know what this is?" he asked.

She'd seen enough Qur'ans to know what one looked like, and was about to make a snide remark when the emblem in its centre caught her eye. She looked closer. Beneath what she recognised as the Arabic word for Allah was the bold outline of the Amarna Stickman; the symbol of Aniquilus.

Aniquilus. The destructor of the Xynutian race. And now its symbol had been adopted by fundamentalists. The irony made her smile.

"Aniquilus," she said. "Although you probably know it better as the *Amarna Stickman*."

The man put the book and the pistol away and stood tall on the walkway. His initial surprise at hearing a new term for the Stickman was quickly hidden. "Absolutely correct, Dr Turner." And without saying a further word, he turned on his heel and left the warehouse.

He returned soon after, accompanied by a much older man dressed in grey. They descended a set of steps to the warehouse floor and made their way towards Gail and George.

"Dr Turner, I presume," the older man said in perfect English. He smiled at his little joke and stuck his hand out towards her. "*Assalaam aleikum!* You are most welcome; I do apologise for the conditions in which you have been kept, these are trying times, and you can never be too careful."

Gail was taken completely off-guard, and accepted the hand in bewilderment, though she stopped short of the formal *waleikum salaam* response. She had just escaped a pistol-shot to the head from this man's sidekick, and now she was being welcomed like an old friend.

"I am sorry, how rude of me not to introduce myself. My name is Omar Abdel-Rahman. I am responsible for Abu Qir. Please, do come this way," he gestured for her to follow him.

George, Ben, Jake and Zahra stepped forward to protect her.

Abdel-Rahman waved them away. "You do not need to worry; we will not harm such an esteemed guest to our country. However, one of you may come with us if it makes you feel more comfortable."

CHAPTER 97

Gail and George were taken to a sitting room, instructed to make themselves as comfortable as possible, then left alone.

The room could only be described as opulent. Not just comparative opulence in bleak times, but the kind of opulence that one would expect of a rich home during the twentieth century.

Gold picture frames held paintings that wouldn't have looked out of place in an art gallery, twin crystal chandeliers hung from richly decorated ceiling roses, plush carpets covered the floor. A display cabinet filled with pottery and glassware occupied one corner of the room, while floor-to-ceiling bookcases filled the remaining wall-space. They sat on one of three Chesterfield sofas, arranged in a square with a large open fireplace making up the fourth side.

George nudged her in the ribs and nodded towards the small coffee table in front of them.

It was stocked with old copies of National Geographic, and a large hardback tome on Islamic art. All were well-thumbed, and Gail noted with interest that the topmost copy of National Geographic was from November 2039, and carried an article on the Amarna Library. Much to the combined chagrin and delight of her esteemed University colleagues, she had been interviewed by the reporter for that very issue, two months before achieving her Doctorate. The chagrin came from some conservative archaeologists who sneered at the sensationalist journalism; she always suspected that they were just trying to hide their envy. The delight came mostly from her old friends Dr Hunt and Ellie.

She had often wondered about them, in the aftermath of the Chaos. About them, Southampton and indeed the rest of the United Kingdom. Britain was such a natural target that it was hard to imagine much of it could have survived. She knew why George wanted to return, she felt it too; the pang of guilt at being safe and well, mixed with curiosity and homesickness. He was a natural optimist, believing that their home was probably safe. There were days when she agreed. In any case, no news of the UK had reached them for many years. It made her sad to think about it, so she tried not to. Jake was more important to her now anyway. Getting him, and his future, away from the dying embers of Egypt and off to a better climate was her only priority.

The sound of the door opening snatched her from her reverie. Turning in their seats they saw that Omar Abdel-Rahman and the man with the hook-nose had entered the room.

Omar sat down on the sofa opposite them.

Gail had already started flicking through the pages of the magazine, looking for the Amarna article.

"I see you have found my favourite magazine," he smiled. "Joking aside, though, it is a poor article. I was particularly disappointed by the way in which they downplayed your part in the discovery. '*Gail Turner sat down to take some rest and found herself sitting on the most important archaeological discovery of the century*', they said." He cocked his head and looked at her. "Surely there was more to it than that?"

"Actually, quite a bit more," she began with a frog in her throat. She cleared it nervously. "Ben, one of your *guests* in the warehouse, did all of the sitting. I saw he was sitting on something important."

"I see!" he slapped his hands together with glee. "But that didn't make for such a good sub-title, did it? The editors took some poetic licence to make it sound more, dare I say it, Hollywood?"

She shifted in her seat. "I'm sure it was an honest mistake. There were more important things in the article, although," she hesitated for a moment before continuing. "Although I do agree with you that it wasn't very scientific."

Omar grinned again with glee. "How interesting! Tell me," he said, leaning towards her and lowering his voice, "what else did you find in the Library that hasn't yet been published?"

"What do you want us to have found?" she asked cautiously.

He raised his hands defensively. "Nothing, I am purely interested scientifically."

"Why do you have Aniquilus alongside Allah on your emblem," she challenged, nodding towards a framed picture on the mantelpiece. "What does it have to do with Islam?" She sensed George tense up at this, and so hurriedly added "if you don't mind me asking?"

"Because Islam is the one true faith, and our way of life is the only acceptable way of life," he answered without batting an eyelid. "And at the same time, we are a proud Egyptian people. Our heritage is the birth of civilisation. The Stickman represents that foundation, the legitimacy of our people to not be subservient to the western world."

"So you brought religion and nationalism together, to take over Egypt and run it as an Islamic state?" she sighed. "That sort of thing doesn't usually end well."

He raised an eyebrow. "And yet it was the liberal west that destroyed humanity, was it not?" Omar leaned forwards and picked up the National Geographic. He flipped directly to a specific page and looked up at her before reading out loud.

"For now, we shall have to call this new symbol 'Stickman'; we don't know if it's a person, a god, a concept, or even a place or time. With the texts studied so far revealing nothing on this enigmatic symbol, we have to accept that we may never know what, or who, it represents."

Gail felt strange hearing her own words, as quoted by the journalist, read aloud. It was like hearing a recording of your own voice. She couldn't help thinking how *naïve* her younger self had been.

Omar placed the magazine back on the coffee table. "Dr Turner, political and ideological differences aside, I would very much appreciate it if you could enlighten me." He crossed his legs, clasping his knee with both hands as he leant back into the sofa.

His body language, tone of voice and even the look on his face told her that she had little choice. And the safety of her friends, husband and son might hinge on her cooperating.

She sighed. "There was a second book, one that was hidden as soon as it was found. I myself only learnt of it shortly before the Chaos, nine years after the discovery of the Library."

He leant forward once more, already fascinated by this new information.

Gail wasn't a betting person, nor had she ever had a keen eye for business, but she knew this might be her only chance. "If you reconsider our request for a boat, so that our companions can leave Egypt, I will tell you everything that was contained within the second book."

There was silence for several minutes, before he replied.

"You would need food, and boats large enough are difficult to come by these days, even for us. You would also need some of our knowledge of safe areas to go to and travel through. It goes without saying you would also need some medical supplies," he said pensively, listing the items on his fingers. "However, we are good people, as you have seen, and I am a good man. More importantly, I am a scholar at heart, and your promise has whetted my appetite."

CHAPTER 98

Jake stood on the deck of the large trawler that Omar Abdel-Rahman had, seemingly out of nowhere, decided to let them use. He looked out over the docks where men busied themselves ferrying various crates and odds and ends from the large warehouses on the dockside to the bowels of the ship.

Before long, the last bundle had been stowed away, and Omar Abdel-Rahman joined Gail, George, Zahra and Ben on the dockside. The man with the hook-nose reported briefly to Omar, but the stiff sea breeze made it impossible for Jake to hear what they were saying.

Jake looked on as hook-nose boarded the ship and disappeared below deck, then looked to his mother in interest. Most of the travellers were now already on board, and had been preparing their living quarters. It did not occur to Jake, until he saw six more men boarding, that none of his own people knew how to pilot such a craft, nor knew how to navigate the high seas.

It dawned on him that they would not be making their trip on their own, and that the vessel was a loan, and not a gift.

"You look confused?" a voice said behind him.

Jake turned with a start and saw hook-nose standing on deck, with a length of coiled rope in one hand and a nonchalant smile drawn across his face.

"It seems," he continued as he extended his hand, "that we are to be ship-mates for the foreseeable future. My name is Mehmet."

Jake shook the hand despite himself. This was the detestable man that a day earlier had threatened his mother and had held them all in dire conditions with little to eat or drink. The man who had looked down on them all from the walkway inside the warehouse and held his mother at gunpoint was now shaking his hand.

"Why –" Jake began, withdrawing his arm sharply.

"This is our ship," Mehmet interrupted. "And you require passage

469

to Italy. And yet none of your people know how the ship works. So you need a crew. The ship is valuable, but the fuel we will use is even more so. We are also keen to communicate and trade with Europe, and so you will be our passengers."

Jake looked back at his mother and father, who were now talking quietly to each other on the docks.

"Your mother and Omar Abdel-Rahman are responsible for this. If it were up to me, then my hospitality would not have been so far-reaching. And yet," he nodded towards the dockside, "they appear to have quite a lot in common, at least academically."

Something about the way in which his parents were talking, their body language, the way in which they were looking at the ship, and at him, suddenly made Jake feel uneasy.

He started towards the gangway, leaving Mehmet behind him.

"I don't know how to do this, George," Gail gasped, fighting back her emotions. "It was difficult knowing I would have to say goodbye, but now –"

"We can go with them?" George suggested, a glimmer of hope in his voice.

She hesitated, but not long enough for George's hope to remain intact. "No," she swallowed and evened the creases in her shirt with her palms. "I have to do this." There was finality in her voice, and it still weighed down on them both as Jake reached them, the one word on his mind escaping on a breath.

"Mum," he pleaded.

She said nothing, but opened her arms wide and accepted his embrace.

"Mum!" he sobbed as he buried his face deep into her shoulder and collapsed against her. "I'm staying with you," he said suddenly, holding her at arms' length. His face was a mess of tears and hurt.

"No, Jake," she said softly. "You're not. You have to go and live your life. This may be your only chance."

"Then come with us! There must be enough room on the boat, and if there isn't then we'll make room!"

Gail looked at him, this man who had suddenly become a frightened little boy again. She had spent her life caring for him, making sure he was safe, making sure he didn't stray too far, and yet here she was pushing him away. She broke down, unable to fight back the flood of emotions she'd been building up for days now.

As she sobbed into Jake's chest, George put his hands on both their shoulders, comforting them.

"Jake, you must go with the group to Europe," he tried desperately to fight back his own tears. "They'll need your language skills, and your strength. Your mother has to return to Amarna. There's something very important that she has to do." He didn't mention the fact that neither he nor Gail had any idea what that important thing was.

They held each other tightly in a circle. George let his statements sink in for a few moments before continuing, his voice more steady now.

"Once we have returned from Amarna, we will be safe here in Abu Qir. Omar has assured us of that. And then we can meet again, here or in Europe." George didn't expect his son or his wife to believe that, but nonetheless it seemed to calm some of their nerves down and they were able, somehow, to enjoy their last few hours together, speaking more than in the past few weeks combined.

There was something quite hypnotic about the boat as it left with the tide, diesel fumes and engine noise bringing back memories of a long-gone era of technological advancement that Gail would probably never see again.

The sun broke through the clouds on the horizon just long enough for the boat to be picked out by its rays, like a tiny insect in the undulating sands of the desert.

And then it was gone, the sea descended into darkness.

She looked on long after it was out of sight and the sun had set, following it in her mind's eye. Willing, and wishing, it well.

George covered her shoulders with a blanket and rubbed them gingerly. She continued to look into the darkness in silence, the cold wind playing with her hair and cooling the warm tears as they ran down her cheeks.

She closed her eyes and wept "I love you, my baby." A gust of wind took the words from her lips and carried them out to sea towards the lonely vessel.

CHAPTER 99

The journey south was far quicker, due in no small part to the role of four of their donkeys, which they had been allowed to keep, and a two-wheeled cart. The last two donkeys had been given to Omar Abdel-Rahman, in part exchange for the safe passage of their people to Europe. The academic in him wanted to go with Gail, to see the wonders that she had described. But with his second-in-command on a ship to Italy, he couldn't afford to leave their stronghold without a leader.

Omar had reasoned, accurately, that after their journey they would return to Abu Qir, for news of their son and friends, possible passage to Italy themselves, and lack of anywhere else safe to go.

He had been more than surprised, shocked in fact, to learn of the Xynutians. And while at first he had been sceptical, he had to concede that there was no real reason for Gail to lie to him.

What had been most difficult for him to accept was the fact that his god had created the Xynutians. He had then wiped the slate clean and created modern humans.

It was a hard concept to grasp.

"The Great Flood," Gail had explained, "is a legend that is present in nearly all cultures in one form or another. God was unhappy with his creation, and so decided to start again."

"Of course, as is the case with the Qur'an with the story of Nuh."

"Noah," Gail agreed. Indeed the story of Noah, present in the book of Genesis in the Bible, was also told twice in the Qur'an, with striking similarities to the Old Testament text. "In China, India, Australia, Finland, Greece, the list goes on: dozens of accounts of epic floods that threatened civilisation."

"You could argue that most civilisations are built near rivers and the sea, and that floods are bound to happen at some stage," George had suggested.

472

"Or," Omar had said in wonder. "You could argue that all the legends have the same root: Man emerged from a cataclysm so great that its memory survived thousands of years until the emergence of written language in the Middle East six thousand years ago."

"And that," Gail added with a smile, "instead of this flood being a recent event it was a much more ancient apocalypse that had been passed on in stories for hundreds of thousands of years."

After a short pause, Omar arrived at the same conclusion Gail had, years earlier, when confronted with the book of Xynutians by Professor Henry Patterson.

"I see a flaw," he started. "In the Qur'an, and also in the Bible, Nuh, or Noah, his family and fellow believers were spared. And yet these Xynutians disappear completely, no record of them in archaeology. Where are they? Why didn't they rebuild?"

"I thought the same thing. It's possible that they, like us, had become over-reliant on technology, and those who were left descended into barbarity quickly, forgetting everything." She paused, and looked him in the eyes. "But since then, I found out what really happened to the last of the Xynutians.

"For a start, the Xynutians and modern man evolved separately. We know that the Xynutians, before their demise, were already fighting with early hominids who to them must have seemed like advanced chimpanzees to us. It's possible that after Aniquilus, there was interbreeding of early hominids and Xynutians.

"Not all Xynutians perished here though, as we've seen with the findings on Mars. Some left Earth behind and fled not just to the red planet, but also to the stars. God only knows how many are left roaming the planets of nearby solar systems, or whether the last of their kind died out hundreds of thousands of years ago, exhausted. It's a fascinating thought that there may be millions of them living out there somewhere; maybe like us they themselves have no memory of where they came from, save for legends and religion.

"Of those who remained on Earth, most were wiped out. Despite their technology, which was far more advanced than our own, whatever rained down on them wasn't simply a flood made of water. They were, effectively, annihilated."

"You say most," Omar enquired. "What remained?"

"The Xynutians left their people to die or fight for their survival on the surface, exposed to the elements, they had no choice. But a select few could be guaranteed safety. An army, their scientists, leaders, workers and farmers were saved. They built an ark deep underground, with animals, seeds, technology; everything needed to rebuild their civilisation from the ground up was stored, ready for a time when they could rise again. This was something the ancient Egyptians discovered, and tried to emulate in their own way."

"Where is this ark?"

"Underneath Tell el-Amarna."

CHAPTER 100

Gail, George, Zahra and Ben reached Amarna less than a week later, to the surprise of the old couple who lived there. They were more than happy to share their house one more time, but Gail insisted that they camp on the banks of the Nile.

As they sat around the campfire that night, George laughed.

"Omar was itching to come with us; that would have been interesting!"

"I don't care how much he's helped us," Zahra sneered. "I would not have held back from saying what I think about him and his men."

Ben grinned and drew her head to the warmth of his chest. "Always fire in your heart, isn't there, my dear?"

"He is an extremist, and extremists want to control things," Zahra said bitterly. "We will see how accommodating our host is when your archaeological stories start to wear thin."

They watched the fire crackling lazily at the remnants of a thick log that Ben had dragged up from the banks of the Nile; sparks rose on the hot air into the darkness, like crazed fireflies disappearing into the night.

"I understand why Omar was so interested," Ben said pensively. "I know we've discussed this, and I know you've told us that *this is something you have to do*, but now that we're here, Gail," he hesitated, trying to find the right words, before settling with the simplest he could think of. "What now?"

She looked across the fire at him and Zahra. Through thick and thin they had followed her; from saving her life before the war, to helping her, George and their new-born child make it through the early years. Now they had sacrificed the option of going with their people to Europe just to be with her.

Gail rose, rounded the campfire and crouched before them.

"Thank you Ben, Zahra, for always being there, and for always believing in me. You have been my dearest friends."

She embraced and hugged them both for what seemed an age, before getting to her feet and going to her tent. She said over her shoulder, "I have to sleep now, as do you George, but in the morning, I hope, you will have all the answers you could possibly want."

And with that she was gone, leaving them with the embers of a dying fire.

CHAPTER 101

G ail woke before dawn and dressed as quietly as possible so as not to wake the others. When she was ready, she woke George, and they tiptoed out of camp and down to the Nile, just as the first light of day started to paint the morning sky.

During their nightly pillow-talk, they had agreed that they would go to the Library alone that morning. Gail still wasn't sure what it was she was going to find, and with that uncertainty had decided Ben and Zahra should be kept out of the way at first, just in case.

"It looks like the clouds may clear a bit today," George commented as they found the group of small rowing boats the old couple had told them about under some overgrown, thorny bushes. They dragged one down the concrete slip to the water's edge.

It was, as usual from George, pointless optimism, designed as much to spark up a topic of conversation as to lighten the mood.

Gail jumped from the boat knee-high into the water on the east bank and George followed gingerly.

"I feel bad leaving without saying goodbye," Gail said as they hiked along the road to the hills.

George had only a minor grasp on what was going on at the best of times, but saw in his wife a trembling sense of excitement and restlessness. Deep inside he sensed that something monumental was about to happen. Good or bad, he didn't know what to expect.

And so they walked on in silence, save for the sound of their footsteps on the ground, as the once tarmacked road gave way to what had always been a rough dirt track that led to the Amarna Library.

The entrance to the Library had changed little in two decades. The burnt out remains of the 4x4s had been taken away, one of the few things to have been achieved by the local government before greater worries came about. However, despite the attempted clean up, the main entrance was still a pile of rubble, with a hastily excavated path cleared down to the Library beneath.

Gail fished a flashlight out of her pocket and tested the bulb. It came on first time, as bright as it had been in Walker's hands eighteen years before. She had rarely used it, to the extent that George was surprised she even had it on her, fully charged and ready.

"I always thought it might come in handy, one day," she explained.

They worked their way through the rubble and down the stairs, and quickly found themselves back in the Amarna Library. Memories came flooding back to them both, but while George sounded excited as they retraced their steps to the huge halls beyond, Gail's humour gradually faded, until when they were standing in front of the Xynutian airlock, her face was sombre and voice passive.

"I need to go in alone, George."

George hesitated, not least because that would mean leaving him in the dark.

"There's light in there, remember? You can keep the torch."

Before he could answer, she had passed it to him, and was entering the airlock, which had suddenly opened of its own accord. He leant in and hugged her, reluctant to let go. "I love you," he said as he eventually loosened his embrace, and looked her directly in the eyes.

The stone-like door of the airlock slid shut, separating them with the faintest waft of stale air.

Any sufficiently advanced technology is indistinguishable from magic. He couldn't remember where the phrase came from, but it described the door perfectly. Thinking about how the door could possibly work; not only its mechanism, but also its longevity, to function so well after countless millennia, and its behaviour, to seem to open and close when *it* wanted. *Magic before the Chaos – now in its wake even more so*, he pondered.

He sat down next to the naked statues of Akhenaten and Nefertiti, and waited for his wife to return.

CHAPTER 102

Gail hesitated as the inner door slid open. After a deep breath, she took a step forward, and almost the moment her trailing foot cleared the threshold she felt the slight rush of air as the door shut behind her.

Did it shut differently all those years ago? She stood in silence for several minutes, until the ambient sound of her pulse and breathing had become almost unbearable. She looked up to the face of the Xynutian statue.

Memories of the traumatic events from before the Chaos came flooding back. She looked to the floor where Walker had fallen, gunned down by George.

Curious, she wondered, and moved round the statue to take a closer look at the floor and walls. Walker and Patterson's bodies had been removed by the local police in the days after their escape. She looked to the opposite wall, against which Patterson had gasped his final warning to them regarding DEFCOMM. It all seemed so distant now, like it was from a different world.

She knew from reports from their friends that the local police and forensic teams had performed a routine clean-up of the scene as part of their investigations, but there had been more pressing matters to worry about, and the amazing finds and criminal events in Amarna had quickly been overlooked and forgotten. The fact that there had been no interest or reporting of the finds hadn't surprised her at the time.

What did surprise her now was that there was absolutely no trace of blood, dirt, fragments of clothing or even marks on the walls from ricocheted bullets.

It was then that she noticed the staff.

She recoiled in shock. She had already seen the statue; it dominated the centre of the room, and as such was impossible to miss. But the fact that it was once more holding the staff aloft, as if she had never ripped it from its grasp years earlier, sent a shiver down her spine.

The room was, as far as she could tell, as perfect as the day they had first discovered it.

It was absolutely timeless.

"The perfect time capsule," she murmured in wonder.

"How else?" said a voice behind her.

She froze. There was something *wrong* about the voice. Something *disconnected*. Gail instinctively knew *what* she would be facing as she turned, slowly, towards it.

The Xynutian stood in the doorway. No, 'stood' was the wrong word; at over seven feet tall and with the muscles of an athlete, it *dominated* the doorway. A simple cloth skirt hung round its waist.

This wasn't a statue, but an *actual* Xynutian; he, as she assumed it was a male, was practically human, and yet not at all. There was something unfamiliar about it. All she could think of was that word, *superior*; this was a *superior* human. A superhuman.

The involuntary whimper in her throat barely made it past her teeth as she stood rooted to the spot.

"How else could we build something that would last through the ages, and allow us to return once more to the surface to rebuild our civilisation?" he said, his lips and jaw unmoving as he stared deep into her mind with his jet black eyes. "This Facility is self-healing. It is at the same time the oldest and newest structure on the planet, constantly regenerating and rearranging itself on an atomic level, like the cells in your body, except with no degeneration whatsoever. It will be here as long as required, waiting for the time for us to return to the surface."

"How are you talking to me?" Gail managed to ask. "You're speaking English, and yet your mouth isn't moving."

"I am creating telepathic communication between us. More accurately, the Facility is creating it, but I am the channel it is using to do so. We are both thinking in our own languages, which are both, in essence, electrical impulses in very specific and controlled orders throughout our brains.

"Telepathy is not beyond your understanding. And before you ask, you heard my voice behind you because that is where I was in relation to you. If your ears can tell your brain that I am behind you, then why would it not be possible for a direct message to the receptors in your brain to give the same impression?"

Her mind was racing. The initial shock gone, she found that she was concentrating now more on the conversation inside her head than the actual Xynutian standing before her.

"So many questions!" it said. "You will shortly know the answers to most of them. But let me tell you first of all that I, indeed *we*, cannot answer everything. You must find some answers within yourself. I will answer the second most important question you have asked of me.

"Why did we not return to the surface after the apocalypse that we suffered? That is an excellent question." He shifted his weight slightly onto one of his massive legs and brought his hands together. "For that, I need to start at the very beginning. I have already mentioned that the Facility is self-healing. It is also self-governing, and the intelligence that governs it is based on the moral and scientific knowledge of my time, and that of my civilisation. Luckily, or unluckily depending on your point of view, morality changed significantly in the years it took to build the Facility. By the time it was complete, my race had become more attuned with the world around it; we felt that we were not at the centre of our ecosystem, but rather an integral part of it.

"And so you are standing within a store of life as it existed nearly *two million years ago*. We saved everything that we could, from the tiniest insect to the largest land and sea creatures, the greatest trees to the most beautiful flower. I can see that that age surprises you, as you have by a great margin underestimated the distance in time between our two species; but it has indeed been that long since any of us walked the Earth.

"So why didn't we come back? Well, we are still waiting. Our best scientific minds, and you can testify for yourself that their minds far exceeded your own, estimated that the devastation of our civilisation on the surface would last a hundred thousand years, after which it would be safe enough for us to return."

"So what went wrong?" Gail asked. She was quietly hurt about the comment on Xynutian brains being bigger before remembering that it could read her mind.

He looked at her for a few seconds.

"By the way, I am not an *it*. I am most definitely a *he*."

She blushed.

"Apology accepted. No, what happened was that instead of lasting a thousand years, it barely lasted a day. What the scientists did not predict is that the apocalypse had very minimal impact on other living creatures and plants. It was almost entirely directed at us. The Facility's first directive was to not allow a return to the surface within the estimated duration of the apocalypse, without exception. By that time, life on the surface had thrived in our absence. The Facility has within its power the ability to propagate all of the species stored here across the entire planet. *However*, its *second* directive is to not let that happen if it is likely to cause unacceptable conflict within the existent ecosystem.

"The Facility made the only logical decision, and decided not to return us. Since then, an opportunity to go back has not come up, and so we remain here." The Xynutian didn't sound in the slightest bit upset about the situation. "An ecosystem is a fragile thing, and for the Facility preserving that is more important than anything else."

"So you've been waiting ever since," Gail said quietly.

"Not exactly; we see the passage of time very differently to you. I am connected to the Facility, which is constantly aware of its surroundings, so I have knowledge of the past two million years within my mind. And yet, I have existed only since the very beginning of this conversation. As for the rest of the Xynutian species, and every other creature and plant here, they are frozen in time. When they are finally returned, they will be conscious of but a few moments since they were laid to rest. We are in no hurry, as the time that has already passed is a mere blink of an eye for Earth. The time of humans is ongoing, and we are happy to sit by and watch."

"You speak of a change of morals," Gail said. "Is this what the Book of Aniquilus was based on? Is that why your race was destroyed?"

"Ah, *the books* are another important question. The books are based on true events, but should be considered to be fiction. This Facility developed a habit, quite some time after the fall of my race, and shortly before the dominance of yours, not to *interfere*, but to try and *help*. It did so by using these vaults to send out emissaries: special messengers with key pieces of knowledge that would, it hoped, lead your species down a more fruitful path. As time passed, nature on the surface evolved, and so new samples of your ancestry were brought to the memory banks of the Facility, to be used in future emissaries.

"At the beginning simple messages and concepts were sufficient enough to guide humans, but as time passed and your society developed, more complex ideas were required. This is similar to pushing a stone: the larger the stone, the more effort required to move it. The Facility encountered two problems. Firstly, the human brain, indeed any brain capable of any rational thought, is so caught up in its own inner workings and thoughts that it is very difficult to plant abstract ideas within it and expect any realistic results. The second, and perhaps the most damaging to the cause, is that you are an extremely social species, and as such find it difficult to act of your own accord.

"Humans are, for the most part, like molecules of water in a river; each and every one of you is critical to the water's flow, but you are individually quite incapable of changing its direction. Sometimes, however, one of the Facility's emissaries would succeed in causing more than just a ripple of change, if only for a short period of time and in a small part of the river. The books you asked about are the result of such a ripple.

"Most of the information in them about my race is accurate, however the emissary lived in her own time, and so many details are simply products of the ancient Egyptian culture and belief system. Having read your thoughts, I believe that it changed even further in translation since then; remember you are a product of your own time, and as such cannot expect to interpret, or even translate, entirely accurately."

"Nefertiti!" Gail gasped.

"Yes. And before you ask of other emissaries, because I can feel your mind wandering there, *He* wasn't from the Facility. Good people occur more frequently and naturally than you might think."

"Nefertiti was sent to warn us about Aniquilus, because your race was destroyed by it," Gail muttered.

The Xynutian cocked his head to one side as if hearing her voice this time, rather than simply reading her mind. "Warn you? Well, it may have come across that way, but that was not the intention; Nefertiti, as I have said, was a human being like you or any other, and as such was allowed to make her own interpretations. But there is no point warning you of the inevitable, and consequently the Facility would not have tried to do so."

"I'm confused."

"You are confused because I mention that Aniquilus is inevitable. For some reason you expect there to be a way of avoiding Aniquilus, but why should there be? Is there any way in which an ant can avoid the ant eater?"

"So if there is no way to stop it, then why did the Facility keep sending emissaries? What would be the point?"

"It is not because the apple tree dies that it did not lead a long and fruitful life, Gail Turner. The Facility's aim was simply to help make minor, and sometimes major, adjustments. And yet, the Facility has a complex, evolving mind, and what may be best for you as a collective may not appear best for the individual. So what *it* thinks is a good idea in the long run, may not be something you can fully appreciate."

There was a long silence, during which time Gail's mind raced back and forth. She had so many more questions to ask this amazing creature.

"We are almost out of time," the Xynutian said.

"What happened to the astronauts?" Gail asked suddenly. It was something that had been in the back of her mind for a long time, and she couldn't stop it leaping out.

"They are safe, frozen in time inside a similar, though smaller, Facility, on Mars." pointing towards the centre of the room, an image of the two astronauts materialised, sleeping like the Xynutians in this vault that she had seen all those years ago. "We cannot let them leave, yet, because they would die, alone on the surface of the planet. Their fate is tied to that of my race, now."

"The Book of Xynutians said that Nefertiti would return. The date it gave was almost sixty years ago," Gail said.

"There are some questions that you already know the answer to, Gail Turner. But I *will* tell you this: emissaries are always created in pairs, one male, and one female. Nefertiti never met her male counterpart, as he was unfortunately killed in his youth in a place you now call France. There have been many emissaries since that young man and Nefertiti; they did indeed *both* return for the first time nearly sixty years ago, but this time it was the man who had the greatest impact. Not just a ripple in a river, but a wave."

"Mallus?" she asked incredulously. "You're talking about Seth Mallus? *He* was an emissary?"

The Xynutian cocked his head to one side and smiled.

"It is interesting, statistically speaking, that the point at which your species' population had reached saturation point is also the point at which, for the first time, the two emissaries sent by the Facility had an opportunity to actually meet."

"Why are you telling me all of this?"

The Xynutian stared deeply into Gail's eyes before disappearing into thin air.

Moments later, the lights dimmed and the airlock opened. It was obvious that she was meant to leave. As she entered the brightly-lit corridor between the Facility and the Egyptian hall where she had left George, the Xynutian's final thoughts echoed inside her head.

We are telling you this, Gail Turner, as we are also telling Seth Mallus, because it is time for you to go. Now is the time of Aniquilus, and it must not find any trace of us here.

CHAPTER 103

G ail and George left the Amarna Library in silence. The shock of what she had seen and heard, and of the chilling final thoughts of the Xynutian, had left Gail feeling weak and confused.

George helped her through the gaps in the rubble that led to the surface. Hands reached down towards her from above and pulled her up into the mid-morning light.

Sunshine, she thought as she squinted, her hand raised to shield her eyes.

"We thought you'd be here," Ben said, in a mildly accusing tone. "What have you been up to?"

George made a sign for him to be quiet as he emerged from the rubble.

Zahra walked up behind Gail and touched her shoulder.

"Are you alright, Gail?" she asked softly.

Gail nodded her head and smiled weakly. She turned to the horizon in silence.

The sky was a deep grey with streaks of black and red. She knew there was something wrong with that but the others didn't seem to notice the sky. Her mind flittered between different realities, straying from Xynutian time capsules to Egyptian prophecies, to the mad Seth Mallus hell-bent on the destruction of the world. Now, she was back at the Xynutians. They had known, all those hundreds of thousands, no, *millions* of years earlier, that Aniquilus was coming. Somehow, they had predicted it, and had protected as much of themselves as possible from it. And yet humans had been so oblivious that they had simply failed to save themselves. Instead they had done Aniquilus' job for him. They had already destroyed themselves.

But it wasn't just anyone who had destroyed humans, it was Seth: an emissary. Everything he had done had been because of that. And he was *still alive*. Even as she had been speaking to the Xynutian, he had

486

been receiving a similar message. After so many years she could barely remember his face, but she fancied she could almost hear his voice, feel his presence. They were, after all, linked.

She had always known that she was different, *after all, who isn't?* she thought. But from that to finding out that she had been sent by the Xynutians. *To do what? Seth destroys the world, and I just get caught up in it all.* And then it occurred to her, that somehow her innate intuition, seeded by the Xynutians, had led her to this very spot, to make her momentous discovery. And without that, Seth would have no book of Aniquilus, no Mars landing site, not even an Armana Stickman.

She was vaguely aware of George kneeling beside her, looking down at her with a worried expression and she realised that she was no longer standing, looking towards the horizon.

She was lying on her back, looking up into the sky. And she could feel herself slipping away.

ANIQUILUS

E ARTH, it thought as it entered the Solar System. Its myriad taste buds tingled with anticipation. The cold depths of inter-stellar space had made it weary and, more notably, hungry.

Nine years later, it passed Mars with a cursory glance, before a carefully calculated slingshot round the Sun brought it perfectly into orbit around the third planet.

It stayed there, observant, for several milliseconds, before unfurling six tentacles round the planet, to join on the other side in an astronomical embrace.

Moments passed, and then slowly, inexorably, it drew closer, tightening its grip on Earth until its body touched the outer fringes of ozone. Any closer would be deadly to it, and so it stopped.

Aniquilus let its senses run free in the thick atmosphere.

Trillions of filaments poured down from its vast body, connecting it with the land below. Most plunged into the depths of the seas, sending back countless readings that were processed and stored with interest. Evolution, intelligence, it seemed, was slow in the waters of this planet compared to others. However, future visits could still be worthwhile, it noted.

Many billions of the infinitely-thin filaments reached solid ground, some penetrating several hundred feet in their quest.

CURIOUS, it thought.

Aniquilus reeled in its first prey: a human.

The harvested mind was weak, both in terms of intelligence and knowledge. The energy gained from absorbing it didn't even compensate for the energy used to harvest it.

Aniquilus knew that one of three higher species was likely to be dominant at this time. It was very hard to believe that with such an outlook after its last visit to Earth, the reality could be so different. In nearly two million orbits of this fertile planet around its star there should have been ample time for intelligent life to repopulate, evolve and expand. It already knew that there had been trips to nearby planets, from radio transmissions it had intercepted on its voyage.

And yet the mind that it had sampled was stale, devoid of nutrition.

It withdrew momentarily, to think things through, and then approached again for a more detailed analysis; it sniffed the ozone cautiously, the tentacles drawing it as close to the noxious atmosphere as it dared.

The upper atmosphere was full of heavy particles, and little light was reaching the ground. It was a miracle that any life had managed to survive at all.

WASTED, it thought, forlorn; a wasted crop.

It knew what had come about on Earth. It was one of those things that just happened sometimes. It was one of the undesired side-effects of intelligent life.

That creatures with so much at their disposal could be so preoccupied by the certainty of their own deaths that they simply forgot to live was one way of ruining a harvest: depression tasted awful.

And this was another undesired side-effect; with intelligence mostly came technology, but not always responsibility. In this case, it was a catastrophic combination.

There was nothing that could be done. It didn't even dwell on the thought for more than a second.

Once more the filaments descended, but this time only as far as the upper stratosphere. They sucked away the pollutant particles and scrubbed the air. Several moments later, they withdrew, and Aniquilus pushed away from Earth.

CLEAN, it thought.

It orbited the planet one last time before heading to the Moon, which it used to slingshot out towards the Sun, which in turn it would use to slingshot to the next solar system, and the next world.

It left a bright blue planet behind, its shroud of deadly grey removed.

EPILOGUE

EGYPT - YEAR ONE

George cradled Gail in his arms and looked down at her in despair. "It's like someone's opened a curtain," she said weakly, looking up at the clear blue sky. Her voice sounded odd, as if she were drunk.

"Don't try and talk," he said. "Zahra and Ben have gone for some medicine. You need to rest until they get back."

She looked up at her husband in adoration. *Screw the Xynutians* she thought to herself. *My only purpose in life was you*, George.

"Hold on, Gail. Everything's going to be alright."

"I love you," she managed to say with a faint smile. A dull pain started to spread across the top of her head, and down her temples to her cheeks, causing her jaw to lock in pain. An involuntary spasm caused her teeth to grate violently against each other. The pain gained in intensity, until her vision blurred and a piercing whine filled her ears.

I love you, George, she thought with all the willpower left within her. *Thank you for always being there for me, for giving me Jake, for loving me so much. I love you.*

George buried his head in Gail's greying hair as her final breath left her body with a sigh. He squeezed her tight and wept as the muscles in her neck went limp. Her hand let go of his arm and fell loosely to the soft sand below.

"I love you too," he whispered.

AUTHOR'S NOTE

SOUTHAMPTON, ENGLAND, FEBRUARY 2013

Firstly, I would like to thank my numerous proof-readers: Nigel Budd, for his technical insights, my brother Alex and my parents, for their efforts to remain unbiased, and Najam Mughal, for her insights into the Qur'an, Islam and Arabic. I would lastly like to thank my wife, Sonia. When we first met I told her of my ambition to become a writer, and without her it would still be just that.

On 10th February 2011, protests began in Egypt against the establishment of Hosni Mubarak. Spurred on by peaceful revolution in Tunisia, citizens occupied Tahrir Square and within weeks Mubarak ceded all presidential power, which he had held uncontested for nearly thirty years. There were hopes that this would be the start of a new democracy for Egypt.

Unfortunately civil unrest and violence have persisted during the two years since this largely peaceful revolution.

One of the sad consequences of this disorder has been a sharp rise in illegal excavations in Egypt. In a country fiercely proud of its heritage and seven thousand years of civilisation, in 2013 there have been reported cases of people simply going to sites and digging, removing any artefacts they find and can get away with.

It is in exactly this environment that Seth Mallus' scroll would be found in 2015. Unfortunately, we may never know what finds emerge from this chaos as they disappear onto the black market and into personal collections. For those that do reach an honest eye, they will have lost all context, something that is hugely important for any archaeologist.

The clay tablet delivered by the two messengers in the prologue, which Ben nearly throws away over three thousand years later in chapter six, was actually part of the famous *Amarna Letters*, a collection of 382 clay tablets that would have originally been housed in a building now referred to as the 'Bureau of Correspondence of Pharaoh.' They were first discovered by a local woman digging for *sebakh* (deteriorated mud bricks from ancient sites, used as fertiliser by farmers) around 1887 and sold on the antiquities market. The vast majority now reside in the Pergamon Museum in Berlin, a few hundred yards away from Nefertiti's bust in the Neues Museum.

The Shuwardata of Keilah, just south of Jerusalem, was indeed asking for help from the pharaoh. As far as we know, his plea went unanswered.

The story of Akhetaten and its erasing from history by subsequent kings of Egypt is the epitome of the old 'winners write history' adage. Were it not for the archaeology, an entire city that was once capital of ancient Egypt would have gone unnoticed.

We still know relatively little about Tutankhamen's father, Akhenaten, and even less about the enigmatic Nefertiti (she was his 'Great Royal Wife', he also had a lesser Royal Wife, Kiya, and at least two other consorts).

Suggestions that one of the two female mummies found alongside Akhenaten (in KV35 in the Valley of the Kings) might be Nefertiti were quashed following detailed analysis of the remains, now known to be those of Akhenaten's mother Queen Tiye, and an unnamed daughter of hers and Amenhotep III. So Akhenaten was buried with his mother and sister.

Nefertiti's burial remains unfound.

There *is* a library hidden under the sands of Egypt, we simply haven't found it yet. The Villa of the Papyri in Herculaneum is an indication that such hoards exist. One can only imagine what future civilisations would learn about us, and think about us, if they uncovered the British Library.

The Backscatter X-Ray the engineers used to peer through walls is not science fiction. Such devices do exist already, and have been used in airports around the world, particularly in the United States and the United Kingdom. I have, however, taken some liberties and assumed that in the next twenty years science advances considerably, making them both more portable *and* powerful. It's a wonderful thought that one day we might be able to see through solid walls and have some idea of what is inside without having to take an articulated lorry-full of equipment with us. The potential applications for search-and-rescue, let alone archaeology, would be worth it.

There has been much debate on the nature of the first manned mission to Mars, and I won't add to it too much here. However in speaking of *Clarke*'s relatively small team of four explorers, it has recently been announced that a crew of two, a married couple no less, may be sent to Mars as early as 2018.

I would love to think that a manned mission to Mars will have occurred already by 2045. Both George W. Bush and Barack Obama made pre-election speeches promising a landing on Mars by the mid-2030s. In both cases, these promises were followed by budget cuts to NASA after they reached office. It seems increasingly likely that private enterprise will make the most daring steps into space in the coming decades, and those steps will be built on business case rather than the spirit of adventure. So while it's more likely we'll land on an asteroid before we reach Mars, I am still hopeful that someone will set foot there within my lifetime.

It does seem unfair to give the ESA the burden of not being part of the manned mission, but there is a very real risk that with funding decisions for the successor of Ariane 5 (tentatively named 'Ariane 6') set to take place in 2014, and current economics being what they are, there simply may not be a European rocket capable of launching large payloads into orbit after the 2020s, so their ability to contribute significantly may be low. The possibility that the ESA will lag behind the Chinese is increasingly likely, and with manned missions being undertaken by others, the focus could indeed centre on satellites and robotic exploration. Getting Beagles 3 and 4 onto Mars would be a worthy consolation prize, though.

Nuclear War is something that seldom concerns people in the 21st century. And yet there have never been so many countries with weapons capability. There could be as many as 250 warheads held by countries that have not signed the Non-Proliferation Treaty, and thousands held in countries that have.

In 2012, the United States spent up to $31 billion on its nuclear weapons activities. In the same period, the NASA budget had been reduced from $18.5 billion to $17.7 billion. And if you think this is an American problem, the annual cost of running the UK's Trident programme in 2008 was $3.3 billion. The UK Space Agency was set up in 2010 with a grand total of $350 million of non-recurring funding.

There's a reason we haven't gone to Mars yet.

In ecosystems, there are particular species that provide equilibrium.

They may not themselves be very abundant, but they play a critical role in maintaining the order of an ecological environment. Their presence helps to determine the variety and population of other species in the community. It could be a certain species of starfish that eats mussels, which have no other natural predators, stopping them from endlessly multiplying and taking over the sea bed. Or a sea otter that protects kelp forests by eating sea urchins, which would otherwise completely remove the kelp from the ecosystem.

Such a species would have been of great interest to Gail's husband George, a marine biologist.

He would have referred to it as *keystone*.

Luke Talbot
February 2013